NECROMANCER
AWAKENING

NAT RUSSO

Praise for *Necromancer Awakening*

"Mind-blowingly good."

Nicholas Rossis, #1 Bestselling Author of the epic fantasy series *Pearseus*.

"Best book I've read this year. Nat Russo could turn into my favorite author."

Phillip Ferriera, Owner of ReviewBoard.Com

"Necromancer Awakening by Nat Russo is one of the finest examples of fantasy genre fiction I have ever seen. I started to say, "seen in a long time," but the qualifier isn't applicable, since Russo is well able to hold his own among such lights as Martin, Gaiman and Gabaldon."

C. L. Roman, Editor, Brass Rag Press

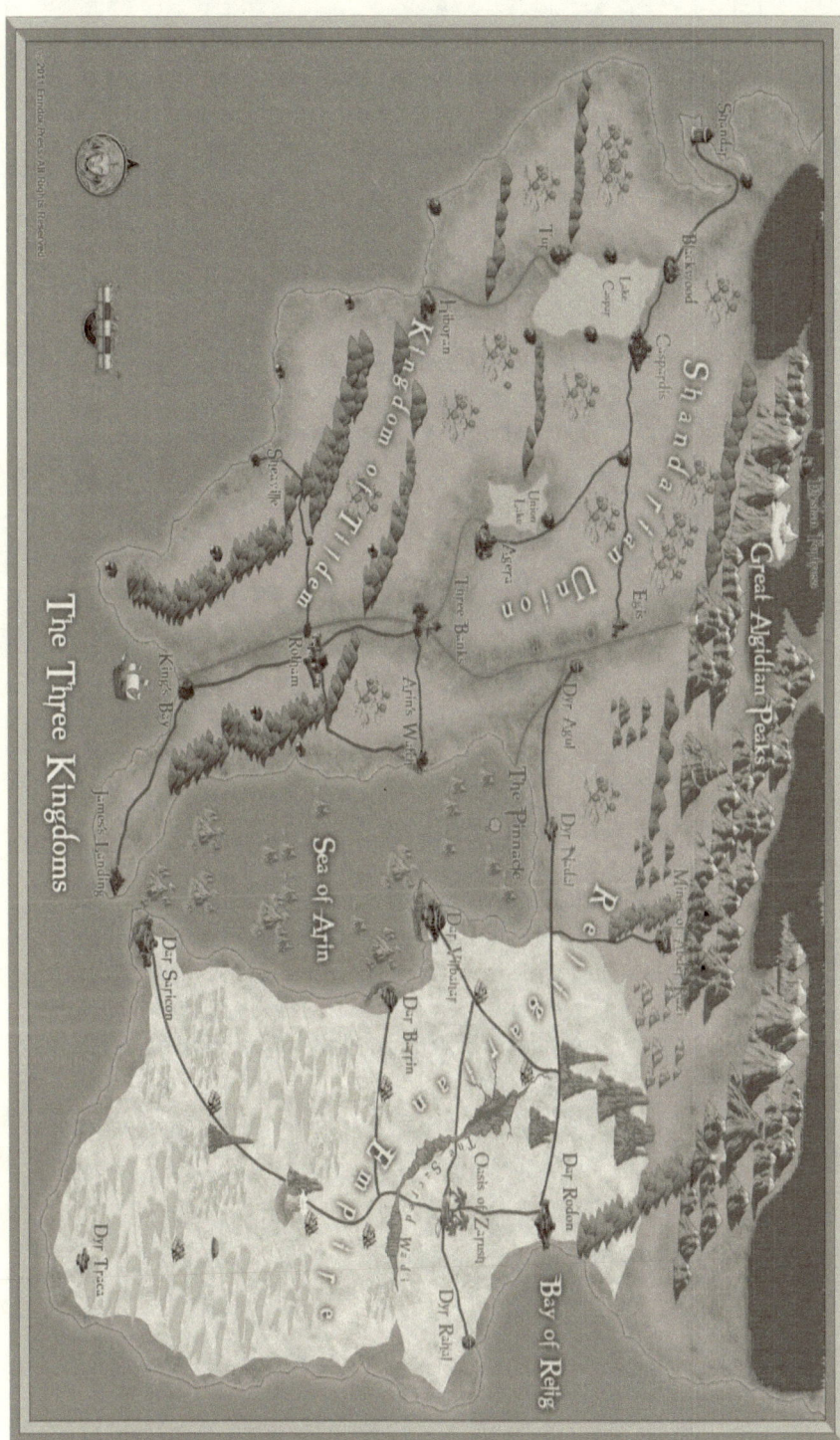

The Three Kingdoms

Necromancer Awakening
Copyright © 2011, 2016 by Nat Russo
All rights reserved.

The Road To Dar Rodon
Copyright © 2014 by Nat Russo
All rights reserved.

Published by Erindor Press
www.erindorpress.com

ISBN: 0-9960059-3-5
ISBN-13: 978-0-9960059-3-7

Cover Art and Design:
Atanas Stoykov

PREFACE TO 2ND EDITION

It's been an amazing couple of years since Necromancer Awakening was first published. When you're a creative type, you never know how your work is going to be received. I expected to publish quietly to little fanfare and live on in obscurity while I completed the little trilogy I had mapped out.

I couldn't have been more wrong. I'll never forget sitting on my sofa, staring at my laptop screen, when I received the following text from a close friend:

Dude! Necromancer just hit #1 in the UK!!!

I can now say I know what it's like to go "weak in the knees", because I tried to stand to go tell Casi and Nic, but I fell off the sofa instead.

Since then, Blackstone Audio reached out wanting to produce an audio version (which we did), and a "Hollywood type" reached out to talk about a screenplay adaptation (which we didn't. But don't worry, I will when the stars align properly).

And now, *Necromancer Falling*, the sequel to the book you hold in your hand, is also making its way onto the bestseller lists. It's surreal in so many ways! In celebration of two outstanding—and completely unexpected—years as an independent author, I've commissioned new cover art from the brilliant Atanas Stoykov, put together a crude map of the Three Kingdoms (I apologize for my lack of cartography skills), and typeset the manuscript in the larger 6 x 9 format for a more comfortable reading experience. And just for the heck of it, this print edition includes *The Road To Dar Rodon* in its entirety.

Thank you all so much for making this an extraordinary time in my life.

Cheers!
Nat
Pflugerville, Texas.
June, 2016

ACKNOWLEDGMENTS

In 1999, I started playing a game called *EverQuest* (a genre-defining game from Sony Online Entertainment). I made friendships in that game that last to this day, including one of my best friends, Joe Smithey.

One day Joe and I rolled up a couple of Dark Elf Necromancer characters; I called mine "Mujahid" and he called his "Nuuan". We became so inseparable that our fellow Enchanted Circle guild members called us the "evil twins". Some time later I wrote a piece of *EverQuest* comedy that I called "*d00d, sow plz - The Discovery of the /who Bug*". Feel free to look it up, though you may need some knowledge of old-school *EverQuest* to get the jokes and style. I shared it with Joe, and he insisted I post it to our favorite site, EQNecro. It went viral before viral was a thing, and it sparked a passion I hadn't felt for quite some time: writing. I owe Joe a debt of gratitude for that and for suffering through the 1st draft of every chapter of Necromancer Awakening.

Writing isn't as solitary an endeavor as many believe. There are some great folks who had a lot to do with my success:

My beta reader, editor, mentor, cheerleader, and brutally honest friend, Joan Reginaldo. I'm a better writer today because of Joan, and there's far less "eyebrow raising" in my work because of her.

My colleagues in software engineering, John Boyd and Ian Mitchell, who were the first two avid Fantasy readers to read my work. Their early feedback was invaluable. I owe a huge debt of gratitude to John for constantly making me feel like "the next great thing" in Fantasy. And my lengthy conversations on magic with Ian, who is equal parts mad scientist, Gandalf, and *The Dude*, kept my imagination working overtime.

I'd also like to thank my son, Nicolas, for insisting I use the name of one of his *EverQuest 2* characters: Zubuxo. The name has taken on a life of its own, and I can't imagine an Erindor without a Zubuxo.

Every writer says this, and I finally understand why. This book simply wouldn't have been possible without the support of my wife Casi. This was a three-year labor of love, and I can't begin to tell you how much time it consumed. Casi never once made me feel guilty for it, and instead cheered me on from the sidelines, surprising me with "writer supplies" and interesting books that I never would have thought to buy for myself. It's no coincidence that two of her *EverQuest 2* character names made it into this book as well.

Yeah, I come from a family of gamers. I'm a lucky man!

For Casi, Nic, Toby, and Bowie.

CHAPTER ONE

Nicolas yanked on Toby's leash and jumped out of the darkened intersection as a delivery truck sped by honking its horn.

"Asshole," Nicolas said as the driver waved his fist. "People live here, you know."

He knelt beside Toby and scratched the startled beagle. "I know, it's too early for us, isn't it?"

Of all the days to wake up before the birds. I'm gonna get us both killed.

"Are you sure you don't need to go?"

Toby whined and pulled him toward home.

"You better not ask me later."

They crossed 24th Street to the six-story apartment building on west campus. Toby got excited when they approached the entry and started pulling at the leash.

The staircase to his third story efficiency was immaculate and well-lit. The building was a few years old, but it had that brand new construction smell, as if the wood on the banister had been cut yesterday.

I forgot to thank dad for putting me up here. He went to a lot of trouble, as always.

His dad had bought him a car, subsidized his rent, and even got him into Archeology school so they could work together someday. Nothing was too much trouble. Nicolas was a teenager when Dr. Murray adopted him, against the advice of his own family, and he did everything to make Nicolas feel like a son.

He pushed the thoughts away and slid the key into the lock, trying his best to keep quiet.

Toby whined.

"Shh," Nicolas said. "Mr. Landing hates you enough as it is. You want him to come beat our door down again?"

The old coot hates everyone, come to think of it. He'd fit in with some of the nuns at Saint John's.

Most of the nuns at the children's home were wonderful, but one or two shouldn't have been around kids. They acted as if they hated everything and everyone, going so far as to ignore the bullies who tormented Nicolas at every opportunity.

Dad helped me with them too. He always said "Intimidation is the weapon of bullies. Don't let them know you're intimidated, and they'll leave you alone."

Nicolas dropped the leash as the door opened, and Toby ran inside, attacking his favorite toy. It looked like a cross between an alligator and a pickle, so Nicolas and Kaitlyn had taken to calling it Toby's *gatorpickle*.

The annoying squawk of his alarm clock drew his attention to the time.

Oh crap!

He closed the door, silenced the alarm, and threw his clothes onto a pile of laundry outside the bathroom as he ran toward the shower.

Nicolas placed his hand against the cold, wet tiles and let the lukewarm water pour over him. He hoped it would alleviate the nausea he'd felt since he got up.

He didn't know what was happening to him. Every night for the last couple of weeks had been the same. He'd go to sleep and have the worst nightmares of his life. A partially decaying head floating toward him, or a group of rotting corpses clawing their way out of cold, ancient rune-covered graves, chasing him until he woke up nauseated and covered in sweat. The skull dreams were getting worse. Last night he could smell the putrid clumps of rotting flesh falling from the decaying head.

He wanted to tell Kait, but she'd downplay it. She'd chalk it up to stress from their upcoming graduation, or do some chore for him, thinking it would make him feel better. But all it would do is remind him of what happened. She wasn't the person he needed to talk to anyway. Only his dad would be able to help him.

An archaeologist who's afraid of dead things. My future looks interesting.

Toby bayed and spun, running too fast for his paws to grip the damp floor tiles. He looked as if he were running on an invisible treadmill. When his feet gained traction he launched himself out of the bathroom.

Kaitlyn's here.

He turned the water off and toweled himself dry. A mountain of clothes stood between him and the door, and his favorite t-shirt sat on top of the pile. He smelled it.

Clean pile.

He tossed the shirt and a pair of socks through the door, hoping it would distract Toby, who was baying as if the place were under attack.

A wave of nausea hit him, and he doubled over in front of the sink.

What the hell? I didn't drink last night.

The nausea passed, and he hurried around the corner to let Kaitlyn in, but he was too late.

"He's a good boy," Kaitlyn said.

Toby stood with his paws on Kaitlyn's thighs. He was all eyes and tongue, licking her face as if he hadn't just seen her last night. She hunched over, massaging both of his ears. One of Toby's paws got tangled in her long auburn hair.

"Yes he is," Kaitlyn said, untangling him. "A good boy with stinky puppy breath, isn't he? Where's your *gatorpickle?*"

Any other day this would be a perfect picture. But things weren't perfect, and nothing brought that home as vividly as the black dress Kaitlyn wore. She hated black.

"Almost done," he said.

She hugged him and laid her cheek against his chest. The warmth of her soft, rose-scented skin always made him feel better. That rose scent was so her.

"It's ok," Kaitlyn said. "We'll get through this together. Why don't I walk Toby for you?"

"No." *Five seconds and she's already starting with the chores.*

"I can make you something to eat?"

"No. I just have a headache. And I want to get this over with."

She walked to the kitchenette on the other side of the small studio apartment and opened a cabinet. It was empty. She shook her head and reached into the sink, taking a dirty glass and filling it with water.

"Take this," she said, handing him the glass and a couple of aspirin.

"I need my jacket."

Kaitlyn glanced down. "Pants wouldn't hurt, either." She handed him a pair of trousers that were draped over his papasan chair. "Change your shirt. You're not putting a jacket over *that* thing. And no boots, cowboy."

He huffed and pulled a shirt with buttons off the clean pile. "The boots are fine."

Kaitlyn patted his back. "When we get back I'll do the laundry and dishes—"

"Dammit, Kait, just stop."

"But—"

"I can do it myself. I don't need—" He covered his mouth with his fist. "Just *stop* ok?"

She rubbed his arm. "Ok. I just...I want to help. But, I get it. I went through the same thing."

"There's nothing anyone can do. I just need to feel like...my life hasn't been changed forever, you know?"

"We'll figure this out. Together."

"Everyone says it'll get better. I just don't...what happens now?"

She touched the side of his face. "It's going to suck for a long time. Then, one day you'll wake up and it will suck a little less. And just when you thought the worst was over, you'll see something, or smell something, and it will flatten you all over again. That's what's going to happen, babe."

"It's like there's no solid ground anymore. He was just handing out food at that soup kitchen a couple weeks ago. And now...Now...."

"You can do this," Kaitlyn said. "And I'm here. Toby's here. And we're not going anywhere."

"Promise?"

She held up her ring finger and light glinted off the tiny inset diamond. "I already did, remember?"

His doubt evaporated and he smiled. He could always count on her to be strong when he needed her.

He put his shirt and pants on and handed her a tie from his dresser.

She smirked. "How old are you, and you can't tie a tie? You graduate in December, you know."

"I'm gonna be an archaeologist, not some pencil jockey."

"You think you'll charm your way into research grants with a trowel and a pair of torn cargo pants? Archaeologists wear ties too, dingus."

"Not *this* archaeologist," he said.

When she was finished with the tie, she gave him a quick inspection, pursing her lips to the side and squinting. He loved how she always did that before they went anywhere.

"I approve," she said. "Now let's get going, monkey butt."

"No. Just...no."

"Well, you ruled out *pookie* and *num nums* too." She frowned. "You're not getting away without a cute nickname. There are rules."

"Ok, you give me a nickname and I get to play connect-the-dots with your freckles."

"Come on," Kaitlyn said. "We have to be there at ten."

"Wait." He took his wallet off the nightstand, which was open to Kaitlyn's picture. He dropped it as he was closing the drawer.

Kaitlyn picked it up and handed it to him. "I hate that picture. I look like I bit into a lemon."

And that was exactly why he liked it. She was never prettier than when she was pretending to be ugly. They had just started dating and he had wanted to take her picture near some flowers. She had leaned over to smell one of the bouquets and didn't like it. When she turned toward the camera, he could see how nasty the smell was by the way her face scrunched. It was his favorite picture.

"You can leave the looking to me." He took her hand and led her out into the hall.

He locked the door behind them and heard someone clearing their throat.

"Boy," Mr. Landing said.

Mr. Landing, from the apartment across the hall, scowled at him over a pair of bulky plastic eyeglass frames.

Even with a slight stoop, Mr. Landing stood an inch or two taller than Nicolas's six feet. In all the time Nicolas had lived here, the old man never had visitors. And he rarely spoke, unless he was complaining.

"I heard that damned dog again this morning," Mr. Landing said. "How many—" He cleared his throat so violently Nicolas thought the man's tonsils would fly out. "Do I have to report you again?"

"I'm sorry, Mr. Landing," Kaitlyn said. "Toby is just—"

"He's my dog," Nicolas said to Kaitlyn. "I can do the apologizing."

"I shouldn't have to sacrifice my peace and quiet because you live with livestock," Landing said. "I pay rent here same as you. And don't think I'm oblivious to what goes on here at night. If you were my daughter, I'd—"

"Listen here," Nicolas said. "I go out of my way to be nice to you and all you do is complain about it. Toby barks because he's a dog, and that ain't gonna change any time soon. Kait is my fiancee, and I don't plan on *that* changing either. And I don't have the time or patience for your crotchety old man horse shit today."

Mr. Landing looked as if he'd been slapped.

"Now if you'll excuse me," Nicolas said. "I'm late for my father's funeral."

The air was crisp in the parking garage, and Nicolas put his arm around Kaitlyn when he saw her shiver.

"Thanks for being so good with lunatics," Nicolas said.

"I was about to bite his head off."

"Landing's the biggest asshole in the asshole kingdom, true. But I was talking about me."

"You're not crazy. You're just...sanity-challenged."

He laughed and ran his fingers through her hair. The red highlights were always brighter when the sun hit her from behind like this.

"We have to hurry," Kaitlyn said. "You can play with my hair later."

"Oh can I?" Nicolas said through a grin.

Kaitlyn rolled her eyes.

Nicolas grabbed her keys away and made a show of opening the door of her beat-up '91 Mustang for her.

They drove out onto the I-35 and he swore. He hated Austin traffic. Always bad, no matter what time of day.

He felt nauseated again but he shrugged it off.

"You ok?" Kaitlyn asked.

"Didn't eat this morning."

"I tried to make you something."

"I'm trying not to throw up here."

The wave of nausea passed as they pulled into the funeral home's parking lot. He felt odd. A few minutes ago he was about to throw up in Kaitlyn's car, but now he could run around the block without breaking a sweat.

The chapel was in the center of a cemetery that ran for at least a mile in every direction, and every time he passed a gravestone his head swam.

"You're not hung over, are you?" Kaitlyn said.

She took his hand and led him into the chapel.

Flowers lined the center aisle, filling the room with a sweet fragrance that intermingled with the colognes and perfumes of the people in attendance. An organist pounded out a hymn as if the solemnity of the ceremony hinged on how hard she could press the keys. Colleagues and family of Dr. Murray packed the pews, and Nicolas worried they wouldn't find seats. His eyes were drawn to a long, brown casket in front of the altar. A portrait of Dr. Murray rested on an easel next to the casket.

Nicolas had taken that photo on Easter Island a year ago. A Rapanui elder was presenting Dad with an award for his self-sacrificing contribution to Rapanui culture. Dad had tried to turn it down, holding up his hand and saying "no" through his grey beard, but the elder insisted. Even his long, graying hair seemed embarrassed, flying away from the elder in a strong gust of wind that had almost pushed Nicolas off the boulder he'd been standing on.

I'll never take another picture of him.

They found seats near other family members and close friends. People took turns greeting Dr. Murray's surviving brother and sister. Both were in their sixties, just like Dr. Murray, and both had the same square jaw and prominent cheekbones. Nicolas wanted to go over and talk to them, but they had been against his adoption, so he doubted they'd want to be close now.

The ceremony began with a hymn before settling down into a biblical reading. Nicolas tried to pay attention, but he felt hyper, like he needed to run and burn some energy off before it burned him up.

The minister stepped up to the podium.

A violent wave of nausea hit Nicolas. He leaned forward in his seat and took a deep breath, trying not to vomit.

The man behind him leaned forward and whispered. "Your dad was a great man. He'll be missed."

"Brothers and sisters," the minister began in a low baritone. "We are gathered here..."

Something solid struck Nicolas's chest with a force that crushed him back into his seat. Images of people and places he didn't know flooded his mind.

"*...today to recall...*"

It felt as if someone had hooked his heart up to a car battery. In his mind, he watched through the eyes of a burly man in mechanic's overalls as he stabbed another man in a tweed suit. Nicolas, the murderer, shouted, "You wanted my wife? You can have her. She's next." He dropped the bloody knife to the floor, and the jealousy and rage of the mechanic consumed him.

"...the life of..."

Another jolt made his heart stutter, and the dead man morphed into a little girl with blond pigtails, who clutched her teddy bear and trembled. This time he was a middle-aged man in a bathrobe, towering over the girl and beating her without mercy. The girl cowered away, but Nicolas, the abuser, punched and kicked her. He felt disgust and hatred, not because of what he witnessed, but because he felt as if the girl deserved it. He was still Nicolas, yet also this monster of a man, kicking and beating a little girl.

"...a great friend and..."

A third electrical shock. The girl blurred into an amorphous blob that transformed into a baby boy. Nicolas was a young woman wearing a white slip extending down to her—his—knees, and carrying the crying infant in his arms. The smells of soap and lotions intermingled as a smooth jazz piano played on an old gramophone. A high-pitched tenor voice threaded through the notes of the piano, singing the lyrics to "Ain't Misbehavin'", but the tenor was drowned out by the sound of running water. Nicolas stroked the child's hair as she—he—stepped into the bathroom. The crescendo of music and lyrics combined to mask the wailing of the infant, and as the music subsided, Nicolas plunged the infant into the tub and held him underwater until the flailing of his tiny limbs stopped.

Nicolas shook his head, desperately trying to erase the horrific images. What part of his mind could harbor these disgusting thoughts?

"...colleague. A great archaeologist and humanitarian."

What?

Had all these things happened in less time than it took the minister to finish his sentence?

He panicked and tried to stand, but another forceful blast of energy, and stream of horrific images, struck him. If this continued the images would kill him. There was no way he could live with that much evil on his conscience.

He looked at Kaitlyn, and the sight of her face expelled the hatred and evil from his mind. He felt an invisible wall go up between him and whatever was trying to kill him.

The force reversed direction.

His heart raced as the energy radiated away from him. There was a primal satisfaction that accompanied this release of power, and it scared him.

Kaitlyn elbowed him and gave him a dirty look. The energy field surrounding him collapsed and his mind was present in the chapel once more.

"What the hell?" Kaitlyn whispered.

He started sweating as the panic grew worse.

I can't be here.

He squeezed past the people sitting next to him. He might not make it out of the chapel, but he was determined to make it out of this pew.

"Nick," Kaitlyn said in a louder voice.

He stumbled over the person at the end of the pew and escaped into the main aisle.

Another wave of nausea struck him. He had to get out of the building.

The parking lot made him feel better, but not much. The energy was there but subdued, just out of reach as if he had passed through an invisible barrier. He leaned onto the hood of Kaitlyn's car and waited for the nausea to pass.

"Are you ok?" Kaitlyn said, running toward him.

He tried to speak, but dry heaves sent him into a fit of retching.

Kaitlyn rubbed his back until the heaving subsided.

When the nausea passed, He stood up and covered his mouth with the back of his fist.

"Better now?" Kaitlyn said.

He shrugged.

"Let's get you back home then."

"Gotta go back."

"Like hell you do." She grabbed him by the shoulders and spun him around. "You're going home."

"But my dad—"

"Isn't here. And wherever he is, he understands. Now get your ass in the car."

How could this happen today of all days? The man who had saved him from life in a children's home and had given him a name and a future was lying dead in a wooden box, and he couldn't attend the funeral because of an upset stomach?

No. He'd sit in that pew if he had to hold a bucket in his lap.

To hell with it!

He stepped forward.

Images of one atrocity after another assaulted him. Light strobed in his mind. He shot three people in the back of their heads as they knelt, then cut the tongue out of a witness to silence him. Strobe. He tied a woman down and injected her with heroin to make her more compliant. Strobe. He lit a cross on fire, and in its merry light, slaughtered the landowner and his family when they fought back. Strobe.

He collapsed and clawed at the ground, pulling himself back toward the car, and as he crossed that invisible line in the pavement, the images stopped.

He pushed himself up onto shaky legs and leaned against the car.

"Ok," he said. "Let's go."

"Give me the keys."

"I can drive."

Traffic was worse on the way back, and Nicolas cursed whoever designed the roads in Austin. Every time the car hit a bump, he thought it was the strange energy coming back.

"We can go to St. David's," Kaitlyn said.

"No hospital. I just need to go to bed."

"Hospitals have beds."

"Toby needs me."

"Excuse me, but Toby wouldn't eat if it wasn't for me. Do you even know what brand he eats?"

"Puppy...dog nuggets."

"Puppy dog nuggets. Wow, Nick. Just...wow."

He pumped the brakes behind a moving van as he turned onto 24th from Guadalupe and swore.

His apartment building was only a block away, but a long line of cars stretched out in front of them.

"I can't see anything," Kaitlyn said. She craned her head out of the window.

"Accident," Nicolas said. "Police and stuff."

"Paramedics are working on someone on this side," Kaitlyn said. "Whoa, they brought out the paddles."

Nausea churned in his stomach. He put the car in idle, leaned out the window to heave, and a blast of energy entered his mind, replacing the nausea with vitality and power.

He could see it this time...a random stream of images accelerating toward him.

"Another ambulance," Kaitlyn said.

He braced himself for the insanity the images would bring, but they carried a different set of emotions this time. He was an older man, swinging a little boy in a circle. The boy giggled with glee, and a sense of love and devotion filled Nicolas. As the boy spun, Nicolas saw his reflection in the window.

"It's Mr. Landing," Nicolas said. A frightening realization formed in his mind. "He's dead."

"No, they're still working on him—"

"He's dead. He was a good man. His grandkids...."

"Now you're scaring me."

A powerful force struck him and he was consumed by a dark stream of images.

He was Mr. Landing, only eighteen years old. The mugginess of the jungle outside of Nam Dong was oppressive, and the VC was out here somewhere. The crescendo of chirping insects made it hard to hear anyone approaching. He checked the twenty-round magazine on his M16 for no other reason than nerves. He knew how many rounds he had left. He'd loaded his usual eighteen and hadn't fired a shot.

But a vicious and unseen enemy was stalking him through the dense foliage. His life was in danger, and his body trembled from an adrenaline rush. Where was the enemy? For that matter, *who* was the enemy? It was impossible to know.

Twigs snapped by a nearby tree, silencing the roar of the chirping insects.

Panic.

He lifted his rifle with unsteady hands and aimed it at the tree.

Movement!

He screamed and unloaded the M16 toward the tree.

The dull thud of a body hitting the ground was amplified by the silence of the insects. Dirty bastard tried to ambush him, but he'd been ready for it.

When he saw the body he grew cold and dropped to his knees.

It was a small child. His face was drawn, gaunt as if malnourished, and he was covered in scratches.

Landing, in a daze, saw the rest of his patrol running over to him, but the sound wouldn't register. His hands trembled, and the shakes spread throughout his body until he collapsed next to the tree. He looked away from the boy, but the trembling grew stronger. By the time the patrol reached him, he was screaming the same word over and over.

"Why?"

The jungle faded and withdrew, taking the hysteria with it, until Nicolas was in the car once more.

"It was a kid," Nicolas said. "He didn't know. He was just scared."

"Stop it," Kaitlyn said. Her voice was raspy.

"It wasn't his fault and he never knew it. He couldn't have known. I can't be here."

"Nick, don't."

He opened the car door and ran toward his building, passing Landing's covered body to his left. The lobby doors were open, and he entered at a full sprint, taking the stairs two at a time until his apartment door stood before him. Everything would be better inside.

The key wouldn't go in. The metal tapped against the lock's core and slid off, scratching the surface of the door. His hands trembled with frustration and he wanted to yell.

He swore.

The key slid into place and the door opened. He stumbled into the apartment, threw his jacket on the ground and pulled his tie off. He needed to sit down and look at something familiar...something peaceful.

A wet nose swept across his face. Toby nuzzled against him.

He grabbed for Kaitlyn's picture and rocked back and forth on his creaky bed with one arm around Toby.

It wasn't Landing's fault. He thought he was going to die. God, what's happening to me?

He hugged his knees to his chest and stared at the picture.

Forty years and he never forgave himself. My god, how do I know these things? I'm losing my mind. God help me. Please!

"You left me there!" Kaitlyn said. She closed the door behind her.

Kait's here. Everything will be ok now.

"It wasn't his fault." Nicolas said.

"It was *your* fault. You took the damned keys. My car's sitting out there."

When Kaitlyn spoke, a strange calm descended on him.

His vision darkened, but another stream of images came to him. An ornate door, etched with symbols reminiscent of Nordic runes, opened in his mind, and he imagined himself walking through it. Two open doorways stood in the room beyond. Darkness shrouded one door, but the other emitted a radiant white light. The white door pulsed, and with every pulse it enticed him closer.

But the white door also emitted a *wrongness*. Something bad would happen if he entered it. He forced himself to look away and, instead, walked toward the black door. The grotesque, decapitated head from his dreams hovered in the air beyond the threshold. Jagged, ripped flesh hung from the base of a torn spinal column. Patches of hair fell from the skull and the smell of burning, putrid flesh made him want to puke. He stumbled backwards in fright.

An unexpected sensation of calm returned. Something was soothing him. And whatever it was, it wasn't from Texas.

Toby growled.

"The hair is burning," he said.

"You're going to the hospital," Kaitlyn said. "I've seen enough."

A pulse of energy threw Nicolas backward and pinned him against the wall.

Kaitlyn screamed.

Every time the energy touched him he learned more about it. It was a life force, vast and powerful, but he wasn't afraid of it. It gave him a sense of security. It took away his fear. It made him feel...loved.

An invisible hand formed around his torso and tightened, threatening to crush him, but the strange calmness blanketed him again. He knew the hand was good in the same way he knew the man—Landing—was good.

Toby started baying.

A low-pitched metallic sound filled the room like someone striking a piece of sheet metal. A small point of swirling black light formed behind Kaitlyn, whipping her hair around her face, and grew larger, morphing into a multi-hued disk with a void of pitch-blackness at its center. As the point became a disk, the metallic sound grew louder.

"What is that?" Nicolas asked.

Kaitlyn looked in the direction he was staring. "What's happening?"

The vortex of light filled him with a sense of belonging, as if his world would be complete if he stepped inside. But he refused. If it wanted him that much, it would have to take him.

The hand of energy lifted Nicolas several feet off the bed, as if in response to his thoughts.

Kaitlyn screamed and grabbed his boots, trying to pull him back down to the bed.

With a violent thrust, the hand pulled him into the vortex, ripping him out of Kaitlyn's grasp. Pain radiated down his spine as his head snapped backward, and lights flashed like a strobe across his eyelids. He tried in vain to move his arms against the force, but it was too strong.

The world disappeared and he tumbled into the black void.

CHAPTER TWO

Nicolas blinked, and light stabbed at his brain like thousands of tiny daggers.

What the heck just happened?

The back of his head was throbbing, so he reached back to rub the sore spot.

Why am I on my stomach?

He spat out the taste of dirt and sat up. His head felt wobbly, like an egg on a spring.

A cool breeze tickled his face. He took a deep breath and a coughing fit seized him. The scent he inhaled wasn't the familiar smells of his apartment, stale with week-old laundry and trash piling up in the corner. It wasn't the scent of car exhaust leaking through cheap windows. It was lavender and juniper mixed with lilac and exotic smells he didn't recognize.

He couldn't decide whether he liked the smell or hated it, but it filled his lungs without suffocating him, and that's all that mattered. His nausea was gone, the pain was bearable, and above all, he didn't feel that strange energy pouring into his body.

Something shrieked above him.

He looked up and his chest tightened.

The sky was pale yellow, lighting the emerald-green meadow before him from all directions. The sun was missing. For a moment he thought the sun had taken on gargantuan proportions and filled the sky. But he could stare at it without pain, and the heat was bearable. In fact, it wasn't hot at all. It was like that spring he spent in Flagstaff studying the Wupatki pueblo with Dad, and a biting breeze made them glad they brought their heavy-duty windbreakers.

He sat against a boulder in the foothills of a vast mountain range. The distant mountains were tall enough to put Mount Humphreys to shame. Snow was absent above the timberline, revealing grey rocky peaks. There was something odd about that timberline, though, as if the foliage below the line had been...removed.

Something shrieked again, and this time it flew over him. He had to look twice when he saw it.

It looked like a bright turquoise bat the size of a pickup truck, with wings the length of an eighteen-wheeler from tip to tip. Its neck was just as long, covered in cascading blue feathers, and ending in teeth surrounded by a feathery mane. Fangs longer than Toby's body formed three concentric rings in a cavernous maw and dripped with saliva. Its six scaled, muscular legs flayed out beneath a lithe body with every beat of its wings, and a distinct saltwater smell followed it.

It shrieked once more, then dove down about a hundred yards away.

Nicolas inched his way around the boulder.

A herd of cows stampeded away from the mountainside. Bells dangled from their necks, filling the air with frantic dull clanks. They ran into a vast meadow, which was bordered by a dense row of tall shrubs. When they reached the shrubs, the entire herd turned left as one.

Those ain't no cows.

He had no idea what else to call them, though. They had six legs, like that bat thing, but their agility was no match for the bat.

The bat swooped toward the herd, unleashing another shriek as it flew over. This time the sound was soothing, like a lullaby, and the animals started grazing as if the creature weren't there.

Dumber than a box of hammers too. That thing's gonna swallow 'em whole.

Nicolas blinked from drowsiness. He wasn't sure where that came from. He was energetic a moment ago.

Another shriek echoed off the rocky outcropping and three of the cow-like creatures staggered. They fell to the ground, but the rest of the herd ignored them.

Nicolas covered his ears and wobbled, but he gripped the boulder in time to stop falling.

The bat's giant wings created a dust cloud as it landed among the cows. A few of them ran away, but the bat ignored them.

Two worm-like tongues snaked up from the recesses of the bat's throat. They slid across the surface of the outermost ring of fangs as if in anticipation of a meal. It lumbered forward until it reached one of the fallen cows and raised its two hind legs in the air.

It faced its leathery hindquarters toward the cow and released a steady jet of liquid, spinning the cow as if on a lathe. The liquid congealed around the cow like a cocoon.

The bat encased two more cows and connected strands of the liquid among all three. With two beats of its massive wings, it lifted the three helpless cows as one, looking back as if to make sure they were secure, and flew up into the mountains.

Nicolas sat back down against the rock and leaned back.

"This ain't Texas," Nicolas said. "It's a dang Spielberg film."

Where the hell am I?

He was still wearing his suit pants and shirt, but he was squeezing his wallet in the palm of his hand.

Kaitlyn's picture.

He was empty, as if a piece of him was missing.

A sting in his palm made him realize he had balled his hand into a fist. He stretched his fingers and tried to calm himself down. There had to be a rational explanation for this.

Portals didn't open up in people's apartments...in *Texas* of all places...and drag them into a world with six-legged cows and giant turquoise bats.

Please, God, just take me back home.

He rubbed his temples.

This ain't helping. I have to do something.

He had to get back to Kaitlyn and Toby somehow, but he didn't even know where he was. He needed information, and he wasn't going to find it behind this rock.

Those things may not be cows, but there was something about them that made him think they were cows in the first place.

They had bells. That means they're domesticated. So where's the rancher?

He turned away from the herd and saw plumes of smoke rising from a cluster of small buildings in the distance, no more than a mile away.

There you go.

That village might have some answers. He wiped a small bit of moisture from his eyes, stood up, and started walking.

T he terrain was rocky on this side of the emerald field, but he thought it wise to avoid the meadow. The jagged rocks rose to sharp points that stood several feet above him, and it was difficult to keep from stumbling. He tripped over a concealed granite nub.

That's all I need right now. A broken leg.

His stomach growled. If the village didn't have answers, maybe it had food.

The sharp crack of falling stone echoed in the crags, as if a scurrying animal had dislodged some rubble. He looked for the source and lost his balance again.

Careful, dumbass.

He steadied himself and continued around the face of an enormous boulder. He looked up at the yellow sky. Something wasn't right about it.

As he climbed over some rocks, his hunger left him. Invigorated by the extra burst of stamina, he scrambled over the remaining boulders. All that stood between him and the village was a few hundred yards of meadow.

There was movement among the thatched-roof buildings. People.

He remembered the cows and decided it would be best to take a good look at the villagers first.

Two legs and two arms. Now we're talking.

He took another step and his senses reeled. The faint sound of falling rocks reverberated through his mind as if he had some kind of sonar. The sound was too faint to know it was coming from the direction of the mountain...but he knew just the same.

An old stone building, surrounded by marble columns and covered by a rock awning, sat nestled in a collection of boulders beside the mountain. The sound was coming from behind that building.

How the hell am I hearing this?

Carvings on the awning drew his attention. He was looking at a runic language unlike any he knew, but something was familiar about it. The energy that had been increasing with every step grew stronger.

A wave of nausea struck him and he doubled over in agony. But as painful as the sensation was, he hoped another invisible hand would pull him back to Kaitlyn.

Rocks crashed nearby. Something was coming toward him.

He began to think at a lightning pace. Small things that would have escaped his attention earlier snapped into focus. He understood the movement of the herd and the shriek of the flying predator now. The reason the predator looked backwards when it flew off had nothing to do with its prey. It had stolen the prey from something else, something terrifying enough to cause it to look over *its* shoulder.

And that *something else* was hunting him.

Nicolas ran back toward the rocks. The sound of feet clacking on the ground ricocheted off the rocky mountainside. There were too many footfalls to be a single creature chasing him.

There was nowhere to run, and if he hid among the crags, whatever was chasing him would find him.

The clicking feet vanished.

He stopped and turned in the direction they came from.

Nothing but the grassy field and stone building.

In a moment of panic he looked up, thinking the creatures could fly. But there was nothing except pale-yellow sky.

Something crashed on the rocks behind him. His face grew cold and his pulse quickened as he turned toward the sound.

Eight solid-black eyes, darker than night, stared at him from a spherical head as wide as Nicolas was tall, and pincers clicked in front of a mouth dripping with rotting ichor. A bulbous abdomen, covered in course hair resembling the spikes of a porcupine, dwarfed the massive head. And the entire repulsive thing rested atop eight grotesque legs that protruded from the abdomen, ending in sharp points that rested on two boulders.

His knees buckled, and he fell to the ground, paralyzed with fear. He was going to die.

A vision of the bodiless skull from his dreams appeared in his mind's eye.

The spider crept closer, clicking its slobber-covered pincers together, and reared back on four of its eight legs.

Nicolas cowered, pushing himself away from the spider with his feet in anticipation of its strike.

The skull in Nicolas's mind crackled with energy and pulsed with a blue light. The energy flowing through him reached toward the skull like a plant reaching for sunlight. When it touched the skull, Nicolas felt the power leave him.

A cloud of dirt formed at the spider's feet and launched itself up into the creature's abdomen, forcing it backwards.

A stream of images entered Nicolas's mind, passing before his vision like a slide show that was too fast to keep track of—pitched battles between infantry in scale mail. Long swords crashing against tower shields. Soldiers being trampled by mounted cavalry.

The ground in front of the spider parted, and a skeletal hand clawed its way up from the dirt. A head appeared, face hidden by a dull grey helmet, worn from years of battle and burial. An armor-covered torso followed the helmeted head, then the last hand appeared, holding a great sword the length of Nicolas's body.

Another stream of images flowed through his mind.

In a single moment, Nicolas saw every foe defeated by that sword.

He struggled against the images, trying to force them out, but bloodlust rose in his chest. He wanted nothing more than to wield that sword...to wield *Lugus*...in battle one last time.

I'm losing my mind. What the hell kind of name is Lugus?

The skeleton leapt from the grave too fast for the spider to react, swinging *Lugus* as if it were weightless. The skeleton severed two of the spider's legs with a single strike, and the giant monster screeched.

The stream of images accelerated, like a movie playing on fast-forward, and this time he saw a giant spider in his mind's eye, identical to the one confronting him. Recognition sparked in his mind, and a foreign presence guided his thoughts.

Crag spider. I know your kind. You cannot defeat me.

He had no idea where the words came from.

This young, starving spider was no match for his martial skill and years of battlefield experience. He rotated the sword twice in his hand and began the deadly dance of blades.

No...not me...I'm not the skeleton. I'm Nicolas...Nicolas Murray.

The skeleton warrior moved with impossible agility, making the spider look clumsy by comparison. The warrior thrust the great sword into the spider's abdomen, spilling a black, stinking liquid onto the ground. The spider screeched one last time and collapsed.

The skeleton faced Nicolas and raised a fist, as if announcing victory.

Thank god it's over.

The skeleton roared a fierce battle cry and charged.

What?

Nicolas didn't have the strength to cry out. There was nothing he could do. He knew the warrior as well as he knew himself. Anything he tried would be like a child fighting a tank.

Out of the corner of his eye, he saw quick motion. A second skeletal warrior charged the first, drawing its attention away from Nicolas. A strange prickling sensation ran over his scalp, like dozens of tiny bolts of electricity.

An old man in floor-length black robes and sandals was walking toward him.

"Fool," the man said in a deep voice. "Take him! What are you waiting for?"

The first skeleton reached Nicolas and raised Lugus over its head.

The world went black, and as consciousness left him, his last thoughts were of Kaitlyn's face and her rose-scented skin.

CHAPTER THREE

Tithian's polished leather boots clacked against the floor of the marble hallway as he raced toward the Archmage's audience chamber. He pulled his black cloak around him to hide the glowing Talisman of Archmages.

This was the moment he had been praying for since the heir was taken forty years earlier.

Arin be praised!

Holding his cloak shut was awkward, so he dropped the talisman down the neck of his robes by its golden chain. He reached for the sigil pouch hanging from a leather cord at his waist when his cloak swung open. It was a habit. The sigils gave him access to the spy tunnels, among other places.

He turned a corner and stumbled over a sconce that had fallen from its mount on the wall.

The Builders would turn in their graves.

The Builders—legendary magi—had built the Pinnacle upon foundations of magic by a power not even the archmage knew. Now, the once grand edifice decomposed like a rotting corpse, rocked by decades of earthquakes.

Four decades, to be precise.

A council magus nodded as he passed and said "Prime Warlock."
Tithian returned the nod, but his thoughts were elsewhere.

How can this be after forty years? Where has he been?

Tithian had no answers. And that wasn't a good position to be in when the Archmage had questions. His title would matter little. The Archmage would banish him as he banished the Mukhtaar Lord all those years ago, and he'd have no difficulty finding another second in command.

Not even the combined might of the dread Mukhtaar Lords was sufficient to stand against Archmage Kagan, and Tithian was no Mukhtaar Lord.

He took a deep breath and tried to calm his nerves as he navigated the twisting Pinnacle complex.

I will be obedient. That is my calling.

The archmage was more to Tithian than a religious superior. Archmage Kagan spoke to the gods face-to-face, during the *Rite of Manifestation*. His voice was the voice of the gods...the voice that kept Malvol, the God of Hate, at bay. Others may be skeptical, but Tithian had witnessed the Rite. It was no idle boast.

How can the archmage have expected good to come from what he did?

Tithian caught his errant thought. Speaking against the archmage was speaking against the gods, and that was a line he was unwilling to cross. If the archmage thought the Great Barrier was necessary, then so be it. Only the demon Hasat'Tan would deny Archmage Kagan's divine prerogative.

A guard snapped to attention as Tithian approached the audience chamber, then heaved himself against one of the thick stone doors.

The hinges groaned as the door gave way and opened wide enough for Tithian to pass through.

The archmage, arms folded beneath the black-fringed, red scapular that covered the shoulders of his black robe, was speaking with ambassadors from each of the three kingdoms. The conversation was heated, from the looks on their faces.

If the ambassadors were here, then layers of political machinations would cloud the discussion, and Tithian couldn't allow himself to miss anything. He drew power into the energy well that rested at the center of his mind. It would sharpen his senses as bladestone sharpens a Religarian sword.

Ambassador Abelard Cooper, representative of the Kingdom of Tildem, adjusted his linen cravat and grabbed his diplomatic top hat from a nearby end table.

"Forgive me, Archmage," Abelard said. "It appears your *jest* was closer to the truth than you may have suspected. You will understand, of course, that I need to communicate this turn of events to the king immediately."

Archmage Kagan nodded, but he looked concerned.

Abelard brushed past Tithian without saying anything on his way to the chamber door. He nearly knocked the jeweled ceremonial dagger off the belt of the Shandarian Ambassador's army uniform.

Odd. It wasn't like the ambassador to be rude. Tildemen were polite to a fault.

"Mark my words," Kagan said. "As sure as I'm sitting here, I will see the Empire and the Shandarian Union in a formal embrace of friendship. Consider it an old man's dream."

A chuckle drew Tithian's attention back to the formal sitting area. It had come from Emissary Chal Ghanix, of the Religarian Empire. Ghanix sat on a cushioned chair in his brilliant-white desert robes. A tightly-wrapped turban, billowing up from the back of the robes, framed a tanned face. Ghanix's flowing black beard extended to the middle of his chest, partially obscuring the Red Dragon of Religar.

"Waters of Arin's Grace, Ambassador Emaldor," Ghanix said. "You are either the most astute politician I've ever met, or an idiot of the highest order."

Tithian wasn't well-acquainted with Emaldor. The previous Shandarian ambassador had died under suspicious circumstances several weeks earlier, and Emaldor was his replacement.

"Archmage, this is outrageous," Emaldor said. "Ghanix goes too far."

"Gentlemen," Kagan said. "Need I remind you that you conduct this business in the presence of a god?"

Ghanix bowed his head in supplication, and Emaldor paled.

"We have more pressing matters to deal with," Kagan said. "Why would a member of your government, Ambassador Emaldor, use you to send a message to the King of Tildem? Unless, of course, you weren't aware you were being used, in which case I'm tempted to agree with Emissary Ghanix's assessment of your competence."

"Kagan, you—"

"Hold your tongue, Ambassador." Tithian said. Politics may be heated at times, but he wouldn't allow sacrilege. "You're addressing the Holy Archmage within sight of Arin's sanctuary."

"Forgive me, Prime Warlock. I misspoke."

Kagan stood and waved Tithian closer.

"Ahh, Tithian." Kagan extended his hand, palm down, exposing an obsidian-encrusted ring.

Tithian knelt and pressed his lips to the ring.

"Rise, Warlock, and give voice to that look of concern on your face," Kagan said.

"Forgive my interruption, Holy One," Tithian said. "This is news that should be heard in private."

Kagan squinted, and then turned to the ambassadors.

"Leave us. Oh, Ambassador Emaldor?"

"Yes, Archmage?"

"If I were you, I would prepare your chancellor for war. Why your nation would choose now to pull out of the Treaty of Three Banks is simply beyond me."

Kagan shared a look with Emissary Ghanix that Tithian would have missed if not for the power he was holding. The two men were complicit in some goal of which Tithian was unaware, and that unsettled him.

As Prime Warlock, magic and knowledge were his powers. It was his job to make sure he was aware of everything. As the politicians left, Tithian thought about what he had heard.

If the Shandarian Union had pulled out of the Treaty of Three Banks, then both the Union and the Kingdom of Tildem were vulnerable to invasion from the Religarian Empire. Neither nation would survive intact. Kagan was right...it made no sense whatsoever.

Tithian grasped the golden chain around his neck and held up the Talisman of Archmages.

A single point of light within a warm, translucent sphere was proof the heir had returned.

Kagan's face was expressionless.

"This was foretold moments ago in the Book of Life," Kagan said.

Tithian's pulse quickened. There was no greater divine revelation than the Book of Life. Holy proclamations flowed from the gods, through the Archmage, to the Book of Life, where they were indelibly scribed in both the Book and the Archmage's mind. He had witnessed the transfer of divine knowledge several times, as had most Council magi.

"Praise the gods," Tithian said and bowed his head.

"You must not reveal his return to anyone. Not yet. I need to know his intentions."

"But this is joyous news. The gods have restored—"

"King Donal flaunts his heresy in Tildem, while Emperor Relig's army crosses the Shandarian border on a daily basis. And now the Shandarians threaten to pull out of the Treaty. Three nations at each other's throats."

"You are the archmage."

"They answer to me because they fear the wrath of the gods. What if they stop believing? How sharp will my bite be then? What if someone...a *Mukhtaar* someone...sets my son's heart on the Obsidian Throne? War comes to Erindor, Warlock."

"I doubt—"

"I'll inform the Council in my own time. Where is he now?"

Tithian studied the talisman.

"Somewhere in the northern provinces of the Shandarian Union."

"Find him," Kagan said. "Before the traitor does."

Kagan went to his desk, which was constructed of enough wood to pay the salary of every soldier in the Pinnacle Guard for a decade. He opened a drawer and two dull black spheres the size of fists rolled to the front. He handed one to Tithian.

It was unusual for Kagan to give someone a translocation orb. The power to travel between two points without moving was a power he reserved for himself.

"It's attuned to a location outside of Caspardis," Kagan said. "Its return point is just outside your chambers...to minimize suspicion. This is an object of power, Warlock. Do not let me discover my trust has been misplaced."

"Of course."

"There is much you don't know, regardless of your former allegiances. What lies beyond the white door is my son's inheritance. I will keep him free of the taint of *death magic*, even if it means his death."

Tithian must have misheard. The archmage would never order such an evil act.

"If he is trained in necromancy, he will cause more harm than good," Kagan said. "You must promise me something."

"My allegiance is to you...to the gods."

"If you find my son has been...tainted by necromancy, you must kill him. Without hesitation. Do you understand? If he is tainted, in the slightest, he must die."

Tithian tried to understand. Had the archmage just ordered the death of his own son to further a political agenda? The archmage was Arin's representative on Erindor and acted with Arin's authority. How could the gods condone such an immoral course of action?

"You cannot mean that, Holy One," Tithian said. "What will happen if you die without an heir? Only an Ardirian can invoke the Rite of Manifestation. The world will fall into darkness and ignorance."

"What makes you so certain I will die?"

Tithian's eyebrows rose.

"It would be better to have no heir than to have a dynasty divided," Kagan said. "You of all people should know I will not suffer a false archmage."

Tithian offered a silent prayer. He had been present, all those years ago, when Yotto, an ambassador from a place called Barathos, informed Kagan of the rival archmage across the ocean. That knowledge led to the creation of the Great Barrier and the banishment of the Mukhtaar Lord, Tithian's predecessor.

"You have your mission," Kagan said. "It's in your best interests to succeed."

Tithian suppressed a shiver. On the one hand he was repulsed by the notion of killing the Ardirian heir. Yet on the other, the voice of the gods themselves had given the order. He looked at the translocation orb in his hand and wondered how it had come to this.

He took a deep breath. The archmage was the voice of the gods. Tithian was wrong to have doubted, even for a moment. There was no choice to be made. He would follow the archmage.

"It will be done, Holy One." He bowed and left the chamber.

As the massive door closed behind him he studied the translocation orb and thought about Kagan's orders. His conscience gnawed at him. How could the archmage order his own son's death? He suppressed another shiver as he offered a silent prayer to Arin.

Arin grant me strength to be faithful...and forgiveness for what I must do.

CHAPTER FOUR

A cold slap made Nicolas bolt upright. He touched his cheek where his face stung.

An older white-haired man with a neatly trimmed grey mustache and goatee knelt beside him. He wore long black robes, and a black scapular, trimmed in a thin red fringe, draped down over his shoulders to the middle of his chest.

"Good of you to join me," the man said. "If you're finished napping, perhaps we can try to stay alive? We can't stay here." The man leaned in. "Your eyes...the resemblance is remarkable."

"Did you need to slap me?"

An image of the skeletal warrior popped into Nicolas's head, and he suppressed a shiver.

"The skeleton."

"I took care of him," the man said, scowling. He leaned forward and pointed a finger at Nicolas's face. "That's something his priest should have done. He was suffering, you fool."

Nicolas looked up at the underside of a large marble awning and realized he was sitting in the entryway of the stone building he had seen earlier. The crag spider lay dead in the field.

"By Malvol, why didn't you control him? You know the danger of an unfettered penitent."

"A what?"

"A patrol could have seen you. You'll bring the Union down on us! Arin's arse, boy, are you an idiot?" He put the back of his fist to his mouth. "Now you have me blaspheming."

"Hold on a dang minute. Where am I? And who the hell are you?"

The man wrinkled his brow, then knelt and touched the side of Nicolas's head.

A strange feeling entered Nicolas's mind, like the tingling sensation of licking a nine-volt battery.

"Your accent is bizarre, boy, but you have no head injury beyond a lump."

"Don't call me boy. My name is Nicolas." Nicolas slapped the man's hands away and rubbed the back of his head. "Now who the hell are you?"

The man tugged at something around his own neck. "How many Halls of Power have you mastered?"

"What's a Hall of Power?"

"Who instructed you?"

"What are you talking about?"

"Calm yourself," the man said. "Strong emotion will make the awakening difficult. Unpredictable even."

The man's eyes flashed brilliant white. Again the feeling of dozens of electrical shocks covered the surface of Nicolas's head. When they stopped, he felt relaxed.

But Nicolas did a double take when he realized the man looked offended.

"What?" Nicolas said.

The man threw up his hands and shook his head. "Your head will heal in time, but your insubordination is anyone's guess. May the gods help us if—"

"How did you do that?" Nicolas stood.

"You wouldn't understand any answers I give you, and there's no time for explanation. The Shandarians are nothing if not punctual."

"I'm not going anywhere until I find out who you are and what I'm doing here."

"Dammit, boy! They will start with this crypt, for reasons that...should be obvious to you but aren't. We cannot be here when they arrive."

Nicolas followed the man's gaze toward the village and saw a cloud of dust on the far side.

"Then I suggest you start by telling me who and what you are," Nicolas said.

"Listen carefully. I am Mujahid Lord Mukhtaar."

"That's a mouthful, Mujeed."

"Mujahid. *Mu...Ja...*oh for Arin's sake. I'm the former prime warlock of Archmage Kagan, and Lord, by Rite of Testing, of Clan Mukhtaar, as is my brother Nuuan."

"Ok."

Mujahid squinted. "For reasons only the gods know, that name means precious little to you. As far as what I am...I'm a necromancer. By blood." Mujahid tapped Nicolas's chest. "As are you."

"You think you're a *what* now?"

"The answers don't help, do they?"

"Necromancer? Really? You don't know me very well, Mujahid, and that's cool. But I'm not an idiot. And I don't play with dead things." Nicolas stepped closer. "I don't know who you are, or who you think you are, but none of this is helping. I need to get home, and I don't think digging up corpses is going to get me there."

Mujahid scowled but his voice was calm. "There are elements of our calling I find distasteful, boy, but I take my responsibility with a seriousness I'll ask you to respect. I won't ask again."

"Our calling? I have nothing to do with this."

"And what's your explanation? You're ripped away from your home, find yourself under attack, and receive help from beyond the grave. Yet you find it difficult to believe you're a necromancer?"

"How did you know that?"

"Have you already forgotten it was I who rescued you from the angry, undead warrior wielding that named sword?" He nodded toward the wall where the sword was leaning.

"Not that. The *ripped away* part."

Hoof beats made Nicolas look up toward the village.

"Come with me and you'll have your answers," Mujahid said. "But we must leave."

The man was right. Whatever was coming was getting closer.

"One more thing," Mujahid said. "If you don't learn control, you'll end up killing yourself. Or worse...me. You should have professed vows years ago."

The ground heaved, tossing him and Mujahid to the marble floor.

"Of all the festering times for a quake," Mujahid said. "Follow me into the crypt." Mujahid ran into the stone building without looking back.

One of the columns supporting the stone awning collapsed, bringing a section down with it. Nicolas darted into the building and hoped he wasn't making the biggest mistake of his life.

H urry." Mujahid cursed as a column came crashing down next to him, missing him by inches. "The ceiling won't last long."

"Then why'd you bring us in here?"

"You'd prefer a crushing death over what those Shandarians will do to you if they discover what you are."

Energy pooled in Nicolas's head, and skulls circled in his mind once more. "I don't think I can be in here."

"Beyond the sarcophagi," Mujahid said, pointing in the direction of two large marble graves.

The mosaic ceiling shattered, filling the air with a cloud of dust. They dodged falling debris while weaving their way among the ornate graves.

The largest sarcophagus had fallen sideways, revealing a dark passageway beyond.

A giant slab of marble crashed down in front of Nicolas and cracked into two pieces.

"Quickly," Mujahid said.

Nicolas leapt onto the cracked marble slab and slid across its shiny surface. He jumped and landed in front of Mujahid, who pulled him through the archway and into the tunnel.

Mujahid's eyes glowed white again.

Nicolas felt dizzy and stumbled. Once more the electrical shocks covered his head.

The pitch black tunnel grew brighter, but there was no light source.

Nicolas squinted. "Where's the light coming from?"

"Your eyes, boy. I gave you the sight. Your power hasn't developed it yet. Keep moving. This tunnel is stronger than that crypt, but not by much."

A thunderous crash behind them announced the collapse of the marble entryway, removing any hope of going back.

"Don't look so bothered," Mujahid said. "If we can't leave, they can't enter."

A wave of nausea tightened Nicolas's stomach, causing him to double over. He could feel the dry heaves starting.

"Oh god," Nicolas said.

Mujahid placed a hand on Nicolas's head.

A wave of power entered, and the nausea left him. Mujahid's eyes had turned a brilliant white again.

When Mujahid's eyes returned to normal he scowled.

"You're well past the age, by five years at least. The rudiments of the art should be second nature to you, yet you stand here retching as if you've never channeled."

"I'm from Texas!" Nicolas said.

Mujahid grabbed Nicolas by the shoulders.

"You must be truthful with me, boy. Your life depends on it. Have you entered a Hall of Power?"

"Mister, you got a hole in your screen door or something? I told you. I have *no idea* what you're talking about."

"The room with two doors. Have you seen it?" Mujahid shook him. "One is light. One is dark. Answer me, boy!"

He remembered them. He also remembered the skull waiting behind the black door, and how the white door tried to pull him in.

Nicolas nodded.

Mujahid balled his hand into a fist and shut his eyes. "Did you enter one?"

Nicolas couldn't stop thinking about the skull floating behind the dark door.

"There was something off about the white door so I left it alone. And there's a floating skull behind the black one. It's always there. I feel the energy, I get sick, and I see the skull. That's how it happens. Am I going crazy?"

"That skull is the reason you exist."

"What do you mean?"

"You're a necromancer. This fact isn't conditional upon your belief. You can't eradicate truth by denying it. You have the blood, and you can't wish it away."

As much as Nicolas hated to admit it, Mujahid struck him as a straight shooter. He was out of options, and he didn't like it.

Nicolas stopped, hoping Mujahid would slow down. The man sure was spry for an old guy.

"Keep moving," Mujahid said. "This tunnel isn't going to wait for me to cure your insufferable ignorance. When did your skull dreams start?"

How does he know about the dreams?

An aftershock caused the ground to heave, and Nicolas stumbled.

"Answer me," Mujahid said.

"A couple of weeks. At most."

"Arin's grace, it's a wonder you're still alive. Stay close. Our destination is near."

Mujahid began running up the passageway.

"Texas, you said?" Mujahid said without turning back. "I've never heard of it. Tell me more."

Nicolas sighed and followed. What choice did he have?

They ran for several minutes, and three aftershocks followed the first.

The tunnel was damp in places, with small rivulets of water running down the porous walls. Nicolas covered his nostrils to block the smell of mold and dirt. He hoped Mujahid knew what he was doing.

"The power will fill you soon, but don't fear it," Mujahid said. "We're approaching a vast source of necropotency."

"A what?"

"I've slowed your awakening, but this will make you weak with the power." Mujahid raised his eyebrow. "Though it's doubtful you'll notice the difference."

Nicolas was getting tired of the sarcasm. Mujahid didn't like him for some reason, and he couldn't figure out why. He'd have to ignore it for now. The man was his only lifeline.

The tunnel curved to the left, and the rivulets of water disappeared. Energy pooled inside him, and Nicolas tried to stay calm like Mujahid asked him to, but when they rounded the curve, he jumped backward.

A crackling blue wall that looked like a force field blocked the tunnel ahead, and Mujahid wasn't slowing down. It emanated a faint humming sound that reminded Nicolas of a transformer at a utility substation...the kind always blowing up and causing power outages.

"What is that?" Nicolas asked.

"Why don't you tell me what you know? The list will be shorter."

Nicolas fought back the urge to insult the man and took a deep breath.

"Let's start with that then," Nicolas said. "I know that isn't a door."

"It's a barrier, boy. Barrier magic, to be precise. Not as strong as the Great Barrier, of course."

"This is the part where I ask *what is that* again."

Mujahid huffed. "The Great Barrier covers all of Erindor like a dome. Barrier magic is a mystical force, which serves whatever purpose its creator imbues it with. I created this one, and therefore it serves my purpose."

"That yellow sky has a barrier in it?"

"That yellow sky *is* the Great Barrier," Mujahid said. His expression grew slack. "The true sky of Erindor is hidden."

"Yeah...so...remind me what Erindor is."

"The Three Kingdoms. Though that name hasn't applied for decades. We're standing in the Shandarian Union, the northwest portion of Erindor. The Religarian Empire spans the eastern half of Erindor, and the Kingdom of Tildem lies to the south, smallest of the Three Kingdoms."

"Only one kingdom in the Three *Kingdoms*?"

"Long story. This small barrier in front of us protects the coven from quakes and intruders. Can we dispense with the lessons and get to safety?"

Mujahid gestured through the barrier, but Nicolas hesitated. The last time he stepped through something mysterious he found himself on another world.

Mujahid stepped through and waved Nicolas forward.

Nicolas tested the surface with his finger. He knew, somehow, he was in the presence of death...in the same way he knew at the car accident. It felt as if he were standing on the border between two worlds.

He couldn't do it. He took a step back, afraid of what would happen if he stepped through.

Mujahid shook his head and pulled Nicolas through the barrier by his shirt.

An electric shock passed through his body. The presence of death grew stronger now that he was on the other side of the barrier.

"Can you feel that?" Nicolas asked.

"Look around you, boy. This tunnel serves more than one purpose."

The natural stone wall of the tunnel turned into course, stone brickwork. The bricks were set in three rows of arched alcoves that lined each side of the tunnel, one row on top of the other. Each alcove contained a simple, unadorned sarcophagus. He expected to see cobwebs stretching from grave to grave, but the alcoves were pristine.

"We're safe from the tremors here," Mujahid said.

"What is this place?"

Mujahid looked down and shook his head.

"There's something you're hiding from me," Nicolas said.

"Oh there's a lot I'm hiding from you, boy. But it gladdens me to see you're not a complete dimwit."

"You don't even know me but you act like I insulted your mother. Why do you hate me so much?"

"You aren't the only one who has to adjust here."

"Are you serious? I got ripped through a black hole in my apartment, bubba. The worst you've had to deal with is a tourist with questions, so don't go thinking you understand me. Because our situations...not the same."

Mujahid pursed his lips. "You're right."

Of all the reactions Nicolas was expecting, agreement wasn't one of them.

"Wait. Did you just say I was right about something?"

"Don't grow accustomed to it, boy. You're correct, and in ways you can't imagine. Our situations aren't the same, except in one way...we need each other. You won't survive without me, and I...well...my concerns are my concerns for now. Trust is earned."

"But I'm supposed to trust you, right? Why? Because of your charitable nature or winning personality?"

Mujahid offered a bemused smile. "Few would speak to me as you do. You remind me of my brother."

"See, I'm not all that bad."

"The difference, boy, is that my brother has the power to get himself out of the trouble his mouth causes."

"Hey—"

"You're either brave beyond justification, or ignorant beyond explanation. Perhaps both. For now, keep walking."

"Where are you taking me?"

Mujahid smiled.

"My home. I'm taking you to Paradise."

CHAPTER FIVE

Nicolas followed Mujahid for what seemed like hours before the path widened in all directions. The moist brick walls sloped outward, and the path descended into an enormous cavern.

Cooking fires dotted the cavern, and people dressed in rags and patchwork shuffled along the pathways, stopping at the fires for food. Shelters made of cloth and bits of metal formed a ring around the center of the cavern, which was set apart by an iron fence. A bright, thick beam of blue energy extended down from a black void in the center of the cavern ceiling more than one hundred feet above their heads.

The smell of damp earth permeated the coffin-lined tunnel, but the dank atmosphere did nothing to suppress Nicolas's hunger.

"I have to eat something."

"A word of warning before we continue," Mujahid said. "I am not a man moved by displays of obeisance, but I am a person of significance in this community."

"How does this apply to me?"

"You will refer to me as *Lord*."

Nicolas rolled his eyes. "Come on. We're practically old friends—"

Mujahid grabbed his shoulder.

"This is serious, boy. My title and my name hold religious significance. Use these words carelessly, and you tread on fractured ice."

Nicolas folded his arms and Mujahid released his grip.

"Our community is hierarchical," Mujahid said. "A necromancer who forgets his place tends to live a short life."

"Someone insults you and you shorten their lives. Lesson learned, *Lord* Mujahid. What a wonderful place this is. Where's your visitor's center? I need to get a post card."

"We hold a sacred position in the infinite order of the multiverse. Our power, relative to one another, determines in what capacity we serve our god. A Mukhtaar Lord serves in the highest capacity of all."

"I told you, I get it," Nicolas said. "I say something the religious nuts find offensive and someone sticks me with a hot poker. Point taken. Do they wear hoods when they string people up? Do you tell them it's for the salvation of their immortal soul when you're lighting the fire?"

One moment Mujahid was several feet away, the next he was in Nicolas's face with brilliant white eyes. Nicolas hadn't seen him move.

An invisible force wrapped around Nicolas and lifted him against the cavern wall.

"Fool! You mock what you don't understand, and I'll allow it no longer."

Something had paralyzed Nicolas. He tried to move but he had no power over his limbs. He was under Mujahid's complete control. He felt cold. The last time something lifted him off the ground was in his apartment...right before he was taken. Was Mujahid somehow responsible for that too?

The glow left Mujahid's eyes, and the invisible force lowered Nicolas to the ground.

"I can't bestow four decades of experience upon you by decree," Mujahid said. "I'm your only guide, and there are some things you're going to have to take on faith."

Faith. It had been a while since Nicolas exercised that particular muscle.

"I, too, had a guide once," Mujahid said. "I, too, had to learn trust."

"Was he as pleasant as you?"

"She. And she is no longer with us."

Nicolas recognized the expression on Mujahid's face. The man looked like Nicolas felt. Confused. Angry. Sad. Nicolas thought of Kaitlyn and could almost smell her rose-scented skin if he tried.

"She meant a lot to you," Nicolas said.

"Mordryn was a remarkable woman."

"I appreciate you helping me. But you're asking me to trust a person who kills people who get uppity."

"A necromancer who forgets his place poses a serious threat to himself and to a divine purpose you know nothing about, much less understand."

Nicolas looked down the path into the underground village and chewed his lip. The reality of his situation was sinking in. The people down there were going to have expectations of him, and right now his only guide was this mysterious and powerful man. Mujahid held answers. Perhaps answers to questions he didn't know he should be asking.

Mujahid's grip tightened on Nicolas's shoulder.

"Come. We'll have much to discuss later. For now we enter Paradise and see about filling that noisy belly of yours."

Nicolas followed Mujahid down the ramp.

The squalor of Paradise surprised Nicolas. The people all shared a look of surrender. Their clothes looked as if they hadn't been washed...ever. The smell was awful. A miasma of mold, wet dirt, trash, excrement, animals and body odor. Whoever named this place must have been a comedian.

Beggars sat along the main path, but no one offered them anything. People were struggling just to survive here. Their gaunt faces and sagging clothes did nothing to conceal their starvation. He felt awkward, as if he had too much...pants and boots, shirt and underwear. He should be doing something for them, but what? He looked up at the cavern ceiling, not wanting to let his eyes linger on anyone impolitely, and again his vision was drawn to the blue beam of energy.

A group of tents obscured the end of the beam, but he got a clear view of it when they rounded a bend in the path. The beam led to a vibrant red sphere, not unlike the Vatican's giant fractured sphere in size, hovering several feet off the ground. The more Nicolas stared at it, and at the tiny wisps of energy that rose upwards, the more he realized the beam didn't end at the sphere. It began at the sphere.

"What's that floating ball, Muj—Lord Mujahid?"

"An orb of power. The barrier surrounding Paradise is powered by it."

"So it's a kind of generator?"

"If you're asking me if it generates power, then the answer is no. It doesn't create power. It *is* power."

"How long does something like that last?" Nicolas said.

Mujahid looked as if Nicolas had asked if water was wet.

"It simply is. Unless destroyed by magic."

Nicolas thought about all of the scientists back on Earth who would give everything they owned for a patent on that thing.

"Texas could use a few of those."

Mujahid chuckled. "Orbs of power are rare. That orb was obtained at great risk to my brother and me. There are many in this world that would see it removed from us, either by force or destruction."

A tiny ball rolled out in front of Nicolas, followed by a little boy, no more than four years old, dressed in rags and barefoot. Nicolas had to sidestep to avoid tripping over the kid. Short blond hair blackened by soot and dirt made the boy look as if he had never bathed.

Mujahid picked up the ball. "Here you are. Be careful now, child. You have no idea how precious you are."

The boy smiled, took the ball from Mujahid, and scampered away.

"You couldn't just make another one?" Nicolas asked.

Mujahid grabbed Nicolas's arm. "Tell me you value life more than that."

"Not the kid! The orb."

Mujahid released him. "Only the gods can create them. There is legend that implies humankind once had the knowledge, but I have my doubts. And there's no record of it in the Chronicles."

"Hard to believe anything could put a dent in it, much less destroy it," Nicolas said. "What's so special about the kid, anyway? You went full-on Gollum back there. Why's he *precious*?"

"There aren't many children left."

"Y'all know about the birds and bees, right?"

"What about them?"

"Ok, I got this. When a mommy loves a daddy, they get married and start kissin'...."

Mujahid gave him a dark look. "Living newborns have been rare since the barrier went up."

"What do you mean, *living*?"

"Exactly what I said. Women still get with child, but more often than not the babe is stillborn. Maybe one child in a thousand survives."

A man approached from the side of a tent. "Lord Mukhtaar. It is wonderful to see you again, Excellency."

"Luven, this is my postulant, Nicolas. He is new to our coven. I will be disappointed if he is harmed in any way."

Luven swallowed. He had the same look Toby would give when Nicolas scolded him for barking.

"Disappointed, Luven," Mujahid said. "Do I make myself clear?"

"Yes, my Lord. Very clear indeed." Luven backed away as if from a poisonous snake.

"Good. Spread the word."

Luven turned and ran down the path.

"Let me get this straight," Nicolas said. "You call this place *Paradise*, but it's actually full of starving religious people who are so dangerous you need to threaten some guy to make sure no one hurts me?"

"I wish I could tell you *religious* and *good* were one and the same. But I can't. 'And the Power looked upon the Tree of Life and was repulsed, for Chaos and Wickedness had become one with the Tree.' Emergentiae five, verse three."

Nicolas blinked.

"A quote from the *Origines Multiversi*. The *Mukhtaar Chronicles*. Like I said, we'll have much to discuss later."

"Well, seeing as how I'm a postulant, it'd be nice if you told me what that is."

"It means if I tell you to bring me food, you will do so before taking your own meal. If I tell you to clean my scapular, you will return it to me as if you had purchased a new one. And you will relish these activities, for it is a rare honor to be the postulant of a Mukhtaar Lord."

Nicolas felt the anger rising again. "Oh, so I'm your slave now?"

"To complain in front of the coven will give up the lie," Mujahid said. "We can't afford to have them asking questions."

Nicolas wasn't convinced. Mujahid had been acting like his boss since the moment they met, and now he was surrounded by people who expected him to act like a slave.

"I'm not going to act like your damned servant, Mujahid."

Mujahid gave him a stern look.

"Oh, I'm sorry, your lordship. Maybe you'd like to share the bible verse that tells me how I'm going to hell if I don't polish your shoes? I almost forgot! Shoe polish. I'll add that to my slave boy shopping list."

"Hell? You know nothing of the Hells."

Some passersby stopped to watch the exchange.

Mujahid stood face to face with Nicolas. His voice became a whisper.

"Get a hold of yourself, boy. You dishonor yourself as much as you dishonor me."

"My name is *Nicolas*."

The murmuring crowd grew larger.

"I'll stop calling you *boy* when I see a man before me," Mujahid said. "Until you learn how to survive in a man's world, I suggest you take your lead from a *man*."

The crowd looked as if they were watching someone defile a holy place.

Mujahid leaned in to Nicolas and whispered, "Follow my lead, you fool."

Power forced Nicolas to the ground, and he landed hard on his knees.

"This postulant has invoked the anger of your Lord, and he will be punished," Mujahid said. "He is as a ghost to you all. He does not exist until I command otherwise. Am I understood?"

The crowd shouted a mix of "Yes, Lord Mukhtaar," and "Yes, Lord Mujahid."

"And if any of you take it upon yourself to be the instrument of his punishment, I won't hesitate to become the instrument of yours."

The crowd shrank away and Mujahid knelt beside Nicolas.

"Your ignorance has served us here, boy. Of course it makes buying my food difficult, considering the merchants will ignore you now."

Nicolas was angry, but he couldn't deny he'd messed up. He had better get some perspective on this, or he'd screw something up that Mujahid couldn't unscrew.

Nicolas stood up when the force holding him vanished.

"These people fear you that much?" Nicolas asked.

Mujahid waved his arm. "The demonstration of authority you saw here was effective because authority isn't something I abuse."

Nicolas rolled his eyes.

"I'll do my best to instruct you, but if this is to work, you must trust me. If you don't, you'll die, and not because of some slip of custom or etiquette. It's that simple."

Nicolas looked away, thinking of the only people in the world he trusted that much. Dr. Murray, his adoptive father and mentor. Kaitlyn. Grief welled up inside. He had never felt this alone.

"Continue walking with me," Mujahid said. "I'll give you answers. That much I promise you. But let's see if you ask the right questions first."

"So instead of just telling me what I need to know, you're going to test me?

"Knowledge in the absence of wisdom is a dangerous thing, boy."

They walked among makeshift tents where vendors hawked their wares; cheap statuettes, old cooking utensils, mismatched earthenware and decorative items. People haggled in loud voices, stepping over each other at the chance to buy a serving spoon, or clay pot.

Everyone greeted Mujahid like a family member who'd been away. They were always deferential, but never fearful.

Mujahid reached into his black robe and pulled out a small brown pouch. He opened it, pulled out a fistful of gold coins, and distributed them among the people. The people thanked Mujahid, each accepting a single gold coin and no more.

Nicolas looked from face to face as the people approached. Mujahid had been right. Everyone was older than him. Aside from that one young boy, there were no kids. He hadn't seen any teenagers either.

They walked for several minutes along the eccentric route of vendor stalls, until the grating sound of a vendor's voice drew Nicolas's attention. He craned his neck to get a better look.

Flesh dangled from the vendor's partially exposed jawbone, revealing a bloody mix of sinew and muscle. One of the man's arms was devoid of skin and flesh, leaving only the bone behind. He had a rib cage and no internal organs whatsoever.

Nicolas couldn't breathe. He grabbed Mujahid's arm.

Mujahid shook his head. "It would appear some celebration is in order. I've managed to find the first necromancer in the history of Erindor who is afraid of the undead."

"Zz...zzz...zomb...."

"Get a hold of yourself, boy. Keep telling yourself that nothing here can harm you."

Nicolas looked into Mujahid's eyes. "Is that true?"

Mujahid inhaled as if to say something, paused with his mouth hanging open, then shrugged.

"Oh god," Nicolas said. He tried to keep his eyes off the other vendors.

They entered an area separated from the rest of the community by a plain metal fence. Fence was too fancy a word. It was nothing more than a bunch of metal bars held up by iron posts, with a piece of fabric serving as a gate. Sick people were lying on man-sized rectangles of sewn material stuffed with something that Nicolas couldn't see.

A man knelt beside one of the nearest pallets and wiped a sick man's face with a cloth. The sick man stared unblinking at the cavern ceiling. A foamy liquid dribbled from the corners of his mouth.

Mujahid stopped and looked at the sick man. "Pray that never happens to you, boy."

"What happened to him?"

"He failed in the Halls. Our numbers dwindle, and now we lose a good man to a foolish mistake. He should have known better."

"I'm sorry," Nicolas said.

"Don't spend time thinking on it now. Come. Paradise lies down another corridor."

"But...I thought this *was* Paradise."

"I know you did," Mujahid said. He started walking again.

CHAPTER SIX

T he crowd parted as they headed toward a large tunnel. A vitrified stone arch rose above the tunnel entrance, made from obsidian so black it absorbed hope.

A fiery orange pictograph surrounded by lettering that resembled Arabic spanned the breadth of the arch, embedded in the obsidian. The picture depicted a figure in a meditative pose hovering above a crowd of people who covered their faces. Beams of light shot out of the hovering figure's eyes and struck the people.

Two skeletal guards snapped to attention. They wore spectral armor from skull to foot. It was like they were wearing the *ghost* of a set of armor. Each had two short swords that were fastened to their hips by decaying leather belts. Their chests heaved as if their missing lungs needed to breathe, and dim blue light shone from their empty eye sockets.

Nicolas suppressed a chill when he got closer to them.

"This is my postulant," Mujahid said to a guard. "You'll allow him to pass, unharmed and without question."

"As you wish, *priest*." The undead guard's voice sounded like Toby scratching a fencepost, and he said the word "priest" like he was swearing.

Mujahid motioned Nicolas into the tunnel.

"I get the feeling they don't like you," Nicolas said.

"Their sentence is a long one, and that doesn't lend itself to happiness."

"Jail sentence?"

"The estate is ahead."

Nicolas chuckled. "Undead criminals. Amazing. You guys got zombie chain gangs too?"

"We're here."

They were at a dead end.

"There's nothing here," Nicolas said.

The nerves in his arms and legs spasmed from top to bottom. He looked up in time to see the glow fade from Mujahid's eyes.

"You did something to me."

"Yes. I did." Mujahid faced the wall.

"You gonna share with the class?"

"I...refreshed your vision. The magic was about to fade."

"It felt different than last time."

"You're an expert on magic now?"

"What's with the tingling on my head? Every time you use magic it feels like I stuck my head in a mini electrical storm."

"The *tingling*, as you call it, lets you know that someone is using magic nearby. How near depends on your abilities."

"But how—"

"What you're about to see is known to few. I'll teach you, but you will tell no one."

Mujahid's eyes glowed white. He pressed one hand against the stone wall and made a bunch of strange gestures with the other. The wall changed from solid rock to grey cloud, then evaporated into nothing. An archway tall enough for a man to pass through appeared in its place, and a field of pure blackness filled the space between.

"Well ain't that something," Nicolas said.

A familiar image drew his attention to the top of the arch. It was the symbol of the floating person with glowing eyes from before.

"That supposed to be a picture of you?" Nicolas said.

"Too much, too soon. You wouldn't understand."

Even Nicolas's enhanced vision wouldn't penetrate the blackness of the void inside the arch.

Mujahid stepped forward and disappeared into the void. Nicolas took a deep breath and followed the old man into the blackness.

He expected to walk into a pitch-black room, but globes of fiery-orange light, varying in intensity and elevation, floated all around the cavern.

This side of the arch was as pitch black as the last, but the pictograph above it was different. This one was in the image of a mountain with three peaks.

A massive structure filled the cavern. This must be the *estate* Mujahid mentioned.

The building, carved out of the cavern wall itself, was as large as the Texas state capital. The top disappeared into darkness, making it impossible to guess its height, but it was at least two hundred yards wide, and it was surrounded by several tall, narrow spires. Intricate patterns of gold and black scroll work decorated the building around the sides and up a stone staircase, which was as wide as the building itself. The stairs led up to three monolithic doors, each at least fifty feet tall and set back from the top of the stairs.

Statues spanned the top of a facade above the doors. But one statue stood above the others—a statue of death. An obsidian robe shrouded the statue, and it carried an ominous scythe. The entire figure cast a macabre shadow on the steps beneath it.

The whole thing reminded Nicolas of the basilicas he visited with Dad in Italy. The beauty and craftsmanship captivated him at first.

But his admiration turned to disgust.

Here, a short walk from the squalor of Paradise, Mujahid's palatial estate grew out of the stone floor, trimmed in gold, as if mocking the destitution that surrounded it.

"You live like this," Nicolas said, "while those people struggle to survive right under your nose?"

"You don't understand what you see."

"How's it feel to walk through that ghetto on the way to your palace? That gold you hand out ease your guilt when you sit on your throne?"

"You understand nothing yet presume to judge?"

"I know—"

"Nothing! Do you know anything about the history of this world, boy?"

Nicolas stared at him in silence.

The man had a point. Nicolas knew nothing about this strange new world, and lashing out at things he didn't understand wasn't going to help him see Kaitlyn again. Worse, it might get him killed.

He followed Mujahid up the staircase.

The room they entered destroyed any doubt the estate held religious significance. Twisting marble columns lined the cavernous room, their tops rising higher than the floating light spheres that bathed everything in an orange glow. Two broad transepts opened like great, arched tunnels on either side of a recessed apse at the far end of the room. A golden altar stood at the center of the apse.

Nicolas couldn't believe he'd stumbled across a baroque cathedral in the middle of an alien world. He wanted to study the place to see how far the similarities went. Why would a civilization build a place like this without any of the religious inspirations and symbolism of his own western civilization?

He wanted to dig. Was there a crypt? Was there an older structure underneath, like at St. Peter's Basilica in Rome? Was this estate part of a larger underground complex or city? What was it about the shape of a cross—formed by transepts, apse and nave—that spanned two worlds?

His questions would have to wait. Mujahid was already leaving through a large golden archway.

They emerged into a room that was smaller, yet vast by any standard.

Golden-framed portraits of men and women wearing long dark-blue robes hung above wooden tables and dainty chairs. The dark-blue scapulars draping their shoulders bore the symbol of the floating person with glowing eyes.

One portrait in particular caught his attention. A bright yellow creature with an enormous head and cavernous mouth sat with webbed hands folded. Chameleon-like eyes the size of basketballs pointed in two different directions. It wore a form-fitting doublet the same color as the robes, and a dark-blue scapular with a black fringe hung to the middle of its chest.

The religious imagery didn't stop with the architecture, it seemed. Catholic clergy back home wore scapulars as well, depending on their status.

Gold tiles and jewels formed a mosaic on the far wall. Multifaceted stones simulated magical flashes of light. Two tall skeletal warriors on the edges of the mosaic carried blades the length of a man's arm. They stood beside two men, each wearing the same midnight blue robes as the men in the portraits. One of them looked like Mujahid, but the other was facing away. Each man held a scythe like the one wielded by the statue outside. But the main subject of the mosaic stood at its center. A cyclops, at least four times the height of the men, swung a massive black hammer. Next to it a perfect sphere floated in the air, its shiny surface reflecting the magical flashes in a cascade of gems.

"Is that what I think it is?" Nicolas asked.

"I told you it was hard won."

"You fought off a cyclops for it?"

"An old, malevolent creature, with a long history of tormenting the people of Erindor. There aren't many left, Arin be praised."

"Is that other guy your brother Nuuan?"

"*Lord* Nuuan, postulant. Remember that. His disposition isn't as friendly as mine."

"You're the friendly one?"

Mujahid walked toward a staircase that ran up the side of the hall.

"Your quarters are on the second level. Mine is on the fourth. Training rooms are on the third."

"Those stairs go down too."

Mujahid turned on Nicolas. "Under no circumstances will you visit the crypts."

"I knew this place had crypts! Can't I just take a look?"

"I don't care what you see, boy. Explaining the death of my postulant will be very awkward, however."

Nicolas swallowed.

"There'll be a penitent outside your room. If you need more food, ask him."

"You said that before. *Penitent.* I know what it means, but I've never heard it used that way."

"The undead serve a penance for the evil committed during their life. And so we call them penitent."

A shiver of anxiety ran down Nicolas's spine. The dead were among his greatest fears, and now he was stuck in a world filled with the undying.

"We'll speak more about it," Mujahid said. "In fact, it's central to what you must learn."

They reached the second level, and Mujahid led him to a stone door at the end of the hall. A skeleton walked out carrying a tray.

Nicolas jumped.

"You'll get used to them," Mujahid said. "Eat. Then get some rest. I'll send for you in the morning."

The room was small and spartan. A bed was pushed up against the far wall next to a stone wardrobe. Next to the wardrobe stood a buffet blanketed with food. The centerpiece was a cooked turkey, but it was unlike any turkey he'd ever seen.

Four drumsticks?

His mouth watered, and he tore off a drumstick.

"Amazing," Nicolas said with his mouth full. "It tastes like turkey."

"What in the six hells do you expect a turkey to taste like?" Mujahid raised his eyebrow.

"But it has four legs."

"I know. It's a turkey."

"No, you don't get it. This turkey has four legs!" He pulled off another drumstick and held it up for Mujahid to see.

Mujahid shook his head and left the room, mumbling something as he closed the door behind him.

It didn't take long for Nicolas to drift off into a turkey-induced coma.

The rotting head dripped with melting skin, and saliva foamed from gaping wounds in the jaw, where missing muscle revealed teeth and sinew. Hair in a patchwork of clumps clung to portions of charred skin that hung from the back of the skull. A jagged, severed spine extended below the head, and blood oozed between the vertebrae.

It pushed itself into the room by coiling and uncoiling its severed spine.

A scream rose in Nicolas's throat, and he scooted backward on the bed.

The head burst into flames, filling the room with the scent of burning flesh, until nothing was left but a pristine skull.

It rose into the air several feet away.

"No," he said.

"Nicolas," the skull whispered.

"No."

"Nicolas." The skull raised its voice and drew closer.

"Get away from me!"

The skull rushed through the air, opening its mouth beyond the limits of human anatomy, unhinging its jaws like a ravenous snake as it reached his face.

Nicolas," Mujahid said. "Wake up."

Mujahid shook him.

"What happened?" Nicolas said. His head pounded like he'd been hit by a rodeo belt buckle.

Mujahid's eyes flashed white, and a wave of energy entered Nicolas's body. The headache vanished, followed by the anxiety.

"This is far worse than I feared," Mujahid said. "We can't delay any longer."

"Morning already?"

"I left you two hours ago."

"What's happening to me?"

"The Hall of Power calls, boy, but your lack of training prevents you from doing anything about it."

Nicolas leaned back against the wall.

"Did the skull explode with power, crackle with energy, or do anything out of the ordinary...that is, compared with previous dreams?"

"It was all on fire and stuff. I could smell it. Disgusting."

"This is important. You must follow my every direction."

Nicolas swallowed.

"Do you remember the sick man?"

"You said he'd failed in the halls, but I don't know what you meant."

"Not just any hall. A *Hall of Power*. Halls of Power are places where necromancers go to advance their knowledge. They are...mental constructs. And each Hall of Power is connected to yet another by a doorway."

"Anyone can do this?"

"Only those who can wield magic...people like us. *Magi*. And only a magus that knows his strength will emerge with his mind intact."

"So that guy that failed...he wasn't strong enough?"

"Strong, smart, agile, wise, compassionate, merciful...there's no way to know to a certainty. His priesthood was his own, and only the gods know the attributes he needed to do their will. Suffice it to say he was tested beyond his measure."

"I don't know about this."

"Your first Hall should be simple, but there is always a chance of failure."

"What do I do?"

"As in everything, begin by clearing your mind. When your mind is at rest, remember the room with the white door and the black door. The black door leads to your Halls of Power."

He imagined the room, and the entrance appeared in his mind's eye—the ornate door with strange symbols.

"If something harms you in the Halls of Power, it harms you out here. So protect yourself."

"Why does the white door feel wrong?"

"It leads to a perversion of our magic. Its arcane pathways run orthogonal to ours."

"Say what?"

"Stay away from it."

"So I should enter the other one?" Nicolas looked toward the black door. The skull floated in midair beyond the threshold.

"The black door is the path of the necromancer. But not yet. Tell me what you see."

"That skull. It's just inside the door."

"In, out, up, down...these are concepts that have no meaning in the Halls, and you must embrace this. For a necromancer, a thing can be both friend and foe at the same time. This is an important function of our work."

"That doesn't make any sense."

"The skull is your foe. It will attack you the moment you approach it. But it is also your greatest ally."

"So do I go in or not?"

"Calm yourself. Lack of focus will cause the Halls to collapse, and you'll have to start over."

"So I'll start over."

"You haven't yet entered a true Hall yet, Nicolas. You merely stand on the threshold. If the Halls collapse while you're inside them, your mind will collapse with them. Do you understand me?"

"Um...sure?"

"Oh for Arin's sake, boy. The skull will attack you *psionically*. Certainly you know what that means?"

"I don't think we have that in Texas."

"It means that the skull will attack your mind," Mujahid said. "But your mind and body are intertwined, so an attack against your mind is an attack against your body. You must never forget this. You'll have to defend yourself."

"But how?"

"Stay calm."

"But how do I defend myself?" A bead of sweat formed on his forehead as he realized he would be alone with that thing.

"You must answer that question for yourself."

"What? How?"

"Each of us brings something different into the Halls, and the opponents we face use our own minds against us."

"You've gotta be kidding me." What if he failed? What if he was killed because of some stupid mistake?

He shot backwards through the ornate door as if a catapult had launched him. He opened his eyes and stared at Mujahid.

Mujahid swore. "You can try the patience of a rock, boy."

"I'm sorry," Nicolas said. "I don't know what the hell I'm doing here."

"An ever present fact."

"I'm sorry."

"Enough with your sorry. Calm your mind." Mujahid took a deep breath. "Focus on the energy around you. I know you feel it."

Nicolas adjusted his position on the bed.

"No more than thirty feet below you is my ancestral crypt and—" Mujahid stopped as if he had almost let a secret slip. "Power permeates this place."

"It's all around me."

"Draw it into you."

"How?"

"Always with the questions," Mujahid said, and Nicolas's eyes snapped open.

Mujahid sighed. He placed his hands over his eyes and squeezed, but after a few moments, he patted Nicolas's shoulder.

"I'm an old man, and it's late at night. And...it's been a long time since I've had to do this. A very long time, indeed."

"You don't look too old."

"Boy, you have no idea."

Nicolas squinted.

"The energy around you is what we call *necropotency*," Mujahid said. "Some refer to it as *death energy*. Think of necropotency like a footprint in the snow. A person walks through the snow and leaves footprints behind, yes?"

"Some deeper than others, yeah."

"More insightful than you realize." Mujahid made a sweeping gesture across the floor with his arm. "The world of the living is the snow. As a person passes from life to death, they leave a footprint behind. Necropotency, death energy, is that footprint."

"Let's say I understand. What exactly does that mean?"

"Necropotency has life of its own, but it has no direction or purpose. The necromancer must imbue that energy with purpose and direct it toward an end...small tasks like moving an object, healing a wound." Mujahid pointed at Nicolas's head. "Taking away a headache."

"Summoning the dead?"

"Oh, Nicolas, that is no small task. That is our very purpose for existing. The undead are the reason Zubuxo has given us this gift. But...we must conquer your first Hall of Power or it will all be moot."

"Can I use this necropotency to calm myself down?"

Mujahid smiled. "The mind finally grasps what has been right before it. Direct the flow of energy to your mind, and let us begin again."

Nicolas wasn't sure how to do this, but he started by seeing if he could command the power to enter his body.

Power! In!

He didn't feel any different. He felt the energy around him, but it wasn't entering him like before.

Necropotency, inside me is where you wanna be!

Nothing. So rhyming wasn't the answer.

Abracadabra?

Still nothing.

So much for magic words.

Mujahid stood and paced. "The energy is like a child. You don't command a child to fish...you show it how to bait a hook. You are the magus. Direct it. Show the power what you want it to do."

The energy was all around him, as before. It brushed against him, making the hair on his arm stand on end like some sort of liquid electricity.

He imagined himself to be the drain at the bottom of a large tub, and visualized the necropotency swirling around the drain and entering him.

Every hair on his body stood on end.

The necropotency turned into a vortex that surrounded him and whipped the linens around on his bed. The food that remained on the banquet table flew up and around him, tracing the outline of the invisible tornado of energy. The vortex, and the objects it carried, compacted at a point in front of him and the room grew silent.

The energy slammed into the center of his chest, along with the food and linens, and threw him back against the wall.

"I see." Mujahid raised an eyebrow. "Might I suggest that next time you leave some power in the crypt for the rest of us?"

Nicolas groaned and sat back up.

He did his best to get comfortable with his back against the wall. He formed an image, but instead of water pouring into a drain, it was a small creek entering his mind.

"Good," Mujahid said. "Now call to mind the entrance to the Halls."

The skull hung beyond the black door, as it had before.

"I'm there," Nicolas said. He felt different this time. Serene.

"The skull will attack in a way I cannot know or predict. Trust your instincts."

Nicolas forced himself closer to the door.

"Doubt is your enemy," Mujahid said. "Doubt will lead you to failure. It is you who are the master of your mind. Keep your purpose ever before you."

Nicolas stepped through the black door.

A feeling of *wrongness* permeated Nicolas's being. He shouldn't be here.

Lord Mujahid told me to do this. So why do I feel like I did something wrong?

A light source above bathed everything in electric blue.

He expected an attack when he stepped through the door, but nothing happened. The skull was gone.

I'm not ready for this.

The light grew brighter.

How can I fight something I can't see?

As the light intensified his panic faded.

There's nothing to fight.

It comforted him to know he had been afraid of nothing all along.

I just need to sleep. Lord Mujahid will send for me in the morning.

The light radiated warmth that made Nicolas want to curl up and sleep. But his bed was missing.

That's odd.

The light was good. It would help him.

Out of the corner of his eye, he noticed his bed against the wall.

But it was gone a minute ago. No, I just missed it, is all.

He remembered sitting on his squeaky bed at home. Something was wrong that day, but he couldn't remember what it was. Mujahid had driven him to a funeral, then they went back home for a huge meal.

That's...not right, is it?

Every time he tried to focus his thoughts, it was like trudging through mud.

The sense of wrongness returned, but the light grew stronger. It called to him, and he wanted nothing more than to bask in its radiant warmth. Everything would be ok in the light.

But, how can light be coming through my ceiling?

The warmth grew stronger, but it was relaxing. He sat on his bed and unbuttoned his shirt. This was going to be the most restful sleep of his life.

The light was his life's purpose now. It was all he needed.

He reached into his pants for the picture of Kaitlyn. He always looked at her picture before going to sleep. He could smell her rose-scented lotion as if she were standing right next to him.

Clarity hit him like a bucket of cold water.

The light was his enemy.

He imagined a bubble of energy around his body, and the power left him, forming a barrier that closed around him. The necropotency shielded him from the radiance and cleared the cobwebs in his mind.

Idiot. I was under attack all along.

The light sputtered out with a loud crackle.

Something moved and caught his attention.

The skull had returned.

The rotting flesh burned away, and the clumps of hair disappeared, leaving pristine bone behind. It emitted a bright blue light, the same light that had tried to kill him. This time, however, it turned inward on the skull.

The skull vibrated, shaking in all directions as if trying to expel the light pouring into it. The shaking stopped and the skull floated backwards toward the far wall.

Nicolas didn't know how he knew, but he was certain something terrible would happen if the skull touched that wall.

He extended his arms and released power into both the wall and the skull. He could feel the wall as if the strand of energy was an extension of his hand. The wall was malleable.

He willed the energy to carve an opening in the wall in the shape of the skull, and it lashed out like an invisible whip, biting into the wall and changing it.

When it was finished he realized it wouldn't matter. The skull would still touch the wall.

The skull was less than a foot away from the wall.

Don't tell the power what to do. Show it!

He imagined necropotency running down his arm like oil and into the skull-shaped alcove. When the image was complete, the barrier around him changed shape and elongated. With a twist of his hand, he detached a smaller bubble and moved it into the opening. The energy coated the alcove like syrup. When the melding of energy and alcove was complete, the alcove emitted a bright, electric-blue light.

The skull slid into place like a brick in a wall. The alcove and skull collapsed together, and the wall's surface became flat.

Blue light sparked along the skull's outline like a blowtorch through metal, then went dim, leaving the image of the skull etched into the wall. It glowed with inner power.

He had won.

He exhaled and willed himself out of the Halls.

When Nicolas opened his eyes, something felt different in his head, but he couldn't place it.

Mujahid was sitting in front of him.

"Well done." A broad smile appeared on Mujahid's face. "You're an awakened necromancer now."

"So I don't have to run around doing your laundry?"

Mujahid placed a hand on Nicolas's shoulder. "You've learned an important lesson, but many more remain. Get some sleep. There'll be no more nightmares for you tonight."

Nicolas realized what was different. He could sense the presence of the glowing skull in his mind. It felt like a tool...or a weapon.

"What's this thing in my head?"

"It's called a symbol of power. Tomorrow I'll teach you how to use it."

"What's it do?"

"It raises the dead."

Mujahid stood and left.

Nick shivered. Dreams or no, he'd get no sleep tonight.

CHAPTER SEVEN

Tithian prayed Kagan would show mercy when he heard the news.

The labyrinthine passageways of the Pinnacle didn't slow him down as much as the new hole in his polished boots, but he was determined to reach the archmage before the general assembly met. It was better to deliver bad news to the Holy Archmage as soon as possible.

The Holy Archmage, who would kill his own son for political reasons.

He shook the thought out of his head. The archmage's holiness was beyond question. If Tithian didn't understand the divine plan, it was his own fault.

He vowed to spend more time praying and meditating. Perhaps he would fast during the month of Mose and make a small pilgrimage. That would cleanse his thoughts.

He turned a corner, found the marble column he was looking for, and made sure no one was watching.

Better to be safe.

He performed the *unlocking ceremony* his predecessor had taught him. The complex hand gestures were nothing more than a ruse designed to fool unseen observers. It was a form of power manipulation that involved symbolic objects that did the real work of unlocking. *Sigilmancy*. And few remained who were adept in its use. He channeled power into a carved wooden symbol in the sigil pouch hanging from his waist. The column turned, creating a grinding noise of dirt and grit, and revealed a hidden archway.

The dust and mildew choked him as he stepped inside. He'd have to thank Lord Mujahid for teaching him that clever trick, if he ever saw the man again.

If he doesn't kill me first for what I did to him, that is.

He cleared his mind and formed a mental image of the secret passage bathed in light. The power obeyed his will, flowing into his eyes and illuminating the pitch-black passage.

He made his way through the secret tunnels in the ancient underbelly of the Pinnacle to a room just outside the main hall.

Servants filled the hallway that led to the Council chamber. As Tithian scanned the mob, he saw the formal robes of the archmage and smiled. He had arrived in time.

"Holy One," Tithian said.

Kagan gestured over his shoulder for Tithian to follow.

"Warlock," Kagan said.

"Your son has been taken to Paradise."

Kagan stopped.

"Forgive me, Holy One, but the Mukhtaar Lord arrived before me."

Kagan grabbed the Talisman of Archmages from Tithian's neck.

"And how do you know it was a Mukhtaar Lord?"

Sweat beaded on Tithian's forehead. The necklace was beginning to dig into the back of his neck, but he didn't dare pull away from Kagan's grasp.

"The sacred light of ascendancy," Tithian said. "I watched as he saved the boy's life. He had the light. There was no mistaking it."

Kagan released the talisman.

"Why do you call him *boy*?"

"He is...that is to say...if it weren't for the talisman, I would never have believed he was your heir."

"Explain yourself."

"Your heir is...he has the appearance of a man far younger than your son."

"Could the talisman be wrong?"

"I don't see how, Holy One. Lord Mujahid himself—"

"Yes, about Lord Mujahid. Tell me about the other talisman. The one you swore you took from him."

The implication stung. He swore because it was true. What sort of man would lie to the archmage?

"It's secure in my chambers," Tithian said. "It was my first priority when you ordered his banishment."

"I want to see it," Kagan said. "Take your place in the chamber and wait for me."

A look of euphoria passed across Kagan's face and he turned. "Announce that I've been delayed. The Book of Life calls to me."

Tithian bowed his head and offered a prayer of thanksgiving for the Book.

It pained him that after all these years the archmage didn't trust him. His former friendship with Lord Mujahid made him guilty by association in Kagan's eyes.

When the archmage sees the Talisman he'll know I'm a faithful servant.

He entered the council chamber and his eyes were drawn to the Obsidian Throne as he walked.

It stood ebon black in the sandstone room, resting behind a small, wooden podium on a dais—a relic of a time when wood was in abundance. The perfection of its color and the history of the men who had sat upon it would intimidate anyone who knew what it was. But it was humble, almost self-deprecating in its shape and size. To those who didn't know better it was nothing more than an uncomfortable black chair.

Tithian climbed the dais and looked down at the assembled council members. Conversations turned to petty disputes between magi maneuvering for personal favors. They disgusted him, these self-aggrandizing politicians. Power-hungry magi who took greater interest in themselves than in the souls of humankind.

He looked at the podium and his hope returned. Today, the Book of Life would rest on that podium. Today, the council would hear the voice of the gods.

Tithian's stomach tightened.

The magi, grouped by nationality into three sections, fell silent as Kagan strode across the oblong room and placed the Book of Life on the podium in front of the Obsidian throne.

"Be seated," Kagan said.

"Yes, sit, you Shandarians." The voice came from Nebuch, a Religarian with an unkempt beard.

"If you have something to say, Magus Nebuch," Tithian said, "perhaps we can discuss the shipment you're expecting from Shandar?"

Magus Nebuch's face paled, and the other magi lowered their eyes.

Nebuch's addiction to Shandarian powder made him easy to control. But Nebuch wasn't the only magus with secrets. Tithian had enough knowledge of every magus in the Council to shame them into self-imposed exile, and he took every opportunity to make sure they knew it.

Kagan gripped the marble bannister circling the dais until his knuckles whitened.

"I have asked you for years—begged you—to help me eliminate the evil of necromancy," Kagan said.

"You cannot eradicate the old religion, Archmage," an older magus said.

Tithian recognized the man as Magus Gregory from the southern coast of Tildem. Tildemen were notorious for being sympathetic toward necromancy.

"The gods defined orthodox worship millennia ago," Magus Gregory said. "Necromancy is a valid Rite—"

"*I* define orthodoxy," Kagan said. He stepped down from the Dais. "*I* define what is valid."

Shouts of "Tildemen" and "blasphemer" rose from the Religarian magi.

Kagan raised his hand. "Come now, brethren. We spend so much time on the heresy of King Donal in Tildem that we often overlook what takes place in the northwest."

Angry voices rose among the Shandarians.

"It has come to my attention that a coven exists in the mountains of the Shandarian Union," Kagan said. "You'll recognize the name, I'm sure. They call it *Paradise*."

Several magi whispered "Mukhtaar" as if it were a holy word.

"Yes, brethren," Kagan said.

"Do the Mukhtaar Lords still live?" Magus Gregory asked.

Kagan looked down. "We have no reason to believe so."

Tithian tried not to betray his confusion. Had the archmage misunderstood him? He had been explicit about the presence of a Mukhtaar Lord earlier.

"Those overblown heretics do not concern me," Kagan said. "What does concern me is the presence of an orb of power within their city."

A hush descended over the Council.

"Our laws on this matter are sacrosanct," Kagan said. "It is forbidden to possess an object of power outside of the Pinnacle."

"If this is the Paradise of legend, there are forces at play we do not understand," Magus Gregory said. "Unless *you* are privy to the secrets of Unification?"

Not even Tithian knew those secrets. One of the greatest mysteries of the last century was how the Mukhtaar Lords unified the twelve necromantic clans under a single banner at Paradise. After Unification, no clan leaders remained except the Mukhtaar Lords, and Lord Mujahid never told him how it was accomplished.

Kagan stepped back up the dais and nodded to Tithian.

"Prepare, brethren, to receive the Voice of the Gods," Tithian said.

Kagan lifted the Book of Life high with both arms extended, and bowed his head. After a moment of silence, he put the book down, opened it to the last page and spread his arms.

A massive release of vitapotency rippled across Tithian's skin in waves.

Multi-hued lights appeared on the ceiling of the chamber, first as tiny points, then as larger spheres of luminescent energy. The lights danced in circles around one another before coalescing into letters. The letters formed words, the words formed sentences, and when the final sentence was complete the lights descended upon Kagan as one, entering him through the top of his head.

Tithian had seen the miracle countless times before, but it never failed to fill him with awe and wonder.

A distinct aura formed around Kagan, cycling through every color of the rainbow. His face contorted with every color change, as if each successive color hurt more than the last.

A shock wave of vitapotency pulsed from Kagan, blowing Tithian's long hair back, and he began to speak.

"People of Erindor, mark this day. The Mukhtaar ancestral home of Paradise will fall and the magic of death will be obliterated once and for all. Obey the archmage."

As he spoke, vibrant orbs of multi-hued light emerged from his mouth and traveled down the length of his arm. When they reached his hand, a parchment materialized next to the Book of Life, and the orbs leapt forward. Fire ignited as the orbs transformed into fiery words that burned themselves into the parchment and fused the parchment into the Book of Life. As the last orb inscribed itself onto the parchment, a visible shock wave emanated from the book, spreading outward in a translucent, golden sphere. That sphere would carry the sacred words to every Temple of Arin in Erindor.

"I take this command as sacred duty," Kagan said. His voice was strained. "This assembly is at an end."

Tithian climbed down from the dais with Kagan.

Kagan leaned in close and whispered, "Now let's see that Talisman of Archmages you stripped from the Mukhtaar Lord."

Tithian nodded and followed Kagan out of the Council chamber. Now he would prove his loyalty. Now the archmage would see.

Tithian's stone desk sat in front of the large polished-quartz window overlooking a courtyard. A four-post bed covered in an opaque red canopy dominated one side of the room. The value of its wood could feed a city for a year, but Kagan long ago forbade him from selling it.

"The talisman is locked away," Tithian said.

"Show me," Kagan said.

Tithian opened a small room adjacent to the main bedroom. The small box that contained the Talisman hadn't been disturbed in forty years. He retrieved the box and set it on a small table next to Kagan.

Three metallic clasps held the box closed, and each clasp radiated a yellow light in the shape of a key. Tithian waved his hand over the clasps and gave a sigh of relief.

"It hasn't been opened," Tithian said.

"Unlock it."

Tithian released power into the key sigil he carried in his sigil pouch and the box sprung open. He looked into the box and felt his heart race.

Kagan leaned over the box and swore.

"I don't understand," Tithian said.

Kagan pulled the talisman out and held it next to Tithian's. They were identical in every way, save one—Tithian's talisman radiated light and heat, but the talisman in the box emitted none.

"You were duped by a Mukhtaar Lord," Kagan said.

"But it was identical to mine when—"

Comprehension dawned. Of *course* it had been identical! The heir was already gone by the time Lord Mujahid was banished, so both *real* talismans would have been inactive. An inactive *fake*, worn by a savvy Mukhtaar Lord, would have passed for the real thing with no way to tell the difference.

"Holy One—"

"I have a task for you."

"You can trust me."

Kagan waved the comment away and smiled. "Your trustworthiness was never in question. You're a man of faith. I know you understand that your salvation depends on obeying my will."

Tithian's skin grew cold.

"Take your agents to the Shandarian Union, and Destroy Paradise."

"My agents are capable, but my duties here require—"

"Find the entrance to the Mukhtaar Estate. It will be hidden somewhere within Paradise. You're the only one I can trust with this."

Kagan walked to the door of the chambers, but turned as he reached the threshold.

"That orb," Kagan said. "Either capture it or destroy it."

"Paradise is protected by barrier magic. My trip may be a short one."

"You're not the only one with spies, *Warlock*. The barrier will come down."

Kagan turned back to the door. "I am a merciful man, Tithian. But if you fail me again, I fear the gods may demand a penance. As your confessor, understand that I will take no pleasure in you living the remainder of your days without skin."

Kagan left without closing the door behind him.

CHAPTER EIGHT

A sharp slap tore Nicolas out of a sound sleep and he drew back to punch the offender.

When he sat up, Mujahid was standing in the doorway more than ten feet away.

"How did you do that?"

"Like this," Mujahid said. His eyes glowed and another invisible slap hit Nicolas.

"Hey—"

"It was a hand on your face or a boot up your arse. I chose the one I thought you'd prefer."

"Real nice."

"You stick out like a virgin in a whore house, boy." He nodded toward the stone wardrobe. "Get dressed. Meet me in the training hall when you're done. Know where that is?"

Nicolas rubbed his face. "You told me yesterday."

"Did I now? Well...go where I *told* you, then."

Something had changed. Nicolas thought the old man had started warming up yesterday.

Mujahid left and a skeletal penitent closed the door behind him.

"Asshole," Nicolas said.

An invisible slap sent Nicolas flying off the bed.

"All right already!" Nicolas said. He heard a chuckle and footsteps fading.

He yanked open the wardrobe. A sour, musty smell permeated the cabinet. *Great. Moldy clothes.*

A single white robe hung inside with a white piece of fabric draped over it. Must be a belt, but there was something odd about it. It was wider in places, and flexible.

He took his pair of black pants off and tossed them in the corner of the wardrobe, but he kept his boots on. When he changed into the robe, he felt like he was swimming in it.

At least he left the belt.

He tied it around his waist, but couldn't figure out where the wide portions should go. They seemed comfortable in the back, where they draped down below his waist. The old man hadn't put any underwear in the wardrobe, so Nicolas didn't wear any. He gave the belt one last tug and ran out of the room.

A large doorway stood before him on the third level of the building. A mix of open and closed coffins lined the sides of the room beyond, and dusty cobwebs covered the entire place, as if its owners had abandoned it decades ago. The room smelled from centuries of burning candle residue, and wax hung like stalactites from the candelabra that stood between the coffins.

A grating noise made him turn. Mujahid was sliding the cover off one of the coffins.

"Real funny, Mujahid," he said.

Mujahid kept his eyes on the coffin. "Good. You're an early riser. You did well last night, boy."

"You can wake someone up without smacking them."

Mujahid looked at Nicolas's clothes for the first time and raised his eyebrow.

"What in Arin's name are you wearing?" Mujahid said. "Those aren't the robes I gave you."

"And just try putting a boot up my ass and see what happens."

"I see," Mujahid said. He closed his eyes and shook his head. An odd smile formed on his face.

"So you do think this is funny?" Nicolas said.

"Any time now, brother," Mujahid said.

The sound of rushing air filled the room, along with the cracking pops of tiny releases of static electricity. A foot stepped out from thin air between them, attached to a black-robed man that followed it. It was like watching someone step out from behind a mirror. The man was laughing and clapping his hands as he approached Mujahid with his back toward Nicolas.

"Brother," Mujahid said, shaking his head. "Torturing postulants again?"

When Nuuan turned around, Nicolas had to question his own eyesight.

Mujahid and Nuuan were identical twins.

"Postulant Nicolas," Mujahid said. "Meet my brother. Nuuan Lord Mukhtaar."

"He's a little long in the tooth for a postulant," Nuuan said. "Don't you think?"

"You didn't have to dress him like a woman, brother."

"What? A woman?" Nicolas asked.

"Look at him," Nuuan said. "He doesn't know teet from arse, and you think he's the one?"

"Excuse me...the one *what*?" Nicolas said.

Mujahid gave him an anxious look of warning.

"I think you'd do well to get your head out of all these books and your arse out of Paradise," Nuuan said. "Now that I think on it, getting your head out of your arse wouldn't hurt either."

"There's too much to be done."

"Hey," Nicolas said. "I'm standing right here, and I asked you a question."

Mujahid's eyes grew wide, and he held up his hand.

Nuuan's expression changed from joy to a mixture of shock and rage.

"On your knees, postulant!" Nuuan's eyes flashed white and something forced Nicolas to the ground by the shoulders. "By the sweat on Arin's festering—"

"Brother," Mujahid said, placing his hand on Nuuan's shoulder. "Please."

Nuuan exhaled a long breath. "Control your postulant, or I will."

"He is unfamiliar with our customs. It was *my* fault, not his."

Nuuan's face relaxed. "You'd wager the clan on him? After what we did to unify it?"

"After what *you* did?"

Nuuan scowled. "I may have been the blade, brother, but you were the hilt."

Mujahid looked down. "What's done is done. I've studied that prophecy for more years than I care to admit."

"Kagan isn't going to wait for him to be ready."

"Leave the worrying to me. It's time to head south."

Nuuan raised an eyebrow. "Tildem?"

Mujahid nodded.

Nuuan whistled. "There's no going back once I open my robe and flash the Pinnacle."

"I know."

"I hope you do, because when it starts, the two of us may be the only ones fighting. This boy-girl over here looks more apt to trip over the power than wield it."

Nicolas wanted to say something but thought better of it.

"King Donal is our best choice," Mujahid said.

"The Union—"

"Can't be trusted. And you underestimate Nicolas's abilities, by the way."

Nicolas wasn't expecting Mujahid to come to his defense.

"Malvol's festering cock, brother," Nuuan said. "My arse has welts from that flea-bitten *adda* they gave me in Agera, and now it's off to Tildem?"

"Blasphemy, brother."

Nuuan waved his hand. "The gods can—"

"Would you rather train him and I go to Tildem?"

"One day," Nuuan said. "Just one day."

Mujahid smirked.

"You're denying the fair women of Paradise their greatest treasure," Nuuan said. He frowned at Mujahid. "How uncharitable of you, priest."

Mujahid smiled. "The brothel has had enough of your treasure this year."

Nicolas adjusted his belt.

"That isn't a cincture, you little girl," Nuuan said. "It's a supporter."

Nicolas looked down at the belt and comprehension dawned on him. Nuuan had given him a bra, and...judging by the looks of it...a training bra.

"The room over there, boy," Mujahid said, nodding to his left. "You'll find some robes and sandals. Take anything that fits."

"And remember this, Postulant," Nuuan said "There are necromancers who would sever their own cocks to learn the arts from one of us."

"Nuuan," Mujahid said.

"You are a postulant of Clan Mukhtaar now," Nuuan said. "Learn what you can, and learn it well, boy. The path you're on—"

"Enough, brother," Mujahid said. He shook his head. "Too much too soon. Not good."

Nuuan chuckled. "You sound like old *fish breath*."

The two men embraced

"Be careful this time," Mujahid said. "This is different."

Nuuan nodded and walked away.

Mujahid looked at Nicolas. "Unless you're getting in touch with your feminine side, I suggest you change your clothes."

"Oh I'll change," Nicolas said. "But I'm keepin' my boots."

N icolas emerged wearing a long brown robe and his brown boots.

Mujahid had removed the covers from the remaining coffins and was holding what looked like a polished femur.

"Before I teach you to summon, tell me what you think necromancy is," Mujahid said as he sat on the floor.

The bone was unnerving, disgusting, but Nicolas joined Mujahid on the floor anyway.

"It's got something to do with raising the dead."

"True. What else?"

"Slapping people with magic and dressing them up like girls?"

Mujahid's expression grew serious.

"Being from another world is both good and bad. It's good because you come here free of preconceived notions about this world. Therefore, you're in the unique position of being objective. But you lack the most basic understanding of how this world functions. The world you're from understands the concept of sacred, yes?"

"We have religion."

"Excellent. How do you practice this religion?"

"It's not like there's just one."

Mujahid raised an eyebrow.

"There are billions of people on my world, and they all believe different things."

"Billions of religions?" Mujahid dismissed the comment with a wave.

"There's a handful of big ones. And they're broken into smaller ones."

"But they all remain the same at their core, no?"

Nicolas chuckled. "Not even close. Some worship a single god, and others believe there are many. Hell, if you landed on Earth and flashed those eyes of yours, somebody would worship your sorry old ass too."

"A world that believes in more than one truth." Mujahid shook his head. "Are contradictions a normal part of life there?"

Nicolas thought back to the nuns who raised him. They wouldn't be happy with the way he was answering these questions.

"I don't know," Nicolas said. "It's kind of complicated. Religion was never one of my strengths."

"Men often complicate the truth to further their own goals."

"I can buy that."

"So let me begin by telling you a simple truth," Mujahid said. "Necromancy is the most sacred gift bestowed by the gods. Through necromancy the spirit is made pure, and the dead are made worthy of their final reward."

One of the nuns would have smacked Mujahid with a catechism by now.

"All necromancers are part of a sacred priesthood. We are priests of Zubuxo, the God of Death."

"The death statue outside is Zubuxo, isn't it? I was right. This place *is* a religious site."

"Far more than you realize. Our charge is to assist Zubuxo in his eternal task of sorting the good from the evil. He takes the good and sees them on to their final reward."

"Leaving you with the evil?"

"Us, Nicolas...and precisely. Never forget, even for a moment, the creature you summon is evil. When it awakens to this world, it will have one wish and one wish only...to kill."

Nicolas wasn't sure he could do this. But if learning how to bring some psycho dead guy back to life would take him home to Kaitlyn and Toby, then so be it.

"There are varying degrees of evil, to be certain," Mujahid said. "Some spirits are so vile they can only be purified in one of the six Hells.

You will not be able to summon those. But the initial instinct of the spirits you *do* summon is always the same, because it's a survival instinct. They will kill anything within reach. You must gain control over your penitent as soon as you summon it."

"I was taught there's only one Hell, and it's eternal."

"There is another...no. Too much, too soon."

"But there's a bunch of different ways to be bad, right? Not everyone's a killer, so why do they want to kill?"

"The person you summon may have been dead for centuries. They are shadows of their former selves, left only with the rotting evil the God of Death saw growing inside them. Many embrace their evil, becoming more and more sadistic over time."

"So, it's our job to get them to see that they're bad?"

"A bad person doesn't look at their reflection and see a bad person staring back. Nor do most people commit evil with the desire to cause evil. We have to help them see the *consequences* of their actions."

"But if they can't remember anything, then how do we get them to see consequences?"

Mujahid nodded and placed the bone between them.

"Outside of the crypt, where we first met, you summoned the warrior without knowing what you had done."

Nicolas shook his head. A spider the size of a car attacked him, true. But he had nothing to do with summoning that homicidal skeletal dude who clawed his way out of the ground.

"Let's get this straight, now," Nicolas said. "All I did was get attacked. And why did it have a sword?"

"You raised a warrior from his own grave, boy. If you summoned a dead baker from under his kitchen, I'd expect him to be wielding a rolling pin."

"Still," Nicolas said. "Who are you to judge anyone?" The nuns told him people didn't have a right to judge others.

"You only saw a glimpse of that warrior's life. When you have control, and you summon with purpose, you will witness every evil act that person has ever committed. But that's often not the worst of it."

"What could possibly be worse?"

"Witnessing the consequences."

"Person does something bad, something bad happens in return. Not exactly a mystery."

Mujahid's eyes took on a faraway look, as if he were staring through Nicolas.

"You will see futures that are no longer possible. You will come to know and love children that will never be born. You will hear songs that will never be written and see great acts of wonder that will never be possible. You will see entire civilizations that will never exist, and in your heart you will know the sentence that must be served by your penitent, for in that instant you will know the blackness of their heart better than you know your own."

Nicolas looked down. "That's...horrible."

"Yes. And I despise every moment of it. But that is our sacred duty."

Nicolas started seeing the bone in a different light. He hadn't thought about those skeletons outside as people before, with past lives of their own.

"Do you understand what I mean by *sacred* now?" Mujahid said.

"I'm just wondering what happens when people die where I'm from?"

"Necromancy will help you understand a great many things."

Nicolas looked up.

"For a start you'll come to understand that there is too much to understand." Mujahid smiled at Nicolas. "And that, my young postulant, is the beginning of wisdom. Spend a few moments clearing your mind. There is more I must prepare."

Mujahid stood and walked to one of the coffins.

E nergy flowed all around Nicolas. At first it rushed in, threatening to force him backwards. But after a few moments he managed to control the flow so that it was a slower, steady stream.

He opened his eyes and saw Mujahid staring back. "Oh, sorry." He shut his eyes again.

"Your eyes don't matter. You may need to summon in the middle of battle, and battle isn't the place to close one's eyes, boy."

Nicolas opened his eyes again.

"First, a word about the energy you've been feeling," Mujahid said. "You must be close to a source of death in order to use it. Necropotency surrounds us in this estate, but beyond these walls that is not the case."

Mujahid took a step back.

"Look at the bone on the ground before you," Mujahid said. "I'm going to show you the first way of summoning the dead."

"There's more than one?"

"The first way uses a corpse. The second does not. Always use the first when possible."

"Why?"

"Summoning without a corpse takes its toll on you. It's called a *pure summoning*, and it uses more energy, because you're pulling someone from the Plane of Death and incarnating them here. They come back as skeletons of whatever race they were when they died. And they have neither armor nor weapons. Just rage and brute force."

Mujahid looked down at the bone. "This belonged to a man I knew personally."

"Was he a good man?" Nicolas hoped so. The thought of seeing all that evil stuff disturbed him.

Mujahid shrugged. "I've never known a good man who had no evil in him. And I've never known an evil man who had no good. Is your mind prepared?"

"I think so."

"That is something you need to know, boy, not suppose."

Nicolas sighed and cleared his mind as best as he knew how. "Ok, it's clear...I think."

Mujahid frowned. "Do you sense the symbol of power in your mind?"

"It's always there now, like a tiny point of energy. It's like I could point to it if I wanted to. Except I can't and...I couldn't. Am I making any sense?"

"Search for a place in your mind where the energy is accumulating. It's a like a pool of necropotency. It should exist close to the symbol of power."

"Yeah, I can feel it."

"Right now there's only one symbol of power in your mind. As you acquire more, they will aggregate around that pool of power."

"How many symbols of power do you have, Mujahid?"

Mujahid's eyes grew dark.

"Don't ever ask that question of a priest. Ever." Mujahid looked away for a moment. "It is rare for a Mukhtaar Lord to take on a postulant."

"Why—"

"Too much too soon."

"Yeah, *not good*. I heard."

"Imagine a pathway between the pool of energy and the symbol of power. Allow the energy to embrace the symbol."

Nicolas tried to force the power to touch the symbol floating in his mind. The power rushed out of him, but it had no other effect.

Mujahid shook his head. "Ordering something to do what it already wishes to do is pointless. The power wishes to assist you by its nature. It wants to embrace a symbol of power. But you must show it how."

Nicolas allowed the necropotency to enter him in a slow trickle. He imagined a small river of energy flowing down a pathway, at the end of which it struck the symbol and wrapped around it.

Energy burst from his well in a torrent and imbued the skull symbol with power. The necropotency pulsed in his head like a throbbing headache, as if it begged him to release it.

"I think I did it."

"Good. The connection will maintain itself until you cast the power or you are cut off from its source. Now, cast the symbol into the bone on the floor."

"How?"

"We should be past that point by now, boy. *Show* it how."

Nicolas imagined the necropotency reaching out like a cloud and touching the bone on the floor. Nothing happened, so he imagined the symbol of power flying forward and entering the bone.

His vision went black, and he started groping around like a blind man.

"All is as it should be, Nicolas. As you grow in power the blinding effect will lessen. Now, watch for the stream."

Images poured into Nicolas's mind. But they were flying past like debris in a tornado. He could hear bones clacking together, so he concentrated on the sound.

"You're hanging on to the present, boy. Embrace the time stream. Merge your thoughts into it."

A sense of goodness filled Nicolas, like the feeling he'd get after meeting a really nice person. When his vision returned, he saw a skeleton standing in front of him.

Nicolas wanted to run. He pushed himself backwards, trying to get away from it.

"No boy. Control it!"

It was the last thing he heard before the world went black.

CHAPTER NINE

Nicolas sat on the edge of his bed, frustrated by his inability to control his power.

"We need to continue your studies closer to the orb," Mujahid said. "It'll make this process easier."

"Why?" Nicolas asked.

"You want to find a way home, don't you?"

"Wait. The orb is my way home?"

Hope welled up inside Nicolas. Could going home be that simple?

"Orbs of power are more than repositories of energy," Mujahid said. "They hold knowledge, but like all objects of magic their range is limited."

"It happened so fast. What was I doing wrong?"

"What you made me do up there was unpleasant, and if you cause it to happen again, there'll be consequences you'll not enjoy."

"Hey, I'm trying as hard as I can here. Maybe I could have focused more on the images, but I'm doing—"

"Not the images, boy."

"Then what are you talking about?"

"How would you feel if you woke from death in the shape of a monster, and had no will of your own?"

"I would probably think I was going crazy."

"You would be suffering beyond measure."

"I didn't—"

"You made me send an old friend back to the Plane of Death, because you couldn't control what any postulant worthy of the title could have controlled."

"I didn't know that would happen. I'm sorry—" He stopped himself as the anger welled up inside. "No, dammit, I'm tired of saying I'm sorry. You're part of some...sacred system of things I don't understand, and you're expecting me to do things no normal person—"

"You're part of this sacred system of things too. Never forget that."

"You think I've forgotten being ripped out of my life, into...this? I was an archeology student a few days ago, and now you expect me to raise the dead?"

Mujahid yanked Nicolas forward by the robes until their faces were inches apart. "I'll give you time to learn control, boy, but know this...I'll kill you myself before watching you torture another spirit like that. Learn. Learn quickly."

Mujahid released him and turned away.

Nicolas looked down. "I'm not even supposed to be here," he muttered.

"I can't see the future, but it doesn't require a prophet to gain insight into what's happening here," Mujahid said. "You think yourself the victim of some cosmic accident?"

Mujahid clutched at the chain hanging around his neck. His robes always hid whatever was hanging from it.

"Did you take control of your friend?" Nicolas said. "I mean, when I couldn't?"

Mujahid's face became a mask of anger.

"*You* were his priest," Mujahid said. "No man interferes with the bond, not even another priest. This was *your* responsibility. This was *your* lesson to learn."

The weight of his failure grew heavier on his shoulders. He couldn't look Mujahid in the eyes.

"Now do you understand?" Mujahid said. "I was forced to kill my own friend because of your incompetence."

Nicolas hung his head.

"Now he exists as pure spirit, in a place you can't imagine, awaiting another chance to be purified. And when that moment does arrive, he'll be ripped away...confused, panicking, not understanding who or what he is, and thinking the only way he'll survive is by killing anything that moves."

"I'm sorry. I mean really sorry. If I only had more time."

Mujahid sat next to Nicolas.

"Time," Mujahid said. "Of all the illusions I've witnessed, Time is the greatest of all. It doesn't always behave."

"I don't understand."

Mujahid shook his head. "When you gain control of your power, you'll live entire lifetimes in a single instant. In the fraction of a second it took me to summon a penitent, I fought in a war that lasted fifteen years. I made friends...comrades in arms. We fought together, killed together, ate together. I killed innocent men because it was my job to do so. I experienced a future that will never exist. A future where I had a wife...and children. I watched them grow, and...I remember their names."

Mujahid's voice became raspy.

"So you mean if I raise more than one penitent, I'll live —"

"Don't try it. You'll only hurt yourself...and others."

"Ok, I'll —"

Mujahid leaped off the bed. His eyes flashed white then returned to normal. "This isn't possible. Come with me."

Nicolas followed him, trying his best not to trip over his own robes.

When they passed through the black portal, screams reverberated through the tunnel. It sounded like a riot was in progress. The screams grew louder as they drew closer to the main cavern, and Nicolas heard cries of rage and what sounded like metal striking metal.

A blast shook the cavern walls.

Explosion? How is that possible?

The main cavern was a churning sea of chaotic fighting. Fire had destroyed most of the vendor stalls, and bodies were strewn on the ground. Many were on fire.

The orb hovered in mid air, like it had earlier, but the energy beam was no longer shooting out of it.

That barrier must not be working anymore.

Charred corpses returned to life and people celebrated like it was some macabre family reunion. One by one, the reanimated bodies transformed into pure white light and vanished.

Black-robed magi were walking through the vendor stalls several hundred feet away, arms outstretched. Fire leaped from their hands, igniting everything in front of them.

A man ran toward them and shouted. "We've been betrayed."

"My penitent told me," Mujahid said. "Save the child!"

A skeleton ran out of a nearby tunnel and stopped in front of the man. No words were spoken, but the skeleton ran toward the black-robed magi as if the man's life depended on it.

"My brother and I have made provisions," Mujahid said. "But we must leave this place to its fate."

"But your estate," Nicolas said. "You said the orb's my way home!"

Mujahid gestured and two undead tunnel guards approached him.

"Slow the attack," Mujahid said and one of the skeletal guards nodded. "It's a losing battle, but you must buy us time."

Mujahid began to turn away, but something stopped him.

"You," Mujahid said, pointing to the skeleton on the left. "Approach me."

The skeleton complied and Mujahid examined it from head to toe.

A look of pure happiness appeared on Mujahid's face. "You know you don't need to do this anymore, my friend."

Something had changed about the skeleton since the first time Nicolas saw it guarding the tunnel to the Mukhtaar Estate.

"I know, Mujahid." The skeleton's voice sounded like rocks grinding together. "But this may be my last chance to help."

"I release you," Mujahid said. His smile grew wider. "You may stay, but know that when you fall, you will rise to new life."

The skeleton touched Mujahid's shoulder, then ran toward the fight.

"You witnessed the miracle of purification, boy." He grabbed Nicolas's shoulders with both hands. "Remember this day. This is why we exist. This is the *sacred order of things* you're so flippant about."

Mujahid's eyes turned brilliant white, and the slab of rock hanging above the tunnel entrance melted, dripping molten stone into the tunnel. A cube of energy, the size of the tunnel entrance, formed around the molten stone like a mold.

Motion drew Nicolas's eyes. A man in robes was running toward Mujahid with a dagger in his hand. He had to act.

He gathered as much necropotency as he could and imagined the power rushing into his energy well.

A wall of necropotency slammed into him, and knocked him to the ground.

He tried to send energy toward the running man, hoping to knock him down and buy Mujahid more time, but the power wouldn't leave him. If he didn't figure this out soon, Mujahid could be dead in a matter of seconds.

All Nicolas could think about was punching him in the face and sending him flying.

The power flowed down into his arm. His hand balled into a fist and Nicolas took a swing. When he hit the man's jaw, an explosion of energy rippled outward from his hand. The blast lifted the man off his feet and threw him back across the cavern, where he struck the far wall and fell in a heap.

Nicolas had never felt his fist touch the man. He heard a chuckle and turned to see Mujahid smiling at him.

"Undignified," Mujahid said. "But there's no denying the result. You work well under pressure."

Mujahid noticed something over Nicolas's shoulder, and a look of pure horror appeared on his face.

More black-robed magi had joined hands and were circling the orb of power. A glow of energy surrounded them, but there was something different about the way it felt. It wasn't necropotency.

"It's too late now," Mujahid said. "We must leave."

Mujahid ran toward one of the tunnel entrances.

Energy from the joined magi flowed into the orb. The orb pulsated and shook, its motion becoming chaotic and violent as it absorbed the energy.

The magi looked at one another and dropped their hands. They broke from their circle and fled, colliding with one another in their haste and terror.

The orb stopped shaking and seemed to absorb all sound and light. Then it exploded in a brilliant blue flash of raw power, sending a shock wave that demolished everything in its path.

When it reached Nicolas and Mujahid it knocked them off their feet, tossing them forward into the air. When they landed, Nicolas glanced backward to see what was happening. His heart sank.

The orb was gone. It was supposed to teach him how to get home, and that circle of magi destroyed it.

"They have Paradise now," Mujahid said, "but the estate is sealed. We'll return someday, but for now we run."

Mujahid ran into a nearby tunnel, followed by two skeletal warriors that were standing on guard.

Nicolas ran after them.

Shouts rose up behind them.

"They're following us," Nicolas said.

"I'm aware of that," Mujahid said. He never slowed or looked back.

The muffled sound of the pursuing invaders echoed off the tunnel walls and grew louder.

Mujahid swore and came to an abrupt stop as they rounded a bend in the tunnel.

Enormous boulders blocked their path. Fractured beams of a collapsed supporting lay strewn across the tunnel.

The sound of feet pounding on stone grew louder behind them.

"Guard us," Mujahid said, and the skeletal warriors drew swords and took a position near the bend in the tunnel.

Mujahid grabbed Nicolas's shoulder and caught him by surprise. "The orb's destruction weakened me. You must overcome your fear of the undead and summon a penitent."

"Mujahid, I—"

"I can clear this passage, but it will take time. I can't summon and melt stone at the same time. Not anymore. You must fight."

"This isn't a good idea."

"When a starving beggar finds moldy bread, he eats it."

Nicolas frowned. "Wait. Am I the beggar, or the mold?"

"Just do it!"

Mujahid turned back to the stone, his eyes glowing white. The stone started melting in small droplets.

"You can do this, boy." Mujahid's voice sounded distant, as if it took great effort for him to speak. "You're a necromancer. This is your calling."

The rattling armor of their pursuers grew louder. Nicolas needed to do this now. He opened his mind to the necropotency surrounding Paradise and allowed it to flow into his well of power.

He imagined a river flowing from the well of necropotency to the skull that hovered over it. But there was nothing to channel the energy into here. The realization nearly broke his concentration, and he struggled to hold onto the power.

He focused on what he thought they needed—a serious badass. A predator killing its prey with ease was all he could think of, so he imagined a cheetah taking down a turtle and visualized the necropotency flowing from the skull to the image of the cheetah.

The power left him, and the ground shook as pieces of rock flew upward, and struck the tunnel ceiling. This time he was ready to embrace the stream. His vision dimmed, and he waited for the images he knew would come.

Time started misbehaving.

A stream of images entered his mind.

He was no longer Nicolas. He was *Ensif.*

He was no longer human. He was an a*rgram*, a creature of nightmare preparing for a battle he craved with every fiber of his being.

Darkness blanketed the hive, causing the drones to burrow deeper in fear, but Ensif embraced it. Only the drones and the two-arms feared the night, and *he* was the night. The two-arms had good cause to fear him. He would pull them apart and delight in their screams. He would make his queen proud.

He flexed all six of his arms and felt the power in his two muscular legs. He looked around at the army invading his home and vowed to make them feel pain for every life they took.

He folded his central arms around his thorax and extended the other four in an x-shape to signal his commitment.

The hive mind reacted with pleasure. *The hive is life.*

The *warrior call* took control of his consciousness. He unfolded the six tarsal swords that grew within his body and attacked. He was a living weapon, tireless, and he flowed through the enemy dropping opponents six at a time.

The images shifted around Nicolas...*Ensif*, and he stood in a village. Screams rose through the night as straw huts burned to the ground, trapping the two-arms inside. He could sense the joy of the hive with each death he caused.

The hive is life. Purge the hive.

This was no longer war. This was extermination. Only one race would rule this world, and he would make sure it was the Argram.

The hive mind cheered in solidarity as his thoughts passed to every one of his nestlings. They were many, yet they were one. His segments quivered in reverence as the queen silenced them.

Purge the hive, my soldiers, the queen said. *Then bring me drones to feed on.*

A two-arm girl, not yet a woman, was hiding in the entryway of a hut that had escaped the fire. She cowered in terror, and his pincers clacked in anticipation of the kill.

His reticulated eyes calculated the distance between them. Twenty-five yards. It would be effortless. He could leap three times that distance if needed. With a single push of his powerful legs he landed in front of her. The girl stumbled and brushed against him. Her grotesque, soft skin touched his scaly carapace and the blood lust filled him.

She disgusted him.

He felt the reaction of his nestlings, and the hive mind spoke as one in his head. *Make it suffer.*

With the simple flick of one of his six tarsal swords he severed one of her arms and legs, and blood drained from her face. He spat resin into the wounds to stop the bleeding. The toxic adhesive would cause the girl great pain. He'd pull her remaining leg and arm off, of course, but it would be the resin that killed her.

The images swirled.

Nicolas was no longer the rage-filled argram. He was an observer this time, as if he were watching a movie play out on a screen in his mind's eye. When the images sharpened into focus, he saw a woman.

The necropotency became a torrent of information and sensation.

The woman was in love, and it was a pure love that radiated through his entire being. She would be married tomorrow, and start her life as a chieftain's wife.

But he knew, somehow, that what he was seeing would never be.

No. This isn't possible.

His mind worked with necropotency-enhanced speed, drawing connections between events with ever-increasing accuracy. She would never marry, because the argram killed her when she was a child. He tortured her after cutting off a leg and an arm, until the torment was no longer fun for him. She died a horrible death, writhing in agony from the venom that flowed through her veins.

Her marriage would never be. This woman would never be.

Fifteen years passed as he observed the woman from a distance, until one day she bore two sons of her own. She taught them how to read and write so that one day the oldest could take over for his father.

The oldest grew into a powerful man, waging war and protecting his people from the argram attacks. Nicolas followed the woman's son through marriage, having children, running the village from day to day, and finally growing old and sick.

In a large building at the end of a muddy road that snaked its way between thatch-roofed houses, the woman's son, now an old man, lay on his death bed.

A son who will never be, born of a woman who will never be. What's happening to me?

"Take care of them, my son," the old man said to a younger man holding his hand. "The argram rage against us because they fear us. And they have good cause. What have we ever brought them but pain? We started this many generations ago. We should have befriended them. Instead, we were selfish and greedy."

"There is no way to reason with them. They are animals," the younger man said.

"No. They are people. You will lead our people when I pass. Promise me you will lead them to peace, not war."

"But father, the elders will never allow —"

"Promise me." The old man's grip tightened on the younger man's hand, and his eyes burned with single-minded intent.

"By our ancestors, father. I will honor your final wish as if it were my own."

After the death of the woman's son, Nicolas walked beside the younger man, her grandson, for forty years, watching as he grew older and worked tirelessly to bring about the dying wish of his father. When the task was accomplished, he stood upon a raised platform and addressed the people of Lasin...his people.

Three argram warriors stood next to the man. And for the first time he saw their faces, insect-like with more eyes than he could count. Articulated, overlapping scales covered their bodies, serving as impenetrable armor. He looked at their powerful legs, remembering the jump he...no, the jump *Ensif* made...and saw that they bent backwards.

Each of their six arms ended in three protrusions that gripped together like fingers, but a single bone in the shape of an elongated razor, no more than two feet long, folded back from the wrist into a slot in the arm, like a knife slides into a sharpener. A tarsal sword.

The man cleared his throat, and all eyes turned toward him.

"Remember this day, people of Lasin. Today is the day we forge peace between Argram and Lasinian."

A peace that will never be, forged by a man who will never exist.

The images swirled again and Nicolas felt as if he were falling. But when he opened his eyes, some unseen force was lifting him into the air. The whole of civilization spread out over the surface of a planet below him. Argram and Lasinian lived and worked together, and their combined intellect produced the greatest works of art, science, and philosophy the world had ever known.

None of this will ever happen!

Nicolas wept.

An entire civilization robbed of its existence because of rage and revenge. How could they let this happen?

It was too much. He felt dirty, as if the residue of a billion sins coated his skin. Rage formed inside him to rival the rage of the Argram, and it threatened to consume him in an outpouring of arcane energy. He calmed his mind, knowing he would make this creature pay for every evil act. Ensif would pay for every life whose existence he had stolen. He would pay for every song that went unwritten. Every painting left unpainted.

Clarity washed over him, and he knew the punishment this creature would have to endure to be purified. Ensif would live as a penitent for thousands of years, and Nicolas would be the instrument of his purification, every step of the way, until the argram had paid every last penny of Zubuxo's price.

When the rage subsided, a comforting thought came to him.

Salvation is possible...even for Ensif.

Time behaved again.

Nicolas was back in the cavern with Mujahid, but he'd experienced over a hundred years in a fraction of a second.

An undead argram stood before him. The creature's appearance hadn't changed much. Dozens of tiny sockets had replaced the eyes he recalled from the images. Ensif's body was thinner, but he had been mostly bone to begin with.

Six tarsal swords unfolded and the argram reared.

Nicolas imagined the argram shackled by a leash, and the creature froze in place.

A pathway to the argram formed in Nicolas's mind, and he knew he was in control. He couldn't help grinning. Mujahid was too busy clearing away rock to have noticed, though.

The sound of swords clashing against swords told him the invaders must have reached the skeletal warriors.

The argram spoke with a hiss. "Why have you summoned me, priest? Why do I no longer sense my nestlings?" The argram folded his swords.

"Go take care of those dudes who are chasing us."

Impotent rage emanated from the necromantic bond. Ensif wasn't happy.

Whatever, bug face. You don't gotta like it, you just gotta do it.

The argram leapt around the bend in the tunnel with one thrust of his legs. Screams of the dying invaders echoed through the passage as Ensif slaughtered them without effort. Ensif returned a few seconds later.

"The task is finished, priest," Ensif said.

Nicolas thought the argram sounded insulted, like a noble being asked to make his own bed.

"Your name is *Ensif*, isn't it?" Nicolas said.

"That name no longer holds meaning for me, priest."

"I'm sorry, Ensif, but you're wrong. I think this is all about knowing yourself. And you don't realize who you are and what you've done."

"Release me," Ensif said. "I served my hive with honor."

"Was it honor when you tore that girl limb from limb for no other reason than she was human?"

"There were many girls. The humans treated us no better."

"And they'll pay for what they did, too. There were no —"

"How are you speaking with it?" Mujahid said.

The voice startled Nicolas. He turned around and saw the passage was clear. Mujahid was staring at him with a strange expression on his face.

"What do you mean?" Nicolas said.

"That language, boy. How could you know it?"

"He's talking the same language we are."

Mujahid's eyes widened, as if comprehending what had happened. "You summoned it? How in Arin's name did you manage it?"

He shuddered when he thought of the images he had seen. No, he could never think of that experience as *imagery* anymore. He had lived another person's life, as Mujahid warned him he would. And more...he had watched an impossible future unfold from the vantage point of a god. He felt as if he was as responsible for everything that happened as Ensif was. He wasn't sure he'd ever feel clean again.

"Gods," Mujahid said. "What else might you be capable of? Maintain the bond, and follow me. We make for Egis."

"What the hell's an *Egis*?"

"The easternmost city in the Shandarian Union, on the border of Religar."

"The Shandar *what* on the *where* now?"

Mujahid rolled his eyes. "Just follow. And keep that thing on a short tether."

CHAPTER TEN

They made camp at a rock outcropping in the foothills of a mountain range.

Magical fire pulsed with a rhythmic hum under the amber sky, sending vapor into Nicolas's face whenever the breeze changed direction. He had asked Mujahid why they didn't build a normal fire and was rewarded with a startled look and something about how he'd sooner burn gold. Mujahid told him wood was becoming less common since the Great Barrier went up, and no one knew why, though he thought it had something to do with the hidden sun.

Nicolas was happy to rest his sore feet. They had walked for hours after leaving the mountain tunnel, and blisters from too many hours in boots were stinging him.

Dwarf trees, no taller than two or three feet in height, peppered the landscape, scattered amongst scrub brush that covered the ground in patches.

Mujahid hadn't spoken two words in the last couple hours. Whenever he did take the time to look at Nicolas, he looked like a person trying to solve a puzzle.

Nicolas sensed the argram even though the creature was out of sight. It was unnerving, as if he had discovered a sixth sense every bit as clear as his vision.

"That penitent of yours is a good hunter," Mujahid said, breaking the awkward silence.

Nicolas snapped out of his thoughts.

"You should send him to fetch game for us to eat. In the morning, we'll go on to Egis and continue your training with the coven there. It will be slower, but...it is what it is."

Nicolas sent the argram away. "What the hell happened back there in Paradise?"

Mujahid glanced up at the sky. "It's night, you know. There was a time when countless stars filled the sky. Now, even the moons are hidden. What you see now is the naked barrier itself, unlit by the sun." He mumbled something under his breath and looked at Nicolas. "It's no coincidence I found you near that crypt when I did, boy."

"I'm listening," Nicolas said.

Mujahid pulled at the necklace hanging from his neck until a glowing amulet emerged from his robes.

"This is the symbol of your birthright. The Talisman of Archmages."

Nicolas reached for the amulet.

"No, boy." Mujahid tried to snap the necklace back, but Nicolas was too quick.

When Nicolas's fingertip touched the amulet, the ground pulled away from him.

The world started spinning and no matter where he looked, everything was rushing away from him.

He emptied his stomach. He couldn't tell which direction was up and which was down for several minutes.

"That was my fault," Mujahid said. "I should have warned you. Don't touch this anymore."

"What the hell happened? And why isn't it doing the same thing to you?"

"What do you know of your past? I mean the world you came from?"

"I wish you'd stop dodging my questions—"

"I'm trying to answer them, boy. Now tell me how much you remember of your past."

"What's to tell? My parents either died, or didn't want me. I ended up at an orphanage run by the church and spent some time in foster homes. There was a man who was like a father to me. But he's gone now." A pang of grief returned when he remembered Dr. Murray and the funeral.

"There's no easy way for me to tell you this," Mujahid said.

Nicolas tried to suppress the lump forming in his throat. "What?"

Mujahid spread his arms. "I held you in these hands when you were a babe. I presented you to your father myself, as Prime Warlock."

Nicolas felt like a man who had just discovered his girlfriend was a guy. "What?"

"It was at the Pinnacle...the center of religious authority in Erindor, ruled by a body called the *Council of Magi*. Their leader is a man known as the Archmage. Kagan."

Heat rose inside Nicolas.

"I was the one who cast the binding spell on this Talisman...I linked it to your soul. It's an object of power...a tool that leads whoever wields it to you. You became dizzy because you were locating yourself. Not a wise thing to attempt."

A war of emotion erupted inside Nicolas, cycling through feelings faster than he understood them. Shock at news he thought impossible. Anger at being a cosmic pawn of some sort. Fear that he might never see Kaitlyn again. Despair over being helpless to do anything about it. But the feelings settled on anger. None of this was true. Mujahid had to be lying to him. Had to be.

"You're crazy," Nicolas said. "I mean, you're nuts." He slapped the rock he was sitting on, making his hand vibrate with pain. "This whole place is nuts!"

Mujahid swore. "Too much, too soon. I should take my own advice." He placed a hand on Nicolas's shoulder. "I know you must feel somewhat—"

"No!" Nicolas said and pushed Mujahid's hand away. "I don't believe any of it."

"Objective truth doesn't require your belief to remain true," Mujahid said.

Nicolas turned away.

"There are those of this world who would see Necromancy wiped from the face of Erindor and replaced by a perversion of magic they call *Life Magic*. It was life magi who led the invasion of Paradise."

"No," Nicolas said. He pushed Mujahid away with a forceful shove. "You're wrong about that. You're wrong about everything."

"I need you to calm yourself and take this in," Mujahid said.

Nicolas tried, but he couldn't deny it anymore. He'd seen too much. In his mind, a link pointed him toward an undead insect he'd called back from the grave, and a glowing skull floated around a well of power. No, he couldn't deny it anymore.

Nicolas turned to Mujahid. Rage simmered under the surface of his emotions, but he trusted the man. "I'm still listening."

"Good. Because there's more to this festering mess."

Mujahid took a seat on another boulder behind Nicolas. He took a deep breath and sighed.

"Archmage Kagan is your father, Nicolas. You are the heir to the Obsidian Throne, next in line to be the supreme religious leader in the Three Kingdoms."

Nicolas stared straight ahead. The words weren't making sense to him.

"He will stop at nothing to find you. He wants you trained in life magic, and I can't allow that. I won't."

"My father is alive, and he lives here. On another world."

"That's all you took from what I told you? Listen, boy. No one in Erindor wields more life-magic than he does. No one wields more political cunning. And no one wields more religious authority. He may not be a king, but that matters little when the world considers him the voice of the gods."

Nicolas thought back to his Western Civilization classes in college. Kings and Queens deferred to the Pope, or their own people rose up against them.

"Ok, let's say you're right and I believe all this. Why would my father want me trained as a life magus? Won't I die if I stop training in necromancy? You said yourself the skull would have killed me."

Mujahid closed his eyes and sighed. "Necromancy isn't the only path through the Hall of Power. Many of those life magi were once necromancers."

"See, that's the kind of thing you tell a guy before he enters a Hall of Power and hangs his hat on one of those doors."

"You've felt the wrongness of the white door in your heart. Passing through that door puts you on the path to becoming a life magus, and it's a difficult path to find your way back from."

Nicolas remembered how much the white door had disgusted him.

"There was a time your father was a good man and friend of mine. But life magic corrupts. It stands against everything we hold sacred." Mujahid glanced at the sky. "In his madness your father created that monstrosity. I watched as he defied the gods and defiled the Pinnacle, and they branded me a traitor for standing against him. That was the day I saw you taken. I had no proof he was lying...that he was a false prophet, so Clan Mukhtaar was driven underground."

Nicolas kept shaking his head. "I can't be this person."

"I'm sorry, boy. But somewhere inside, you know I'm right."

Nicolas wanted to cry out in rage. He wanted to pick up the boulder Mujahid was sitting on and turn it over.

"Remember what I taught you about clearing your mind," Mujahid said. "Necropotency heightens your senses. When emotion battles reason, it can help."

"I don't feel much around here."

"You must be close to a source to use it. There are few nearby, so your power is limited."

Nicolas drew some power into his well.

"I've lived my entire life away from here," Nicolas said. "Why pull me back now?"

"The gods have a plan for you that I can only guess at. A guess based on wisdom, but a guess nonetheless." Mujahid put his hand on Nicolas's shoulder. "I've waited for you for many years, boy."

Nicolas squinted. "How'd you know I'd ever come back?"

Mujahid clutched his necklace. "This isn't the only Talisman of Archmages. Its twin hangs around the neck of my successor. Because of it, the archmage knows you've returned, and he knows where you are."

"So what now?"

"If there's one thing we can count on from your father, it's arrogance. He doesn't know all of my secrets."

A rhythmic pounding on the ground drew Nicolas's attention, but he couldn't see where it was coming from. The sound seemed to come from all directions at once.

"Arin's arse," Mujahid said. "Follow me, and make as little noise as possible."

"What is it?"

"Did you not hear me the first time? The archmage tracks your every move. If I can find you in the middle of nowhere, so can he."

Mujahid wove a path through the shrubs.

The dull pounding grew louder and Nicolas struggled to keep up with Mujahid.

"Your argram, boy. Call to him."

"Ensif!" Nicolas yelled.

Mujahid smacked him on the back of the head.

"Fool! Use your link, not your voice. The whole festering Shandarian Union knows we're here now."

Nicolas concentrated on the link in his mind, but he didn't see any way to communicate with Ensif. "I don't know how."

"Direct the energy, boy."

Nicolas imagined the argram running back to him and sent the image through the necromantic link.

The argram replied with an image of a vast plain. Ensif was far away.

Another image came to him. This time, it depicted empty hands. Ensif had found no game on his hunt.

"Drop your weapons." The voice came from farther into the brush. It was a deep voice, like it reverberated out of a huge barrel instead of a man. "There's no use in it. You know damned well there's no way past us now. Drop your arms and you'll live to see the inside of a Shandarian jail cell. I think you'd prefer that to the inside of an *adda-ki*, no?"

Mujahid gestured for Nicolas to stop, and he whispered. "We must tread with caution. Don't use my name or title if you value either of our lives. Better yet, say nothing."

Several large animals approached from all directions with catlike grace. They blended into the surrounding countryside, and all but their outline was invisible. Nicolas focused on the closest shape. It had six legs, like the cow beast from days ago, but it was different. The animal was at least twice the length of the largest horse he'd ever seen.

The creature appeared to have no rider at first, but the outline of something man-shaped stepped down from it. Whatever was dismounting was as transparent as the horse creature. The man shape turned its head and Nicolas jumped in shock. Two eyes floated in the air as if disembodied. They were feline, and glowed from the reflected light of the amber barrier.

Mujahid looked down and swore. "Shandarian Rangers."

"Are they cats or something?"

"Human...mostly. Religious warriors. Animalists. They're under holy vows that give them some magic."

"Wait...mostly?"

"You think Necromancy is the only form of magic?"

"What the hell do I know about magic?"

Nicolas didn't know what to do as the cat eyes approached him, so he held out his hand in greeting, hoping it was the right gesture.

The man shape knocked Nicolas's hand out of the way with one arm and struck a painful blow to his face with the other.

Nicolas grabbed his jaw, checking for any breaks, but everything was intact. He had a nasty cut on his lip, though, and his mouth filled with the metallic taste of blood.

"You don't touch a Shandarian Ranger," Mujahid said in a whisper.

Would have been nice to know sooner.

"May Arin bless us through your presence, Ranger," Mujahid said. He gave a slight bow at the waist and spread his arms.

"And may my passing leave you elevated," the voice said. "Captain Saren. What are you doing skulking about in the middle of nowhere?"

The man pulled something off his head and a disembodied face floated in midair. Whatever was causing the rangers to appear translucent had something to do with what they were wearing. A thick, curly mustache and beard hung below the floating face, which was human in all ways except for the feline eyes.

"My young friend and I are Union citizens on pilgrimage to the Pinnacle, Captain," Mujahid said. "We travel to Egis to book passage on a riverboat to Three Banks."

An image of the argram entered Nicolas's mind. Ensif was close now.

Saren stared at Nicolas. "He *is* young at that, ain't he. Don't see that much these days." He turned back to Mujahid. "There's not much left of Egis. And what little there is ain't gonna help you. Harbor's gone." Saren spat on the ground next to him. "Small group of Religarians broke off from the main force and headed inland. To what ends, only Malvol's festering arse knows."

"For a Ranger to invoke the god of hate, it must be serious," Mujahid said.

"Damned border skirmishes get worse every year, but this is the first time they've had the bollocks to set fire to a whole town. I'd sleep in cold camps, if I were you."

Mujahid pursed his lips.

"If you head south, you'll be safe enough," Saren said. "Keep your heads up for shrillers, though. Nasty buggers are mating. You'll see the big blue bastards long before they get to you if you're alert."

So those bat things were *shrillers*. Nicolas would have to remember that.

"Well, my friend," Mujahid said as he turned to Nicolas. "We'll make straight for Agera instead. Two unarmed pilgrims won't last long against trained Religarian soldiers."

"A sword, Sinner Charles," Saren said.

A sword materialized out of nowhere. It came flying at Mujahid, who grabbed it out of the air with remarkable dexterity.

"A worthless practice sword, but it's pointy," Saren said. "Do you or your mute friend here know how to use one?"

"Undead!" a voice shouted, followed by "Necromancer!"

Ensif had caught up to them.

An image emerged from the necromantic link. Ensif knew one of the rangers had struck Nicolas, and he wasn't happy about it. He was signaling that he planned to attack.

The rangers unsheathed translucent swords, but Ensif stood there like a defenseless child.

"Ensif," Nicolas shouted, "No!"

"Don't make him attack!" Mujahid yelled.

Ensif charged and the rangers contorted their bodies in impossible ways, dodging every blow the skilled argram directed at them.

When Ensif passed through the group of rangers, they charged him from behind and hacked him to pieces. It didn't take long before Ensif was nothing more than a pile of bones on the ground.

The mystical link disappeared from Nicolas's mind. Ensif was gone. A sense of loss and disappointment filled the gap left behind by the link.

"Why didn't he defend himself?" Nicolas said.

"Fool boy," Mujahid said.

"Bind them with Arinwool." Saren said.

Invisible hands placed silk-like bindings around Nicolas's wrists. Like the swords and the rangers themselves, the silk was invisible. They tied Mujahid in similar fashion.

"Guard that boy, Sinner Charles," Saren said. "He's the necromancer. Let him escape and you'll have more than the loss of your *adda-ki* to worry about."

"Yes, Ranger," Sinner Charles said.

The outline of another man approached.

"You can't believe the boy is a necromancer, Captain," Mujahid said.

"He lies." The voice came from two disembodied cat's eyes that floated behind Mujahid. "I heard this one tell the boy to keep the penitent at bay. Strange order to give if the boy don't have the power to do it, no?"

"He wasn't being quiet at all, was he?" Saren said to Mujahid. "He was sending messages to that thing the whole time. And you were helping him."

"Absurd," Mujahid said.

Captain Saren's disembodied face turned toward Nicolas. The feline eyes squinted. "We're taking you to Caspardis, necromancer. You too, old man. I don't know what part you play in this yet, but I'm dragging your arse to Caspardis as well. Sergeant."

"Yes, sir."

"Have the prisoners placed on mounts. We leave immediately. You know the drill. Draw straws for Sinner Charles."

"Yes, sir."

"And make it quick or *I'll* decide."

The man called "Sergeant" picked up his pace.

Rough hands pushed Nicolas up into place behind a ranger on one of the translucent beasts. They lashed him to a saddle using more of the silky Arinwool. It wouldn't stretch or tear, no matter how much force he used.

Nicolas drew a little power into his well and regretted it. The Arinwool around his wrists glowed and seared his skin. When he released the power, the burning stopped.

"Won't be trying that again, will you," the ranger sitting in front of him said. "Just so we're clear...I get so much as a twitch on my arse cheek, and you won't live long enough to feel the pain of the Arinwool burns."

Nicolas grabbed the handhold. "Look, I don't understand what the hell's going on. I'm not trying to hurt anyone."

The disembodied voice chuckled. "Not that difficult to understand, really. You're going to be executed in Caspardis. After a fair trial."

The rangers laughed and prodded their mounts forward.

CHAPTER ELEVEN

T ithian swore.

Chal Ghanix, the Religarian emissary, stood outside Kagan's audience chamber wearing his white desert noble robes. It was bad enough Tithian had failed to capture the heir, but now he would have to wait to deliver the news.

Two guards stood on either side of the entrance to the audience chamber, staring straight ahead. Their quartz-tipped, golden spears created a prism effect on the wall as the Great Barrier's ubiquitous yellow light struck them. Beyond the entrance, Kagan sat on a stone chair smoothing his red ceremonial cassock.

A liveried page led Ghanix and Tithian into the chamber. Ghanix dropped to his knees and bowed his head.

Kagan stood and extended his ring of office.

"Emissary Ghanix," Kagan said. "I trust all is well with the Empire?"

Ghanix pressed his lips to the ring.

"May the Grace of Arin be with you, Holy One," Ghanix said. "I bring a request from my Emperor."

"Rise," Kagan said. "Let us discuss the matter of Egis, and your nation's recent act of aggression against the west."

Ghanix's eyes widened, and Tithian grimaced.

Few played at politics as well as the archmage. Ghanix was going to have a difficult time justifying the Religarian invasion of the Shandarian Union.

The archmage led them to a less formal sitting area beneath a monolithic quartz window.

Ghanix's eyes kept flashing from Kagan to Tithian and back again.

"The Emperor regrets not attending to this personally," Ghanix said. "Matters of state keep him in Dar Rodon for now."

Kagan ambled around a large wooden table to a padded chair that had raised armrests. He sat down and adjusted his cassock.

Ghanix cleared his throat. "The recent *unsanctioned* action taken by the citadel commander at Dyr Agul was most unfortunate."

Kagan smoothed the folds of his red cassock over his knees.

Ghanix blinked. "The Emperor wishes to inform you it is being dealt with internally."

Tithian had expected many different explanations—from the aggression being a response to a wayward Shandarian patrol, to the empire's belief in their divine right of manifest destiny. What he had not expected, however, was the emissary to sacrifice a garrison commander. Smart move. The accusation allowed the Emperor to save face and reduce tensions, while getting rid of an expendable border officer in the process. The garrison commander's downfall had been set in motion the day he was banished to the border.

Tithian's pulse quickened. Ghanix had used the word "request" earlier. There could be only one request the emperor would make. Any advantage Kagan began with was fading fast. It would be his turn to think on his feet. The prospect entertained Tithian.

Kagan stopped smoothing his cassock and looked at Ghanix.

"A rogue commander taking matters into his own hands isn't going to comfort Chancellor Rillick," Kagan said. "Hundreds of Shandarians lost their lives at Egis, not to mention the loss of livestock and the precious timber that was burned. *Burned*, Emissary!"

"All the more reason for this request," Ghanix said. "The Emperor wishes a peace agreement brokered between the Empire and Shandarian Union."

There it is. A request the Holy One can neither grant nor deny.

"The Emperor would seek peace personally, of course," Ghanix said. "But since we share a common faith in Erindor, he defers to your divine office. If the request for peace comes from you personally, Holy One, Chancellor Rillick will embrace it, however reluctant he may be."

"They are going to want compensation," Kagan said. "What is the Emperor willing to provide in reparation?"

Ghanix smiled, and Tithian felt a chill. It was a trap, and Kagan had blundered right into it.

"Religarian stone *and* masons," Ghanix said. "We will provide the Shandarian chancellor with a suitable amount of stone and cutting services. We merely seek an exchange of resources and the possibility of fair trade in future. By Arin's Glorious Helm, of course."

Tithian was nonplussed. He had never seen Kagan outmaneuvered before. Chancellor Rillick would accept those terms without question if the amount of stone were sufficient.

"How soon will the Empire be able to deliver?" Kagan asked.

"Quarrymen are filling warehouses in Dyr Agul as we speak, and we have already begun construction of masonry workshops."

Kagan stood. "I will discuss the matter with the Shandarian ambassador."

Ghanix appeared troubled by this. "I must express the Emperor's sincere regret to Ambassador Emaldor personally."

Kagan smiled at Ghanix and guided him toward the entrance of the audience chamber. "I think you'd agree it would be better if I smoothed things over first. The divine nature of my office may serve to...stay the hand of the Union. No one wants peace more than I." Kagan extended his ring hand.

Ghanix kissed Kagan's ring of office and left the audience chamber.

"Summon Ambassador Emaldor," Kagan said to a nearby guard.

Tithian was confused. Kagan had agreed to something that didn't make sense.

"I hardly think a peace treaty is in your best interests," Tithian said.

"Of course not," Kagan said. "There will be no peace."

"How do you intend to—"

"Leave the politics to me, Warlock. When this is finished I would have your report."

Tithian felt the familiar chill settling deep in his spine.

Tithian stood as the chamber echoed with the tap of boots striking the marble floor. Dan Emaldor, ambassador from the Shandarian Union, entered the chamber in the uniform of a Shandarian Army Officer.

Kagan extended his ring.

"Forgive me, Archmage," the ambassador said. "I am not here on religious pilgrimage." He bowed at the waist and placed his hand over the seal of office on the jeweled ceremonial dagger hanging from his belt, as if it would fall to the ground if he wasn't careful. The dagger had no cross-guards, and the new ambassador must still be getting used to it.

Kagan shared a brief look with Tithian. A look Tithian took to mean "watch and learn."

"I admire your directness," Kagan said and gestured to the seating area.

Emaldor sat without waiting for Kagan.

Tithian shook his head at Emaldor's pathetic attempt at manipulation. It may have worked on a local Shandarian mayor, but this was the Pinnacle. He'd have to work harder than a simple breach of etiquette to put the archmage off balance.

Tithian sat in the chair reserved for him. Kagan liked to have him there as a power play, to intimidate visitors. But even Tithian could see intimidation wouldn't work on Emaldor. A man new to politics would be expecting it. No, Emaldor was about to learn what true manipulation looked like.

Kagan took a seat in his armed chair and leaned forward. "I have unfortunate news for your chancellor. The implications of what I am about to tell you must not be underestimated."

Emaldor pressed his lips into a thin line.

"I'm sure that by now you're aware of the border skirmish that caused the near destruction of Egis," Kagan said.

It wasn't possible for the ambassador to have this information yet.

Emaldor's eyes widened for a moment, before his face became expressionless. It was too late, though. Kagan would have seen his reaction, and was, no doubt, planning to exploit it.

"The Overcourt hides nothing from me," Emaldor said.

"A man of your influence must have many sources of information at your disposal," Kagan said. "Being appointed by the Shandarian Overcourt is no small accomplishment."

Emaldor sat erect in his chair.

"I was once new to the world of international politics as well, Ambassador," Kagan said. "I see much of myself in you. I wish to guide you so that you may avoid some of the pitfalls I stumbled into along the way."

"Your tutelage is appreciated."

Kagan smiled and Tithian smiled along with him. This was all part of the game, but Tithian was waiting to see how Kagan was going to sabotage the peace process.

Sabotage. The word made him shiver when used in connection with the holy archmage. Kagan's motives must be pure. This must all be part of a divine plan.

"The plot against the Shandarian Union threatens to catch your chancellor unaware," Kagan said. "That will reflect poorly on you in the Overcourt. They may reconsider their appointment if they discover this through other channels. I only wish to see you succeed, of course."

Emaldor swallowed.

"And now the empire is building up arms in the city of Dyr Agul," Kagan said. "This is a prelude to war. But then, I'm sure you've read the reports already. Forces gathering along the border. The recent annihilation of Egis. And now, as you know, they fortify their garrison with new construction and daily shipments of arms. It does not surprise me you would see war on the horizon, Ambassador."

So that was it. Kagan would know Shandarian spy networks were reporting a buildup of forces along the Shandarian border. There was no way for them to know the shipments to Dyr Agul were for their own benefit. The sheer size and frequency of the shipments would convince the Union that Religar was preparing an invasion force.

Emaldor nodded. "It appears war is indicated, Archmage."

"Know the Council of Magi understands the course of action you must take. A difficult position you are in, ordering your country to war, all because of Religarian greed and aggression."

"This is...I will need to think on—"

"I, of course, stand behind your decision to take Dyr Agul, and I will have no trouble convincing the Council to do the same. They'll see the wisdom of this strategic plan."

"Archmage, the chancellor will not go to war on my word alone. The Overcourt will want to investigate these matters. Our constitution demands it. The chancellor cannot make that decision alone."

"Unfortunate," Kagan said. "If anyone understands the restrictions of office, it is I. But I'm afraid that by the time you take action there will be no Overcourt left to do any investigating. Or a constitution left to uphold, for that matter. A shame the chancellor is powerless."

Emaldor looked down for a moment. "Not *exactly* powerless. The chancellor may commit to limited military action while the Overcourt debates."

Kagan leaned close to the ambassador. "Understand I am no military strategist, such as you. I would send a small force across the Orm into Dyr Agul...perhaps no more than, say, a brigade? The sooner you take their military surplus, the safer the Union will be—the safer *Erindor* will be."

"I think we would need a larger force than that, Archmage. The Religarians are well-trained soldiers. I would think at least two brigades are necessary."

"You will have to raze the entire city, of course," Kagan said.

Tithian's face grew cold.

"Excuse me?" Emaldor said.

"The surplus could be stored anywhere," Kagan said. "The empire is notorious for storing arms in civilian homes."

"They would do such a thing?"

"Even worse, I'm afraid. They sometimes disguise their soldiers as civilians. Barbarians."

Tithian fought to understand the emotions he was feeling. What the archmage was so casually suggesting would result in the deaths of hundreds of innocent people who, in all likelihood, had never held a sword a day in their lives. If the archmage—the infallible voice of the gods—could lie about this, then what else was he capable of lying about?

"We can leave no one alive in Dyr Agul, Archmage. I hope the Council will understand."

Kagan leaned back in his seat. "I must say, Ambassador, I'm impressed by you. Your suggestion to send two brigades across the Orm demonstrates you are more skilled at matters of war than I am."

"You flatter me, Archmage. I will notify the Overcourt. This Religarian aggression must be stopped once and for all."

"No truer words have been spoken," Kagan said.

When Emaldor had left the audience chamber, Tithian faced Kagan. "I would never question you in front of the ambassador, but—"

"I would prefer you never question me at all," Kagan said. "To question me is to question the gods. Is that your intent? Perhaps you are aware of some morsel of information of which they are not?"

Tithian lowered his head and suppressed a shiver. "I would never do such a thing, Holy One."

"Of course you wouldn't." Kagan tilted his head back and looked down at Tithian over his long nose. "You are a loyal and pious man, and that is what I prize about you. All men suffer from breaches in judgment now and again. Now, tell me of my son. What of the attack on Paradise."

"Paradise is destroyed, as is the orb of power." Tithian swallowed. "But the Mukhtaar Lord escaped with the heir. The talisman indicates they head toward Caspardis."

Kagan's face was expressionless. "What is he called? Do you know?"

The question caught him off guard until he remembered the child disappeared from the Pinnacle before his naming day.

"I don't know."

"Do not think for a moment you will be invulnerable if the Council moves against me. When you assumed the privileges of that traitor's office, you also assumed the risks. If there is a fall...we fall together."

"The heir is my primary concern right now, Holy One."

"You know your task. See it done. But there is something else."

Kagan turned and started walking back to his seat.

"Retrieve the Shandarian ambassador's ceremonial dagger and place it inside my desk," Kagan said. "I trust you have your ways?"

"I do."

"I wish to examine it...without his knowledge."

Tithian bowed and left Kagan alone in the audience chamber. What could the archmage want with that blade? He offered a silent prayer to Arin, and hoped the God of Life would guide him.

As he turned the corner out of the audience chamber he stumbled against the door jam and tore another hole in his favorite boots.

CHAPTER TWELVE

Nicolas was sticky from the humidity, and his bindings kept him from wiping the sweat from his forehead. The dwarf tree forest turned to grassy plain as the patrol made its way to Caspardis. The plain sloped downward toward a walled city on the horizon and beyond to a vast sea whose surface frothed from the wind that whipped it up. Ships were anchored in a harbor that dominated the length of the city.

It had taken most of the first day for him to get used to the odd sensation of floating through the air. The adda-ki, the creature the Shandarian Rangers used as a mount, was an agile creature. If it weren't for the wind on his face and the passing landscape, he wouldn't know he was moving. He spent much of his time battling an ever-present fear that threatened to spin him into a panic. Mujahid had always been there to save him, but now the older necromancer was as much a prisoner as he was.

Necropotency was all around, but it felt different from before, as if it existed just beyond the reach of his mind.

The city spread out for several miles to the north and south in one uniform, light brown color, as if each building had been carved from the same type of stone. Towers with crenelated parapets punctuated the massive wall that surrounded the city, flying red flags with a cat's eye in the center.

They passed a signpost on the outskirts of the city. The sign contained two words, one on top of the other, written in a strange language. An arrow on the top pointed toward the city, while an arrow on the bottom pointed toward a large camp.

They turned toward the camp and wound their way among large, mud-covered canvas tents, which were arranged in concentric circles. The rangers removed the mysterious fabric that rendered them translucent and revealed their faces to the guards standing post.

They did the same for their adda-ki, revealing only the creatures' heads, and Nicolas took a sharp breath when they removed the first hood.

The adda-ki was a brilliant red and its head was feline, resembling a panther with a bright red lion's mane.

The roar of the adda-ki caught several of the soldiers by surprise, and the rangers laughed in response. Multiple rows of razor-sharp blades lined its cavernous maw. Nicolas was glad to be on the creature's back and not standing in front of it.

The smell of meat roasting over fire reached Nicolas's nose, and his stomach growled. He couldn't remember the last time he ate.

"Hold," Saren said.

The rangers brought their mounts to a quick stop. Captain Saren dismounted and handed the reins of his adda-ki to a stable hand.

"Sinner Charles. Have the prisoners taken to the holding area and fed," Saren said.

"Ho rangers." An older man, dressed in leather armor, and bald except for a beard and mustache, approached the group. "May Arin bless us through your presence." The man stopped and bowed, spreading his arms in the same gesture Mujahid used when they first met the rangers.

"And may my passing leave you elevated," Saren said.

"What news of the north?" the man asked, standing straight once more.

"We come from the east," Saren said.

"Even better. We march east."

Saren's head jerked back. "What would cause a full brigade to march east?"

"We've been ordered to march on Dyr Agul."

"And what do *you* know of Dyr Agul?"

The man shrugged.

"Agul is a merchant city, nothing more," Saren said.

"Fifth Mounted is already on the march."

Saren swore. He did a double take when he saw Nicolas and Mujahid standing there.

"What are you waiting for, Sinner Charles?" Saren asked.

The man they called "Sinner Charles" nodded and led Nicolas and Mujahid into a tent, where he lashed them to the central tent post, leaving one arm free—which struck Nicolas as odd, not that he could do much with it. He had a scar in the center of his forehead, but the longer Nicolas stared at it, the more certain he became it was no scar at all. It was a brand.

"Why do they call you that?" Nicolas asked.

"Nicolas, no," Mujahid said.

"My shame isn't great enough for you?" Sinner Charles said. "Don't be so smug. I prefer my fate to yours. Now don't go anywhere, ladies." He stood and left the tent.

"I didn't mean to offend the guy," Nicolas said.

"The man lost his mount."

"So what? I just asked him—"

"I'm answering your question, boy. The Rangers revere the adda-ki as a holy animal. They hold the creature's life more valuable than their own. Sinner Charles will bear the title *Sinner* until he is granted another mount. And he will bear that mark on his face for the rest of his life. If it happens again, his life is forfeit."

Mention of the ranger's possible execution rattled Nicolas. "What's going to happen to us?"

"Shandarian justice. They are going to conduct a trial, at which they'll find you guilty of necromancy and me guilty of assisting you. This way they can kill you legally and go to bed with clear consciences. All neat and proper, the way Shandarians like it."

"They won't execute you?"

"They don't know who I am yet."

"I don't get it. What the hell did we do that was so bad?"

"You really need to work on your listening skills. Necromancy is illegal in Erindor."

Shadows on the front of the tent caught Nicolas's attention. Two men were setting up a table out in front, and they were in the middle of an argument.

"When's the last time the sky brought a building down on that big-boned head of yours, Gant?" one of the voices said.

"I'm saying it would be nice if the sky didn't look like piss every day, Boll, that's all," Gant said in a low pitch.

"That's my point, you monkey's arse," Boll said. "The sky turns yellow, and then the whole festering world starts shaking like it's riding on the back of a mating shriller. And what do those *adda*-buggering council magi have to say about it?"

"How am I s'posed to know? Ain't never been to the Pinnacle."

"Purger's bollocks, you're a thick one," Boll said. "Piss off and feed the prisoner's already. I don't want to spend the next three days shoveling shite because of you."

One of them entered the tent and set two bowls on the ground. He looked at Nicolas and quickly turned and left.

The dude's bigger than all hell and he's afraid of me?

The smell of the stew made Nicolas's stomach growl, and it became clear why they had left one arm unchained. He ate as fast as possible.

"Was that true?" Nicolas asked. "What that guy said about the quakes starting when the barrier went up?"

"He had his reasons for making it," Mujahid said.

Nicolas squinted.

"Your father. He thought he was serving the people."

"Is he keeping people in, or keeping people out?"

"Ahh...there's activity in that brain of yours."

Nicolas rolled his eyes.

"An empire from across the ocean, the Barathosian Empire, once declared war on the three kingdoms. They sent an armada that anchored off the coast of Dar Rodon. There were so many ships you could walk the breadth of the Bay of Relig without stepping in water."

"Why did they want a war?"

"Your father killed their ambassador."

Nicolas wanted to feel something, anything, after hearing his father was a murderer, but the archmage was still more hypothetical than real. Regardless of what Mujahid said, he had no real connection to that tyrant or his Pinnacle. The only person he had a true connection with was Kaitlyn.

"So what did the ambassador do that pissed Kagan off so much?"

"The Barathosians have an archmage of their own. They worship the same gods and keep the same rituals. Your father saw that archmage as a rival rather than a colleague. He was certain Arin had forsaken him."

"Still...all-out war? I may be new around here, but I ain't stupid. There must have been an attempt at a diplomatic—"

"The Barathosian ambassador was heir to the throne of Barathos," Mujahid said.

Nicolas whistled.

Mujahid finished eating and put his spoon in the bowl, which was sitting on the ground in front of him.

"You never answered about the quakes," Nicolas said.

"They started the day the barrier went up. Many believe it's the god's anger that shakes the ground and destroys our buildings."

"You too, I take it?" Nicolas smirked.

"I was there the day humankind gave them reason."

Nicolas wanted to roll his eyes. He didn't put much stock in this *gods* business.

"No, boy. Whatever the source, it isn't the gods. I believe these quakes are a consequence of acting on partial knowledge. Arin could have stopped Kagan, on that day, yet he chose not to. He spoke of things I don't fully understand...about souls that have yet to be born into this world, as if they already exist and are simply *waiting*."

Nicolas put his spoon down.

"I know it will be hard, but try to get some rest," Mujahid said.

Mujahid stretched out as much as the lashings would allow.

Nicolas pushed the bowl aside to clear a place for his legs, and tried to rest his aching back against the lashing post.

The sound of Captain Saren's loud voice drew Nicolas's attention.

"Get them up and on mounts, Sinner Charles," Saren said.

"Yes sir," Sinner Charles said and entered the tent. He untied Nicolas's lashings and pulled him to his feet. Another ranger was doing the same for Mujahid, and Nicolas realized they were no longer translucent. He was relieved they appeared human in every other way.

Sinner Charles marched them out of the tent to the waiting ranger patrol. Many of the men were already mounted, and Nicolas's jaw dropped when he saw the adda-ki. They were no longer translucent either. Their bright red coats stood in stark contrast to the drab surroundings of the camp. Their extra legs made them seem nightmarish, and Nicolas found it unnerving to look at them, like staring too close at a spider. The adda-ki appeared bred for agility, with long, lithe figures and legs that were capable of quick bursts of speed.

Someone forced Nicolas up onto an adda-ki, behind the same ranger he rode with the day before.

"You know the drill," the ranger said. "Grab the pommel and draw no energy."

"Don't worry," Nicolas said. "There ain't any."

"I'll drink to that," the ranger said.

They rode out of camp the same way they entered. When they approached the sign with two arrows, they turned and trotted down the grassy plain toward the city. The adda-ki stood out against everything they passed, as if they had been taken from some alien, multi-hued world and inserted into a colorless environment.

The outside of the city was falling into ruins. A section of wall had collapsed, and three of the numerous parapets had crumbled to the ground. Parapet flags whipped above the heads of the armored wall guards, and ships unfurled their sails in the distant harbor.

As they made their way down the sloped plain, the view of the harbor disappeared, and the ruined wall loomed large in front of them. Uniformed guards snapped to attention as they trotted through a great arch and under a set of iron gates.

The crowd of people parted and cowered as the red adda-ki entered an enormous plaza.

The buildings were falling apart, and several leaned together at odd angles. Merchants set up their wares in tents that lined the edges of the plaza and people congregated amongst three large fountains that dominated the center of the place. The fountains were no better off than the buildings—there was no running water, and the statues were crumbling.

City guards chased one of the merchants between two tents. The merchant was putting up a good fight, but it didn't take long for the guards to subdue him. They led him away from the plaza down a wide avenue.

Nicolas reached out with his mind. Like before, the necropotency was there, but it retreated whenever he reached for it. It was like trying to grab water with his fingers.

A burst of pain erupted in the center of his face.

"Try that again and I'll show these people how an adda-ki keeps its prey alive while it eats."

When his vision returned he saw the ranger's arm moving away from him, and blood dripped from the man's elbow.

"Don't think my threat empty, boy. You know the worth of a ranger's word."

Nicolas wanted to wipe away the blood dripping down his face, but there was no slack in his bindings. He would have to do his best to ignore it.

Everywhere he looked, he saw destruction. It was as if the end of the world had come and gone, but the people hadn't noticed. Instead, they went about their business, ignoring debris and avoiding the rangers.

What he didn't see bothered him more than what he did see, however. As in Paradise, there were no young children or teenagers in the streets.

After several turns an expansive fortress came into view. The fortress, like other buildings in the city, was also falling into ruin. The main building was circular in shape, and the wall on top gave Nicolas the impression of teeth on a saw, as if the entire roof were an enormous battlement.

They entered a large sandy plaza in front of the fortress.

Two large poles topped with metal hoops stuck out of the dirt, and the ground between them was darkened, like wet sand. A gigantic bell tower had been set into the wall next to a gate that led farther into the keep, but Nicolas didn't see a church nearby.

They passed through the gate and dismounted in the courtyard beyond. The rangers untied them and led them down into the basement of the fortress through damp tunnels permeated with mold. Water dripped in the distance, from some unseen source, echoing off the stone walls with every splash. But even with blazing torches spaced several yards apart, causing an alternating pattern of light and dark on the walls, Nicolas still had a difficult time seeing.

A fortress guard jumped as they turned a corner in the hall.

"Why are you taking them through here," the guard said. "We're not—Rangers?"

The guard's face paled in the shimmering torchlight.

"Just unlock the door and get back to doing nothing," Saren said.

The guard nodded and swung the door aside. Beyond it, prisoners stood huddled in a group of jail cells. One of the cells was open, and two guards flanked the entrance.

A ranger untied Nicolas's lashings.

"Remove the other prisoners," Saren said. "Take them to the cells near the crypt"

Mujahid turned his head at mention of a crypt.

"Arin's bollocks," a guard said. "I don't care who you are, they don't pay me enough."

Saren turned on the man and his feline eyes squinted.

"This is a necromancer, you idiot."

The guard swallowed then nodded toward the other guard.

When the last of the prisoners had been moved, Captain Saren gave Nicolas a firm shove in the direction of the nearest open cell.

"In you go," Saren said.

Mujahid followed, and the cell was locked shut.

"Welcome to Caspardis," Saren said. "I'd tell you to enjoy your stay..."

Saren turned to leave.

"Wait," Nicolas said. "What happens now?"

Saren glanced over his shoulder. "You won't be here long."

Nicolas spun to face Mujahid as panic rose in his throat. "What now?"

"We wait. There's nothing else to be done. We're without power."

"What about the crypt he was talking about before?"

"Unless you can find a way through these walls, the crypt won't do us any good. Just look, listen, and speak as little as possible."

"But there has to be—"

"Powerless is powerless, boy!" Mujahid looked away. "Without necropotency, I'm just a man like any other."

Somehow, Nicolas doubted that.

Two days passed. Servants fed them twice each day, which was more than Nicolas had expected.

The cell was stone blocks on three sides, twelve feet long by eight feet deep. It was closed off by a flattened iron-lattice grate with a steel door through which the guards would bring their meals. The grate formed small squares barely large enough to fit an arm through. A single torch, in a sconce on the moldy wall outside of the cell, burned an acrid fuel that made Nicolas's eyes tear up.

The hay in the corner reeked of urine and feces. The guards were quick to take away empty bowls, but they ignored the hay.

An odd tapestry hung on the wall outside the cell. It looked like the skin of a bright orange fish, if the fish were larger than a man.

Nicolas attempted to draw power, but it kept retreating from him.

"If I could summon another argram we wouldn't have to sit here like this," Nicolas said.

"You shouldn't have been able to summon one the *first* time," Mujahid said. "Count yourself lucky you're still alive."

"Have you ever summoned one?"

Mujahid looked away. "At least they're feeding us. We should—"

"No. I'm not letting you change the subject. Something happened when they killed Ensif—is that even the word for it?—and I don't understand it. I feel like I lost a part of myself."

"You did, boy. A very important part of yourself."

"I only knew him for...."

"We're getting somewhere now. Finish the sentence."

Nicolas looked away. There was no frame of reference for him to know how long he had been with Ensif. The concept of time didn't seem to apply.

"Was it hours?" Mujahid asked. "Or was it years? I'm guessing you lived several years of that creature's life during the summoning."

Nicolas looked down.

"Longer? How many decades did you wander through the consequences of that creature's actions?"

"You wouldn't believe me if I told you."

"I've heard the songs, boy. I've read the poetry. But those songs and poems have never been written, have they? Nor will they ever be."

"So you *have* summoned an argram."

"When you summon a penitent, regardless of who or what it is, you form a priestly bond with that creature stronger than any other bond. And when they fall before they're purified...it's as if you've failed your sacred duty and caused someone else to suffer as a result."

"What do we do about it?"

"We leave them to the mercy of Arin."

"That's it? That's all you got?"

"And then we find the festering bastards who bring evil into this world and make them question their life choices."

"So we've got *that* to look forward to at least."

Mujahid grinned.

"What's the deal?" Nicolas asked. "Why can't I pull any power in? It's like it runs away from me."

Mujahid shook his head. "There *is* no power here."

The door at the end of the hall opened with a metallic clang.

"Guard," Mujahid said. "Tell me of Caspardis minor. I don't recall seeing it last time I was here."

The guard stared at Mujahid, saying nothing.

"I'm not the necromancer here," Mujahid said. "And he'll be dead in a day or two anyway."

Nicolas swallowed. Was Mujahid bluffing or had he come to terms with the inevitable?

"I'm still a citizen of this Union," Mujahid said. "And I have yet to be found guilty of a crime."

The guard faced Mujahid. "We're taking the fight to the Religarians this time."

"We invade Religar?"

"And it's about time, if you ask me."

"King Donal agrees to this business?"

"The Tildemen have their own problems, apparently. That's ok, if you ask me. Next time Religar challenges the border with Tildem, maybe we'll have *our* own problems."

"And the empire will pick us off, city by city, until neither Tildem nor the Union remains," Mujahid said. "Why would the chancellor invade a country he cannot hope to defeat? Why pull out of the Treaty of Three Banks now?"

The metallic sound of a key entering a lock rang through the air, and the door at the end of the hall swung open. The guard at their cell turned and nodded to someone standing beyond the door.

The expression on Mujahid's face changed from frustration to terror.

"Guard," Mujahid said. "Can I have a word?"

Mujahid sounded like a kid in a snake pit.

The guard huffed.

"Unless you want this necromancer to escape you'd better hear me out," Mujahid said.

"What the hell?" Nicolas asked.

"He's threatened to kill me once already," Mujahid said. "I can't bear the thought of being raised up as his servant. Please. You have to help me!"

This couldn't be happening. Mujahid had turned on him to save his own life.

Nicolas stepped toward Mujahid. He'd fix that old bastard.

"He's lying," Nicolas said. "He's Muja—"

Mujahid kicked Nicolas square in the chest with a speed and strength that terrified him.

Nicolas fell to the floor and landed hard. If he'd had his eyes closed he'd think the old man picked up a refrigerator and hit him with it.

Mujahid clasped a hand over Nicolas's mouth and leaned in close.

"Quiet you fool." Mujahid spoke in a whisper. "Our only hope is that they put me in with the other prisoners near the crypt."

He wanted to believe Mujahid, but how could he? He closed his eyes and started shaking his head.

"You're stronger than you realize, boy. Look toward the Pinnacle. That's where the answers will be. Go to Arin's Watch. I can track you with this." Mujahid pointed to the amulet concealed beneath his robes.

Two guards entered the cell area.

"Arin's helm," Mujahid said. "There's so much you don't know. You'll need the *tithe* from Pilgrim's Landing to enter the Pinnacle. You must not forget. The tithe."

"You there," a guard said, pointing at Mujahid. "Let's go."

"Thank the gods," Mujahid said as he walked toward the cell door. "I had to defend myself. He was going to kill me."

The guard tied Mujahid's hands behind his back and shoved him toward the door.

Nicolas wanted to yell, but Mujahid's kick had knocked the wind out of him.

"There is a prophecy," Mujahid said as a guard pushed him.

"That'll be enough," the guard said.

"It's all about the energy. Give yourself over to the water. There's a—"

The guard backhanded Mujahid across the face, knocking him into silence. "Shove your prophecy up your arse and keep moving."

The stone door slammed closed.

Mujahid was gone.

CHAPTER THIRTEEN

Mujahid had been gone for two days.

Nicolas spent the first day in complete despair, convinced his life was over. He kept going over Mujahid's last words but they didn't make any sense.

The first night was difficult. The guards kept him at a distance the same way he'd treat a rattlesnake—never taking his eyes off it and worried that one strike would kill him.

He didn't get much sleep that night. He dreamed about Kaitlyn. But every time she would appear she'd pass through his hands like mist, leaving nothing but a hint of her rose-scented skin.

The last dream he had was bizarre. He'd been sitting against the cell wall when the ground in front of him opened up with a ripping noise. A single bone, a large femur, floated up from the newly formed crater and stopped when it was at eye level. The bone hummed and the room shook and vibrated around it, as if the bone were the only stable object in the world. The shaking stopped, and the bone transformed, its top end sharpening into a point, as if whittled by an invisible knife that sent bone shards flying. The bottom sprouted feathers like an arrow's fletching complete with a nock that burned from within by a fiery light. The arrow turned its point toward him and a cacophonous hum erupted as it flew through the air, traveling straight for his chest.

The shock of the sudden attack had jolted Nicolas from his sleep, and he woke up, bathed in sweat. It was like the skull dreams, only this time it was a homicidal arrow trying to kill him. At first he ignored it, as he had with the skull. But every time he fell asleep the arrow would appear and fly toward him, closer and closer to striking, and each time he would wake right before the arrow penetrated his chest.

The most recent dream, however, was the worst one. He felt the tip of the arrow pierce his skin and he woke in a panic. He could feel the sting where the arrow dug into his chest, so he reached into his robe to touch the sore spot. A small pool of moisture that felt too slick to be sweat clung to his finger. When he pulled his hand away blood dripped onto his robe, but there was no wound.

He swore. It wasn't just any dream...it was *the* dream. The arrow must be a symbol of power. Mujahid was right—if he didn't wrestle this thing into submission in the Hall it would kill him, just like the skull would have if Mujahid hadn't intervened.

He sat up and tried to calm his mind, but the power still slipped through his mental fingers. He had no other choice except to enter the Hall without Mujahid *or* necropotency.

He imagined the room with two doors. The white door called to him, as it had in the past, tempting him to take a step toward it, but he ignored it. The more he resisted the door, the easier it became to resist, like strengthening a muscle. He gathered his newfound confidence and stepped over the threshold of the black door into the room beyond.

The skull symbol, encased right where he had left it, glowed from its internal blue light. Another black doorway was present this time, and the bone arrow hung in midair beyond the threshold. He kept repeating Mujahid's words—*Doubt is your enemy.*

He took a deep breath and stepped through the second black doorway.

N icolas had been daydreaming in class.

"Your project is late," Dr. Murray said. "You're just going to have to lose the grade on this one."

"I worked really hard on that," Nicolas said. "I get it, but I have a really good reason for being late."

He felt confused, and seeing Dad's square jaw and horn-rimmed glasses made him sad for reasons he didn't understand.

"Such as?"

He couldn't remember. Was it because he took a wrong turn on the way to the funeral? No, he didn't think so. Nuuan made sure they got there on time.

Lord Nuuan, he corrected himself.

He remembered puking all the way to the funeral, and Nuuan making fun of his clothes. Then there was the accident...an overturned orb truck on the freeway.

This isn't right.

"I'm sorry, Nick," Dr. Murray said, "but I have another Hall of Power starting in five minutes. Consider this a character-building moment. I know you. It won't happen again."

Nicolas headed for the door, leaving his notes on Dr. Murray's desk, but stopped and turned when he reached it.

Confusion.

He was going to say something...to someone. But no one was there, and he couldn't remember what it was he wanted to say anyway.

Wasn't I talking to someone?

He reached for the door but felt dizzy and had to look down. His sight went blurry, as if someone were spinning him around. When his vision cleared, cars filled the small parking spaces that surrounded the Archeology building. He felt the warmth of a familiar light but couldn't find the sun.

A door? I'm losing it. Why would you expect to find a door in a parking lot, you idiot?

The light made him feel at home. He'd be content to walk in circles as long as the warmth of the light stayed with him.

Parking lots make me happy.

The absurdity of that comment caught him by surprise. Why would parking lots make him happy?

There was the parking lot at the orphanage, where Dr. Murray would pick him up and take him out to eat. There was the parking lot at the Mukhtaar Estate where the floating orange cars parked. And then there was the parking lot at the funeral parlor, where someone had been chasing him.

That sounds important.

He needed to remember who was chasing him, but he couldn't. He remembered having chills, though. And puking. Lots of puking.

The light intensified. It was a wonderful feeling, like when he had spent time inside the computer lab at school and then stepped out into the warm Texas sun to thaw out for a few moments. He could walk in this light forever.

Dangit! Who was chasing me?

Something bad was going to happen if he couldn't remember.

A flash of light and heat blinded him and he collided with something he couldn't see. When the light subsided, he saw the side of his own car.

But it hasn't started in months.

He reached for the handle and lifted, but it wouldn't open. He always locked his car. He patted his robes down, looking for his keys.

Figures. I left my keys in my other robes.

His hand stopped at an object in his pocket, but every time he tried to see what it was, the light would flee from him. He needed the light. He wanted it to stay forever.

The light was telling him the object was bad and he should forget about it. He ought to wander around the parking lot for a while instead. Everything would be all right...if he kept wandering.

Light can't talk, dumbass.

He reached into his robe and felt the object in his pocket.

I doubt these are keys.

A saying popped into his mind...*doubt is your enemy*. He didn't know where it came from, but it was popular in his Latin class these days. The teacher would recite it before the ritual meditation.

Doubt is your enemy.

Every time he'd focus on a thought, the light would intensify and make it difficult to think.

He took the object out of his pocket and held it up.

It was his wallet. And it smelled like roses. He opened it and found a picture inside.

A picture of a beautiful girl.

My girl. Kaitlyn. Kaitlyn!

A chill went over him as if someone poured cold water on his head. The fog in his mind cleared, and he was aware. He knew what was happening. He knew where he was and what he was doing. This was a Hall of Power. And he'd almost failed.

The parking lot vanished, leaving him in a room with a single door. The arrow hung in the air in front of him. It rotated until the sharp tip pointed straight at his chest. This time he wasn't afraid. He knew the arrow for what it was now, and that knowledge strengthened him. It was a symbol of power, and he would take control of it.

The arrow floated backwards toward the wall, and he reveled in the sensation of the necropotency that surrounded him. He used the power to spin the arrow so it pointed towards the ceiling. He channeled necropotency into the wall to carve a place for it, just like he had for the skull.

The wall and arrow collapsed into one, and the arrow imploded, contracting from three dimensions to two. An electric-blue light radiated from its edges.

He had won the battle...all because of Kaitlyn.

He ran for the entrance of the Hall until he reached the room with two doors. He willed the Hall to collapse and opened his eyes to see his prison cell.

Two symbols of power floated in his mind. A skull and an arrow. He had no idea what the arrow was for, but he was safe now.

He understood, at last, why Mujahid couldn't tell him what he'd be up against in the Hall of Power. The Hall used people's own minds against them. But the Hall didn't understand him. He had memories and concepts from two different worlds in his head, and the Hall was combining them as if they belonged together.

He shivered. If it was this easy to confuse him when he knew the images didn't make sense, then how easy would it be for someone who had never left Erindor?

Two guards entered his cell. He was so focused on the arrow he hadn't noticed them earlier. One of them grabbed him and lifted him to his feet, while another bound his hands.

"Where are you taking me?" Nicolas said.

"Don't you think four days is enough to prepare for trial?" the guard said as he led Nicolas out of the cell.

This was it. There was going to be a trial and Mujahid hadn't been able to do anything about it.

He was in a daze as two men led him through the fortress. The reality of what was happening was too much to absorb. When the men stopped shoving him he realized he hadn't been aware he was moving.

A row of men, dressed in purple robes trimmed with gold, sat together on one side of a long stone table. They wore funny hats that reminded Nicolas of a chef's hat, except puffed out at the center like a beach ball. Something told him there was nothing funny about what they were going to do to him.

"Bring the prisoner forward." The voice came from an older man sitting in the middle chair. He didn't bother looking up from his scroll as he spoke to Nicolas. "The Province of Caspar will read the charges, according to the Shandarian Justice Protocols. Scribe, if you will."

A man stood up, unrolled a scroll, and cleared his throat. "The prisoner is charged with the practice of necromancy, as witnessed by the accusers, the Shandarian Ranger Patrol of the Province of Elegar, under the leadership of Captain Elis Saren."

"Saren himself bears witness?"

"Yes, Magistrate," the scribe said.

"The Ranger's testimony renders the prisoner's plea unnecessary," the magistrate said. "Therefore, this tribunal finds you guilty of the practice of necromancy."

Nicolas's chest tightened. He wanted to say something, to fight back, anything except stand there doing nothing.

But he couldn't. The fear wouldn't let him.

"You are sentenced to death by drowning," the magistrate said. "You will be taken to Lake Caspar, bound, weighted, and sunk."

Panic turned to terror, and he felt the blood drain from his face. He wasn't sure whether he was going to pass out or throw up. He was suffocating. One of his knees gave out, and he fell. The guard standing next to him grabbed him under the arm and hoisted him to his feet. He tried to draw power, but the energy wouldn't respond.

"Guards, prepare the prisoner for execution," the scribe said. "And notify Captain Saren."

"Have him flogged, first," the magistrate said. "If there are any other necromancers lurking about, we would do well to discourage them. Double the number of lashes of the other prisoner."

"Yes, Magistrate."

Nicolas's knees buckled and they dragged him out of the grand room.

The bell reverberated like a deep gong being struck every few seconds as the sandy plaza filled with people. Every strike threatened to penetrate the comforting numbness that had settled deep within Nicolas.

The guards led another prisoner into the plaza, and the man trembled and cried. Like Nicolas, he was bound at the wrists and ankles, and chains extending between his bindings made it difficult to walk.

Nicolas recognized the other prisoner. He was the man the guards had chased through the plaza a few days ago.

The crowd grew louder as a man in a simple gray robe climbed a platform in front of them. Guards escorted Nicolas and the other unfortunate man onto the platform with him.

The robed man turned, and Nicolas recognized him. It was Captain Saren, the Shandarian Ranger who had arrested him and Mujahid. Saren wasn't wearing the Arinwool that rendered Rangers invisible, but there was no mistaking the feline eyes reflecting the yellow light of the Great Barrier above. A white stole swept from Saren's left shoulder down to his right hip, and it was covered with images of red *adda-ki* in different poses.

A hush settled over the plaza, and the bell rang one last time.

"People of Caspardis," Saren said. "The men you see before you have been found guilty of crimes against the Union. They are sentenced, in part, to public flogging."

A cheer rose, and Saren gestured for silence.

While the crowd settled, Nicolas used the growing quiet to calm himself, but his heart wouldn't cooperate. It raced and pounded as the inevitability of what was about to happen grew more and more real.

"Take the first one," Saren said.

A guard grabbed the other prisoner by the arm and led him to two poles jutting from the ground. He refastened the man's chains to the tops of the poles, one wrist bound to each pole so that the prisoner's arms were spread out, and he dropped a cloth sack next to one of the poles, toppling it with his boot.

As the sack spilled some of its crystalline contents, the last of Nicolas's numbness vanished and he became aware of every detail. He saw the smiles on the faces of the people in the crowd. He heard the clinking of the prisoner's chains against the poles and every creak and groan of the nearest guard's leather armor. He smelled sweat and something else. Urine?

The guard who knocked the cloth sack over tore the bound prisoner's robe down to his waist, exposing his back. When he turned, Nicolas saw something in the guard's belt, and his stomach quivered.

A scourge.

Nicolas knew too much about history to pretend that thing couldn't kill him. A wooden pole, twelve inches long with leather strips attached to the end, and each strip tipped with a metal or stone bit. The leather strips alone would slice the skin. But those bits of metal...they would rip the flesh right off his bones.

"The first convict has been found guilty of violating the Shandarian Merchant Statutes," Saren said. "He's sentenced to fifteen lashes by loaded whip. Proceed at will, guard."

The guard carrying the scourge detached it from his belt and raised it back over his shoulder. The crowd was silent.

The scourge struck the prisoner and blood sprayed backward, covering the guard's face and armor. A gurgling scream escaped the wounded prisoner's mouth. The guard pulled the scourge away, tearing bloody chunks of flesh from the man's back and scattering them into the crowd.

The cheering crowd drowned out the suffering man's plea for mercy.

Nicolas shook, and his heart drummed in his ears. He was next. Food rose in his throat, and he vomited onto the platform.

He felt a splash of water. The other prisoner had lost consciousness, and a guard was emptying a bucket of water on him.

The man returned to consciousness and screamed. His back was unrecognizable. It looked like a piece of striped meat rather than human skin and flesh.

The scourge struck...over and over...tearing flesh and sinew from the man's back. The man opened his mouth, face contorted in agony, but no sound came out.

The guards left him unconscious for the last few strikes, and he hung limp from the posts, bleeding and drawing ragged breaths. Blood and torn chunks of flesh covered the onlookers.

"Take him back to the dungeon," Saren said.

Blood ran down the guard's face as if he had bathed in it. He dropped the scourge and approached the post, where he unlocked one of the binding chains. Something stopped him.

"He's dead, Ranger," the guard said. "Or close to it. Odd for fifteen lashes."

Saren glanced at Nicolas with a look of concern.

Nicolas felt hope when the guard pronounced the prisoner dead. His fear overpowered any sense of right and wrong. He wanted the man to die. Death meant necropotency, and if he had the chance, he'd kill the guy himself to get it. But it was no use. The prisoner clung to life with a tenuous grasp. There'd be no surge of power to use for escape.

"Remove him and make way for the next prisoner."

Saren pointed at Nicolas and raised his voice over the crowd. "This man is a convicted necromancer."

Murmurs spread throughout the crowd.

"He's been sentenced to death by drowning, under the Shandarian Justice Protocols," Saren said. "Before this sentence is carried out, we're going to give him thirty lashes by loaded whip."

People in the crowd gasped, and incredulous cries of "thirty lashes" echoed around the plaza.

One voice in the crowd shouted "Drowning? He'll never survive the *whip*."

Nicolas was vaguely aware of guards leading him to the poles, dragging his feet through the muddy blood and sand. They tore his robe open and pulled it down to his waist, as they had with the previous prisoner. When they finished lashing his hands and feet to the posts, spread wide like the last prisoner, they retreated.

The scourge struck his back for the first time and the world exploded. The edges of the scourge dug into his right shoulder, tearing trenches down to his left hip, and he screamed.

When the scourge landed its second blow, it tore a path from his left shoulder to his right hip.

He had lost his voice from the volume of his screams, but screaming was involuntary now, and neither the pain nor his raw vocal chords would allow him to stop. Blood poured down his back as more flesh was ripped away, and he tried to pull against the right post.

He couldn't feel his right arm anymore.

After the third blow he could no longer sense the pauses between strikes. He drifted into unconsciousness.

Water ran down his face, and he couldn't breathe.

He felt every fiber of his back—every jagged tear, every empty hole, every sharp cut.

Something—a piece of himself—ripped away from the back of his neck. Pain spread across his body like liquid fire, always growing in intensity and never abating.

His vision went black and the image of Kaitlyn faded from his mind.

He coughed water out of his mouth and nose, and the feeling of molten metal pouring down his back returned.

The ambient power around him grew stronger, and he tried to reach out and touch it, but again he couldn't.

I have to live.

He clung to the vision of Kaitlyn's face, having no idea how many lashes remained. He could no longer tell if the scourge was striking him or not.

A guard walked passed his field of vision.

"He lives," the guard said.

He heard a sound at his right foot and saw the guard opening the cloth sack. A small shovel, more a scoop than anything else, lay on top of a crystalline substance. The guard reached in and scooped up the powder and disappeared from Nicolas's sight.

White hot torture spread across his back, but it paled in comparison to the torment in his mind. His life was about to end and he was powerless to change it. He'd never see his home again. He'd never see Toby again. He'd never see Kaitlyn again. He tried to keep an image of Toby and Kaitlyn in his mind as he began to pass out.

An armored fist struck his face, and his jaw shattered.

"We'll have no more of that," a guard said.

Agony defined his existence. Pain was no longer something he experienced. Pain was who he was.

A sword hung from the guard's hip, and a brief glimmer of hope flickered through Nicolas's mind.

He mustered as much breath as he could, and through vocal chords he thought would never work again, he uttered the two words that had the power to set him free.

"Kill...me."

"Don't worry," the guard said. "We will."

They untied him from the posts. One of the guards lifted Nicolas's robe and covered his ravaged back.

He fell, face down, into a bloody quagmire of flesh and sand.

"Help him to his feet," Saren said. "Carry him, if you must."

Several guards cleared a path through the crowd as they led him away. His hair dripped with moisture from the spitting onlookers, but he was oddly at peace.

These people weren't spitting on him. They were spitting on what he represented. Even now, though he was bound and minutes from death, they feared him. It was like the humans and the argram, only now he was the argram in their eyes—a vicious monster who would rip them apart if given a chance. These weren't bad people. They were *scared* people.

When they reached the harbor, they led him up a gangplank to a waiting ship.

Bells began to toll throughout the city. People ran away, and what had been an orderly march became a chaotic stampede. Guards looked at each other as if they didn't know what to do.

"Your duty is here," Saren said. "The garrison will sort the alarm."

Nicolas felt the smallest amount of power enter his mind as the boat sailed farther from the shore. It was faint, but he accepted it for what it was and drew as much as he could into his well. It allowed him to see Kaitlyn's face, and that was all that mattered.

A small platform, large enough for three men to stand abreast, floated in the water no more than a hundred yards from shore. The boat came to a slow stop as it pulled up alongside it.

Crewmen lowered the gangplank and grabbed Nicolas's arms. The slightest touch to his body caused him to convulse with pain.

Two guards draped large chains around his shoulders and shackled his ankles to two iron weights. When they were finished, they led him down the gangplank.

"Necromancer," Saren said. "Do you have anything to say for yourself?"

Nicolas tried to speak, but he had no voice left.

"If there is nothing more," Saren said.

"He's trying," a guard said.

Nicolas was long past trying to summon a penitent. Even if he could gather the power, he'd never be able to subdue it.

He released some power into his throat, soothing his damaged vocal chords.

"You're wrong about us," Nicolas said. "But I understand. And I forgive you."

"Do it," Saren said.

Strong hands pushed against his back, reigniting the pain. Water rushed up to meet him as he fell off the platform. He inhaled as much air as he could.

He plunged into the cold water and sank, struggling against the bindings and chains, but it was clear he would never break free. As the weight dragged him deeper into the darkness of the water, images of Kaitlyn flashed brightly in his mind.

He smiled when he remembered how they met, but his broken jaw forced him to stop. She didn't like him at first but he was used to fighting for what he wanted. His life had been a series of fights—fights with the nuns over going to church, fights with the teachers over his behavior in class, and fights with himself over who he was and where he came from. Kaitlyn changed all that. He gave himself over to her, and she brought him peace.

Mujahid's last words came to the forefront of his mind, and this time he understood them. The water was peaceful. It was a type of energy, in a way. It would release him from suffering and bring him rest, as Kaitlyn had released him from the trials of his former life and brought him rest. He should give himself over to it, as Mujahid told him to do...as he had with Kaitlyn.

He could smell her perfume and rose-scented skin, feel the softness of her kiss. He imagined her holding him, and as he sunk into the depths of the lake, her embrace soothed him.

When he lost his sight, the last image he saw was her face, and he smiled without pain.

I love you, Kaitlyn.

The world disappeared around him, and he dissolved into nothingness.

CHAPTER FOURTEEN

Mujahid sat up in bed, awakened by a gong-like bell tolling in the distance. It had been two days since he saw Nicolas, and he had no idea how they were going to get out of this.

His plan had failed. He was counting on them putting him in with the prisoners near the crypt. Instead, the guard captain isolated him in a room in one of the guard towers.

If that fool boy hadn't called for the argram.

He shook the thought away. One way or another the rangers would have discovered the truth.

It wouldn't be long before they sentenced the boy to death. The word of a ranger was considered infallible. If Nicolas were to survive, it would have to be by Mujahid's hands.

He reached deep within his mind, past the diaphanous fog that crackled with energy and surrounded his symbols of power, past the symbols themselves that formed a sphere around his energy well, toward the symbol at the center of it all. The symbol of ascension. It was in the shape of a levitating human, legs crossed, arms spread outward as if to embrace. Resplendent white light illuminated its eyes from within. It simultaneously repelled and bound the other symbols together, and it allowed a Mukhtaar Lord to weave complex patterns of magic.

But Mukhtaar Lord or not, he needed power to cast like any other priest, and there wasn't a drop of necropotency anywhere. If he could get closer to the crypt, he'd have all the energy he needed. But he didn't think the guards would take him on an excursion any time soon.

His mind drew back, out from his well, out past the symbols and into the fog. The fog was still a mystery. It had appeared when he ascended, and only he and Nuuan could sense it.

He abandoned his futile attempt to gather power and instead, concentrated on the Talisman of Archmages that hung from a leather thong around his neck. It was guiding him toward the plaza in front of the fortress.

That's not good.

He tried to sense the boy's unique energy pattern, but it wasn't there. He must be too far away.

The bell stopped tolling.

The door to his small chamber swung open and a guard entered. He was a burly man in a Shandarian soldier's uniform — loose-fitting pants and pullover shirt, both dyed forest green — with the triple cat's eye insignia of a sergeant. A skinny man dressed in gold-trimmed purple robes followed him.

A court official. Mujahid had dealt with them before.

The official cleared his throat and spoke. "Sinclair Thomry," he said with a yawn. "Attendant to the provincial magistrate. He'll see you now."

Perhaps this was just the *excursion* Mujahid needed. He debated whether to start imprinting the man's energy pattern in his mind — another benefit of ascension — but it would take days to become permanent. And if this went to plan, Thomry's remaining life would be measured in minutes.

Thomry dusted his robes with his hands.

Mujahid saw his opening. *It won't be difficult to provoke this fop.*

"Mr. Thomry, is it?" Mujahid said. "I dare say those are the finest robes I've seen in some time. Pure silk?"

Thomry looked up from his preening and spread his arms. "A discerning eye. Spun from the finest shriller silk in the Sea of Arin. As soft as it gets."

"Well, let's be honest," Mujahid said. "It's not as soft as crag spider silk. Though, spider silk would be pricey for someone of your rank."

Thomry looked baffled. "Are you daft, man?"

"I own several spider robes myself. Far softer. They hold the dyes better, as well. Not that yours aren't...*nice*."

Thomry gaped. He held out his arm and took a step toward Mujahid. "Feel this and tell me—"

"Hold, Thomry," the guard said. "You may be good with a mirror and comb, but you're shite around prisoners."

Thomry stopped and lowered his arm.

Looks like I'll have to do this the hard way.

Mujahid needed the guard alive and intact if this was going to work. He sprang for the guard and planted a boot in the man's chest, taking care not to injure him. The kick sent the big man sprawling.

Thomry darted toward the door.

Mujahid caught him by the back of his robe, yanked him to the floor with one hand, and drew back a closed fist.

Thomry screamed and passed out.

Mujahid shook his head.

The guard climbed to his feet and lunged at Mujahid.

Mujahid put up a token struggle, trying to make it look as real as possible. After a few missed swings, he crumbled to the floor in a ball, feigning a moan of pain.

The guard helped him up and bound his wrists with cords. "That was about the stupidest thing I've ever seen anyone do, old man. Now I have to drag your decrepit arse to the dungeon."

Mujahid felt a surge of relief. "What about my trial?"

The guard chuckled. "There'll be no trial for you today once the magistrate hears about this. Move."

Mujahid nodded toward Sinclair, who was lying unconscious in the middle of the room. "Aren't you going to wake your friend? He's had a long enough nap on the citizen's gold, don't you think?"

The guard shook Thomry. "On your feet, you useless dandy."

Thomry rose. When his eyes came to rest on Mujahid he backed away.

"He thinks he's tough," the guard said. "So I'm putting him in with the rest."

They led him down a winding tower staircase and through a hall lined with rubble from years of continuous earthquakes.

Mujahid felt the first stirrings of power as they approached a pitted stone door. It wasn't much, but he welcomed it.

The door opened with a loud creak, revealing an unkempt graveyard beyond.

Mujahid smiled. He wouldn't have to wait for the crypt after all.

When he stepped over the threshold, a pulsating wave of necropotency washed over him and filled his well. Now they would learn their mistake. Now they would feel the wrath of a Mukhtaar Lord.

"Tell me," Mujahid said. "Was the necromancer taken through here as well?"

Thomry snorted. "Do you have any idea how many bodies are buried here?"

"Oh yes," Mujahid said. "A very good idea."

The ground erupted in front of them as Mujahid raised a penitent. A skeletal warrior, wielding two long daggers, clawed his way up through the dirt and was on his feet within seconds.

Mujahid lived a lifetime in a single moment. When the stream of images stopped, he gained control over the skeleton before the guard had a chance to react. He sent the skeleton into the passage across the graveyard and turned to face his captors alone.

The symbol of ascension ignited, and he wove threads of energy through several symbols of power, bringing them together in a symphony of mystical forces. He turned his gaze to the guard, who was unsheathing his sword, and unleashed a cone of disease. The guard crumbled to the ground, clutching his throat, as his skin turned black and erupted in pustules. He was dead within moments, and the stench from his rapid decomposition overwhelmed the graveyard. The guard was a fleshless skeleton before Mujahid could face Thomry.

Thomry screamed and slapped Mujahid with an open hand.

Mujahid shook his head. Thomry was a waste of life force, and he was going to change that.

The symbol of ascension pulsed, and Mujahid sent a thread of energy through two symbols he hadn't used in a long time. With a simple act of will, he hurled their combined necropotency at Thomry. When the energy struck, a vortex of arcane power formed between them and lifted Thomry off the ground.

Mujahid took a deep breath in preparation for what would follow.

Thomry's life force drained, passing through the mystical maelstrom into Mujahid. The primal power of the vortex lifted Mujahid off the ground until all of the force was absorbed. Thomry's lifeless corpse fell to the ground, dried and shriveled, as if every drop of moisture had been squeezed out of him.

The energy coursed through Mujahid's body, rejuvenating cells that had begun to decay, and repairing aged muscles and tissue. He opened and closed hands that had been arthritic. A burst of adrenaline made newly strengthened muscles quiver, and his back straightened. He looked down at his arms and hands and marveled at his newfound flexibility. His long white hair, hanging down into his face, darkened until it turned jet black.

Mujahid's youth had returned. The vortex collapsed and his feet touched the ground once more.

He ran toward the sound of strangled screams coming from a doorway across the field.

Corpses of guards and servants paved the hallway inside. His penitent had turned it into a slaughterhouse.

An image of a man clearing a path with a machete flowed into Mujahid's mind—his penitent was making the fortress safe for him.

Mujahid ran down the hall in the direction the skeletal warrior had gone. He heard a clash of metal and shattering bones, and the necromantic link vanished.

He channeled necropotency into a nearby guard's corpse and the body rose.

"To the plaza," Mujahid commanded. "Leave nothing alive except my friend."

The undead guard turned and ran, sword in hand.

When they reached the plaza, Mujahid saw the bloodstained sand between the flogging poles. This wasn't good. He had seen enough public floggings in his day to know there wasn't much time left, if the boy had been flogged already.

Mujahid and his penitent wove their way in and out of the streets of Caspardis in a southerly direction, toward the docks that ran the length of the south end of the city.

Bells began to toll. The garrison must have raised the city alarm.

Mujahid swore when the docks came into view. He was too late. The ship that carried Nicolas to what was likely his death had already sailed.

Torn between a futile dash to the harbor and escaping detection by
the city guard, Mujahid chose the latter and ran back into a small
side street. If the garrison swarmed him, it didn't matter how
many symbols of power he had, they'd defeat him by sheer number.

He released his penitent and the corpse dropped to the ground,
concealed behind the corner of a building. The dagger in the guard's belt
could serve as a last resort, so he took it and hid it in the sleeve of his
robe. He dusted himself off and walked out into the throng.

He crossed the plaza, keeping his eye on the arch that led out of the
city. He had to get through the gate before the Authority ordered
Caspardis sealed.

Two guard officers in Shandarian long coats emerged from a side
street and ran to the gate. Within moments the portcullis slammed shut.
Someone must have discovered the carnage in the fortress. Again he was
too festering late.

This was going to be a blood bath, but he had to get out of the city

The dead guard wasn't close enough to draw necropotency from, so
he'd have to get creative this time. Guards had spread out along the base
of the wall, and six of them stood post at the gate under the arch,
including the two officers. More were emptying into the plaza, and
Mujahid's chances were growing thinner every moment.

The guard in the northeast corner of the plaza was the last in the row,
and therefore the least likely to be noticed. Mujahid hunched to hide
some of his height and started walking. He wanted to radiate a sense of
weakness and vulnerability so he wouldn't startle the guard, but his
newfound youth would betray him if he wasn't careful.

When he was within speaking distance, he folded his arms, tucking
his hands into his sleeves.

"What causes the alarm?" Mujahid said.

"Don't know. We were just told to double up, is all."

Mujahid stepped closer until he was an arm's length away. He didn't
want this to take any longer than necessary.

"You were all in such a hurry. Did you run far?" Mujahid said. The
guard was young. He must have entered the city watch as a new recruit
this year.

The guard shrugged. "What's far? Was down at the dock, so suppose
some would say that's far. Not far for the guard. We march three leagues
a day. Full gear."

"I don't usually have the pleasure of speaking with the city guard. What's your name?"

The guard smiled and began to speak.

In one deft motion, Mujahid unfolded his arms, sliced the dagger across the guard's throat and placed it back in his sleeve before the guard started bleeding. With his other hand, he pushed the man against the wall, propping him up in an effort to draw no attention from the people passing by.

"I'm truly sorry, young man," Mujahid said. "Know that your penance will be short and your reward great."

Life slipped away from the guard until Mujahid was certain he was holding a corpse. His well of power started to fill, but escaping the city was going to take more power than this. There were more guards here at the main gate than in the fortress.

He willed the guard back to life.

When the flood of images stopped, he knew the dead guard better than guard knew himself. The boy's sentence would, indeed, be a short one. He was a kind soul.

He felt a cold sensation at the center of his chest, and dismissed it. Killing the guard had upset him more than he cared to admit.

Kill them, you fool. Feel sorry for yourself later.

Mujahid sent his new penitent to kill the next guard. The penitent decapitated his former comrade, and the headless corpse dropped, filling Mujahid's well further. They made their way through six other guards, and by the time anyone noticed what was happening it was too late for the remaining gate guards.

His penitent waded into battle, and Mujahid released a cone of disease that dropped two men to the ground. Mujahid grew stronger with each death, and his chest grew colder, but if he didn't find a way out of this soon, the size of the guard force alone would overwhelm him.

The guards across the plaza had noticed the fight and were getting closer. He wove fire together with wind, preparing to unleash a storm of flame in the plaza, but he stopped when he saw the people. Killing the city guards had added enough penance to his soul for one day. He wouldn't add mindless slaughter of innocent civilians to the tally. If he didn't get past that gate quickly the death toll would continue to rise.

He wove a thread of power through disease and shield, binding them together into a single deadly purpose. He cast them forward into the air, and a green cloud materialized between him and the oncoming patrols.

It was risky. The slightest breeze would disperse the crude wall, and he'd be just as vulnerable if the wind changed direction.

He sent a small amount of necropotency into his throat to amplify his voice. "This can end without your deaths," he said. His voice reverberated off the buildings. "But if you attempt to stop me I won't hesitate to unleash hell on this city."

The coldness in his chest became concentrated at a single spot, as if icy water had dripped onto his robe. He felt his chest, but there was no dampness.

His warning had fallen on deaf ears. The first patrol hit the wall of green sickness and fell to their deaths, clutching their throats as their bodies erupted in blisters of puss. They were young. Too young to know what it meant to face a necromancer in battle.

The wall weakened. Mujahid wasn't sure it would withstand another hit. He turned to the arch and ignited the symbol of ascension.

"By Arin, his eyes," the older of the two officers said. "He's a Mukhtaar Lord. Retreat!"

At least the leaders have some festering sense.

His chest was much colder now. Something was wrong. He was upset, but not enough to make him feel as if there were ice in his robe. The blood drained from his face when he realized the source. He reached into his robe and examined the Talisman of Archmages. It had grown cold, and the inner light was extinguished.

He staggered. This couldn't be possible. The words of the prophecy given him by the goddess Shealynd ran through his mind.

"In Erindor's time of greatest need, He Who Walks Between Worlds will come to bring down the sky. The banished lord from Paradise will cradle him like a babe until the water takes him...." He couldn't finish the words. It was too painful.

He didn't understand. The prophecy was specific. The barrier would come down, and Nicolas would be the one to do it.

The rage he kept at the center of his being began to boil and bubble to the surface.

No. I can't release it. Not yet.

With measured breaths, he quelled the storm inside until the rage was back in its place, bound and shackled, where it would stay for as long as Mujahid could manage to keep it there.

A cry of pain drew his attention. Only one guard remained at the portcullis, and Mujahid's penitent was making short work of him.

The symbol of ascension glowed in his mind, and he released a thread of power into the telekinesis symbol. He cast it forward, grasped the gate's locking wheel, then spun the wheel around until the portcullis began to rise.

When the portcullis was high enough, he ran and slid under it.

The undead penitent attempted to follow, but Mujahid released the locking wheel, and the portcullis crashed back down, trapping the penitent inside the city.

Emotions warred inside Mujahid. How could the gods allow the boy to die? For decades he had carried that prophecy with him, and now this?

Caspardis would be held accountable. Kagan would be held accountable.

He absorbed as much necropotency as he could and prepared to level the city. He warred within himself, as if another consciousness had entered his mind and took control—an evil and twisted consciousness—forcing him to observe from outside of his body.

They'll write songs about this day.

Images from the guard's life entered his mind and wrested control from the evil that was directing his actions. These weren't random thoughts. They came from his penitent through the necromantic link.

Caspardis wasn't the source of evil in this world. They were every bit the victim that Nicolas was.

The rage subsided and it was as if the foreign consciousness released its hold on him. He allowed the necropotency to spill back into his well of power.

Gods, what was that? If some entity ever took control of me, the power they'd wield would be...

He stopped himself and shook off the disturbing feeling.

"It seems you have been *my* priest on this day," Mujahid said to his penitent, who was smiling at him through the portcullis. "I release you, my friend. Your penance is at an end."

In a burst of radiance, the undead guard transformed into pure spirit.

"Thank you, Mujahid," the spirit said. "But know that you have incurred some penance yourself on this day."

Mujahid smiled at the spirit. "You don't know the half of the evil I've wrought upon this world, friend. My penance will be legendary."

"There is a force that will consume you if you do not complete your ascension."

Mujahid squinted. "Explain your—"

The spirit vanished.

What could that mean?

Mujahid turned and ran toward the coast, determined to bring the barrier down alone if necessary. He'd have to puzzle out the mystery some other time.

CHAPTER FIFTEEN

Tithian sat on the edge of his bed, hoping he was wrong.
He had turned his back on everyone he cared about because he
believed the archmage was the voice of the gods. But how could
the gods speak lies? Perhaps Kagan wasn't their voice after all. That
could be the only explanation.

He closed his eyes and recalled a conversation with Lord Mujahid in
better times.

"Faith is wonderful to have when it is well considered," Mujahid had
said. "Never allow another to do your thinking for you."

"'But what of faith, my Lord? You ask me to set aside centuries of
revelation in favor of my own conclusions?"

"The gods gave us Faith, yes, but they also gave us Reason."

"Faith is more valuable, obviously."

"And on what measure do you base that decision? Did you somehow
reason it out, or is it mystical knowledge that requires faith? How are we
to decide which is the measure of the other?"

"The archmage is divine. It's blasphemy to suggest otherwise."

"The archmage is a *man*, and that is a fact you forget at your own
peril. There will come a day when he reveals his true nature, and if you
hold him in too high regard, you may not be able to accept it when it

happens. If you build your faith on the foundation of a single man, what will become of that faith when the man crumbles under the weight of his own sin?"

Tithian opened his eyes and donned his favorite boots. They were worn and threatening to fall apart, but he had a hard time letting go of them.

In hindsight, the Mukhtaar Lord's words had been prophetic. The image of a perfect archmage who communed with the gods and served the good of humankind seemed naive after the things Tithian had witnessed. He had built his faith on a foundation of sand, and now that sand was shifting.

He couldn't continue to serve a man and an institution that he doubted. He would give the archmage one more chance to prove his divine nature, and then he would act...one way or another.

He considered the dual nature of the role he played at the Pinnacle. On the one hand he had to be a docile man, devout in his beliefs, and fierce in his devotion to the Archmage. But on the other, he had to be a cunning man who understood manipulation and how the powerful kept their power. The two natures had become tightly-woven, and he was adept at switching roles as the situation required. But in all his years at the Pinnacle he never expected to use those skills against the archmage.

No, not against. He may still prove himself true.

Docile Tithian would never be able to ferret out the truth. That Tithian would be subservient and unwilling to ask the questions that needed asking.

But *cunning* Tithian would have no such problem.

He approached the wall on the other side of the storage alcove in his quarters and performed the opening ritual. He knew where he had to go and what he had to do when he arrived. He only hoped that what he saw wouldn't shatter what was left of the foundation of his faith. He had precious little sand to spare.

This treachery cannot be allowed to stand, Holy One," said Chal Ghanix, the Religarian Emissary.

Tithian could see and hear everything within the archmage's private study through a necromantic lens the size of a man's head. The *necrolens* made the wall look as if a perfect circle had been cut out of the stone, but no one would know he was there. A necrolens was undetectable to all but its creator.

Ghanix was in the middle of an unofficial audience with Archmage Kagan. Tithian always tried his best to ignore these secret meetings, but he couldn't anymore. If a meeting was taking place between two heads of state, he needed to know why, even if that meant ignoring Kagan's prohibition of necromancy. Reason told him the archmage was planning something best kept secret, but faith made him cling to the hope he was wrong.

"I demand an audience with ambassador Emaldor," Ghanix said. His face had turned as crimson as the Dragon of Religar embroidered across his desert robes. "We welcome them into our city, and they thank us by destroying it?"

Kagan made a placating gesture with his hand and sat in the high-backed chair behind his desk.

"First," Kagan said, "thank you for agreeing to meet with me here, Emissary Ghanix. The Pinnacle sometimes has ears of its own. Please, have a seat." Kagan gestured toward one of the chairs in front of Ghanix.

"I am comfortable standing, thank you."

"I will remind you to recall who provoked this response," Kagan said. "The Shandarian Union did not invade your nation on a whim. Technically, Emissary, the actions of *your* nation could be considered prelude to war."

Bile rose in Tithian's throat. Kagan had caused the invasion, and now he tried to blame the Emperor of Religar. That sand under his faith was shifting again.

"This entire matter disgusts me," Kagan said. "Two nations fighting like shrillers over a wounded adda."

"With all respect, Holy One, the Pinnacle doesn't have to fight for basic resources. The faithful bring gifts to your doorstep every day, in spite of how lavish this place is." Ghanix stopped and bowed. "By Arin's beneficence, of course."

"The Council does not wish for war to come to Erindor, but under the circumstances we can hardly stop you."

Ghanix tilted his head to the side. "The Pinnacle...bastion of peace in the three kingdoms...would accept war between Dar Rodon and Shandar?"

Tithian listened in disbelief. If the archmage didn't act to stop this escalation, war would be inevitable.

Ghanix smiled. "No. I think it's time for cooler heads to prevail. I will not advise the Emperor to go to war when war is precisely what he wishes to avoid. The Empire can't afford a war on two fronts."

"Surely you don't expect the Barathosian armada to come crawling back," Kagan said.

Tithian shook his head. Kagan was reminding Ghanix of the vast power he wielded.

Ghanix chuckled. "If the armada ever breaches the barrier, the three kingdoms will cease to exist. Perhaps even the Pinnacle itself would cease to exist. Arin forbid, of course."

"The world will always need an archmage, Emissary."

"Barathos has no need for a *second* archmage, or have you forgotten? With Barathos in charge you'd be little more than a temple priest...if their archmage even let you live. Tell me, would you let their archmage live if placed in that position?"

Kagan lost his smile. "Is there a point in your rambling, Emissary?"

Ghanix bowed. "Forgive me. I am not blessed with magic, as you are, and my mind is more prone to distraction as I get older. I was referring to Tildem as the second front."

Kagan opened his desk drawer and retrieved the ceremonial Shandarian dagger Tithian had placed there.

A rush of vitapotency swept past Tithian. Kagan was drawing a massive amount of power into his well, and Ghanix would have no awareness of it.

An ethereal hand formed in front of Kagan and reached out toward Ghanix. The hand appeared fashioned of smoke and wisps of cloud, and it crackled with energy. It grew big enough to wrap itself around a man's torso, and with each pulse of energy dagger-like claws protruded farther from the tips of the fingers, stopping when they were as long as the fingers themselves.

Ghanix backed away from the bladed fingers.

An expulsion of force sent the emissary flying backwards, where he struck the wall opposite the necrolens and collapsed onto the ground.

Tithian gaped as the ethereal hand inched closer to Ghanix. He had never seen such a use of magic before, but he knew it wouldn't be good for Ghanix if it touched him.

"Listen to me, you sun-addled fool," Kagan said. "This war will happen and it will be your own festering emperor who makes the declaration."

Ghanix screamed but no sound came out of his mouth. He panicked as the hand drew closer to his chest.

Tithian hoped Kagan was bluffing, trying to strong-arm the emissary, but that hope was tenuous.

Kagan's face became a mask of contempt.

The smoky hand drew back then plunged into Ghanix's chest. The ghostly fingers squeezed, and Ghanix's body convulsed once before going still. When Ghanix stopped moving, the hand dissipated.

Tithian felt a presence that had been absent from the Pinnacle for decades. A surge of necropotency filled the small chamber.

Motion caught Tithian's attention, and when he saw the source he took a step back from the necrolens.

The corpse of Chal Ghanix rose and approached Kagan, and it was obvious Kagan knew it was happening.

Tithian focused his thoughts. He couldn't make an accusation like this without confirming the facts. He tapped into the smallest amount of necropotency, taking care to not draw attention to himself. When the power entered his well, he concentrated all of his strength into enhancing his vision. The faint trace of a necromantic link extending from Kagan to Ghanix became visible.

There was no longer a question. Ghanix was Kagan's penitent. The man who proclaimed the evils of necromancy to the world was now, himself, using necromancy to control the corpse of Emissary Ghanix.

Which was the lie? Did he lie about necromancy being evil, or did he lie about what the gods said?

Facts Tithian never imagined he would question, much less doubt, he now rejected outright as the delusions of a naive man. If the archmage could lie...if such great evil were possible...what of the ceremonies and rituals he followed? Were they lies too? What about the gods? Were they not gods? Were the sacred writings all lies, written by men to serve their own purposes? Was the *Book of Life* itself a lie? Was there nothing remaining of his faith at all?

He looked at Kagan and for the first time saw him for what he was — nothing more than a man.

Mujahid, old friend, you were right. I should have listened. I cannot accept this.

Kagan lifted the Shandarian dagger and vitapotency entered the chamber. The blade began to glow. He placed the dagger's point on the center of Ghanix's chest, then pushed the blade deep.

The ceremonial dagger had no cross guards, allowing Kagan to insert the blade up to the seal of office, which was etched into the jeweled handle. Any blood escaping Ghanix's body was concealed by the Red Dragon of Religar on the front of his robes.

The events Tithian witnessed had numbed him. He wanted to feel something — to have the desire to scream, to have the desire to cry, the desire to lash out at Kagan. But he had none of the rage those things required. All he could do was watch as the last vestiges of his faith slipped through his fingers like so much sand.

"Guards," Kagan said.

The door to the study swung open and two Pinnacle guardsmen entered.

"Inform the Shandarian ambassador that I'm waiting in my study with the Religarian emissary. We have much to discuss. And summon magi Winston and Samnal."

The names didn't surprise Tithian. Winston and Samnal were the youngest members of the Council. Kagan needed men who lacked necromantic training. Even a newly-awakened necromancer would be able to sense Ghanix's corpse, so allowing Council elders to enter the room would give up the lie.

Mujahid had been right to question Kagan, but Tithian had turned away from him out of religious duty fueled by faith. He had cast Mujahid out of the Pinnacle and foreswore his oaths to the clan. Mujahid could never forgive him for that...because Tithian would never forgive himself.

A knock on the chamber door drew Tithian's attention.

"Enter," Kagan said.

Ambassador Emaldor entered, followed by magi Winston and Samnal, and the animated corpse of Ghanix rose.

"Ahh, Ambassador Emaldor," Kagan said. "I thought you should be here for this discussion, since it relates to the recent hostilities between your two nations."

To Tithian's astonishment, the corpse of Ghanix spoke.

"Ambassador Emaldor," the corpse of Ghanix said. His voice was no different than before he was murdered. "We finally meet face to face. May Arin bless your descendants. I've been informed of your political prowess, so I will speak directly."

Tithian noticed a near-imperceptible struggle taking place between Kagan and Ghanix's corpse, but when it was over Ghanix spoke.

"My emperor expresses his deepest regret for the unfortunate choice of locations for our arms warehouse, Ambassador," Ghanix said. "In return for an agreement of peace between our two nations, my emperor is willing to grant the following concessions."

Ghanix's corpse laid out the details of the original peace agreement, changing only the location of the stone warehouses and masons.

Emaldor looked taken aback, and Tithian couldn't blame him. Nothing about this made sense.

"Remarkable," Emaldor said. "Access to the stone cutters will allow my nation to rebuild from the earthquakes."

"It would appear we have reached some agreement, gentlemen?" Kagan asked.

Kagan faced Ghanix and Emaldor. "I told you gentlemen some time ago that I would see you in a formal embrace of friendship someday. If there ever was a day for it, I believe that day is today."

Ghanix's corpse took a step toward Emaldor.

Emaldor returned the gesture and opened his arms to embrace the Religarian emissary.

Kagan smiled as the men embraced and the Council magi applauded in the background. But the applause was short lived.

Ghanix's corpse dropped to the floor with a sickening thud and the council magi stared, mouths agape. Emaldor's blood-covered ceremonial dagger was visible, standing several inches out from Ghanix's chest. Blood dripped from the dagger and ran down Ghanix's robe.

It had happened so fast that it took a moment for Tithian to understand what he was seeing.

"Gods, man, what have you done?" Kagan said. "I hardly believe I'm saying this...arrest the Shandarian ambassador immediately."

Guards brushed past the Council magi and grabbed the ambassador.

"I don't understand," Emaldor said. "I had nothing to do with this."

"We saw the deed committed with our own eyes," Kagan said.

"The archmage is right," Winston said. "Ambassador Emaldor killed the Religarian emissary."

Tithian felt sick. He had unwittingly made this entire situation possible, and now he wanted to shout the truth at the top of his voice, but he stopped himself. An impulsive move like that would ruin any chance he had of setting things right.

The guards led Emaldor out of the room as he shouted his innocence.

"My brothers," Kagan said. "I had expected this to be a joyous occasion."

"I can hardly believe what I just witnessed, Holy One," Samnal said. "You understand I must inform the emperor of Shandar's betrayal?"

Kagan nodded. "Of course. And I am certain Magus Winston understands as well. What could possibly have driven the Union to this madness?"

"Do not accuse the Union of the treachery of a single madman," Winston said.

"I doubt the emperor will agree with that sentiment," Kagan said. "Wars have begun for far less than the assassination of a diplomat."

Winston stared at the corpse expressionless.

"It is imperative that both nations hear the truth of what happened here today," Kagan said. "We will not be able to end this war, once it begins, if its cause is not rooted in truth."

Tithian's face contorted in disgust. How dare that man utter the word *truth*?

Kagan lifted his head and closed his eyes. "The Book of Life calls to me, brothers. Perhaps the gods will instruct us."

Tithian released the power, and the necrolens closed. His world was different now. Everything he had once believed faded like a dream.

Tithian the Prime Warlock was dead. But Tithian the former priest of Clan Mukhtaar had grown stronger by the power of truth. He knew it was a partial truth, but he would find the rest, one way or another. Either by himself, or....

There was one man in this world who would understand what he had seen. He wasn't sure if that man would accept him or kill him on sight, but he had to try.

He had to find Mujahid Mukhtaar.

And, somehow, he had to keep Kagan distracted while the Mukhtaar Lord gathered more necromancers. For necromancy is what it would take to bring the Council down, and Tithian wouldn't rest until that happened.

He kicked off his tattered boots. It was high time he found a new pair.

CHAPTER SIXTEEN

T he arrow floated like a compass needle in the periphery of
Mujahid's vision, pointing him toward the nearest source of
necropotency. It had been years since he last navigated the
narrow, twisted passageways under the city of Caspardis, but the arrow
would lead him to the coven's orb of power, an artifact he needed if he
had any hope of bringing Kagan down by himself.

Mujahid felt like he was piloting a ship without a sextant. Prophecy
had guided his actions for decades, and now it appeared to have proven
a false guide. He needed to speak to William, the leader of the coven of
New Caspardis. That old necromancer understood the inner workings of
necromantic prophecy better than any magus in the Mukhtaar
Chronicles. William would help make sense of this mess.

Something wasn't right. He should have passed the barrier into the
coven by now.

*By Zubuxo's scythe, where is it? William wouldn't have lowered the barrier
without sending word to me.*

Barrier magic had become central to the clan's defenses, but a shield
didn't work if it wasn't there.

Mujahid released the tiniest amount of power into his eyes, and the
tunnel before him illuminated. He sent power into his ears, and the silent

passageway exploded in a cacophony of sound. Necropotency amplified the smallest of noises, but he was ready for this change in perception. Few knew better than he that the underground was teaming with life.

He concentrated, searching the surrounding tunnels for any familiar energy patterns, but didn't sense anything. Patterns worked in much the same way as the sense of smell. Like the smell of a mother's perfume transports a person back to when they were a child, a pattern would take him back to the moment it was first imprinted in his mind, conjuring an image of the person it represented. But there was no image of William here. There were ways to conceal one's pattern, though, and William could be a hair's breadth out of range with Mujahid being none the wiser.

As he continued down the corridor, the source of necropotency he had been following grew larger, and its size began to worry him.

There's too much.

He made his way down a spiraling tunnel, lined with coffins and burial chambers, toward the large cavern at the center of New Caspardis. The stench of death and decay was overpowering. When he reached the bottom of the spiral, he looked out into the central cavern in disbelief.

Corpses paved the ground. Judging by the state of the bodies, they were a few days old. The invaders had spared no one, regardless of age. He offered a silent prayer to Shealynd that William had somehow survived.

Light reflected off shiny objects on the floor, and Mujahid's heart sank. Remnants of the orb of power were scattered into millions of shards around the cavern.

Gods no. Not this orb too.

With Nicolas dead, the clan orbs were his last and greatest hope. Now, both of the priceless objects were gone. When the initial shock of the orb's destruction passed, his focus returned to the dead that carpeted the cavern floor. Countless shards from the destroyed orb pierced the corpses from head to toe.

How could this have happened? He understood how Kagan's forces had found Paradise, but the Talisman of Archmages couldn't have led anyone to New Caspardis. Someone in the coven must have turned traitor and led the local authorities here. But who would do such a thing? How could they have passed through the barrier? And even if they did, how did they destroy the orb?

His enhanced hearing caught the faint sound of falling rock in one of the side tunnels. Someone was here, and they were trying hard not to be heard. Several large pack animals stirred and trotted away. He turned to the tunnel where the sound came from and cursed as he caught a glimpse of a dead adda-ki.

Shandarian Rangers had been here.

Mujahid shook his head in disbelief. Even if the rangers had found a way through the magic, he couldn't understand how they destroyed the orb. Such a feat would require an enormous amount of energy directed into the orb itself. The rangers were many things, but they weren't magi.

More rocks hit the ground. Mujahid proceeded up the tunnel, stepping around dead adda-ki. He walked for several minutes before the sound of breathing lifted his hopes.

He had to be cautious. He cleared his mind and the symbol of ascension flooded with power.

He molded sheets of energy into an invisible platform that lifted him off the ground. It would only lift him a few feet into the air, but that would be enough to silence the rhythmic tapping of his boots against the stone ground. He hovered for a moment, and then glided forward.

The breathing grew louder as the tunnel twisted to the left. The source would be close now. Mujahid turned the corner, and the voice of a woman surprised him.

"My lord?" The voice came from an older woman lying on the ground in front of him. He could have kept levitating down the tunnel without ever seeing her, so covered in dirt and debris was she. He examined her face to see if he knew her.

By Zubuxo, does Arin show no mercy?

The face he beheld told the story of the destruction of New Caspardis in wounds and disfiguration. The woman tried to stand but collapsed. Instead, she raised her hands to cover her eyes, and several more people who were sitting against the tunnel walls, unseen until now, repeated the gesture.

He struggled against the desire to pull her hands away. He didn't like the rituals people performed when they saw the light in his eyes. It smacked of worship to him, and if any person in this world knew he wasn't a god, it was Mujahid.

He dispersed the energy and descended. He needed information now, not ritual.

"The light has passed," he said.

The crowd responded in unison and uncovered their eyes. "May it bless us in its passing."

"How did this happen?" Mujahid asked.

"The rangers destroyed the orb with an object of power, Lord Mukhtaar," a weak male voice said. "The blast did the rest."

Mujahid knelt next to the injured man and began to heal him, but he noticed, with no small amount of irritation, that people had covered their eyes once more.

"Uncover your eyes," Mujahid said. "I'm suspending the ritual for now."

"Yes, Lord Mukhtaar," a voice said.

"Did Magus William survive the attack?"

"He is hurt badly," a voice said. "He sleeps farther up the tunnel."

A great feeling of relief lifted the weight off Mujahid's shoulders and he offered a prayer of thanks to Shealynd. He hoped he had arrived in time to heal him.

"I am awake now, my Lord," the familiar, aging voice of William said. He spoke in a labored way, as if it were difficult to breathe. "Lord Mukhtaar? You haven't aged."

Mujahid ran to his side and knelt. He cleared his mind and sent tendrils of power into William's body, gathering information about the old man's injuries. He suffered from several broken bones, which Mujahid was able to mend, but when the probing tendrils reached William's head, the power vanished into an abyss. Mujahid knew all too well what that meant. A bridge was forming between William's spirit and the Plane of Death.

William was dying. There was no way to tell when it would happen, but it would be soon.

Mujahid released the power.

"You've discovered what I have known for more than a day now," William said.

Mujahid raised an eyebrow. "So you have the healing gift now, Magus?"

"No. But a man knows when his time approaches. Did the attack bring you here, my lord?"

"Don't presume to tell me about a person's time, old man. You'll outlive me, and you know it."

William laughed. "Not even you are that powerful, Lord Mujahid."

"You're still sharp enough to tell me and my brother apart, yet you turn your back on life so easily?"

"Your lack of profanity and beer breath aided my mental acuity."

Mujahid smiled and shook his head. "And don't presume to tell me about my own power, either."

He had a difficult decision to make. William was a dear friend, but saving his life would violate an oath...an oath to a god. He wasn't sure what he would do yet, but he believed in the virtue of being prepared.

He nodded to a man standing nearby. "You. Fetch one of those pack animals. And quickly. The rest of you...leave us."

The people murmured assent as they crawled and limped back toward the main cavern.

"I know our time grows short," Mujahid said, "but you are among the wisest of Clan Mukhtaar."

"You honor me," William said. "What of the heir, my Lord? Is he here with you?"

"How do you know about the boy?"

"I received word from Lord Nuuan. Boy, you say? Most curious."

Caspardis wasn't on the way to Tildem. Once again his brother had too many secrets. "I found the heir. But...."

Mujahid retrieved the darkened Talisman of Archmages and held it up by its leather thong.

"Then it is worse than I had imagined," William said.

"This changes everything." Mujahid shook the Talisman.

"This changes nothing, and Mordryn would be the first to remind you of that fact."

William's words caught him off guard, and for several moments he wasn't sure how to react.

Prior to finding Nicolas, Mujahid hadn't spoken her name aloud in more than thirty years. She was everything to him back then—mentor, confidant, partner, lover. She taught him more about necromancy in the short time they were together than he had learned in all of his previous years combined. She had an intuitive knowledge of energy that was beyond anything he had seen before. He remembered her insisting that necromancy was a religion of love, not death. She had changed him in many ways, and without her guidance he may never have attempted the Rite of Testing at all. He asked her, after he ascended, why she didn't attempt the Rite herself. She looked at him with her piercing blue eyes and said "I don't need to *become* a Mukhtaar Lord, my love. I have one of *my own* right here." And he knew in his heart she was right, for she wielded a power over him that no one could ever duplicate with magic. When she went missing, all they found was her broken blade in the corridor outside of their chambers at the Mukhtaar estate. That and a Rose of Shealynd. It had been Mordryn's favorite flower.

He couldn't allow this memory to linger.

"Mordryn is long gone," Mujahid said.

"Forgive my presumption, but I believe you know what she would tell you now."

Mujahid turned away. The feelings came flooding back and he remembered everything—the way she smelled as if she had bathed in rose water. The way she tasted. The way her blue eyes shone with an inner light. The way her skin glistened as she lay next to him. He raised his palm to his forehead and tried to push her image out of his mind by sheer force of will, but it wouldn't go.

"She would tell you that Kagan must be stopped," William said. He tried to stifle a cough, but didn't succeed. "You must find a way to press on without the heir and bring this course of events to fruition. Too many lives...too many *undead* depend upon it."

"The prophecy was specific."

"You worry too much about that prophecy of yours, regardless of its source."

"Why would Shealynd give me a prophecy that served no purpose? Her voice was —"

"Prophecy is a strange thing that is not often fulfilled in ways predicted by man. I warned you of this many years ago but—and I beg your pardon—you are too thick-headed to heed my advice."

"There's only one thing that prophecy could mean."

"If you shared it with three men you would hear three different interpretations. And strangest of all is that all three could be correct...simultaneously. Yet you consider your interpretation sacrosanct, petulantly refusing to hear any alternatives."

Mujahid raised an eyebrow. "Some would say that's my prerogative as a Lord."

"I require no reminding of your exalted status. But you are nothing more than a postulant in matters of prophecy...and a stubborn one at that. You may flay me for my insolence, if it pleases you."

Mujahid smiled. "Your hide is safe...for now. But the prophecy was given to me. Shouldn't my interpretation carry the most weight?"

"When prophecy causes you to lose sight of the present, it ceases to be useful. Prophecy only illuminates events viewed in hindsight."

"Then prophecy serves no practical purpose at all, and we would do best to ignore it."

William smiled. "It does my heart good to see the birth of wisdom in my Lord before I shuffle off beyond the veil."

"You study prophecy your entire life, then tell me it serves no purpose?"

"Prophecy is a torch designed to illuminate the path behind us," William said. "Not the path ahead. It is a guidepost that tells us everything is unfolding according to divine plan."

"Well, this particular guidepost was quite specific about the boy bringing down the sky."

"You have understood nothing. Forgive me, but you simply do not know that to a certainty. Neither of us do. Now, use that head of yours and tell me why this is the case."

Mujahid had been giving the man some privilege because of their friendship, but the old priest was beginning to test his sense of decorum. "William—"

"Tell me why, *postulant*."

Mujahid closed his eyes and reminded himself that he trusted William for a reason. "We don't know because the sky hasn't been brought down yet."

"You have spoken the words better than I could have. His very death could be the efficient cause of a chain of events leading to the destruction of the barrier. This, too, would fulfill that prophecy of yours."

"I seek truth, not philosophical supposition."

"The natural order of the universe itself requires Kagan be stopped. That is what I know to be true."

Mujahid waved his hand and turned away.

"Either you continue fighting for what you know to be right," William said, "or you hand the world over to Kagan because of a poorly-interpreted prophecy that refuses to obey your preconceived notion of how the future should unfold."

"You have a way with words."

"So I've been told."

"I'll fight, William. Never doubt that. As we speak, my brother sows the seeds of resistance in Tildem. But I fear the resistance will fall short without more knowledge of what we're up against. Kagan knows more about that barrier than we do, and that is something we must remedy."

"The Great Library is within reach."

"What?"

"You say Lord Nuuan travels to Tildem. The Great Library of Rotham has ever been a repository of both arcane and spiritual knowledge. Not to mention...you'll find sympathetic ears in Tildem."

Mujahid considered William's idea for a moment. King Donal was the only monarch to offer resistance, though passive, to Kagan's prohibition of necromancy.

"I'll consider it, William. But my instinct is leading me straight to the Pinnacle."

"Do consider it, if only to suggest the idea to your brother."

A man drew close with a beast in tow.

It was time to decide.

Mujahid fought with himself as he remembered the oaths he swore when he had ascended. There was magic only a Mukhtaar Lord should be aware of, lest the Clan grow corrupt in some futile quest for immortality. But William was the only surviving prophet of Clan Mukhtaar. And he was Mujahid's friend.

Mujahid made his decision.

"The clan needs you now more than ever," Mujahid said.

William coughed. "You will have my services for a little while longer, I think. I only regret you never told me how you united the clans. But I suppose all will be clear once I stand before Zubuxo's throne."

Mujahid placed a hand on the top of William's head. "You are wise beyond your years. But there is still much you don't know about the nature of our magic. Cling to life, William, and I promise to tell every detail."

Power flooded through the symbol of ascension in Mujahid's mind. He wove the necessary pattern, spread his arms in front of him, and cast the melded symbols at the pack animal. A great rushing wind swept through the underground passageway like a gathering storm.

When the symbols struck the animal, a vortex of energy appeared in front of him like a whirlwind. Mujahid turned the vortex's hungry mouth toward the unfortunate animal, and within moments the great rush of wind changed directions, feeding the mystical eddy of power. Life drained from the animal into the rotating miasma of energy, and a stream formed between Mujahid and the vortex's funnel. The life force of the pack animal entered his body and rejuvenated him, as the animal drained to an empty shell and collapsed.

Mujahid's skin tightened and his muscles grew stronger. He reached out with a tendril of energy and rotated the vortex, turning its mouth toward himself. Arcane wind tossed Mujahid's hair around and sent rocks and debris crashing through the tunnel all around him.

"There is so much you don't know, my friend," Mujahid said. He opened a channel between the vortex and William, and as the transfer of energy began it was as if something reached into his chest and squeezed his soul. His muscles grew weaker with every passing moment, and small wrinkles formed on his skin as if he had aged ten years in a moment.

With a concentration that left him shaking and weakened, Mujahid severed the link to the vortex and released the power. The rush of wind disappeared, and silence blanketed the tunnel.

William sat up. "How is this possible?" His injuries were gone, and to all appearances he looked ten years younger.

"I won't tell you, and you wouldn't understand anyway, so hold your question."

"By Arin's shining helm, you look younger," William said.

"Try not to judge me harshly for keeping some for myself. Now, you and the rest of the survivors will travel with me to Agera. What was once Clan Catiatum maintains the coven there. They'll offer you a home for the time being."

"Clan Catiatum," William said. "Savages." The note of distaste in the man's voice was unmistakable.

"We are all Mukhtaar now."

"If I'm not mistaken, my Lord, I believe you made a promise to me a few moments ago. The story?"

"You may see your Lords in a different light once you know the truth," Mujahid said.

"Knowledge is to be preferred over ignorance."

Mujahid leaned in close. "You remember how it used to be...before the Ascension. The clans thought Ascendancy nothing more than a myth."

"Yet you both ascended."

"Indeed."

"I remember a disagreement between you and Lord Nuuan at the time."

"The rediscovery of Ascendancy changed everything. Clan unification was necessary. Inevitable. We called a General Assembly of the clans. We were certain they would see the logic of it."

"They refused?"

"Quite the contrary. We led the clan leaders straight to the threshold...the very entrance to the Rite. We told them to ascend or step aside."

"It bears the mark of logic, my Lord. The hierarchy would be uncertain, otherwise."

"It was a trap, William." Mujahid looked down and exhaled. "One by one the clan leaders stepped over the threshold to enter the Rite, and one by one they died."

"I understand your concern, but it doesn't change the fact the hierarchy needed to be secured for everyone's protection."

"We knew they couldn't ascend. We knew they would die."

"Yet you also knew unification was necessary. You will object, my Lord, but sometimes the ends justify the means."

Mujahid didn't expect to hear that from William. "Even if the means are intrinsically evil?"

"You overstate matters," William said. "Questionable, perhaps, but evil? A complete and utter absence of good?"

"The story isn't finished. I didn't fully appreciate what Lord Nuuan had done until the clan delegations returned to their homes to prepare the heirs for succession."

"That must have been problematic. You don't simply take over a clan that has clear succession."

"You do if there aren't any heirs to succeed."

William's eyes widened.

"Now you understand. When the clans returned home they found their heirs dead or missing, leaving them without clear paths to succession. It was all handled...most efficiently."

"Lord Nuuan did this, my Lord?"

Mujahid looked away. "Within weeks of the General Assembly the clans swore fealty to us, dissolving their old ties and uniting under Clan Mukhtaar."

William whistled.

"When the leader of the old Catiatum coven sees me, he is more likely to soil himself than refuse to aid us."

Mujahid was certain it was a story William would never forget.

CHAPTER SEVENTEEN

The refugees from New Caspardis were welcomed into the coven of Catiatum in much the way Mujahid expected...without enthusiasm. But the leadership obeyed, and that was enough for him. They asked him to stay and assist with the transition of the refugees, but there was no time to spare.

William insisted on accompanying him to the surface, so he selected a handful of refugees to go along. He didn't want William to have to make the journey back alone.

Recent quakes had decimated the underground tunnels, and Mujahid was thankful they were able to find any path at all. They cleared a blocked passage and emerged from a concealed tunnel east of Agera.

"You would do well to enter the city prepared," William said.

"We've been over this. I merely intend to make my way to the harbor and book—"

"My Lord, please hear me out. What you did in Caspardis will not be allowed to stand. Your reputation will precede you in Agera. The provincial government will have circulated your description by now. The local garrison may have already been alerted."

Mujahid hadn't considered that. He was expecting Agera to be aware of what happened in Caspardis, but if the local garrison had a description of him, this could be a short journey.

"I don't believe they've had enough time to do that."

"You are probably right, but are you certain? I do advise you to exercise caution."

"I appreciate your concern. But right now I would take greater comfort in knowing you'll take care of the survivors."

"I would have it no other way."

"Apart from what I may have said before...don't be too free with your trust around the old Catiatum priests. They're a work in progress."

"Of course, my Lord."

"We will speak of rebuilding New Caspardis when I see you again, so don't grow too used to leisure, old man."

William smiled and nodded. "Forgive my presumption, but...."

"You've no need to mince words with me. Speak your mind."

"I have known you for many years, and Mordryn changed you for the better. Do not push her out of your mind. She plays an important role in your priesthood. Love always does. We don't know what happened, but as sure as I am standing here, I know, in my heart, one day you will have your answers."

"Is that a prophecy, old friend?"

"Call it hope."

Mujahid smiled.

"About this Pinnacle business...do reconsider, my Lord. I fear the worst if you were to make an attempt on the Pinnacle prematurely."

"The world falls further into decay with every passing moment that barrier stands. I've spent years waiting for the one person that could bring an end to this, and now that person is gone. I'll tolerate no more madness. I'm going to the Pinnacle to confront Kagan once and for all. There are only two men alive powerful enough to stand a chance, and my brother is doing his part. If I fail, perhaps he'll succeed."

William frowned. "You gamble with your life, Lord Mukhtaar."

"Shall I gamble with the countless lives who live under that abomination in the sky instead?"

William sighed and nodded. "Be safe. The clan cannot survive without you."

Mujahid headed into Agera, wondering whether the clan would survive *with* him.

Mujahid approached Agera with caution.

Most of the city's buildings lay in ruins, and only the sturdiest of stone structures remained standing at all. The once beautiful city was a jumble of fallen towers and debris-filled streets. Merchants watched him eagerly from within voluminous patchwork tents along the main avenue. There wasn't a customer in sight.

A dozen Agera militia emerged from a concealed alley and Mujahid swore.

He didn't recall such a strong military presence the last time he was here, but he wasn't about to stick around to find out why. He ducked into the nearest merchant tent, and a miasma of scents assaulted his nostrils.

Great. A fragrance trader. Now I'll smell like a Religarian brothel.

A loud snore caught his attention and he saw a lanky man lying on the floor at the back of the tent. Business must be bad indeed for a Religarian to be napping around money.

Mujahid pretended to examine the various fragrance vials until the patrol passed the tent and turned down another avenue.

He had to get out of Agera as soon as possible. All a guard patrol needed to detain him was a general description, and judging by the military presence it was likely they'd have one.

He cast his mind outward, searching for sources of power that must exist in a city of this size. A familiar sensation told him he was right. He was too far away from the necropotency for it to fill his well on its own, but he was close enough to draw it in.

Ruined buildings provided ample cover as he covered the distance to the harbor. The docks formed a natural border on the western edge of a large plaza, which was ringed on three sides by well-maintained buildings. The harbor was busy. Travel over land was treacherous, so most trade flowed through an intricate system of riverboats and barges that all stopped here.

Several boats anchored in port, and Mujahid made his way across the plaza to get a better look. He studied them from behind a fountain, looking for any that were preparing to leave.

Healing William left him looking younger, but his facial features wouldn't have changed much. He pulled his hood up to minimize the chance he'd be recognized.

The sound of boots drew his attention as lightly armored militia entered the plaza from a nearby avenue. There were no ruins nearby for him to hide in, so he ran back across the plaza toward a narrow street, cursing as he ran.

Something was wrong. The militia weren't on a routine patrol. They wore barely enough armor and were moving with haste, glancing around the plaza as if looking for something specific.

Three more militia, dressed like the first group, stepped out from a building a few feet in front of him, catching him off-guard.

One of them looked at Mujahid's robes with a blank expression. "Religarian," she said. "You've got a lot of nerve—"

Mujahid bolted for the corner of the building.

"Get him," she said.

"Why?"

"He's running, ain't he?"

Mujahid picked up speed as he turned the corner into a side street.

A fine festering mess. I manage to hide my true identity only to look like something worse! A Religarian!

Shouts told him the patrols were flanking him, driving him farther east. One way or another he had to evade them. Between what the Shandarians thought he had done in Egis as a Religarian and what he *actually* did in Caspardis, there'd be no hope of escape if they caught him this time.

The street made a sharp turn to the right, and Mujahid ran into a wall. He was at a dead end.

A door opened behind him.

He began to weave two symbols together, intending to unleash a cone of disease at whoever tried to capture him. When he saw who had opened the door, he stumbled backwards and released the power harmlessly, unable to believe his own eyes. A man he hadn't seen in forty years stood in the open doorway.

"Mujahid," Tithian said. "Quickly. Before the militia arrives."

Tithian's pattern was undetectable. The man must be concealing his identity. There was no doubt in his mind it was Tithian, however. This was the man who had refused to come with him all those years ago. This was the man who had stayed behind, valuing the promise of title and riches over the sacred vows of the priesthood. This was the man who led the *Great Purge* that resulted in the deaths of entire necromantic blood lines.

The shouting grew louder, and Mujahid could hear the boots of the lightly armored soldiers striking the ground not far from where he stood.

He was out of choices. He would either have to trust this man—a man who didn't deserve his trust—or take his chances with the militia. With a curse and a burst of speed, Mujahid ran through the doorway with Tithian.

"This way," Tithian said. "It will take the patrols hours to search all of these buildings individually. We'll be long gone by then."

"Tithian?"

Tithian stopped and turned.

Mujahid stared at the man, and a rage that had lain dormant for forty years boiled to the surface. How many nights had he lain in bed, imagining what he would do if he ever got his hands on this traitor?

He closed on Tithian in two strides and pressed his dagger to Tithian's throat. "Give me a reason I shouldn't kill you and make this world a better place."

The leather pounding of boots, and the metallic rattle of sheathed swords echoed in the street outside.

"If my wits haven't dulled I'd say there are two dozen reasons out there," Tithian said.

Mujahid considered.

"I have limited influence here," Tithian said. "Time is at a premium."

Mujahid released him and placed the dagger back in his sleeve. When Tithian didn't move, he gestured through the archway and said, "Get on with it."

They came out of the building on the opposite side. Mujahid wanted to leave Tithian behind, but he needed the man's help right now. Besides, if Tithian wanted him captured, all he had to do was let the militia catch up. Instead, he had chosen to help, and somehow that was more unsettling.

The buildings they moved through were a collection of ruins. The surrounding stone structures remained standing, but most of the interiors had fallen into disrepair or had been looted for wood.

They came to a building with a partial second story and climbed up a precarious staircase.

Tithian stared through a demolished quartz window, scanning the streets below.

"I think we've lost them." Tithian examined Mujahid. "The years have been kinder to you than to me. I wouldn't mind learning that little trick."

Mujahid's old emblem of office, now hanging from Tithian's neck, caught his attention. He cared little for the office, or the illusion of power that came with it, but the emblem brought back painful memories.

"Ahh yes," Tithian said. He glanced down to where Mujahid was staring. "I didn't take pleasure in succeeding you."

"You've had forty years to voice a complaint."

"Can't say I blame you for your suspicions. But I'm here to tell you something, old friend."

"And what would that be, *old friend*?"

"Something went horribly wrong that day—the day the heir disappeared. I did everything I could to turn Kagan from his course, but he would not listen to me."

"You address the *Most Holy Archmage* by name now?"

"You have no idea how fine the line is that I walk. He sent me to find the boy. But you know of his return already."

Mujahid's suspicions were confirmed. Tithian was aware of the forged talisman.

Tithian waved his hand in a dismissive gesture. "I understand why you did it."

"Then you must know that he's gone."

Tithian retrieved his Talisman of Archmages, hanging from a golden chain around his neck, and stared at it. "Of course," he said. "The gods bring us hope, then yank it from our grasp. Typical. But then a god has the luxury of whim, whereas you and I—"

"Much has happened in forty years for you to blaspheme so casually," Mujahid said. "There was a time you would have flogged someone for less."

"Forgive me. It seems I've forgotten your religious sensibilities."

"Only mine?"

"Come now, Mujahid. This should be a joyous reunion, not one filled with—"

"Are you delusional, man?" The heat rose in Mujahid's face. "Forty years. Not a single attempt to reach out to my brother or me, and yet you have the audacity to seek me out now under the guise of...what is this, friendship? Have you completely forsaken your vows? I should kill you where you stand and be done with it."

"The vows," Tithian said. "They seem quaint now."

"Quaint?" The anger rose higher in Mujahid's throat. "Is the color white so tempting after all?"

"Does it get lonely on that pedestal of yours, Lord Mukhtaar?"

Mujahid stood and turned toward the decrepit staircase. "If you try to—"

"You weren't the one to stay behind. You have no idea what it was like after you left...the atrocities I witnessed, all in the name of Religion."

"Now you hold Religion accountable for the evils of humankind?"

"I hold Religion accountable for being more concerned with the good of Religion than the good of humankind. If you can't...please, let's stop this. We have much to discuss and this isn't helping."

Mujahid channeled a small amount of power, allowing the symbol of ascension to pulse. He knew the effect it would have on his appearance, and he wanted to drive home the point.

"Never forget what I am, Tithian. I am not concerned with your existential crisis. Nor am I concerned with your revision of history. You placed a sacred purpose above yourself the day you took the vows. I am your superior, *priest*, and I will hold you to your sacred duty, with or without your obedience. Now, I would know your intentions, and the span of time you have to fill the gaps in my knowledge grows shorter with every breath you take."

Another bead of sweat formed on Tithian's brow. He held up his hands. "I am here to *help* you."

"Oh happy coincidence." Mujahid released the power and his vision returned to normal.

Tithian leaned forward. "I knew two things." He held up a finger. "One, you hoped the boy would return. You took your talisman and left me with a fake. Why else would you do this? Two." He held up a second finger. "When the boy was killed—near Caspardis I believe—I knew you would charge off to the Pinnacle yourself, feeling you had nothing left to lose. When word reached me of the *godlike* feats you accomplished in Caspardis—something along the lines of slaying the entire army and raping their loved ones, if the stories are correct—I knew you'd have no other choice but to come to Agera. You are here. I was right. No mystery. No scheme. No coincidence. Logic."

"You'll forgive me if trust comes slowly."

"I'm here to help."

"You're correct in one thing...I intend to make for the Pinnacle—"

"My friend, I don't—"

"And I need to get out of Agera. Either you'll help me, or you won't. I don't advise attempting a *third* course of action."

Tithian took a deep breath and exhaled. "That's why I'm here. You can't approach the dock during the day. You discovered that yourself. We should wait for darkness."

Mujahid nodded. Tithian might be a traitor, but he was right.

Tithian settled in with his back against the wall, glancing through the opening to the street below from time to time.

"Tithian," Mujahid said. "Just so there's no misunderstanding...if you betray me, there will be no place in the multiverse for you to hide. If I have to consume the life force of a thousand innocents to see your end, I'll gladly pay Zubuxo's price."

Tithian looked away. After several moments, he nodded, his expression inscrutable.

Several hours passed in awkward silence, save for the occasional rodent scampering about. The sun set, blanketing the room in darkness as a humid chill swept through the air. When it was full dark, Mujahid stood and followed Tithian out of the building.

No militia patrolled, which made no sense to Mujahid. But if the absence of militia on the streets made no sense, their absence at the docks was madness. Not a single guard patrolled what would be, in any large city, the most crime-ridden area. Something wasn't right...and it grew less right the more Mujahid considered it.

Tithian stopped and pointed ahead. "The captain of that boat owes me a favor."

Mujahid wasn't sure what would kill him first, local militia lying in wait or an ambush of Tithian's fashioning. But he knew that sometimes the best way to avoid a trap was to spring it.

An older man emerged from the wheelhouse of the boat and called for a couple of deckhands. He nodded when he saw Tithian and Mujahid, but the way his eyes darted between them made Mujahid feel uneasy.

"Lord Tithian," the man said, and Mujahid's eyes widened.

Tithian saw Mujahid's expression and shook his head as if to suggest Mujahid should ignore the comment.

"I won't be long," Tithian whispered.

Mujahid grabbed Tithian's shoulder with a firm hand. "Captain Roberts addressed you as *Lord*. Surely you intend to correct him?"

"Kagan bestowed the title years ago, nothing more. The captain isn't suggesting I'm a *Mukhtaar*—"

"You're damned right, nothing more," Mujahid said and released Tithian. Outrage boiled beneath the surface. Better men than this traitor had lost their lives to the Rite of Testing.

"You don't say no to Kagan," Tithian said.

"*I* said no. You were there. A Lord says no when no needs saying."

"Is this the passenger?" The captain jerked his head toward Mujahid.

"Captain Filo Roberts, I present to you Mujahid Lord Mukhtaar," Tithian said, introducing the two men according to the old custom.

Captain Roberts lost all color when Tithian pronounced Mujahid's title.

"You were expecting us, Captain," Mujahid said, reaching out to shake the captain's hand. "My companion gets around most efficiently, it seems."

"Lord Tithian and I are old friends, Lord Mukhtaar," Captain Roberts said, bowing his head when he pronounced the clan name.

"I engaged the Captain's services before you arrived," Tithian said.

Mujahid had suspected Tithian would betray him at the first possible opportunity, but knowing with certainty was like a knife in his back. He weighed his options and decided he had better chances on the riverboat than dealing with the Agera militia.

The boat's deck was flat, like a barge, except for the aft wheelhouse, which rose two stories above the deck. A deckhand led them toward a row of doors on the first story.

They settled into a room below the wheelhouse and the deckhand announced the ship would be leaving momentarily. Tithian prepared his bunk and sat on the side of it.

Mujahid needed time to think, and he couldn't spend another minute in that room with Tithian. He walked over to the door and opened it.

The cool night air was refreshing as it rushed into the room. He stepped out onto the deck, careful to keep an eye on Tithian. Two deck hands ran down the gangplank, as if something had gone wrong with the launch, and Mujahid took a closer look. He thought better of it and looked back toward the room.

Tithian was no longer on the bunk.

Mujahid ran into the room, thinking he had missed another door, but there was only one way in or out. Tithian was gone.

Mujahid ran out on deck.

The sound of creaking wood startled him and he spun around.

Tithian was sitting on the bunk as if he had never left.

"Why so frantic?" Tithian said.

"Where did—"

The boat heaved away from the dock and pulled a portion of the pier with it. Mujahid fell to the deck and rolled before he could stabilize himself against the wheelhouse. He watched as the river drained away, pulling the boat and part of the pier along in its wake. The river appeared stable as always, but the world tilted at an impossible angle, making Agera appear to be up in the sky, while the opposite bank of the river appeared to be the ground.

"Quake!" Captain Roberts said.

One of the deckhands shouted and pointed back at the dock. A mooring line was coiled around the upper thighs of a trapped crew member like a giant snake, and the man was struggling to free himself. The boat lurched farther from the dock and the serpentine lines pulled tight, severing the man's legs from his torso and dropping them into the chaotic river below. The man's torso convulsed on the dock as his life drained from him in a pool of red death.

Mujahid prepared a symbol that would put the man out of his misery, but the river heaved once more and broke his concentration. When the waters receded from the dock, the suffering man was gone, swept into the churning waters.

The quake lasted less than five minutes, but the damage it had caused to the Agera docks was considerable. Mujahid thanked the gods that dry rot had chosen the pier instead of the boat.

"Is the boat sound, Captain?" Mujahid said as he stood.

"No way to be sure without climbing up under it myself. But she's seen worse."

Between the quakes and the archmage's lackeys, Mujahid wondered if *he* would survive.

The city of Three Banks, the northernmost city of the Kingdom of Tildem, received its name from the convergence of the great Orm River with a tributary that originated from Union Lake at Agera. The two rivers came together to create a large triangle of land pointing due south, which locals referred to as *North Bank*.

North Bank was the city's commercial center, and docks lined both sides of the great triangle for mooring riverboats and barges of all sizes. The Sea of Arin was too treacherous for commerce, only navigable at certain times of the year, and then by only the most knowledgeable captains. The Orm provided a safe alternative for merchants to transport their goods.

A great signal tower at the point of the triangle was the largest feature of North Bank, standing several stories higher than the tallest buildings in the city. Men in the tower carried flags of various colors to regulate the flow of water traffic.

The trip from Agera had been a long one, and Mujahid had grown tired of keeping a close watch on Tithian. He was sure the man was up to something, but conversation had been minimal. Whenever it was unavoidable, however, Tithian would warn Mujahid against traveling to the Pinnacle. Mujahid wasn't sure what to make of it, but he had to admit Tithian looked genuinely concerned about him. The man had more layers than a Turian onion.

"Make ready," Captain Roberts shouted from the wheelhouse, and deckhands darted about. The boat drifted away from North Bank, heading toward the docks on what the locals called East Bank.

"You can't put in here," Mujahid said.

The captain gave him that nervous look again. "Ship took a battering in Agera, and it's still a long way to Dyr Agul. I know a shipwright on East Bank."

Mujahid swore.

"What is it?" Tithian stepped out onto the deck.

"I'm grateful for the help, but this is where we part ways."

A look of worry appeared on Tithian's face. "I've told you. The Pinnacle isn't going anywhere, and your chances may be greater in the future."

Mujahid shook his head. "If I could will myself into Kagan's chambers we wouldn't be having this conversation."

Tithian sighed and tapped his lower lip with his index finger. After a few moments of silence, he clasped his hands together. "I can still be of use. There must be a ship leaving for Dyr Agul today."

Mujahid considered refusing, but the more time he spent with Tithian the more curious he became. Tithian was an oath breaker and a traitor...but he was also an old friend. Part of him hoped the man was sincere in his offer of help.

The ship came to rest and several dock workers secured the mooring lines, but they were clumsy for a port this busy. Mujahid wasn't an expert, but the workers were making mistakes that an apprentice would have avoided. One of them struggled to untangle himself from a line, narrowly escaping the fate of that poor soul in Agera. Another pulled a breast rope tight to the point of snapping. He shook his head and wondered if any of them had ever spent time around water at all.

Tithian stopped before they reached the bottom of the gangplank. "There is still time to reconsider."

"I can't sit idly by and—"

"I'm not suggesting you do nothing. Just do nothing for *now*. You're all action and no plan, old friend. This isn't like you...not the Mujahid I knew forty years ago."

"I don't know which is worse...bad men doing evil, or good men doing nothing."

Tithian sighed and rubbed his forehead. "All right. We'll do this your way." He nodded to one of the dock workers.

Mujahid turned to respond, but quick movement caught his attention. The dock workers had burst into a flurry of activity, but one of them stumbled over a mooring line and fell to the dock. As he fell, his jacket opened and Mujahid's stomach clenched.

The golden helm of Arin was emblazoned across the man's shirt. The dock workers weren't dock workers at all. They were Pinnacle guard.

Mujahid cursed. His dagger was in his hand and slicing toward Tithian's throat in an instant.

When the blade was a hair's breadth away from biting into flesh, an invisible force seized it in a vise-like grip. Foreign energy entered Mujahid's mind and wrapped around his well of power, coating it in an impenetrable oily residue. His power was unusable.

Tithian nodded toward Captain Roberts.

"Now," Captain Roberts shouted, and the dock workers converged on Mujahid, binding his arms and legs together and guiding him to the ground without a struggle.

Mujahid felt as if all the fight had left him. There was no longer any doubt that Tithian had set him up. Certainty was like a blade in his stomach, twisting and wrenching.

"I'm sorry about this, old friend," Tithian said. "But I tried to stop you. I hope you understand in time how I've helped you."

"Tithian," Mujahid said. "Whatever you've become...it's not too late. The gods would welcome you back if you reached out to them."

Tithian knelt beside Mujahid and whispered. "I have a secret for you. The last time you saw the gods was the last time I saw them. Kagan is the only one they speak to now. And his power is absolute." He adjusted his robe and turned to one of the Pinnacle guards. "Prepare him for the trip."

Mujahid sat in stunned silence. What Tithian said wasn't possible. The gods appeared to the Archmage and Prime Warlock every year during the Rite of Manifestation. If the Prime Warlock didn't witness the event, there was no one to confirm the authenticity of the god's words.

Mujahid shuddered at the implications.

Four guards placed him in the back of a wagon. Within minutes they were away from the docks, leaving the city of Three Banks behind them.

CHAPTER EIGHTEEN

T he power began as a trickle creating a tiny pool of energy in his mind. Consciousness brought the pain back, and with each drop of energy his existence solidified, until at some point between two moments he became self-aware.

I...exist.

He was about to inhale when something stopped him.

I'm Nicolas Murray. Son of the archmage. Heir to the Obsidian Throne.

The memories came flooding back in a burst of images and emotions until all confusion vanished.

He was about to drown.

Breaking free from his bonds was impossible, so his mind turned inward. Two symbols of power, a skull and an arrow, danced around a well of energy.

I'm a necromancer.

There wasn't enough power for the skull, and the burning in his lungs was so intense that his other injuries seemed dull by comparison. He had one chance to succeed.

He created a pathway between his energy well and the arrow, and when the power embraced it he cast it into the water, not knowing what to expect.

Nothing happened. His heart sank and he waited for the inevitable. Part of him wanted to inhale to just get it over with.

When the last bit of power touched the arrow, it leaped to the forefront of his mind, pointing down and to the front. With some effort he could guide his descent by small increments, so he angled his course in the direction the arrow pointed.

The effect was instantaneous. What had been a slow trickle of power became a torrent, filling his well to capacity. The arrow faded from his periphery.

His mind went to work, and the first thing he remembered was how he summoned the argram. If he had any hope of succeeding, he had to know what he needed. He made a mental list.

Air.

If he didn't find air, he would be unconscious within minutes. Necropotency was reducing his need for oxygen, but it wouldn't last forever.

Freedom.

Without it he'd never reach the surface. Not in his current condition, anyway. And that reminded him of the third thing he needed.

A damned doctor.

Without healing, the other two didn't matter.

The skull ignited and vibrated with energy, he formed an image of himself breathing and healthy, with his arms spread like a priest at the altar. He cast the symbol through the newly-formed image and into the water. His energy well drained but was replenished by the ambient death energy that seemed to be coming from everywhere.

A series of images resembling nothing he had ever experienced before assaulted him, and once again he lived an entire lifetime in a single moment. The creature he was summoning wasn't human...or argram, for that matter.

In some images Nicolas swam like a fish, and yet in others he walked on two legs, but he knew they represented the same person.

Yes. Person. This is a person *I'm summoning.*

It was a person with culture and society, strengths and weaknesses, and yet none of them made any sense. In some ways it was more alien than the argram.

A word stuck to the tip of his tongue. He'd heard it countless times in the lifetime of this creature, but he just couldn't spit it out.

The images stopped and a mystical link formed in his mind. He had complete control over his new penitent. *Cichlos.*

The creature was a *cichlos*, whatever that meant.

And it was here.

He opened his eyes to look at it. The skeleton was humanoid, but its head was enormous, too large for its body. The eye sockets alone were the size of a man's skull. A large, flat bone bisected the top of the skull, ran down the center of its back behind ribs that looked like thin filaments, and ended in a pelvic bone. The hands and feet had more than five fingers each, but they were more like fins on a fish than fingers and toes.

The pressure in his lungs was unbearable. He needed air.

The creature grabbed Nicolas's wrists and the world became a blur of motion. Water rushed around his aching body, causing more agony as skin tore away from the mutilated muscles of his now-useless right arm.

He felt an odd sensation, as if his mind had formed goose bumps. It was the same feeling he felt when Nuuan and Mujahid used magic. The water rushed past his body, but he no longer felt anything against his face. He tentatively opened one eye, expecting water to rush in, but nothing happened. Instead, drops rolled down his face as if he had surfaced. He opened both eyes and saw a large, shimmering bubble surrounding his head.

He sent a mental image of the bubble to the strange creature.

A grassy plain, its blades of grass rippling and waving in a strong wind, entered his mind in response. When he tried to express his confusion, an image of a fish moving its gills came back through the link.

Breathing. The fish was breathing.

He inhaled.

It was the scent of the wind sweeping down off the Grand Tetons through a forest of pine trees. He hadn't thought of that trip in years. It was the only time he'd been away from the orphanage for any length of time. Dr. Murray had taken him to the Rockies for his sixteenth birthday.

Nicolas turned his head inside the bubble and regretted it. He struggled to remain conscious through the pain.

An image of his bones turning to stone entered his mind. The cichlos creature was strengthening his body, making it adapt to the environment around him.

A moment ago he was floating in darkness, but now he could see as clearly as when Mujahid enhanced his vision in the tunnel.

They were moving through a vast underwater cavern, tall enough for the Eiffel tower to pass through standing on end, toward a massive underwater mountain range that spread out for miles in front of him. The cichlos took him underneath a rock structure, then turned upwards with surprising dexterity.

They broke the water's surface in a small cavern. The cichlos laid him down among the rocks and removed the weighted chains that bound him. It tossed them aside as if they were nothing.

The creature opened its mouth, and the most beautiful singing Nicolas had ever heard filled the cavern. His pain lessened with every note the cichlos sang.

As the song came to an end, Nicolas's back was healed.

"You summoned me, human," the cichlos said. "This should not be." The creature laughed. His laughter sounded like a chorus of voices singing a beautiful melody.

"*Should* and *shouldn't* don't mean too much lately." Nicolas said. "What are you? Some kind of fish?"

"Are you some kind of monkey? Your speech patterns are strange, even with the bond of death between us."

The cichlos smiled, stretching his flexible jaw bones in a wide grin.

"I saw more of you in the images. Answer my question."

"It was not my intent to offend, necromancer, merely inform. The bond of death allows communication, but you have no connection to my living brethren."

"I saw huge cities," Nicolas said. "Underwater, on land, even in the air. How's that possible?"

The cichlos chuckled. "I'm not used to speaking like this. Yes, I walk on land and swim in water. My people adapted to both environments eons ago."

Nicolas delved back into the images, looking for the creature's name. He could command the cichlos to tell him, but he wanted to see if he could find it himself. The word he was looking for leaped into his mind, as if on command.

"Your name is Cisic."

"Not when it's pronounced *correctly*." Cisic laughed.

"I almost died," Nicolas said. He reached behind to touch his back and felt smooth skin, as if the flogging never took place. "How did you heal me?"

"Few would choose to suffer what you suffered."

NECROMANCER AWAKENING 183

"Yeah, I ran into Caspardis asking to be flogged and executed."

"Why would you do such a thing?"

"No," Nicolas said. He was getting tired of his sarcasm not translating well. "They lynched me, dragged me up in front of a kangaroo court, and damned-near killed me."

"My question stands. Why would a necromancer allow himself to suffer such a thing?"

"Did you hear what I said? They *lynched* me."

Cisic shook his giant head back and forth and sighed. "The language barrier is even worse than I thought."

He saw an image of an argram folding its tarsal swords while a feeble old man beat it with a stick.

"It wasn't like that." He formed an image of a necromancer attempting to cast a spell with an empty well.

"What you show me is impossible. A necromancer can never be severed from his power."

What Cisic said went against everything Mujahid taught him. In fact, Mujahid couldn't escape from the dungeon because he had no power.

"Can you teach me?"

"I am no *siek*," Cisic said, using a word Nicolas had never heard before. "And even if I were, our time grows short. I will journey to the Plane of Peace soon. What of your own people?"

"Not sure I know what that means anymore."

Cisic chuckled. "Strange words, priest. Strange words indeed." The laughter continued and Nicolas smiled.

After a moment, Cisic stopped laughing, and Nicolas could tell he was deep in thought.

"Perhaps...no," Cisic said.

"What's on your mind?"

Images resolved into Nicolas standing in front of hundreds of angry cichlos. He lifted the ocean with one hand and they welcomed him.

"I can take you," Cisic said. "But the danger is great. If you command me to fight my brethren, I will lose. They are powerful."

"I don't get the ocean part."

"You have swum with my fins and walked with my feet. I was once a great necromancer, but what do you remember most about me?"

"You were an asshole, *that's* what I remember."

"You have only lived my life, not my death. My spirit is nearly pure, and a joy fills me that I never knew in life. My people do not know this joy. They are honor-bound to ancient tradition."

"Yeah...*assholes*."

"Concentrate."

Nicolas recalled the summoning. Cichlos people were separated into castes that were strictly segregated. There was no upward mobility possible, and any attempt to change one's status met with punishment. Sometimes violence. Their system of honor was so well defined that a large percentage of their language and physical gestures was dedicated to the proper way of addressing people in specific castes. As a human he had no status among them at all. He understood the image now. He would have to gain their respect, and *that* would be an impossible task...as impossible as lifting the ocean.

"Take me," Nicolas said.

"As you command. We go to the city of *Aquonome*."

Cisic lifted Nicolas and plunged back into the lake. The bubble of air reformed around Nicolas's head, and within moments the world was rushing past him.

Distant ribbons of light ran for miles along a gigantic crevasse and formed the underwater city of Aquonome. The ribbons were translucent tubes, similar to the bubble around Nicolas's head, constructed by barrier magic to keep the water out.

Aquonome glistened in all colors of the rainbow like far away Christmas lights in a distant neighborhood. Two massive domes formed the city center, one larger than the other, and twelve barrier tubes extended from the smallest, six on each side, giving Aquonome the appearance of an underwater insect. Tiny bubbles moved between tubes at random intervals. A bubble would form in the wall of one tube and crash into the next, collapsing on impact.

Cisic led them toward the closest barrier tube, which projected out from the right side of the central dome. The scale of the place impressed Nicolas. If he laid every high rise in Austin end to end, it wouldn't equal the length of one of these tubes. Small dots moved about, but he couldn't tell what they were.

Power drained from him in a steady current of energy as they drew closer to the city. Except for Cisic he would be defenseless when they got there, and that knowledge tightened his chest with panic.

They passed through the barrier wall into one of the tubes and Nicolas felt the same electric shock as when he first entered Paradise. The bubble around his head collapsed and he inhaled.

He wished he hadn't.

Aquonome smelled like a giant aquarium. All the decaying fish food and algae in the biology lab didn't come close to *this*.

They emerged into a large open area that resembled a crowded mall. The barrier wall generated a bluish light that surrounded everything in a cool glow.

The small dots he had seen earlier were people—*Cichlos* people—humanoid fish of all different colors, each one brighter than the next, and they stood about two feet taller than Nicolas. He had been right about the webbed hands and feet, but seeing flesh on those enormous heads was a sight to behold. He had been wrong about their heads being too large for their bodies, though. That may have been true about Cisic the *skeletal* cichlos, but everything was in proper proportion on the *living* cichlos.

Rows of teeth filled their mouths, but the cichlos weren't scary-looking...merely different. In some ways they were amusing. Their chameleon-like eyes were able to move in independent directions, making it look like they could stare in two different places at once, and they kept moving their heads up and down as if to examine him from head to foot and back again.

They all wore the same bluish grey clothing, in stark contrast to their otherwise colorful bodies. Every seam, every stitch, every tint appeared identical. Nicolas knew a thing or two about civilizations, and there was no way those clothes were the product of a preindustrial society. They were mass produced.

The tube vaulted over them into a giant arched roof about sixty feet high. Walls seemed to grow out of the tube floor itself to form small buildings not much taller than the cichlos.

The crowd had stopped and people stared at him, speaking words he didn't understand. One of them yelled something, and another ran farther into the tube.

The sound of marching filled the plaza, and danger pulsed through the necromantic link. The crowd parted as a large cichlos...larger than the others...came toward him, surrounded by several undead cichlos skeletons. He must be a necromancer.

As if in response, an image of a general defeating an army of argram on a battlefield appeared in Nicolas's mind. This wouldn't end well.

The undead cichlos looked like fish bones come to life, enormous heads and skinny bones. They were unarmed.

The large cichlos stopped in front of him while the undead circled around. A midnight-blue cowl draped over the cichlos's leathery shirt and pants down to what Nicolas assumed were the cichlos's knees. That cowl would be a robe on a human. In fact, it looked like the robes worn by the Mukhtaar brothers in the mural at their estate. But on closer look it was a material Nicolas had never seen before, rippling in the breeze like cloth one moment and shining with a metallic glint the next. None of the other cichlos wore a cowl like this, but that wasn't the only difference.

While the other cichlos were all colors of the spectrum, this one's skin—if skin was the right word—was pure white, accented in places by orange stripes and splotches, and his eyes had a distinctive pink tint, which reminded Nicolas of some of the albino tribes he had studied.

The albino made a show of looking Nicolas up and down, and then glanced at the tube wall from where he and Cisic had emerged. The cichlos said something, but Nicolas didn't understand what he was saying. At least he *assumed* the albino was a man, but he didn't know for sure. There was something masculine in his bearing.

The albino turned toward Cisic for the first time and grew agitated. He uttered something unintelligible and waved his hand. A tugging sensation grabbed at Nicolas's chest, and the necromantic link disappeared from his mind, leaving him with feelings of loss and guilt. Cisic didn't crumble to the ground in a pile of bones...he *vanished*.

Mujahid had told him a necromancer couldn't mess with another priest's link. It seemed Mujahid had been wrong about that too. The albino had banished Cisic with no discernible effort, and there was nothing Nicolas could have done about it.

He opened his mouth to speak and the cichlos backhanded him with an armored fist, filling his mouth with the metallic taste of blood. He could feel his lip swelling already.

Two penitents lifted Nicolas up, squeezing his arms in vise-like grips.

As the albino turned and walked away, the undead guards dragged Nicolas behind.

CHAPTER NINETEEN

Nicolas, confused and afraid, tried to stand but couldn't break the grip of the large cichlos skeletons.

Questions raced through his mind. Where were they taking him? How did Mujahid not know a necromancer could make another's penitent disappear? And what was his deal with never trying to summon more than one? This albino had four.

His captors came to a stop and released him. They stood like bony columns circling Nicolas.

The albino spoke with another cowled cichlos, but he couldn't understand them. They were loud and used a lot of hand waving.

He sensed power all around him, so he did the only thing he could think of—he attempted to fill his energy well.

The albino flinched and leaped toward Nicolas with an angry guttural sound.

Nicolas closed his eyes, expecting the full weight of the albino to land on him. Instead, he felt a powerful blow to his head, and his head snapped sideways. He drew as much power as he could, but an impenetrable wall rose up around his energy well, making the power useless.

The albino snorted and kicked him again, this time in the side. Sharp, cracking pain tore through his chest.

The albino tried to kick him again, but the other cowled cichlos yelled and stopped him. The albino snorted, as if frustrated, and withdrew farther down the tube with his undead penitents.

The other guards helped Nicolas to his feet and led him in the same direction the albino had gone. He clutched the side of his chest and winced, doubling the pain when he gasped.

They walked for several minutes then came to a halt so fast he stumbled. There was nothing special about where they stopped. The place was empty. One of the guards turned toward the tube wall and Nicolas had a terrible thought.

They're going to throw me out!

A hum emanated from the barrier wall, and those mental goose bumps returned. There was a vast ocean of energy just beyond his reach that recoiled every time he tried to draw it in.

A tearing sound startled him, and three bluish-grey wisps of barrier energy, liquid in form, emerged from the thin veil that separated them from the lake. They coalesced into two transparent walls spanned by a liquid ceiling ten feet above the ground. When the viscous energy had formed a hollow cube, it stopped moving and solidified into an opaque barrier wall.

Unlike the wall of the tube, which swirled with multihued wisps like the surface of a soap bubble, this cube looked as if the barrier had transformed into something as hard as metal.

The guards threw Nicolas into the cube, which forced him to grab his side in pain as he hit the far wall. Another aqueous wall rose up out of the floor and sealed him inside the cube. This wall was different from the others, however. It remained translucent and crackled with an energy that gave it a green tint. The guards stared at him and waved their hands around.

Nicolas looked at them through the green barrier as he stepped toward it. Their faces were expressionless, as far as he could tell, but the closer he got to the barrier the faster their gestures became.

He'd been captured, tortured, and even executed on this strange world. He'd survived his own drowning for what? To be beaten for no good reason? Enough was enough.

"You enjoy this, don't you," he said.

They backed away.

"You like torturing people? I didn't even do anything!"

Speaking made him wince in pain, but he didn't care. The broken rib was nothing next to what he'd already gone through on this hellhole of a world.

A light breeze danced into the cube through the green barrier and tickled his face. He raised his hands, palms out, and placed them about an inch away from the surface of the crackling energy. He moved them across surface of the barrier without touching it, and the cichlos waved their arms faster.

"Oh, *this* upsets you, but kicking my ass is perfectly fine," Nicolas said.

He took a deep breath and pushed both his hands through the green barrier.

White-hot energy blinded him, and all sensation disappeared as he was flung backward into the cell. He felt nothing—neither the ground beneath him, nor the breeze that had been circling around his face. He shook his head and sensation came flooding back. His hands felt like they were on fire, and when he looked at them, he wished he hadn't. His right hand, which must have taken the bulk of the force, was unrecognizable, and the barrier had burned the other to the bone.

The crackling noise stopped, and two of the guards who had been waving ran over to him. One of them knelt beside him and examined his hands. He uttered something unintelligible and waved to the other guard.

Nicolas started shivering, and he didn't know whether he was going to throw up or pass out.

The sound of marching returned and the crowd parted. The albino had returned. The pink-eyed bastard had probably come to gloat. He didn't enter the cube, though. He just stood there, staring at Nicolas like a scientist at a lab experiment.

A slow trickle of energy entered his well of power as the albino drew closer, and a patrol of undead cichlos took up position in front of his cell.

A beautiful song filled the cube, giving him a sense of calm that banished the pain. His anger and frustration drained away. Webbed hands brushed hair out of his eyes, and he stopped shaking.

The pain had subsided but it hung at the edge of his consciousness like the memory of a bad injury.

As Nicolas watched, the crowd parted again and another cowled cichlos, orange-skinned with black stripes and splotches, knelt beside him. Nicolas felt his well of power fill.

The guard that had been singing bowed his head and backed away. The orange cichlos examined the injured hands and sang.

The mental goose bumps returned. Intense pain shot through his chest and down his arms to his fingertips. For a moment he thought he was having a heart attack. Then he felt his rib snap back into place, and a tingling sensation, as if the bones were stitching themselves back together. The skin on his mutilated hands began to stretch and pull until they covered the burned flesh, hiding the injury as if it never happened.

Within a few moments his hands and rib were whole again. The orange cichlos stepped toward the albino, who was standing outside the entrance of the cube, and Nicolas's well of power drained.

Nicolas couldn't see the orange cichlos's face, but the albino bowed his head and looked down at the floor. After a few uncomfortable moments, the orange cichlos left and the green barrier returned. The crowd bowed as he passed.

The albino looked at Nicolas through the barrier with both of his enormous, articulated eyes. They moved up and down in their giant orbs, as if examining every inch. He closed one hand into a fist. With his other hand he pointed at Nicolas's face and said something in the cichlos language. When Nicolas didn't answer, the albino repeated himself and made the gesture again, more forceful this time.

The only thing Nicolas could think of was to step away from the barrier. The green barrier faded from existence and the albino smiled and entered the cell.

As the albino stepped closer, Nicolas's energy well filled. Somehow the cichlos were a source of power. No, that wasn't it exactly. His well only filled when he got close to the cichlos wearing blue cowls.

A section of flooring tore away, the way one large bubble becomes two without breaking. It rose a few feet into the air and hovered, morphing into something that resembled a bench. When the morphing stopped, the bench legs grew down into the barrier floor and formed a seamless connection.

The albino sat on one end of the bench and gestured to a place next to him.

Nicolas saw little choice but to sit. He had no desire for another confrontation.

The cichlos struck his own chest twice and uttered a noise that sounded like *jurn*. Again the cichlos struck his chest twice and said "jurn".

Nicolas struck his chest twice and said "Nicolas."

Jurn looked him up and down again. Then he pointed to Nicolas and said "Nee-kluss."

Nicolas nodded and repeated "Nicolas." Then he pointed at the albino and said "Jurn".

Jurn made a sound similar to *harrumph* and sat straighter on the bench. He said a word that Nicolas couldn't understand and the undead guards broke apart, one bone at a time, until they were nothing more than a pile of skinny fish bones on the floor. He turned back to Nicolas and said something that sounded like *sabnamo*.

Nicolas had no idea what to do. He pointed at the bones and repeated "sabnamo".

Jurn made another *harrumph* sound and the goose bumps returned. Nicolas waited for an unseen hand to strike him, but no strike came.

Jurn said "sabnamo," and an undead guard rose from the pile of bones and entered the cell.

Nicolas didn't understand what Jurn was trying to do or say, so he repeated the word. "Sabnamo."

Jurn growled. "Sab Nee-kluss. Namo!"

"Look, I don't know what the hell a *sabnamo* is. I'm not trying to piss you off, I just—"

Jurn roared. He raised his right hand, and the hair on the back of Nicolas's neck stood on end. A ball of crackling blue energy surrounded Jurn's fist.

Nicolas was at his mercy. Worse, he didn't think mercy was Jurn's strong suit.

Jurn smacked his chest twice again and yelled "Sabnamo!" Another undead guard rose and entered the cell.

And then Nicolas understood.

When Jurn first saw him it was with Cisic. Jurn must be testing him to see if he was a necromancer.

Nicolas sat back on the bench, rubbing his sore jaw, and turned his mind inward. He drew power into his well and created a pathway to the skull symbol. He extended his hand toward the pile of bones on the floor. He didn't know whether pointing would do anything, but somehow it felt right and helped him focus. With an act of will, he cast the power into the bones.

Images came and went and the undead guard rose from the ground. Its bones aligned perfectly, and Nicolas could feel the rage radiating off the skinless beast like heat from a stove. He subdued the guard without difficulty and the necromantic link wove itself into his mind like a thread.

Jurn leapt from the bench. One of his eyes examined the guard Nicolas had raised, while the other looked Nicolas up and down.

Nicolas pointed at his undead penitent and said "Sabnamo?"

Jurn *harrumphed* once more. He waved his hand and the undead cichlos fell to the ground in a pile.

Nicolas felt as if a piece of himself had been torn away.

"How did you do that?" Nicolas said.

Tendrils of energy entered his mind. It was an odd sensation, like someone was tickling his memories. After a few moments they withdrew.

Jurn snorted. He yanked Nicolas off the bench and pushed him out of the cell.

The undead guard rose behind him and followed him out, bony feet clicking on the surface of the barrier floor.

The undead guards led him farther down the tube. He was tempted to draw more power, but that temptation died when another wall went up around his well.

He had no idea whether being a necromancer was a good or bad thing in this place. But he had a feeling he was going to find out the hard way.

The barrier tube spanned two hundred yards across and had a gentle curve to it, making it impossible to see all the way to the end. Judging by the direction they traveled relative to where Nicolas had entered the city, it looked like they were heading toward one of the large domes at the center.

Every time Nicolas slowed down a guard would shove him forward toward Jurn. There had to be a way out of this...something he could use to escape or overpower them. But where would he go if he *did* escape?

Multi-hued columns of barrier material jutted up from the floor and connected to the arched ceiling above them. Each column had a refrigerator-sized hole cut in one side, and two blue-cowled cichlos handed out trays of fish to a line of cichlos in front of them. It reminded Nicolas of a bodega or cafeteria—except the shopkeepers never took anything in return.

Could he escape through those columns? Maybe they led out into the lake. But how would he breathe? And could he even get there before Jurn killed him?

The guards led him toward an open room that projected away from the tube. It was one of those crashing bubbles he saw when he and Cisic were approaching the city.

They pushed him in and followed close behind. The bubble sealed and the city rushed by at a frightening rate, though he felt no acceleration.

The bubble raced toward one of the central domes along the outside of the tube, which Nicolas judged to be about a mile long.

All motion ceased. He heard a strange liquid noise, like a water balloon bursting. The front of the bubble opened, and the patrol led him out into the dome.

He glanced around, looking for another avenue of escape.

The center of the dome was dominated by three gigantic, spherical bubbles, each different in size. Did they work like these strange transport bubbles? Could he use one to reach the surface? Even if he could, he wasn't sure how to reach them. They floated gracefully, one on top of the other, never coming into contact with anything else, and a barrier grew upwards from the floor in a large circle underneath them, creating a fence-like ring about waist high. Three grey-cowled cichlos reclined on chairs inside the ring, and they appeared to be sleeping.

A guard shoved him out of the central hub, and they crossed into a larger dome with opaque walls. While the hub had been bustling with activity, this one was nearly empty. The expanse of the place made Nicolas feel tiny by comparison. It must have been a thousand yards from end to end and more than one hundred yards tall.

A massive statue, standing as tall as the ceiling, stood at the other end of the dome. It was the figure of Death, in black, hooded robes, carrying a scythe with a blade that was half the length of the statue itself. A cichlos skull looked out from beneath the robe's hood.

Jurn walked toward the statue, and the guards followed along behind, making sure Nicolas stayed with them.

The detail of the dome was amazing. Etched and embossed images decorated the wall, depicting scenes he didn't understand. Some images showed a purple sky, with red-skinned cichlos performing a ritual around an altar. Others depicted great battles between armies of cichlos—one army with white skin, like Jurn, and the other army with a mixture of orange and black, like the one who healed him.

The floor had murals too, though they seemed more abstract— sparkling blotches of light in no particular order or shape.

There wasn't a single source of light. Instead, the images on the dome walls and ceiling gave off light in all the colors they were painted in, if paint were the right word.

As they drew closer to the statue, Nicolas could see a large grey sphere hanging in midair. He knew what it was immediately.

An orb of power. It has to be.

They stopped when they reached the orb of power. The statue of Death towered above them, menacing in its visage, yet comforting in its familiarity.

A group of cichlos at the bottom of the statue all wore midnight blue cowls, similar to Jurn, and they were in the middle of a ritual. Another group of blue-cowled cichlos entered from an opening to the right of the statue. Jurn began to speak and gesture frantically, and this time Nicolas thought he heard a familiar word: *Zubuxo*.

Encouraged, Nicolas pointed at the enormous statue and said "Zubuxo."

Jurn leapt toward Nicolas with a closed fist.

Nicolas tried to summon a penitent, determined to put a stop to this once and for all, but before he remembered the shield surrounding his well of power, the shout of a deep voice broke his concentration.

"Jurn," the voice said. It came from behind Nicolas.

Jurn backed away as if his life depended on it. He bowed at the waist and spread his arms to the sides.

Unseen hands turned Nicolas around, gently, until he came face to face with a tall red-skinned cichlos, taller than most, dressed in ornate midnight-blue robes. The skin on his face sagged like an old man's. Pearls stitched into the material reflected the light of the dome. More pearls covered the massive scythe the tall cichlos carried.

The old cichlos shouted and Jurn dropped to the floor, prostrating himself before the colossal statue. The orb of power hummed, and Jurn's undead guard winked out of existence.

Jurn began to say something, but the old cichlos stopped him.

When the old one had finished speaking, one of the other cichlos ran to the opening behind the statue. He returned a minute later carrying a white cowl.

The old one said something to Jurn, and he stood back up. When he was on his feet, the cichlos holding the white cowl forced it into Jurn's hands. Jurn stared at it as if he were looking at something hideous. Another cichlos stripped the blue cowl off Jurn's shoulders and led him away.

"Zubuxo," the old cichlos said. He reached out and nudged Nicolas, gently, into the circle of cichlos who had formed at the foot of the statue. The cichlos joined hands and began to sing.

A band of black energy formed among them, passing through each of them and creating an oily black circle of power that caused the hair on Nicolas's arms to stand on end. The black energy created a wind that whipped their cowls around. When the wind reached a strength Nicolas thought might destroy the entire dome, arcs of black energy flowed out from the seven cichlos, forming a cone over the circle. A beam of oily, black power emanated down from the cone and struck the old cichlos in the head. His head jerked back, and he chanted words that were different from what the rest of the cichlos were chanting.

The cone rose into the air and picked up speed as it approached the top of the mammoth statue. When it passed the statue's face it transformed into a translucent bubble that surrounded Zubuxo's head.

The chanting stopped.

The ring of energy vanished, and the air became still. All eyes turned upward and the bubble began to descend. The cichlos forming the circle gasped and started speaking.

The bubble transformed in midair, shrinking as it descended. By the time it reached the circle, it was the size of Nicolas's head.

It stopped mere feet above the circle for a moment, then dove into the center of the circle and enveloped Nicolas's head.

Bolts of black energy arced from the inner surface of the bubble and reached into his mind like thousands of tiny fingers. When the sensation ended, he heard shouting.

"This can't be," one voice said.

"The People will never accept this, Sabba."

"Be still and watch, brethren," the elder cichlos said. "You behold the fulfillment of the siek's prophecy."

"But he is not of The People."

"Be silent for now, brothers."

It took Nicolas a moment to realize he understood their words.

"Did it work?" one of the blue-cowled cichlos asked.

"I can't be certain," another voice said.

"Rest assured, brethren," the elder cichlos said. "He understands every word you speak."

"How can you be so certain?"

"He lives." He turned to face Nicolas. "You live, human *sab*, do you not?"

Nicolas had no idea what a *sab* was.

"Zubuxo has blessed you," the old cichlos said. "But we did not expect the prophecy to be fulfilled in this manner. Who trained you in the use of necropotency, and how are you capable of summoning one of The People? This should not be possible."

Nicolas shrugged. "It's not the first time I've summoned something strange."

"Find us strange, do you?"

"I didn't mean—"

"I take no offense, hatchling. I seek only information."

Nicolas considered mentioning Mujahid, but decided to honor the man's desire for anonymity for now.

"I trained under a master necromancer above the lake, for a short time."

"A very short time, indeed. Had you summoned a penitent to fight Jurn, it would have ended your life, and we would not be having this conversation."

"Jurn," Nicolas said. "So his name *is* Jurn. And yours is Sabba?"

"Do not use that word," the elder said, and his expression changed. "It holds no meaning for you, and so you abuse it by speaking it. Sabba is my title. I am the high priest."

"No one stands above him, human," a cichlos said.

The elder waved the cichlos away.

"I take it this was some sort of test," Nicolas said. "This black bubble thing on the statue."

"You are perceptive, for a human."

"Not like it would take a detective. These ones over here acted pretty surprised when that bubble started coming back down."

"Blasphemy," one of the cichlos said.

Nicolas gestured toward the cichlos who had spoken. "And that one almost wet himself when it hit me and I didn't die."

"The prophecy is fulfilled by a human," the high priest said. He seemed surprised.

"I'm tired of no one telling me anything! First Muj—" His anger almost made him slip. "First my teacher, and now you. So if I failed your little test, what then? Another ass-kickin'?"

The high priest looked Nicolas up and down as if considering something. "You would have been cast out of Aquonome without air or assistance."

"Nice," Nicolas said. "And since I passed?"

"Let there be no misunderstanding. You do not want to fail the tests that follow." He turned to the group of cichlos and said "Take him to the *siek*."

Nicolas shook his head. "More guards?"

"They are not guards, human," the high priest said. "You have sufficiently demonstrated you are a member of the priestly caste. You are not our prisoner."

"You're saying I can just walk out the way I came and you'll leave me alone?"

"Yes. But there is something you should know first."

"It involves ass-kickin', right?"

"You will never find your *cet* if you leave this place. The humans cannot teach that which you need to learn."

"What the hell's a *cet*?"

"I am not your *siek*, human. Stay and learn, or leave and remain ignorant. That is my offer."

"How can you allow him to decide?" a cichlos said. "If you are correct, then you know what is at stake as well as—"

The high priest held out his hand. "The choice is his. That is how it must be."

Nicolas closed his eyes. It didn't take long for Kaitlyn's face to appear, followed by the impotent longing that raged like a storm in his mind. Mujahid said getting back home had something to do with learning as much as he could about necromancy. But for all he knew the man was already dead, executed by the court in Caspardis. Leaving wasn't an option. Not a good one, at least. So if a fish could teach him what he needed to know...then he'd learn how to swim.

"I'll stay, if I can be taught."

The high priest nodded. "Take him to the siek."

A cichlos nodded and walked toward the opening behind the statue. He looked back over his shoulder and said "Follow me."

CHAPTER TWENTY

They entered a small dome behind three formations of white-cowled cichlos. A blue-cowled cichlos at the head of the group was speaking in a rhythmic, sing-song voice, and with each beat of the rhythm, the students conjured a ball of electric-blue light that pulsed in their hands. There must have been close to a hundred students total.

Nicolas's escort held up a bundle of white fabric that unrolled into a set of white robes and a large white cowl, which he held up against Nicolas's back.

"This will do for now," he said. "It's the smallest I could find."

"What's wrong with the duds I'm wearing?" Nicolas asked.

The cichlos looked him up and down and Nicolas followed his gaze to his own tattered robes. It hadn't occurred to him he looked like he'd been flogged, dragged through mud, then drowned in a lake.

"They are not white, among other things," the cichlos said, as if giving Nicolas the time of day. "You are a student. You wear white, not brown. Someday you wear midnight-blue. And your boots won't do at all."

"Now why is every damned body in this damned place trying to take my damned boots all the time?"

The cichlos was unmoved.

Nicolas pursed his lips, feeling uneasy about having to change here.

Thank god for gym class, he thought, coming to terms with his lack of underwear. He pulled his robes over his head and let them drop to the floor, leaving nothing on except his brown boots.

The room grew silent. He looked up and saw everyone in the dome staring back at him.

"What are you doing?" The cichlos demanded. His eyes spun in circles on both sides of his head. "You change in there." He pointed to a small room that had emerged from the floor.

"Really? You couldn't tell me that a minute ago?"

He took the clothes from the frantic cichlos and clutched them against the front of his naked body.

"I'm keepin' my damned boots," he said and marched into the room.

The robes were too long by far, and two men could fit inside them.

"The siek is expecting you," the cichlos said. "You may approach him now."

"Somebody ever gonna tell me what a *siek* is? I'm not from around here."

The cichlos made a *harrumph* sound. "I hadn't noticed." He turned and walked away.

"So y'all *do* get sarcasm here," Nicolas said.

The blue-cowled cichlos paced in front of the students, his sagging skin orange with black striations and splotches. He looked like someone in authority, so Nicolas hiked up his robes and started walking.

Energy entered Nicolas's mind. Not the sort of energy that would fill his well of power, but fingers of electricity that slid along the surface of his brain. The sensation was unsettling.

The blue-cowled cichlos stepped toward Nicolas. Arcane energy filled the air like static electricity. When they met in the middle of the formations, Nicolas wasn't sure whether he should speak. Every time he opened his mouth he got in trouble.

The cichlos looked him up and down, then huffed. What was it with the cichlos examining him from head to toe every five seconds?

The blue-cowled cichlos was shorter than the high priest, and his cowl wasn't as ornate, but one distinguishing feature stood out—a large gold necklace hung down into his shirt.

"I am Lamil Jiskossa," the cichlos said in a deep, soothing voice. He was the image of serenity. "I will be your siek. It appears you have much to learn."

"Why, because I'm human?"

"Because you are ignorant."

Nicolas opened his mouth to speak but his breath struck an invisible wall and rebounded into his mouth.

The siek continued in the same soothing tone. "We could have had this conversation in silence, yet you did not hear me. Perhaps you did hear, yet refused to respond. If you did not hear me, then you know little of your own power, which makes you ignorant of yourself. If, on the other hand, you *refused* to speak to me, then you know little of your place in this world, which makes you ignorant of everyone around you. Either way...you are ignorant. Knowledge and wisdom are the enemies of ignorance. Therefore, it would appear you have much to learn. Does my explanation satisfy your need for logic, human?"

Nicolas had expected many things but an actual explanation wasn't one of them. "Yes it...does," he said. The invisible wall was gone.

"Yes it does...*Siek*."

"I don't like to use words I don't understand."

Siek Lamil looked him up and down with one of his independent eyes. After a moment, both eyes came to rest on Nicolas.

"Then I shall tell you, and together we will decrease your ignorance." Lamil placed his hands behind his back. "*Siek* has many meanings. In some ways it means master. In other ways it means wise one, or teacher. You may take your pick. But whichever meaning suits you, you would do well to begin using it."

"All it is with you people are threats. Either I succeed, or—"

"Calm yourself, student. Your ignorance causes you to hear threats where none exist. The danger with ignorance, however, is that it can also blind you to *real* threats. Ignorance in a priest is a danger to all. Using my title is a sign for others that you have taken your first step on the journey towards wisdom."

"You sound like Mujahid."

He regretted saying the name as soon as it left his mouth, but Lamil didn't react.

"An ignorant person who wields great power, is a dangerous person," Lamil said.

"I wasn't ignorant when Jurn opened up a can of whoop ass on me, *Siek.*"

One of Lamil's eyes turned, and Nicolas followed its gaze until he saw Jurn, dressed in a white robe that blended with his albino skin. There were other albino cichlos in the room, but none looked more like a chastised child than Jurn did.

"Actually, you were ignorant in many ways," Lamil said.

"You can't be—"

"I seek to instruct, not excuse behavior. If you were less ignorant of yourself, then what Jurn did would not have been possible."

"You're implying it was my fault?"

"Strange." Lamil tilted his head. "You inferred blame from my words. Causality does not imply moral culpability. Do you not know this?"

Nicolas had to repeat the words to himself. "I didn't do so well in Philosophy."

"Jurn's ignorance lies outside your cet, and therefore is not your concern." Lamil's tone was patient, like a parent teaching a child to use a fork. "It was my poor judgment that elevated him to the midnight-blue cowl of mastery. Your ignorance, though a factor in the causal relationship that resulted in your beating, does not imply you are morally culpable for that beating. No blame. You see?"

"Uhh...no."

Lamil rotated one of his eyes, and with the other he looked up and down at Nicolas. "You each shoulder a unique burden. You would do well to focus on your own journey, and leave Jurn to Jurn."

"I keep hearing that word...*cet,*" Nicolas said.

"It is the place wherein your inner peace dwells. Knowledge I can give you, like food to a hatchling. But your cet is a place you must find on your own if you ever hope to achieve wisdom."

"Helpful."

Both of Lamil's eyes came to rest on Nicolas before turning to face opposite directions.

"Dismiss the students," Lamil said in a loud voice.

Three cichlos emerged from the formations and called the students to attention. Soon, a continuous line of students left the dome.

"Walk with me," Lamil said and turned away.

Nicolas followed him toward a table made from barrier energy.

"It is no coincidence that brings you here, Nicolas."

"You know my name."

"Few things related to the priestly caste happen in Aquonome absent my awareness. But I have known you would come for a very long time."

First Mujahid and now this guy. Enough was enough. "Everybody has a prophecy in this dang place, but nobody ever tells me anything. What good's a prophecy if you keep it secret?"

"There are many prophecies, just as there are many...." Lamil stopped for a few moments and his eyes spun around in his head. When they came to rest he continued. "Your language is limited. Let's call them *gods* for the sake of simplicity. There are many prophecies, just as there are many *gods*. Some are intended for multitudes of people to hear, while others are meant for the ears of a few or even one. A prophecy meant for one is meaningless to another, and prone to misinterpretation. Therefore it is best left unspoken. The people you refer to are acting appropriately."

Nicolas wanted a straight answer, and his frustration levels were climbing. He felt the probing fingers of energy in his mind, and he suspected the siek had something to do with it.

"You are an impatient person," Lamil said. "This keeps you far from your cet." He glanced toward the top of the dome. "I could say the way home for you is up...but we both know it is not that simple."

Nicolas's eyes grew large as he realized what Lamil was implying.

"In order to find your way home, you must first understand why you left."

"It's not like I got lost wandering around the fair grounds. Something *did this* to me."

Lamil looked Nicolas up and down. "When you find your cet, you will find your direction. You cannot have one without the other."

Nicolas rolled his eyes.

"Do not take these words lightly, for I do not offer them lightly. I can teach you more about necromancy than you have imagined possible. But I cannot teach you anything if you are unwilling to learn."

"I want nothing more than—"

"Your impatience is a form of unwillingness. To be impatient, by definition, is to be unwilling to suffer delay. But wisdom requires delay, for wisdom is a thing that takes time to acquire. And knowledge in the absence of wisdom is dangerous."

That last sentence was almost verbatim what Mujahid had said. He looked away, thinking about the first day he had spent in Paradise, and wondered if he would ever be powerful enough to get back home.

Lamil chuckled and said "Too much too soon is not a good thing."

Nicolas's head snapped back toward Lamil, and his heart raced. This was more than a coincidence.

"Of course it is no coincidence," Lamil said.

So that was his trick. Lamil was using the strands of energy to read his thoughts.

"The Mukhtaar Lords were among my finest students."

"You're more powerful than they are?"

Lamil *harrumphed*. "Your question betrays your ignorance. I do not offer power...not in the way you expect. I offer a journey towards wisdom."

Lamil raised his hands and spread his webbed fingers in front of Nicolas's face. "Now, in order to reach a destination, one must first know one's starting point. I am going to delve into your mind to see how much of the art you possess, and how much you are capable of possessing."

Nicolas's neck shook with an involuntary spasm as the probing energy dove deeper into his mind. Strands of energy intertwined themselves around his symbols of power and probed the depth of his energy well.

"You have a basic understanding of the source of your power, but not its purpose," Lamil said.

The energy strands grew tighter and dissolved into the symbols of power, and images ran through Nicolas's mind. They resolved into a single image, repeated over and over—the entrance to his hall of power.

A strand of energy touched the white door, entered it and recoiled away from it. When it entered the black door an image of Kaitlyn appeared, and Lamil inhaled.

He tilted his head. "You have come into the second tier of your power." Lamil tilted his head to the opposite side. "Now...let's have a look at what you may be capable of."

The strands reached deeper, opening door after door in the hall of power. Every time a new door opened Kaitlyn appeared for just a moment before dissolving into mist. Deeper and deeper the energy probed, and Lamil's hand trembled, yet the energy delved deeper still, racing through rooms too quickly for Nicolas to keep track. Again he heard Lamil inhale.

"Potential runs deep. You have as many halls as a Mukhtaar—wait...there is another."

The probing strands reached a large, circular room in Nicolas's mind. Multiple black doors dotted the room...too many to count. This was something different, and, judging by Lamil's reaction, unexpected.

The room was a hollow, tubular column climbing to a height beyond the limits of his vision, ringed with black doors stacked one on top of the other that reached up into a black, starless sky.

There was a presence in the room he hadn't noticed before, and he spun around to see what it was.

Kaitlyn stood no more than two feet away, holding a rose and smiling her infectious smile. He reached out to touch her, but she dissolved into wispy strands of cloud that rose up through the hollow column and became one with the starless sky.

Lamil pulled his hand away and he circled Nicolas, as if wanting to see him from every angle.

He might not be able to read the expression on Lamil's face, but he could see the siek was shaken. And the siek wasn't the only one. What in blazes was Kaitlyn doing there?

Lamil completed the full circle and stopped.

"I need time to meditate on what I have just seen," Lamil said. "There are things I do not understand about your pathways...and that is saying something. I will seek the High Priest's council. Let us continue your studies tomorrow. You will train with me. The formations are for cichlos, not human."

Nicolas looked down.

"Learn to develop your patience. We have a long journey ahead of us." Lamil nodded to a nearby student. "Take Nicolas to the sleeping dome."

The student bowed and led Nicolas from the dome.

Nicolas couldn't help wondering what Kaitlyn had to do with his hall of power.

earn anything useful, human sab?"

The voice surprised Nicolas as he left the dome. He was expecting to find Jurn waiting for him, but instead he saw a red-skinned cichlos wearing the white cowl of a student, leaning against the archway that led into the dome. The cichlos was standing in such a way that the left side of his face was hidden from view. His right eye, however, was staring straight at Nicolas.

"Nicolas. The name's Nicolas. Not *human*, or *sab*, or...whatever the hell the cichlos equivalent of *dumbass* is. Got it? Nic...o...las."

The cichlos made an unfamiliar noise and turned away from the arch. When the left side of his face came into view, Nicolas took a step back. The fish man's left eye was completely black, as if the pupil had dilated and remained that way. It was hard to tell with the cichlos, but the skin surrounding the black eye looked burned, as if the entire side of his face had been engulfed in flame at some point. Nicolas couldn't stop staring at the scars.

The cichlos's right eye crossed to the left, as if trying to see what Nicolas was staring at.

Nicolas realized what he was doing and looked down.

"You don't look so pretty to us either, you know," the cichlos said.

"I'm sorry. I didn't mean—"

"Personally, I find it hard to believe you're the one he's been waiting for. You're not even one of us."

This was getting old. "We now continue with the verbal abuse portion of the program, I see. It doesn't have quite the effect you're going for when you do it all the time, you know. Someone should teach you people about that."

"Toridyn," the cichlos said.

Nicolas laughed. "And there it is. The cichlos word for *dumbass*. I knew we'd get there eventually."

"Toridyn is the cichlos word for my name, human...I mean...*Nicolas*."

Ahh hell. I am a dumbass.

"You haven't been treated well by us," Toridyn said. "I understand. But we're not all like Jurn. Few of us are." He paused when Nicolas didn't react. "It was a training accident."

"Jurn was an accident? That explains some things."

Toridyn made a noise like a chuckle. "Not *Jurn*. My face. You were curious. About a year ago, I conjured an energy sphere and something went wrong. It blew up, I cried like a hatchling, and now I have this to remind me." He pointed to his left eye.

"I didn't mean to pry."

"Why wouldn't you be curious? Even my own people stare at me from time to time."

"Well, they don't seem like the most sensitive bunch."

"And the best part is I'm not even supposed to be here."

"I know the feeling. So how'd you get trapped here?"

"It's a sad story."

"Well the universe seems to think I've been too happy lately. I could use a little more depression in my life."

Toridyn looked away as if considering something, and then he took a step toward Nicolas.

"I wanted to work with the chimeramancers, and then the stupid skull dreams started," Toridyn said. He spoke with animated gestures, and his voice grew excited.

"Excuse me...the *whatmancers* now?"

"The grey cowls...never mind that. My point is once the skull dreams start, it's all over. No one cares what you want anymore. It's all *sab* this and *priestly caste* that. And don't even get me started on the prophecies. *'You are destined for greatness, Toridyn, but your ignorance blinds you.'*" He spoke the last in a fake, deep voice that sounded remarkably similar to Lamil's.

Nicolas let a small laugh escape before he realized it. This was incredible. Toridyn was just like him.

A snapping noise caught their attention, and Nicolas turned to see one of the instructors giving Toridyn a strange look.

"Come on," Toridyn said. "There'll be time for talking later. I'm supposed to show you to the sleeping dome. There isn't really a place for you, so you're going to have to bunk with me."

"Works for me."

Nicolas followed Toridyn toward another archway leading out of the temple dome.

"Can I ask you a question?" Nicolas said.

"Sure."

"Just what the hell *is* a cet, anyway?"

Toridyn chuckled and led him into the dormitory.

Nicolas lost track of the days after eight weeks of training, and every morning was the same—a breakfast of raw fish and water, an hour of meditation, and several hours training with the siek. Meal times were difficult for him, but hanging out with Toridyn helped.

The cichlos students lived in pods, small rooms made from barrier material that were large enough for five or six students, and these pods were stacked from floor to ceiling around the dome, leaving a large common area in the center. Ladders hung from pod entrances and small platforms. In a way, it reminded Nicolas of Montezuma's Castle in Arizona. He'd gone there with Dr. Murray on their Rocky Mountain trip.

There was something disturbing about Aquonome, however. Just like in Paradise and Caspardis, there were no children here...or hatchlings, as the Cichlos called them.

He got up earlier than usual to watch an orb ritual in the temple. Cichlos would bring small objects to a temple priest, who would walk behind the orb for a few moments, then bring the object back. Nicolas was just as confused as the first time he'd seen it. After a few minutes staring at the murals on the dome ceiling and the strange sparkles on the floor, he headed back to his dorm to eat.

He sat on a bench, which Toridyn had fashioned for him out of barrier magic, and stared at his breakfast plate, wishing he had some tartar sauce. He took a bite of the disgusting fish. They didn't even clean it for him. They just tossed it on a table, fresh from the lake, and expected him to dig in, fins and all. The one time he asked to cook it they looked at him like he'd farted in church.

He heard a noise at the entrance to the room they shared and assumed his friend had come to join him as usual.

"Hey Tor," Nicolas said without looking up.

"Siek Lamil wishes to see you now," Jurn said.

"Tell him I'm on my way."

Jurn turned Nicolas's plate over and the fish, guts and all, landed in Nicolas's lap.

Nicolas tried to stand but ropes of energy bound him to his seat.

"Be thankful the siek warned me not to harm you."

Jurn left, and as he disappeared into the temple the ropes of energy dissolved and Nicolas was free again.

Nicolas picked pieces of fish off his robes, telling himself Jurn wouldn't be so lucky next time. He took one of the less disgusting pieces and swallowed it. He'd need more fuel for two extra hours of training today.

Toridyn's head peeked around the corner into the room. "*Cheerful* make a special trip to lighten your mood?" Toridyn said.

Nicolas had taken to calling Jurn "Cheerful" in the preceding weeks, and Toridyn was making a habit out of copying his speech patterns.

"Yeah, right," Nicolas said. "I better not keep the siek waiting."

Toridyn grabbed a towel from beside his bed and began brushing Nicolas off.

"This should mask some of the smell," Toridyn said. "Just remember Cheerful's still out there somewhere. Try not to piss on him."

Nicolas was shocked for a moment until he realized what Toridyn was trying to say.

"Piss him *off*, Tor. Try not to *piss him off*."

Toridyn made a strange face. "But that makes no sense."

Nicolas smiled as he stood up and made his way out across the temple and into the training dome.

The familiar tendrils of energy entered his mind when he stepped into the training dome. He looked around for Siek Lamil and saw him standing at the front of the room, waving him over.

Nicolas had learned to see subtle differences in cichlos facial expressions. But, as always, Siek Lamil was inscrutable.

"Another day passes, and yet you remain ignorant," Lamil said.

"I'm sorry," Nicolas said. "I'm trying—"

Lamil lifted his hand. "I accuse you of nothing. Once more you see blame where it does not exist. A necromancer must learn the proper purpose of blame, for blame can be a destructive force as much as a positive one."

"But our job is judging people, ain't it? How can we do that if we can't blame them for the things they've done?"

Lamil rotated his eyes independently of one another in a gesture Nicolas had learned to interpret as deep consideration. After a brief pause, his eyes came back to rest on Nicolas.

"What is the Prime Duty of a necromancer?" Lamil said.

"Not this again."

"What is the Prime Duty of a necromancer?"

Nicolas knew the siek wouldn't stop until he received an answer.

"The Prime Duty of a necromancer," Nicolas said, "is to raise the dead and help them achieve purification."

"Correct," Lamil said. "Tell me where the Prime Duty instructs us to place blame on our penitents."

Nicolas squinted. He was sure the siek was leading him into another verbal trap. "Nowhere?"

"Is that a question or a statement?"

"Statement."

"Correct again," Lamil said. He paced for a moment, keeping one eye on Nicolas and another on one of the training formations. "Blame should never be wielded by a necromancer in the course of purification. It does no good to place blame on someone for the evil they commit."

"That doesn't make sense. We're supposed to make them understand the consequences of the bad things they did when they were alive, right? Don't we have to hold them responsible?"

"What is the Prime Duty of a necromancer?"

"Oh my god! What...the frick...was wrong with my question?"

"What is the Prime Duty of a necromancer?" The siek never raised his voice or sounded flustered.

Nicolas took a moment to control his frustration. He'd get nowhere fighting Siek Lamil's process. "The Prime Duty of a necromancer is to raise the dead and help them achieve purification."

"Correct. Now tell me where in the Prime Duty it instructs us to place blame."

"Nowhere, Siek."

"Correct again. When one person blames another, the accused raises a wall around their mind, rendering it impossible for them to be objective. They cannot step outside of themselves and gain a different perspective, because they have walled themselves up within their own justifications. To be purified the dead must accuse themselves. The necromancer is their guide, not their judge. We lead the dead on a journey through their own lives until they judge themselves. It is the only path to true purification."

He'd heard this before, in different words, but something struck a chord this time. Whenever it happened to him, because of an overdue assignment, or forgetting something Kait had told him, he'd usually spend more time trying to explain himself than understanding what he did wrong.

"Now," Lamil said. "Tell me the First Law of Necromancy."

Nicolas tried to recall the words Lamil taught him a few days earlier.

"Death is a...wait," Nicolas said, bringing his fist up to his forehead.

When the words came to him he snapped his finger. "Death is an extension of life."

"Correct," Lamil said. "The First Law is why I brought you here early." Lamil reached into his voluminous shirt and took out a sphere that looked like a smaller version of an orb of power. When he placed it on the ground between them Nicolas felt a trickle of necropotency.

"Touch the power within the siborum," Lamil said. "Draw it in."

These siborum things must be the cause of the power surge he felt every time he got close to a cichlos necromancer.

He reached out with his mind and sensed a small source of power. It was faint, but he knew he could touch it. He focused and allowed the power to fill his energy well.

"Very good," Lamil said. "You have transferred power from the siborum to your mind. Intuitively, I might add. Now, release the power and repeat."

Again Nicolas reached out and touched the small power source. It was easier this time.

"Continue," Lamil said. "But this time, I want you to turn away from the siborum."

Nicolas turned and drew the power in once more. If the siek was expecting it to be more difficult because he was facing away from it, he must be surprised.

"Continue," Lamil said.

Nicolas repeated the process several more times, and each time it took less effort. Confident in his newfound ability, he emptied himself of power and reached out to touch the siborum one last time.

Nothing happened.

He must be getting overconfident. He calmed himself and reached out once more, prepared to feel the flow of power enter his well.

Nothing happened again.

"Turn around," Lamil said.

Nicolas turned and saw Lamil holding the siborum in his hands. Goose bumps prickled at Nicolas's mind, telling him the siek was manipulating necropotency. The siborum started glowing, and after a moment it popped and separated into two hemispheres.

"What is the First Law of Necromancy?" Lamil asked.

"Death is an extension of Life."

"Correct," Lamil said. "Behold Life." He took the top half of the siborum away and showed Nicolas the bottom.

Resting within the hemisphere was a small flower, dried and shriveled, as if it had been dead for some time.

"How is that possible," Nicolas asked.

"What is the First Law of Necromancy?"

"Death is an extension of Life."

"Correct," Lamil said. "Now tell me, where in the First Law does it refer to sentient life?"

"If what you're saying is true, then—"

"Tell me where in the First Law it refers to sentient life?"

Nicolas blinked as the implication of what he had learned settled in. "Nowhere, Siek."

"Correct." Lamil looked Nicolas up and down with both eyes. "The Second Law of Necromancy teaches us that death surrounds everything. Repeat. What is the Second Law of Necromancy?"

Nicolas repeated the words.

"This flower once possessed life, and as such left a small footprint on this world as it passed through death's door."

Nicolas remembered something. "I've seen cichlos necromancers take sibor...rums...to the priest at the orb of power. The orb recharged them."

"Siborum. And you are partially correct. You assume the Orb of Zubuxo filled the siborum with energy. But you overlook something."

Nicolas replayed the orb ritual from this morning in his mind. "The temple priest."

Lamil nodded.

"He's the man behind the curtain, isn't he? He takes the siborum behind the orb and puts a flower in it while the ritual is going on?"

"Flowers," Lamil said. "Vegetables. Any object that once possessed non-sentient life is a candidate. The remains of a small creature could be used, but...that is distasteful. In practice, a functional siborum is filled with vegetation. This one was merely for demonstration."

"Why can't we just carry some with us, in our robes or something, or focus on the weeds growing all over? Why the fancy ball?"

Lamil harrumphed. "You've seen the physical reality so you discount the mystical."

"What do you mean?"

"The footprint of non-sentient life clings tenuously to the fabric of this plane. The ritual imbues the siborum with a protective ward that contains the fragile life force indefinitely. Outside of a siborum the life force simply disperses into the world around us. Death surrounds everything."

"Death surrounds everything. I understand. I think I'd like to learn this ritual, Siek."

Something subtle changed in Lamil's eyes, and Nicolas realized the siek was smiling.

CHAPTER TWENTY ONE

Nicolas had become adept at drawing power from the smallest plants and leaves, and the siek remarked about how fast he was learning. But whatever force had pulled him here was still a mystery.

His friendship with Toridyn was a welcome surprise. He found a kindred spirit in the friendly cichlos, and found him to be the only other person he could relate to.

During a recent summoning he saw cichlos traveling between two worlds, using an orb of power. The orb looked a lot like the Orb of Zubuxo, and he couldn't help wondering if an orb was the way home. If it worked for the cichlos, why not him?

The siek said his knowledge of necromancy was growing at an astonishing rate. Small failures no longer frustrated him because he knew each success would lead to a way home.

Again, Lamil summoned Nicolas to the training dome before his usual meditation hour, and again those fingers of energy entered his mind.

"Another day passes, and your ignorance remains," Lamil said.

"Yes it does, Siek. Maybe I'll get some wisdom today. You never know."

He had come to understand that Lamil wasn't berating him...Lamil was grading him, as any teacher would grade a student, and it was a simple pass-fail system.

"Your wisdom grows every day. You simply have a long path ahead of you." Lamil looked away and mumbled, "Not too long, I hope."

"Why the rush?"

Lamil flinched. "You heard me?"

"You're standing right next to me. You feelin' ok?"

Lamil harrumphed and straightened his shoulders. "We are often wise in some ways and ignorant in others. That is at the core of what it means to be a...person."

If Nicolas didn't know any better, he would say the siek was about to call him a cichlos.

"You have mastered the first symbol of power," Lamil said. "You are quite adept at raising the dead now. It is time to focus on the second symbol of power."

"The arrow."

"The *guide*. Interesting that you see it as a weapon."

"Any tool can be a weapon. I once saw my dad scare off a grizzly bear with a plumb bob. It's not about what it *is*. It's how you *use* it."

Lamil took a siborum out of his robes and called one of the other students over. "Hide it somewhere in the dome, then have the formations dismissed."

"Yes, Siek," the student said and hurried off.

"When you were dying in the lake," Lamil said, "you channeled power into the guide symbol and cast it outward. You acted correctly. But I'm not sure you understand the implications of your success."

"It knew what I needed and it led me there."

"It knew no such thing."

"Say what?"

"The guide symbol serves two purposes and two purposes only. The first you discovered accidentally—it will guide you to the nearest source of power beyond your reach. Necromancers without siborum use this technique to travel over land. It allows you to move from one source of power to another."

"So in the lake, it was telling me where I'd find power."

"Correct," Lamil said. He retrieved another siborum from his robes and handed it to Nicolas. "Use the same process you used in the lake. I want you to locate the nearest source of energy."

Nicolas focused his necropotency and the arrow grew large in the corner of his eye, like a spec that he could never quite look at. It turned, and he felt drawn toward the opposite side of the dome. Not a physical tugging, but a mental certainty that he should go in that direction. He started walking and Siek Lamil followed.

The arrow led him to a small supply room and began to turn faster on his periphery. Subtle movements of his head or body would cause the arrow to spin toward a single point. As he uncovered the hidden siborum, the arrow shrank down to its place.

"Master this and you will rarely be without power," Lamil said.

"You said something about a second purpose."

Lamil retrieved the gold necklace that was hanging down into his shirt and handed it to Nicolas.

"This is my sister Tamil's. Cast the guide into this necklace."

Nicolas formed a mental image of pushing the symbol into the necklace. When he released the energy...nothing happened.

"I don't understand," Nicolas said. He could feel his frustration rising again.

"The necromantic symbols are allies, not enemies. You need not command the symbol to do that which it already wishes to do."

Mujahid had told him the same thing.

"I know," Nicolas said. "I have to show the symbol what to do."

There could be only one reason the siek would hand him a necklace and ask him to cast the arrow on it, but he wasn't sure how to visualize that. How could he depict something acting like a cosmic hound dog?

Toby! Toby's a beagle!

He created an image of Toby getting a scent from his favorite toy—the *gatorpickle*. Toby nosed his way around every nook and cranny, just like he nosed around the ankles of Nicolas's pants after a long school day. When Toby took his last sniff, Nicolas imagined him morphing into the arrow, and then imagined the *gatorpickle* morphing into the necklace.

The arrow leaped into his mind's eye and guided him out of the training dome.

Nicolas chuckled. It wasn't the complexity of the tasks that kept throwing him for a loop. It was the simplicity. He needed to stop over-thinking everything.

It took a few minutes for them to cross the expansive floor of the temple dome, but soon they emerged into the central hub. This was the first time he'd seen the city proper since they brought him here as a prisoner.

The arrow led him into a throng of cichlos. They deferred to him, nodding and backing away as he walked through the crowd. He couldn't help feeling self-conscious about it.

"Why are they bowing to me like that?"

Lamil regarded the people. "You wear the clothes of the priestly caste. All other castes are beneath ours. It would be dishonorable for them to show you any disrespect, regardless of your...species."

Nicolas huffed and shook his head.

"You disapprove," Lamil said.

"Damn straight," Nicolas said.

"Disapproval takes one of two forms," Lamil said. "Either a person understands what they see and therefore has good reason to disapprove, or they are ignorant of what they see and disapprove out of that lack of understanding. Tell me what you find distasteful."

Nicolas faced Lamil. "What's not distasteful about it? We sit in our spacious temple next to an all-you-can-eat buffet and do nothing but train all day, while these people are out here...how can you consider this just?"

"Justice is ever at the forefront of a necromancer's mind, and rightly so. Your wisdom grows, but your ignorance is formidable. It is born of years perceiving only the surface of matters and not being critical of what lies beneath."

"That wasn't critical enough for you?"

"I speak not of being prone to finding fault. In that sense, yes, you are critical. I speak of a sense of discriminating judgment that will allow you to see beyond appearances to the truth of the matter. Very few things are ever what they appear to be."

"Enlighten me."

"Look around you and tell me what you see."

"We have a power they don't have or understand, and they fear it. They live to serve us and we live to rule."

"I must reconsider my estimation of you, for you are blind as well as ignorant."

It had been a while since he'd let the siek get the better of him, but something about this society was touching on issues at his core that he didn't understand. All he knew was that it wasn't right, and he wasn't doing a good job of explaining himself.

"Perhaps you will be better served by a description of what I see?" Lamil's eyes moved in independent directions, as if taking in the entire central hub at once. "I see a city of love and light."

"You're two sandwiches short of a picnic now."

"You mistake gratitude for fear. They regard us with love for the service we render to society."

"We can do things other people only dream about."

"You have experienced the *namocea* many times," Lamil said, using the Cichlossean word for the moment when a necromancer lives their penitent's life. "These people fear the namocea more than any power we wield. Voluntarily living the life of an evil person, experiencing the torment and suffering they cause, not to mention living through the consequences, is seen as one of the greatest acts of love a person can perform. They honor and respect us. But they do not serve us, Nicolas. How many servants have you seen in the temple that were not priests?"

On reflection, Nicolas had never seen a person in the temple that wasn't a priest. Was it possible he'd missed something? Something huge?

"It is we who serve them," Lamil said. "You know of our pods and the hunting schedule we keep. Yet you've never questioned the amount of fish we caught. Look carefully at the columns of energy in this dome and tell me what you see."

Nicolas examined the structures with the refrigerator-sized cutouts as they walked through the dome. He was about to dismiss the siek's question when he realized something. The shopkeepers wore midnight-blue cowls. Only one caste wore midnight blue in Aquonome—priests. The shopkeepers were priests, and they were distributing food amongst the cichlos, taking nothing in return.

Just like dad at the soup kitchen.

"I can feel sight returning to your eyes," Lamil said.

"Only priests are divided into hunting pods."

"Correct," Lamil said. "It is our duty to take care of these people in life as well as death. The *Third* Law of Necromancy demands this."

"Third law?"

"Too much, too soon."

Nicolas looked down, uncertain of what to say.

"There are many things you do not understand," Lamil said. "We shall remedy that. Back to the task at hand."

Nicolas concentrated on the arrow. When they reached the far wall, he stopped and gazed through the barrier. If a fish swam close to the city he could see it, but beyond that it was dark as a barrel of crude oil.

"I don't understand," Nicolas said. "It's leading me through the barrier."

"Release your control over the guide."

The arrow vanished from his mind's eye.

"There is a part of cichlos life you have not experienced yet," Lamil said. "My sister died many years ago—may the water return her to us someday."

"But—"

"She, too, was of the priestly caste, and this necklace was one of her favorite possessions. Had we continued, the guide would have led you to a burial cave. There you would have found Tamil's final resting place."

"The arrow sniffs out bodies?"

Lamil gave him a disapproving look. "*Guide.* And partially correct, however crude. Had I given you the High Priest's scythe instead of this necklace you would have been led to his chambers. And that would have been an unpleasant surprise for both of you."

"So it can find the living as well as the dead?"

"The Third Law will give you clarity. For now, remember that all life is energy. We are, all of us, beings of a dual nature—material, and energy. When a person cares about an object, or even another person, they impart a certain amount of their life force—their energy—into that object. The guide leads you to the strongest source of their energy. For a person who is alive, this means locating that person. For a person who has died, however, this means locating the site of their burial."

Nicolas nodded, though he was confused.

"How can—"

The entire dome heaved, pushing Nicolas upward, and screams erupted all around him.

His momentum wanted to propel him towards the ceiling, but he was stuck to the floor. He watched in horror as the dome's massive roof rippled in a gigantic wave. It was like those news reports he'd seen of bridges waving about during a hurricane. The ripple groaned like bending metal, and he feared the entire barrier would tear itself apart. When he remembered how far underwater they were he panicked.

Necropotency burst from his mind and wrapped him and the siek in a sphere of energy. Nicolas stared at it, wide-eyed. It resembled a liquid bubble, oozing from his hand and surrounding them.

Lamil's giant eyes grew larger when he saw the shield. "Stay calm. The quake will pass and Aquonome will release you. Dismiss this...barrier."

Nicolas had no idea how he'd created the shield to begin with. He could release his hold on it if he tried. It was the mental equivalent of exhaling. The ball of energy vanished, and he tried to step closer to Lamil. A small section of the floor had reached up and entwined itself around his body like a snake, holding him in place. It did the same to the siek.

He was confused until he looked around the dome. Everyone stood still as if nothing was happening. Barrier energy wrapped around objects that would have become projectiles, binding them to whatever surface they rested on. The city was in the middle of a massive earthquake but nothing moved. Even the screaming stopped.

Everything returned to normal after the first violent heave, though the quake continued. He could hear it like the claps of a thunderstorm.

"How is this possible?" he shouted over the intense rumbling of the quake.

"It is an art unlike necromancy," Lamil said. "It will end soon, and all will be well."

When the rumbling stopped, the floor of the city retracted, allowing everyone to continue about their business.

"Erindor mourns for my people," Lamil said. "The cichlos are not accustomed to the strange movements of this place. Like you, we are from another world. When the first quake hit...the losses were catastrophic. Some of our walls failed because we had not conjured them in a way that would make them flexible."

"You can breathe under water, though, can't you?"

"When such a mass of water converges into a small place, the problem is not one's breath. People were thrown violently into one another. Loose tools or other objects killed many others. Come. Let us begin the journey back to the temple complex."

Now was his chance to ask about the orb in his dreams. He followed Lamil.

"During the namocea, I've seen cichlos use an orb to travel between your home world and Erindor."

Lamil's expression changed, but it was unlike any expression Nicolas had seen. Both of the wise man's eyes rotated straight out to the sides, then down to the ground.

"Do not cast the net of hope into a lifeless sea. What you experienced in the namocea is no longer possible."

"But they used an orb of power, just like the Orb of Zubuxo—"

"It was not the Orb of Zubuxo. It was the Orb of Arin." Lamil's large eyes focused back on Nicolas. "And it has been hidden from us for decades."

An awkward silence persisted for the next few minutes as they entered the massive temple. Nicolas tried to distract himself by staring at the beautiful artwork on the dome and floor. He'd touched on a sore spot with the siek, but he had to know more about this Orb of Arin. That iridescent sphere in his visions was the only solid clue he'd discovered.

"How'd it happen?" Nicolas said.

"This is a subject that brings us—that brings me much pain. I have not seen my mate or spawn in...."

The awkwardness returned. Nicolas had never seen the siek this emotional before.

"Forgive me, Siek. But you know I can't let this go. If the orb isn't the solution, fine. But I deserve the opportunity to figure that out for myself. What was it you said? Something about discriminating judgment and seeing beneath the surface of things?"

Lamil stopped walking.

"I'm not trying to put salt in your wound," Nicolas said. "I just want to understand. You always say wisdom isn't the same as knowledge— that it's the combination of knowledge and experience. Well, isn't my experience different from yours? Isn't it different from any of The People? Why hide what happened when maybe I can help us both?"

"I have hidden nothing from you." Lamil raised one of his giant hands and made a sweeping gesture around the temple.

Nicolas followed the hand, but he didn't get it. The temple was empty, except—

The murals. That has to be it.

Most of the scenes were alien, by his standards, and they numbered in the hundreds. One image depicted cichlos and humans eating a feast together, which he always thought strange. They didn't exactly have the same eating habits.

His eyes scanned from picture to picture but there was nothing that looked like the Orb of Arin in any of them. There were just too many murals to study.

He shook his head and looked down.

When he saw it he wanted to laugh. It had been right in front of him all along. Right beneath him, rather. He saw the murals on the floor every day, the strange sparkles of light, but he never really understood them. The temple was vast, making it impossible to view the entire scene from his height.

But there it was. The iridescent Orb of Arin, hanging in mid-air in the apse of a great temple behind what appeared to be a giant winged helm. Cichlos and humans entered the orb and emerged from it, as if stepping through a gateway. Beyond the orb was a vast field of stars in the shape of a spiral galaxy—the source of the sparkles. On the opposite end of the galaxy was a similar orb in another massive temple behind another giant helm.

Another picture in the mural caught his attention. One figure held an outstretched arm, reaching across the vast galaxy toward another group of cichlos in the same pose. Another figure reached back. Cichlos on both sides of the galaxy held their heads in their hands as they wept.

Nicolas covered his mouth and swallowed a lump. Is that what this place was? Some sort of cosmic trap that sucked people in and never let them go?

Lamil pointed to the orb on the far side of the galaxy. "We traveled by using an object we called *Arin's Gate*. Its twin on this world is called the Great Orb of Arin."

Dr. Murray's training started to claw its way out of Nicolas's memory.

"This is no coincidence," Nicolas said.

Lamil harrumphed. "Coincidence is a word used by fools when they fail to see what is right before their eyes. You may be ignorant, but you are no fool."

"You worship Erindorian gods, or they worship yours. Your cultures must have intermingled for decades, if not centuries." Nicolas recalled how the ancient Romans had adopted first the Etruscan gods, and ultimately the Greek gods. "So, who borrowed from whom?"

"Your question, while understandable, is presumptuous. The gods simply existed, long before The People. Long before the humans. In my culture they look like us. In human culture they resemble the humans. I would think it obvious they are neither."

Nicolas shook his head. He wouldn't get far if he tried to question Lamil's superstitions. "I *see* what happened. But I don't *understand* what happened."

"Before the Erindorian sky turned yellow, we were friends of the humans. We traded with them, and shared knowledge. One day the orb was there, and the next—for reasons that elude us—the humans retrieved it from the great Temple of Arin and brought it to a place they call the Pinnacle. Those of us who remained in Erindor found ourselves cut off from *Terilya*, our home world."

"No one thought to ask them? Not so much as a *hey, about that orb*?"

"You think we hid underwater and did nothing? In the same way that the sky turned yellow, a yellow dome also appeared over the Pinnacle. We tried swimming under it, but those who tried said it was without end. It extended down into the foundation of the world. Many cichlos tried to go through it, in much the same way we can travel through our own barriers, but every attempt resulted in death. Whoever tried simply vanished."

Nicolas remembered the barrier in his jail cell and what it did to his hands. Not all barriers were equal, and he knew that with a certainty. "They must have wanted something."

"The man they call the Archmage declared necromancy illegal. Humans believed all cichlos were necromancers because only the priestly caste ventured to the surface."

"There are cities right above you," Nicolas said. "Don't they hunt you down too? Why don't they just come down here and wipe you all out?"

"That is not possible. Aquonome not only protects us from the shifting sea floor. It also renders its inhabitants undetectable. It is, quite simply, impossible for them to find us by magical means. And were it not for summoning a cichlos priest, you would have died during your descent. The pressure of the sea would have killed you."

"That orb is your only way back home?"

"The only *practical* way, yes."

"You've said, over and over, I need to discover my purpose if I ever want to get back home," Nicolas said. "I think I know what that is. I think I need to find this orb and make it so your people can use it again." Nicolas looked down. "And maybe, if I'm lucky, I can use it too."

"I caution you against misplaced hope. Hope can be a driving force.

But, when unfulfilled, it can be violently destructive. You think you recognize your purpose because you hope this is your purpose."

"It's more than that."

"How can you be certain?"

"Archmage Kagan is my father."

The siek's face was unreadable. He placed his webbed hand on Nicolas's shoulder as they entered the training dome.

Nicolas wondered whether Mujahid learned the gesture from the siek, or the siek had learned it from Mujahid.

CHAPTER TWENTY TWO

T he next day was the same as usual for Nicolas. He was
summoned to the training dome and kept busier than a one-
legged man in an ass-kicking contest.

He and Toridyn sat together in silence, while Nicolas practiced his
summoning. He was tired. Not that he needed sleep—more like he
needed a vacation. Living the lives of every person he called back from
the grave was beginning to take its toll on him.

I'm too young to feel like this.

"Cheerful," Toridyn said, and he nodded to his right.

Nicolas dismissed his penitent, causing the cichlos skeleton to
crumble to the floor. The other students in the training hall ignored him
and continued summoning their energy spheres.

Siek Lamil was crossing the dome with Jurn and two undead cichlos.
They must be Jurn's penitents. Bile rose in Nicolas's throat.

The siek stopped between two student formations and waved Nicolas
over.

Toridyn excused himself and walked a short distance away.

"It is time to move on to areas you have not yet been tested in," Lamil
said. "Areas in which you must excel if you are to succeed at your task."

"What areas?"

Jurn chuckled.

"Combat," Lamil said.

"You don't have to worry about that," Nicolas said. "I don't plan on picking any fights."

Jurn made a sound that Nicolas didn't recognize.

"Outside of Aquonome your *plan* will count for nothing," Lamil said. "Many will hate you, and most will fear you. Combat will find you, even if you do not seek it."

Nicolas pursed his lips. He didn't like the sound of that.

"The only way I can learn how much knowledge you have, is to discover how much knowledge you lack," Lamil said. "I will do this by observing you as you duel. Send your penitents away, Jurn."

Nicolas realized what was happening, and it chilled him. Jurn had beaten him without mercy, and now he'd get to do it again? This wasn't a fair fight. Jurn had already been a master necromancer once.

Nicolas looked at Toridyn, whose eyes had become even larger.

Jurn commanded his two penitents to stand at the entrance of the training dome.

"I'll have them guard the exit," Jurn said. "In case you decide to run away."

Lamil gave him a disapproving look.

"There are rules," Lamil said. "You will not injure one another. You will not attempt anything, mystical or physical, that could result in the death of your opponent."

Nicolas felt a wave of relief. At least he wouldn't have to fight for his life.

"Perhaps I should leave, then, Siek," Jurn said. "My breath alone could snap him like a trout's spine."

"You can say that again, fish man," Nicolas said.

Jurn reared back with one of his massive arms but Lamil stopped him.

Lamil's deep voice sounded like walking through gravel. "Do anything to cause him harm, student, and you will know what that trout feels like."

Jurn looked like his grandmother had threatened him with a switch.

"You may summon the dead for this exercise, if you wish," Lamil said. "They may do anything except injure your opponent. Your duel will remain confined to the training dome." Lamil faced the three training formations. "Students, clear the center of the room."

The other students, Toridyn included, formed a single line around the perimeter of the dome.

"You may begin at will," Lamil said.

Two cichlos skeletons materialized and charged at Nicolas before Lamil finished his words. Nicolas had yet to begin summoning a penitent of his own, and the speed at which they came at him broke his concentration. He dove between the two oncoming warriors. His power-enhanced agility made the dive easy, but he landed hard on the dome floor. He channeled energy into the symbol of the skull.

The namocea took hold, and thirty years passed in a single moment. When his consciousness returned, he no longer felt disoriented as he used to. He took control of his penitent and launched it at one of the attacking skeletons.

Nicolas circled Jurn, attempting to find any advantage he could. Whenever he summoned a warrior penitent his knowledge of combat improved, as if he absorbed some of the penitent's wisdom. His newfound battle prowess told him it would be better, this time, to remain on the defense and try to draw out an attack.

As he crossed between Jurn and one of Jurn's penitents, he felt a strange surge in power, as if he'd stepped through a beam of energy.

Nicolas's necromantic link vanished without warning and his penitent collapsed. Jurn's two skeletons turned on him, forcing him to circle around to the left. A faint beam of light passed through his body from side to side as he stepped in front of Jurn. It was coming from Jurn, but the moment he became aware of it the beam disappeared. He must be going crazy.

Jurn made a chuckling noise and an alien energy entered Nicolas's mind. It felt like what he imagined being dipped in oil would feel like. Like there was something he just couldn't shake off. He tried summoning another penitent, but the energy struck the oil slick and slid off.

"I have seen enough," Lamil said.

Jurn banished his penitents, causing their bones to separate and fall to the floor.

"Jurn," Lamil said. "Form up the students and return to your training."

"Yes, Siek," Jurn said. Some of the other students congratulated Jurn as he walked away.

"From where I was standing, I didn't see a fight," Lamil said.

"I couldn't think fast enough, Siek."

"No one would be able to."

"Jurn obviously can."

"Jurn defeated you for two reasons and two reasons only—his experience, and his instincts. He did not defeat you because his thought processes were faster than yours. You lost this battle before it began."

"Between him and his penitents I'm like china in a bull shop."

Lamil paused and looked Nicolas up and down. "All of your successes share one thing in common—your actions were instinctual, not planned. Think of the shield you created. You didn't create it because you planned it carefully. You created it because you needed it, and you instinctively engaged your necropotency to bring about the desired effect. Instinct and necessity are a powerful combination."

"But I had a plan. I couldn't draw any damned power. It's like he hog-tied my brain."

"The cichlos general, Erasces the Great, once said 'The first casualty of combat is a warrior's battle plan.' What makes a combat necromancer great is not his plan … it's his ability to adapt when his plan is no longer feasible."

"Erasces never met *Jurn*."

"Erasces defeated an army of thirty-five thousand with fifty priests, securing freedom from our oppressors. I do not think Jurn would have posed a challenge."

Nicolas swallowed.

"You have not yet flaked a scale off the surface of your potential. We are going about your training the wrong way."

Nicolas squinted. He had a feeling he wasn't going to like what was coming next.

"You don't need less danger to find your potential," Lamil said. "You need more."

"Now hold on—"

"The next time you face Jurn, there will be no restrictions. He will be free to kill you, and you will be free to do the same."

It took an act of will for Nicolas to suppress the panic that rose in his chest. "He's too strong. I can't beat him."

"Then tomorrow you will die, for tomorrow you will face Jurn once more."

Nicolas gave up on sleep after several hours of fitful turning, opting instead to spend the rest of the night in the Temple. There was something peaceful about the place. It reminded him of the chapel at the orphanage, where he'd sometimes go to be alone. Unlike the chapel, however, priests wandered in and out throughout the night refilling spent siborum and performing other rituals he couldn't identify.

For the last week he felt as if the orb were calling to him, drawing him closer. But every time he approached it, wanting to touch it or place his ear against it, tendrils of energy entered his mind. It was Siek Lamil searching for some piece of information in his brain, no doubt.

His mind drifted toward Kaitlyn while the rituals went on around him. Seeing life through the eyes of so many others had given him perspective. He understood her now. The way she always wanted to lay out his clothes, walk the dog, do the dishes and any number of other chores, wasn't because she felt he was a baby that couldn't take care of himself. It was just her way of showing him that she loved him. He was better able to deal with the sense of loss now, but there were times when he wanted nothing more than to hold her and smell the rose scent of her skin, to run his fingers through her auburn hair, and to hear the lilt of her voice as they walked Toby through Zilker Park.

But that would never happen. Because today he would die.

It can't end like this.

His body ached the way he imagined an old man would ache. Thoughts of Kaitlyn made the pain bearable, though. He could practically feel the warmth of her body against his skin, and how soft her hands were. He let himself get lost in the memory of her face; the way the right side of her mouth curled up in a crooked smile. Serenity radiated through him like the warmth of the sun and he was at peace.

Do you remain ignorant? Lamil's voice rang like a bell in his mind.

Kaitlyn's face disappeared, but the peace remained.

"I have no idea how Jurn messes with my penitents. Mujahid said that wasn't possible. He was wrong, obviously."

Or perhaps just testing you, as I do.

"I don't know. I see my reflection and don't recognize my own face anymore." *I feel so...old.*

That is natural, Nicolas. Your spirit has lived many lifetimes, and the wisdom it has gained is far beyond your physical age.

But why does my body feel like this?

Your mind is no longer ignorant. Your spirit is now much older than your body so your body grows confused. It will adjust with time. And you will learn...other ways to care for the body.

Nicolas jerked his head back in realization. The siek was standing across the dome. He had done it.

Yes, you have. You are ignorant no more. You have found your cet.

"Kaitlyn."

"She is a deeper part of you than you know," Lamil said. "She is both the source of your strength and of your peace. And *far* more than that, if my instinct serves me."

Nicolas squinted at him. *You know something about my future.*

"Does this surprise you?" Lamil smiled.

Nicolas couldn't help smiling in return. He stretched and yawned.

"I wish it were that simple, though," Lamil said. "Prophecy is the least understood concept in our religion."

"I've always thought prophecy was more about the past than the future."

"You are not far from mastery," Lamil said. "And I do not use those words lightly. But remember that the future is not determined. You change it with every decision you make and every action you take."

"Not sure I have many decisions left."

"I will not go back on what I told you yesterday. You will face Jurn, and he will be free to kill you."

"You'd let one of your students die?"

Lamil looked Nicolas up and down. "Other priests live years between visits to the halls of power, sometimes decades. Yet you have mastered two symbols in a matter of months. The futures of many, cichlos and human alike, depend on your survival. But if you're asking me if I would allow Jurn to kill you in open combat...my answer is yes. And you already know why."

Lamil was right, though Nicolas didn't want to admit it.

Necromancy was dangerous. If the wrong people attained mastery the results could be catastrophic...to the dead as well as the living. Lamil was the gatekeeper of the priesthood for the cichlos people—The People—and he would never allow the wrong person to wield its power. If Nicolas was a casualty of that principle, Lamil would consider it a blessing to have weeded out an incompetent priest.

Nicolas faced the Orb of Zubuxo. "I've been thinking about how your people used the Orb of Arin to travel."

"I warned you against hope."

"What about this one?"

Lamil approached the orb and Nicolas followed him.

"If this orb does allow travel, it would take the traveler to a place they'd rather not be," Lamil said. "A place where the dead stand on a vast plain before Zubuxo's throne and await purification. There's only one way back from the Plane of Death, and that is to be summoned by a priest."

Nicolas's hopes sank. Lamil had spoken of the Plane of Death in his lessons; the endless field of souls, the giant throne, the gate to the Plane of Peace.

"The only way you will return home is to fulfill your purpose here," Lamil said.

"I don't even know where to begin, Siek."

"Could you summon the dead on your home world?"

"Does waking a sleeping beagle count?"

Lamil faced the orb. "Let the future worry about the future. You would do well to concentrate on your present instead. Time remains for you to prepare. I suggest you do so."

Lamil left toward the training dome.

Nicolas followed the siek in a surreal daze, knowing this could be his last walk through the Temple of Zubuxo.

Nicolas meditated at the center of the training dome as Toridyn and the other students lined up in three formations. He was serene. His love for Kaitlyn played some part in his necromantic power, and that brought him a measure of peace. Trying to keep her out of his mind had been the wrong thing to do. It was a mistake he wouldn't make again.

Are you prepared?

Nicolas recognized Lamil's telepathic voice.

As much as I'll ever be.

"Students," Lamil said. "Against the dome wall."

There was a flurry of activity as the formations backed against the dome. Jurn approached the siek with two undead penitents, each carrying large, curved swords at their hips, but wearing no armor. Jurn barked an order and the penitents took up guarding positions at the entrance to the dome.

Nicolas knew Jurn was trying to intimidate him. It was the secret weapon of bullies everywhere, just like dad had told him.

"You will restrict yourselves to arcane combat," Lamil said as he placed a hand on Jurn's arm. "Lay down your weapon."

Jurn retrieved a small dagger. Its blade glinted blue as he laid it on the floor between them with its black jeweled hilt facing Lamil.

"Nicolas, do you have a weapon?" Lamil said.

"No," Nicolas said.

"It is each combatant's right to search the other for weaponry. Do wish to search Jurn, or are you satisfied with his honor?"

"He's ok," Nicolas said. "We're both priests."

Lamil nodded, and Jurn made a noise that sounded like a laugh.

"Jurn," Lamil said. "Do you wish to search Nicolas, or are you satisfied with his honor?"

"The human has no honor," Jurn said. "I invoke my right."

Lamil harrumphed, but allowed the search to proceed.

Jurn was rough. Every time he'd touch Nicolas he'd hit him with the back of a closed fist, or squeeze a muscle until Nicolas winced. Lamil either didn't notice or didn't care.

It didn't matter. He had found his cet, and he didn't know how or why, but Kaitlyn lived at its center. He focused on her face and let the serenity radiate through him. He was aware of Lamil repeating his instructions and Jurn taunting him again. But words no longer mattered. Jurn no longer mattered. Neither the past nor the future mattered any longer. There was only now. There was only his cet. There was only Kaitlyn.

Nicolas shifted his focus back to the training dome.

"You may begin," Lamil said.

Nicolas saw everything as if time had slowed.

He had control over an armed human penitent and had begun summoning a cichlos before Jurn had a chance to move. He sent his first penitent straight at Jurn, raising its long sword in an attack position.

The namocea left him weakened. Mujahid had been right. Summoning without a corpse was no easy task. He couldn't let his weakened state destroy his focus.

Jurn's new penitent met Nicolas's half way, and the two undead warriors clashed in battle, the steel ringing of swords reverberating through the dome as the fight swung back and forth. Jurn's penitent got the upper hand and split the human penitent's torso from shoulder to hip.

Nicolas's necromantic link vanished and his penitent crumbled to the ground.

As Jurn's second penitent materialized behind Nicolas, an energy beam shot through Nicolas's torso.

Nicolas looked down and saw a spectral beam of light connecting Jurn to his newest penitent. So he *wasn't* going crazy yesterday. There *had* been a beam coming from Jurn.

The deeper Nicolas retreated into his cet, the more visible the beam became. Three more emanated from Jurn, each one ending at a different penitent.

Nicolas concentrated on the beam passing through him. It pulsed with necropotency.

A skeletal hand the size of his head slammed into his chest and tossed him backwards, breaking his concentration.

As he flew into the air, Jurn fired a sphere of necropotency toward him.

Nicolas reacted instinctively. He channeled energy into the skull symbol and hurled it at a point between him and the oncoming sphere.

A penitent materialized and absorbed the full blast of the sphere, exploding and sending jagged bone fragments flying in every direction.

As Nicolas landed hard on his back, he summoned a penitent and directed it toward Jurn.

The air rushed from his lungs, as it had done in the cell when Mujahid kicked him, and Mujahid's last words echoed in his mind.

It's all about the energy.

The beam that had been passing through him hovered above his face, and realization dawned as if the beam itself had shed light on Mujahid's meaning.

Mujahid wasn't talking about the lake. He was talking about necromancy. It's all about the energy!

He willed the beam to feed the well of power in his mind, treating it like any other power source, and the necropotency poured into him.

The beam vanished and Jurn growled.

Jurn's penitent disappeared, leaving no bones behind.

He'd done it. He'd done something Mujahid told him was impossible.

Jurn roared, but Nicolas remained at peace. He no longer feared the sadistic albino. Instead, he saw Jurn as an object of pity—a cautionary tale he would never forget.

He repeated the process with the next beam of energy, and the penitent at the other end disappeared.

Something began to pull at his necromantic link. The beam extending to his own penitent was curving, creating an arc that moved toward Jurn at its apex. As the arc grew more pronounced it grew weaker. It would snap if he didn't do something about it.

Nicolas released energy along the surface of the necromantic link, coating it in a protective barrier of energy. Jurn's pull grew stronger, so he modified the spell he was casting. The protective barrier became slick, as if coated in oil.

Jurn lost his grip on the link, and the rebounding burst of energy threw him backwards into the air. He crashed into the dome wall behind him.

Nicolas ordered his penitent to attack, and the skeletal warrior charged. Jurn was lying in a heap on the floor, recovering from the whiplash of energy as the warrior reached him. The penitent shouted a battle cry and lifted its hands as if preparing to rip Jurn apart.

"Stop," Nicolas said. The word wasn't necessary, but Nicolas wanted Jurn to hear him. The penitent lowered his arms and took a few steps back.

Nicolas knelt next to the albino who had become the bane of his existence.

"Are you gonna stop acting like an asshole?" Nicolas said. "Or does that friendly skeleton over there have to stomp a mud hole in you?"

Jurn grunted and looked away.

"Siek," Nicolas said. "Should I walk away?" He hoped with all his strength that Lamil would say yes.

Lamil looked from Nicolas to Jurn. "The rules of engagement are specific, and you are both honor-bound to fulfill them. Withdraw at your own peril, Nicolas."

Jurn's remaining penitent leaped toward Nicolas from the entrance of the dome.

Nicolas reached out with his mind and banished the skeleton, drawing the beam of energy into his well. Now that he understood the process, it was effortless.

"Jurn," Nicolas said. "You can end this. We can both walk away."

"You have no honor," Jurn said.

Another penitent materialized in front of Nicolas, and he banished it without hesitation. As Jurn's power waned, his own well filled from Jurn's absorbed penitents.

Jurn couldn't sustain this much longer. Even with a siborum he'd run out of power soon.

Nicolas sensed a penitent materializing behind him and he faced it. He banished it before it had a chance to attack.

Without turning back, he said "I'm done with this, Jurn. The next words out of your mouth better be *I surrender*."

"I'm better than you, human," Jurn said. "You don't even have the honor to kill me."

Nicolas didn't want to kill Jurn. He didn't want to kill anyone. Why couldn't Jurn see reason? The fight was over.

The students along the wall drew back in surprise, as if they'd seen something horrible.

"No!" Toridyn yelled.

Pain exploded between Nicolas's shoulder blades as something sharp dug into his back. He sank to his knees and reached for the source of the pain and felt the hilt of a dagger.

The black jeweled dagger was right where Jurn had left it, on the floor near Lamil. He must have had a hidden one.

Toridyn and Lamil ran toward him.

A group of students converged on Jurn, dragging him towards the wall. They weren't being gentle about it either.

"No," Nicolas shouted at the students. "Leave him."

They stopped in place, as if unable to believe he had spoken.

Strength seeped from his body with every drop of blood that ran down into the small of his back.

Lamil stopped where he was, staring at Nicolas with a look of shock and disbelief, but Toridyn kept running until he was Nicolas's side.

Toridyn knelt and helped Nicolas to his feet. "Your back, Nicolas. You're losing a lot of blood."

Nicolas stumbled backward and almost fell. He faced Lamil, hoping the old teacher would stop the duel, but Lamil stared back, saying nothing.

Nicolas released a small amount of necropotency into his wound. The dagger slid out then dropped to the floor. He shuddered from the pain, but he'd survived worse. Far worse.

He reached out with a tendril of energy and lifted the dagger off the ground, spinning it so that it pointed at Jurn. The dagger floated through the air until it was mere inches from Jurn's face.

"Not like this," Lamil said, shaking his head.

Nicolas realized what he had been about to do and let the dagger drop to the ground.

He wanted this to end, but he knew too much about Jurn.

As long as Jurn lived, Nicolas would be in danger. The albino would never relent. If he let Jurn walk away from this dome, he would kill Nicolas at the first opportunity.

Nicolas felt the weight of the world sit on his shoulders. He knew what he had to do.

Jurn glared at him.

Nicolas recognized the pure hatred in that look, having seen it time and again in the countless lives he lived. He was watching his own life play out, as if he had stepped into his own namocea, into a world devoid of quaint definitions of *good* and *evil*, a world turned on end. He judged himself and what he was about to do from outside the confines of his battered body.

The command wasn't complex.

Two simple words.

Two simple words, which he never thought he'd hear himself say, began as a tightness in his chest, igniting war in its wake...a war of emotions with no clear victor. One side would get the upper hand, only to be pushed back in the ebb and flow of battle.

Two simple words that would forever change him into something he never imagined he would become.

As the words left his conscious mind and passed into the necromantic link, he knew them for what they were—a choice that would haunt him for the rest of his life.

Kill him.

Nicolas's penitent lunged forward and plunged his fist into Jurn's chest. He twisted his hand and tore Jurn's heart out of his rib cage, crushed it, and threw it on the floor. Jurn's corpse collapsed onto the ground and Nicolas felt the life leave him.

"The duel is over," Lamil said. "Nicolas has emerged victorious."

Bile rose in Nicolas's throat. Victorious? The word angered him.

"No, Siek," Nicolas said. "*Both* of us died here in this room. Both of us."

Nicolas stormed out of the training dome toward an uncertain future, leaving his innocence behind him.

CHAPTER TWENTY THREE

Mujahid was powerless in a cage on a wagon, and it wasn't helping his mood. A group of ten guards marched in front of the wagon, which was pulled by two horses, and two guards marched behind. That's how it had been for the last several hours since his capture at Three Banks.

He had allowed himself to hope Tithian had changed, but the man was a traitor through and through. If Mujahid managed to get out of this cage, Tithian would pay a dear price for his treachery.

The wagon had bounced its way along East Bank's bumpy streets until it left the busy city behind. The terrain turned to dusty plains, and the sky changed from its ubiquitous pale yellow to amber.

Mujahid tried in vain to break free of the shield around his energy well. If he didn't escape soon it would be too late. The route they were on was taking them toward Arin's watch, where Tithian would have a ship already prepared. The man was a fool if he'd cross the Sea of Arin at this time of year.

The wagon slowed and Mujahid looked out through the bars of his cage. He had to look twice for fear he was hallucinating. A half league to the east, down a hill in a large valley, an army flying the banner of the Red Dragon of Religar was preparing a camp.

There must be twenty thousand soldiers in that valley.

The Union must have gone forward with its insane plan to invade Religar, and that would render the Treaty of Three Banks null and void. The only festering agreement keeping a full-scale war from erupting was no longer worth the paper it was written on. That army was here because Religar was certain the Shandarian Union wouldn't join the fight.

Tithian's betrayal seemed like a trivial irritant next to this.

The army filled the valley from one side to the other. Siege engines were spaced evenly twenty yards apart. This was more than retaliation for a border violation. This was conquest.

And it doesn't make sense, Mujahid thought.

The Emperor could scarcely afford the border skirmishes with the Shandarian Union. How could he sustain a war with the Kingdom of Tildem?

"Guards," Tithian said as he walked around to the rear of the wagon. "Leave us."

Two guards saluted and left.

Tithian stopped behind the wagon, never taking his eyes off the army.

"Now do you understand?" Tithian said.

There were questions that Mujahid needed answered. Was there a secret alliance between the Shandarian Union and the Empire? Had the border skirmishes been a ruse? Stranger things had happened in Mujahid's lifetime.

"You see an army," Tithian said. "Men, catapults, ballistae, mounts, whores, and everything else that takes part in the games of men. But you don't see the real evil—the puppet master with his hands on the strings, making nations dance to the music of a divine plan. *His* plan."

Mujahid squinted at Tithian.

"He killed him. And I watched through the necrolens as he raised him up and brought war to Erindor."

"Speak plainly, man," Mujahid said. "Who killed whom? Who raised whom?"

"I was a fool. You were right all those years ago. He was just a man all along."

"This is Kagan's doing?"

Tithian told Mujahid how Kagan had killed the Religarian emissary and used necromancy, a magic Kagan himself had forbidden, to start a war.

When Tithian had finished, Mujahid pitied him. It had taken decades, but Kagan had betrayed Tithian just as he had betrayed Mujahid.

"And I know why," Tithian said. "He needs the eyes of the world focused away from the Pinnacle."

"No." Mujahid swept his gaze across the valley. "This is consolidation of power. He'll use the Religarian Empire to conquer, and then he'll assert his *divine leadership* over that fanatic of an emperor, who will, no doubt, hand Kagan control on a platter. The Three Kingdoms will cease to exist. Kagan will rule all of Erindor."

"You can't confront him now."

"That army is on its way to Arin's Watch. I can do something about that."

"Arin's watch is lost already, man. That valley holds twenty thousand battle-hardened Religarian soldiers. Even if I join you, how long do you think two necromancers would last against *that*?"

"What do you mean *if* you join me?"

"Kagan doesn't know I'm aware of what he did. I can still try to subvert his plans from within the Pinnacle."

"This smells of—"

"King Donal is the only sovereign in the Three Kingdoms who takes a stand against Kagan. Your place is with him...for the sake of us all."

Mujahid considered. As much as he didn't want to admit it, Tithian was right. If Mujahid had any hope to gather a coven of necromancers to go against Kagan, he'd have to protect Tildem. He held up his arms and clanged his chains against the bars.

"Will the king be joining me in my cage?"

Tithian retrieved a small sphere from his cloak and handed it to Mujahid. "I believe you know what this is. It will take you to a cave outside Rotham."

"I should have known. This is how you disappeared from the boat."

"No," Tithian said and held up a second orb. "*This* is how I disappeared from the boat. The one you're holding is what I went back for. I wasn't betraying you, Mujahid. I was saving your life."

The shield around Mujahid's well disappeared and his chains broke free. A guard turned at the sound of metal hitting the cage floor, but Tithian waved him away.

"I'll forgive you for trying to kill me if you forgive me for arresting you," Tithian said and smiled.

Mujahid looked out over the valley once more.

"Let's survive this war," Mujahid said. "Then we'll tend to forgiveness."

Mujahid channeled power into the orb and the world disappeared in a flash of blinding light.

Mujahid materialized inside a small cave, which was no more than six feet across by ten feet deep. He glanced around, making sure no one had seen him appear. A lone snake hissed in the corner, dark-brown jasper in color with no identifying marks. A harmless *anklebite*. Other than that he was alone.

At least he found a private place to attune the orb.

He dropped the orb and crushed it under the heel of his boot, grinding it to a black powder. It wouldn't do to be in possession of a magic object if he was captured again.

The anklebite slithered through the remains of the crushed orb toward the entrance, tasting the stagnant air with its forked tongue as it passed.

The cave opened onto a dusty plain that looked much like the one he had just left.

Such a shame.

He'd gotten used to it over the years, but of all the evil he expected the barrier to bring, he never expected this. Tildem had once been a land of rolling green hills. Now, lifeless tree trunks stood like statues in a cemetery, arms outstretched over a land that would never rise again. If he couldn't bring that barrier down, the whole of Erindor would be a cemetery.

The Great Orm River flowed less than one hundred yards to his left, rushing south on in its eternal march toward King's Bay. He estimated it was close to a mile across. The river only reached that breadth at Rotham. He was close.

As he made his way toward Rotham on Orm, Mujahid tried to remember when he'd last seen it. It was before the creation of the Great Barrier.

He remembered the brilliant turquoise sky over the castle of the Tanmor kings, and how a person could eat off of the streets without fear of getting sick. The citizens of Rotham took great pride in their city.

They were unlike any he had met elsewhere. He remembered people approaching him on the street who wished to show him around, or teach him about the history of the streets he walked.

He recalled how majestic the city's two main plazas were. Marble fountains surrounded by intricately carved obelisks, which detailed the history of Tildem, beginning with its war for independence from the Erindorian Empire, and ending with the reign of the last Westbury king. The story played out in two parts, and a person would have to visit both plazas to see all of it. Strict laws kept merchants out of the plazas, forcing them to ply their trade along the many twisting city streets, creating a bustling atmosphere of citizens, businessmen and street sweepers.

The city gates rose in the distance, as did the power in his well. He'd enter through the northern gate, close to his favorite inn, The Dancing Shriller. The building was a marvel of non-magical construction, shaped like a triangle with a rounded front corner, at the intersection of two streets that met at an acute angle.

He knew he should lower his expectations, but nothing could have prepared Mujahid for what he saw.

Rotham had become a ghost town. The remains of stone pathways lay strewn in pieces, intermingled with debris from once grand buildings lying in ruin. The few people walking toward the gate crossed to the other side of the street when they saw him. He could almost smell the fear.

The fetid stench of death reached Mujahid's nostrils and he covered his mouth and nose. His power increased as he approached the gate, but now it came upon him in a great wave. Disgust mingled with confusion as he watched two men drag a corpse toward a pile of bodies stacked against the northern wall.

Is it a plague?

"You there," he said to a woman passing by. "What is the meaning of this?"

She looked down and picked up her pace.

Mujahid swore.

Tithian had once asked him what he thought would happen if the world abandoned the old religion and forswore allegiance to the gods. The answer was written on every corpse in that pile.

The scene repeated itself every couple of blocks. People piling corpses into reeking stacks of decay. This was madness.

He came to the triangular intersection where he had hoped to find his favorite inn. It was no longer recognizable as a building. A familiar turquoise shape caught his attention in the rubble and he stooped to take a closer look. It was the remains of a sign. The lower half of a shriller.

Exhaustion and depression overcame him. Destruction and decay surrounded him, pressing in on him, and he laid the blame squarely at Kagan's feet.

Nuuan should be here, somewhere.

There was no time to lose. William's idea had been sound. The Great Library was no more than a few blocks away, and if anything had been written about barrier magic it would be there.

The sound of boots clacking against the pavement caught his attention and he turned, but there was no one. And the sound had stopped as quickly as he stood.

He shook off the uneasy feeling and left The Dancing Shriller behind, praying silently that he'd learn something of use at the library.

There were no death piles this far into the city, but the smell permeated the air through shifting winds.

Mujahid was on guard after hearing the boots near the ruined inn, but the sound never returned.

The library was easy to find. The shining white structure, capped with five domes, four smaller domes at the corners and one large dome at the center, soared high above the skyline of ruined buildings.

A polished marble staircase leading up to the library was cracked in various places, but the main structure was intact. The library was a masterwork of masonry. The building and everything in it was carved from a single piece of marble, predating the Kingdom. Some said it predated the Erindorian Empire.

The interior was a maze of stone bookcases that rose to the ceiling, carved out of the floor itself. Massive inset slabs of quartz in the ceiling, spaced every fifty yards, allowed natural light to fill the building. Mujahid made a mental note to be far away from those slabs if another quake began.

"May I be of assistance," a voice said, catching Mujahid off guard. He squinted through hazy light.

A gaunt man, who looked as old as the library itself, approached with the assistance of a walking stick.

A brief wave of nausea passed over Mujahid. The sensation reminded him of his awakening, many years ago. He felt disoriented and lightheaded, as if his mind wasn't processing what his eyes were seeing.

"You'll be safe enough under the stone, sir," the man said. His face was devoid of expression. "They'll not be falling to the ground any time soon." The man glanced up at the ceiling before settling his gaze on Mujahid. "And if they do, you'll not live long enough to care."

Mujahid smiled. "Perhaps you can be of help, librarian."

"My name is Saul," the man said, his face never changing from that stony expression.

"Saul," Mujahid said. "I have a problem, and I believe the answer lies somewhere within these tomes of yours."

"And you would be Mujahid Lord Mukhtaar."

Mujahid's chest tightened. Not only did the old man know he was a Mukhtaar Lord, but he knew *which* Mukhtaar Lord.

"Your identity is safe with me," Saul said. "There is no knowledge in Erindor that does not exist under this roof, and knowledge is dangerous. I don't merely give it away because someone asks for it."

"Lower your voice, man." Mujahid looked around to see if anyone had heard, but if there was anyone else in the library, he couldn't see them.

"What type of problem could one such as yourself have?" Saul said.

"A *historical* problem."

"The historical references are deeper within." Saul ambled up the path between two massive bookcases.

The stacks reached from floor to ceiling and were filled with bound works of all shapes and sizes. They stood like monoliths in yellow beams of light that shone through the quartz windows, casting ominous shadows on the floor below.

The place seemed empty, but Mujahid couldn't shake the feeling that he was being watched.

"What period of time are you interested in?" Saul asked.

"The creation of the Great Barrier."

Saul stopped. After a moment he faced Mujahid. "Excuse me, my Lord, but I was under the impression you were present when it was created."

"Many plans were hidden from me during my tenure at the Pinnacle. Plans I would seek to understand now. I did not support, nor take part in the creation of that monstrosity in the sky."

"I would think not, given how much the archmage hates you," Saul said.

"Which Order did you profess vows to, Saul?" There wasn't a library in Erindor that wasn't operated by a religious order, and something about this Saul intrigued him.

"I'm partial to the Order of Arin, but I profess no vows. I am content to play my part while the priests of this world worry over theological and philosophical matters. I am a layperson, one might say."

There was something odd about Saul's choice of words, but Mujahid couldn't determine what it was that triggered his suspicion.

"Any tome covering world events around the time of the barrier's creation will be helpful," Mujahid said.

Saul's eyes moved back and forth, as if he were trying to remember something.

Saul gestured toward a large table and chairs. "I will select some reference works. But understand that without specific direction, this may be a futile search."

Mujahid spent the next couple of hours reading through texts as Saul brought them to him. Most were standard works of history that every Mukhtaar clan necromancer had read. He skimmed through them anyway, hoping to find some spark of knowledge he hadn't considered before, but he found nothing new.

A dull thud made him turn toward the nearest stack. Again the sensation of being observed washed over him. But no one was there. It was probably the old man dropping a book.

Saul walked out from behind the stack, confirming Mujahid's suspicion.

Maybe I'm approaching the problem the wrong way.

"Let's focus on histories that are...somewhat less popular," Mujahid said.

"What did you have in mind?"

"Do you maintain histories of the religious orders here?"

"Religion often drives the course of world events. One cannot fully understand history without considering the influence of the temples."

"Let's start with the Order of Arin. I'll work my way through more obscure orders if I find nothing interesting."

"As you wish."

Saul returned a few minutes later with a stack of three large books. He took the first off the top and handed it to Mujahid.

The title intrigued Mujahid — *The Great Debate*. Mujahid was well versed in philosophy, but he wasn't aware of any world event that could bare the lofty title of *The Great Debate*. The book was covered in dust that threatened to start him coughing as he opened it, but the reason for the title became obvious after the first paragraph.

The author identified himself as the Chief Scribe of the General Superior of the Order of Arin. This book wasn't intended for the public. This was a secret history of the Order of Arin. Religious orders believed theological discussions were above the comprehension of the laity, so they often kept such discussions secret until they came to consensus. The records of these discussions were kept in a secret history, which the Order used in the theological training of novices.

In several places, the book referred to something it called the *Last Word of Arin*, but it was short on details. It was as if the scribe assumed the reader would know what he was writing about.

A passage about the archmage so surprised him that he had to read it a second time. Kagan had approached the Order of Arin for help in constructing the Great Barrier. Mujahid was never aware of this. According to the history, the priesthood rejected the archmage's request, quoting the Archbishop of Arin as saying "I cannot agree to be complicit in such an act without calling a general assembly. It is my opinion that our god would reject this request outright, and therefore we will debate this matter as an Order and act as one body, as our god would wish us to do."

The Great Debate took place at the Temple of Arin, here in Rotham. The order sided with the Archbishop and rejected the creation of the barrier as violating basic tenets of their theology. When the Archbishop of Arin informed the archmage of the Order's decision, Kagan declared the possession of magic items to be illegal outside of the Pinnacle and removed the Great Orb of Arin from the High Temple.

The Order declared every divine communication from that point forward, as relayed by Kagan, to be treated as false prophecy. They agreed to keep this knowledge secret from the world until definitive proof could be obtained.

Mujahid laid the book down and leaned back in his chair. This was unprecedented. Kagan, as archmage, was the conduit of the voice of the gods. It wasn't possible for him to utter false prophecy. There were safeguards. *Divine* safeguards.

What would cause an entire Order to turn against its own god?

The archmage was the Order's conduit to Arin through the Rite of Manifestation. Without the archmage, and the Rite, there would be no communication scrolls. The Order existed to serve the archmage, so that the archmage could serve Arin.

What they did was tantamount to rejecting their calling.

He needed to speak to the order himself. He'd pay a visit to the Temple of Arin and see what information he could rattle out of the local bishop.

The click-clack of hard-soled boots echoed on the marble floor.

He had been right all along. He was being watched.

Mujahid turned to see two Tildem Royal Guardsmen approaching. The royal guard wore no armor except blue linen coats, fastened from neck to waist with large gold buttons, hanging down over snug leather breeches. Sabers hung in ornamental scabbards, covered in gold leaf, giving the impression they were more ceremonial than practical.

Mujahid stood and the chair fell backward with a loud crash.

One of the guards raised his hands, as if in surrender.

Knocking the chair over had been unintentional, but it had a pleasing effect. He didn't embrace the power, knowing that his eyes would give him away.

"We're not here to arrest you, sir," the guard said.

That's a first.

"We're on the business of King Donal. We've been following you...on the King's orders, of course. We mean you no ill will. He wishes to speak with you."

"Why the dramatic entrance? Why not just ask me out on the street instead of spying on me?"

"As I said. We're on the business of the king."

Refusing would just make a mess of things. Besides, he was here for this very reason.

Mujahid smiled. "How can I refuse the king?"

CHAPTER TWENTY FOUR

Mujahid entered the audience chamber and all eyes turned to him. Members of court were gathered in small circles in private discussions, but everyone became silent as he approached the king.

The audience chamber of King Donal Tanmor rested at the heart of Rotham Castle. Functional tapestries depicting the crest of the Tanmor dynasty and its vassals hung from the wall. Where other royal families surrounded themselves with gold and other precious metals, there was nothing here that didn't serve a practical purpose.

King Donal sat on a large stone chair at the far end of the chamber, behind a small table, dressed much the same as the Royal Guard.

The king was young, close in age to Nicolas. He had not yet been born the last time Mujahid visited Rotham. His father, the first Tanmor king, had been an imposing figure with long hair and beard, but Donal was average of height and build. His hair was as long and unkempt as his father's, and his face hadn't seen a blade in too long. His bearing was statuesque, regal, and Mujahid would know he was the king even if he dressed like a pauper. But there was something violent just beneath the surface that Mujahid couldn't identify.

Mujahid bowed at the waist. Protocol demanded he avert his eyes, but Mujahid stared at Donal. Was the king's authoritative presence real, or would it collapse under the gaze of a forceful personality?

"Your Majesty," Mujahid said.

Donal stared back, expressionless as he rested his chin in his hand.

Mujahid lowered his eyes. He had his answer.

"Was it your mother or father who believed you would be a 'fighter for the gods', *Mujahid*?" Donal asked. "Or are you a zealot?"

"Your Majesty's grasp of the old tongue is impressive. It was my father who named me. After—"

"After one of the Thirteen. Yes, I've read the *Origines*. I've even studied the *Coteonic Commentaries*. It was a different time when a father felt comfortable naming a son after one of the first necromancers."

"Indeed, Majesty."

"Rise," Donal said. "Please, take a seat."

Mujahid sat in the chair Donal had indicated and gathered his thoughts. It was vital he leave this meeting with Donal's friendship.

"Tell me, Magus, do you hail from Religar?" Donal asked.

Was the king being cautious or paranoid? Mujahid hoped the former, but whatever was hiding under Donal's composure made him wonder.

"I consider myself politically agnostic, your Majesty." Donal's support of necromancy notwithstanding, necromancy was anathema, and a ruler who violated religious decree soon felt the wrath of his own people.

"If you are indeed Religarian, you would do well to mention it now." Donal said. His gaze swept downward at Mujahid's robe. "You favor their...mode of dress." He looked straight into Mujahid's eyes without lifting his head.

This wasn't about Religar at all. Mujahid dressed like a Council magus, so Donal would think him sympathetic to the archmage. He would have to quell this fear immediately.

"I merely seek sanctuary within your borders."

That should grab his attention.

"Sanctuary?" Donal smiled. "You've missed your mark by about three hundred miles. The Pinnacle is in the Sea of Arin."

"It's the Pinnacle I need sanctuary *from*, Majesty."

Donal lost his smile. He leaned forward in his chair. "Clear the court."

Definitely grabbed his attention.

The doors shut with a loud crash, Donal spoke. "You are leaving me with few choices. I need to know *precisely* who you are and why you're here."

"I was an acquaintance of your Majesty's kingly father. He was known for his sense of honor and fairness. Unusual quality for the first king of a dynasty. I was sad to hear of his passing. But the king I see before me assuages my sadness. A powerful man rules in Tildem."

"I would prefer your identity to flattery, magus."

Mujahid straightened in his chair. "Then know that I am Mujahid Lord Mukhtaar, banished Prime Warlock of the archmage Kagan."

The king's face lost some of its color.

"Need I remind you that necromancy is outlawed in the three kingdoms, *Lord* Mujahid? Mukhtaar Lord or no, if the archmage closes the temples, the people will revolt. Tell me why I should help you, and choose your words with care."

"Many years ago I was granted a prophecy by the goddess Shealynd," Mujahid said. "I believed in the fulfillment of that prophecy for decades."

"You no longer believe?"

"May I ask your Majesty how much you know about the creation of the Great Barrier?"

"An armada of Barathosian ships threatened Erindor, and the archmage created the barrier to keep them out. He blamed the attack on necromancy and outlawed the old religion. I've read the histories."

"I've *lived* the histories," Mujahid said. "They're incomplete. Did your father tell you of the infant who disappeared when the Great Barrier was formed?"

"A rogue necromancer kidnapped the babe. Some say *you* were that necromancer."

"The child was kidnapped, but not in any manner you or the chroniclers suspect. The boy was taken to another world by a force I do not yet understand, and returned to us by that same force."

Mujahid recounted Nicolas's story. Donal appeared awestruck that Nicolas was gone forty years, but seemed to age only twenty.

Donal stood and paced for a short time, furrowing his brow. His expression became deadpan once more.

"What I'm about to show you could bring about the downfall of my dynasty," Donal said. "I trust you'll see we hold each other over the same barrel."

Mujahid felt a release of power, and for a moment he expected an attack, but no attack came. A crackling sound filled the room, and an undead penitent appeared from nowhere and stood before Donal. A brief struggle registered on Donal's face as the penitent raised its arm over its head to strike. Mujahid embraced power, preparing to expel a wall of force.

The penitent lowered its arm and backed away.

Mujahid sat in stunned silence before finding his voice. "I was correct in more ways than one when I said a powerful king rules in Tildem."

Donal was a necromancer, and that changed everything. But Mujahid was concerned. Donal had awakened to his power, but his skills were no better than a novice.

"You lack control," Mujahid said.

"I have had no one to guide me other than a letter from my father. I would appreciate your wisdom, Lord Mukhtaar."

"This explains your position on necromancy," Mujahid said. "My first advice to you, King Donal, is tell no man about this unless you are certain you can trust him with your life. As for my *second* advice...you may find it disturbing."

"Speak your mind."

Mujahid told Donal about the army setting up camp across his northern border.

Donal swallowed.

"Do not lose hope just yet, Majesty. There is still time to gather information and deal with the *real* threat."

"I know of no greater threat to my kingdom."

"If you sever the head of a snake, its body withers and dies."

"Did you find anything in the Great Library?"

"I must speak with the Bishop of Arin. He knows something he hasn't shared with the rest of us."

"The bishop is an approachable man."

"There's a complication," Mujahid said.

Donal cocked his head.

"I discovered this information in a secret history of the order," Mujahid said. "It's a wonder the book was there. Were it not for your librarian, Saul, I would have never thought to search for it. The idea of finding—"

"What did you say?"

"It was in a secret history. The order will never divulge—"

"No. The librarian," Donal said. "The Great Library of Rotham did, indeed, have a librarian named Saul. He was my tutor when I was a child. But he's been dead for ten years."

Mujahid recalled the feeling of nausea when he met Saul. But Saul was flesh and blood.

"Majesty, with respect...the man who stood before me was alive. I am sure you know enough of the art to understand how I am certain of that."

"I'll pay a visit to the library myself. If my old dead tutor is roaming the halls, I would know of it. In the meantime, I can assist you with the complication you mentioned."

"I would be indebted to you, Majesty. That is no small thing."

"I'll have quarters prepared close to mine. A sealed letter will arrive there shortly. Present it to the Bishop, seal intact. It should loosen his lips for you."

"Thank you, your Majesty."

"About that debt you spoke of," Donal said. "You mentioned my skills lack control?"

Mujahid smiled and nodded. "I will train you personally, Majesty, throughout the length of my stay in your city."

King Donal nodded and left the audience chamber.

Mujahid had never met a ruler worth protecting...until today.

Mujahid waited in his quarters reeling from the knowledge that Donal was a necromancer.

A Tanmor king who was a necromancer was precisely what the world needed right now, and Mujahid was certain Zubuxo would have known that decades ago.

Zubuxo's hand was all over this. A Mukhtaar Lord could offer his clan mystical protection, but a king could offer political protection. And sometimes political protection was more valuable.

It didn't take long for the sealed letter to arrive, which was a relief. He was anxious to be off for the Temple of Arin.

Every couple of blocks he saw another stack of rotting corpses, which, he was told, the people had taken to calling *death piles*. He had to cover his nose and mouth to protect himself from the fetid odor whenever the wind would shift. Religious law forbade cremation and mass graves, but certainly leaving a pile of decaying bodies in the street was worse than violating a moral code of questionable origin.

Two guards pulling a wagon approached the rotting stack and started loading it with bodies.

Finally. Someone is doing something.

"Where are you taking them?" Mujahid asked.

"Where do you think?" A guard said. "The Orm." He lifted the legs of the next corpse as his partner grabbed the arms.

Mujahid had a hard time concealing his shock. "These are people. You can't dump them in the river like trash."

The guard looked at Mujahid. "You been living in a cave? The Death Collectors take them. We load the barges, and off they go to the gods know where."

"Why aren't they buried? Don't their families object?"

"Don't you get it? Quakes are killing people faster than we can collect the bodies. The temple priests can't keep up with the funerals. If you want to be helpful, grab an arm or shut up."

"What about—" He almost said *the undead*. With necromancy outlawed, a prime source of manual labor was no longer available.

Mujahid passed two other death piles on the way to the library, but he saw no other wagons.

He tried to refocus on the task at hand. He needed a cool head and a discerning eye.

Similar to the Great Library, the Temple of Arin shone like a white gem in the otherwise filthy streets. Great stone buttresses leaned against the sides of the Temple as if the builders thought it might fly apart. Crenelated towers, slightly taller than the main building, surrounded the temple, and the entire structure was crowned by three domes, the center dome being the largest. A statue of the Great Helm of Arin rested on top of the center dome, almost as large as the dome itself.

The smoky interior offered some respite from the smell of Rotham. Candles made from fragrant insect wax gave off a mild honey scent and cast ethereal shadows that danced around the marble columns lining the nave.

Quartz panels, stained in numerous vibrant colors, lined the temple's apse and formed a mosaic of the god Arin, resplendent in his golden helm and armor. A multihued orb rested at Arin's feet, and the spiraling iridescent colors on its surface reminded Mujahid of how they swirled around the surface of the real orb.

Chanting priests brought his attention to a funeral taking place in the apse. The bodies of several people lay across a table while the priests performed some invented ceremony designed to assuage the grief of the friends and loved ones.

In days past, a necromantic funeral—a *real* funeral—would take place in a temple of Zubuxo. Surviving members of the family would be allowed to communicate with the deceased, if the state of the corpse didn't make such an act unseemly. But now the temples were gone, destroyed during Kagan's *Great Purge* of necromancy. Arin's temples became flooded with people who had questions the Arinian priests couldn't answer.

Mujahid reconsidered. He would have to show these priests more respect. Their job was more difficult than his, because they possessed no real power.

The ceremony ended and Mujahid began the long walk down the temple's nave. The Bishop and priests started toward the sacristy, a room used for ceremonial garments and vessels, but when Mujahid approached, the bishop stopped and turned.

"May I be of assistance, Magus?" the bishop asked.

Mujahid had to look twice. It had been forty years, but he recognized the man as Archbishop Jonathan Kalim, General Superior of the Order of Arin. The archbishop once ran the largest community of Arinian priests in Erindor, at the High Temple on Pilgrim's Landing, until Kagan claimed authority over the temple and banished the archbishop.

An expression of surprise appeared on Jonathan's aging face. "I know you. But no, he had a twin. Forgive me sir, but may I presume it is Nuuan Lord Mukhtaar that stands before me?"

"No, Excellency," Mujahid said. The look of relief was obvious on Jonathan's face.

"Mujahid Lord Mukhtaar," Jonathan said in a hushed voice. "I wouldn't believe it if I didn't see you standing here with my own eyes. You survived the Purge."

"I wish our reunion was under better circumstances. I come to you for clarity on a matter I've recently become privy to."

"I will try," Jonathan said, shrugging. "My aging mind may not be up to the challenge, I'm afraid."

"You're as clever as you ever were, I'm sure, Excellency," Mujahid said. He was under no illusions about the archbishop's mental capacity. There was a fine line between religion and politics, if one existed at all, and a man didn't rise to the top of his order if he wasn't a master politician.

Jonathan smiled, but Mujahid knew his friendly demeanor wouldn't last.

"What do you know of the Great Debate?" Mujahid said.

Several of the priests gasped, and Mujahid offered them an innocent smile. On the list of things he enjoyed in this life, surprising people was near the top.

"Forgive me, Lord Mujahid." Jonathan's face became an expressionless mask. "You're straying into territory I cannot assist you with."

Mujahid handed the archbishop the sealed document from King Donal, making sure the Tanmor royal seal was visible.

Archbishop Jonathan read the letter and looked up.

"There is a reason that information is privileged, Lord Mukhtaar." The anger in Jonathan's voice was unmistakable, and he waved the letter at Mujahid. "These are matters not meant to be discussed outside of the order. If you have a shred of decency, you would reconsider your request."

"I'm usually a decent person. But I'm afraid you caught me on a bad day."

"I'm tempted to have you removed, necromancer, and deal with the king myself. He was probably misled by your air of authority. There is no greater god than Arin."

The archbishop threw the royal letter at Mujahid's feet.

Mujahid stepped toward the archbishop until he could feel the man's breath on his face. "I wish to neither reveal your order's secrets, nor use them against you. But if you don't give me the information I seek, I'll slit your throat and take your secrets from your corpse. Then you'll discover just how expensive the sins of a priest are."

A bead of sweat rolled down the archbishop's face and splashed on the ground next to the letter.

"Leave us," Jonathan said over his shoulder.

When the last priest disappeared behind the veil of the sacristy, Jonathan faced Mujahid. "Ask your questions."

"Why did the Order refuse to help the Pinnacle?"

"We acted in your defense, you know."

"Me?"

"We knew the archmage planned to outlaw necromancy, but none of us understood why. Not until he requested the use of the orb. There can be no purification without necromancy, everyone knows this. I'm no fool."

"Why did he need the orb?"

"Some of us deduced he intended to channel a new form of energy — vitapotency—into the orb. He believed it would stop the Barathosian Empire."

Mujahid raised his eyebrow. "Channeling energy into an orb of power is usually ill-advised."

"The Orb of Arin is the only means we have to verify the authenticity of the god's communication scrolls. As far as we know, if the orb were destroyed, Arin may not be able to communicate with us at all. We could not allow him to have it."

"Yet he has it."

"The Pinnacle guard overpowered us and took it by force. Archmage Kagan commanded our silence."

Mujahid remembered entering the Grand Sanctuary with Kagan during the Rite of Manifestation all those years ago. The orb shouldn't have been there...but it was.

"Was that what your order refers to as the 'Last Word of Arin'?" Mujahid asked.

Jonathan shook his head and frowned. "No. You don't understand at all. As far as we know, communication with Arin ceased forty years ago."

"That's not possible." Tithian's chilling words returned... *The last time you saw the gods was the last time I saw them.*

"We may not possess mystical powers like the priests of Zubuxo, Lord Mukhtaar, but we do recognize our god's voice when we hear it. And I can assure you, his voice is not to be found in any Pinnacle proclamation since the formation of the Great Barrier."

"This...no. You must be mistaken."

"There is something you should see."

Jonathan turned and headed toward the sacristy.

Mujahid picked up the king's letter and read while he walked.

> *Archbishop Kalim,*
> *You may find yourself reticent to divulge the*
> *information requested by Lord Mukhtaar. You have my*
> *understanding and sympathy. I do, however, caution*

*you against refusing. The climate at the Pinnacle is not
conducive to good health for renegade bishops.
His Majesty, Donal Tanmor.*

Mujahid was going to get along well with this king. He tucked the
letter into his robe and followed the archbishop.

T he sacristy was a long, rectangular room, ten feet wide by twenty
feet deep. Incense and the honeyed scent of candle wax hung
heavy on the air from centuries of constant ritual. But there was
another smell that caught Mujahid by surprise. Wood. A *lot* of wood.

An ornate maple cabinet, with inset cherry borders and copper
fixtures, hung on a wall above a long mahogany counter. A matching
mahogany kneeler, inlaid with gold leaf images of Arin and the Great
Orb, rested beneath it next to the counter. A reddish-brown hickory
wardrobe ran the length of the opposite wall.

The wood in this room, if divided and sold, would feed Clan
Mukhtaar for a century.

Jonathan side-stepped the kneeler and opened the cabinet, taking
from it a large cherry box covered in gold and silver filigree. The ends of
two maple posts stuck up from the top of the box, which Jonathan was
careful not to catch on the rim of the cabinet. He kissed the filigree
pattern, and then carried the box to the mahogany counter, where he
unlatched a locking mechanism and opened it. Inside the box a fabric
scroll wound around the two carved maple posts, which Jonathan also
ritually kissed. He took the scroll from the box and laid it down on the
counter as if he were handling a precious egg. He reached under the
counter to a mahogany shelf and retrieved a collection of loose
parchments. He set them on the counter next to the scroll and rolled the
maple posts apart.

"The wood you're ogling is nothing next to this," Jonathan said. "This
is the most valuable relic we possess. Within this scroll are the collected
words of our god, spoken throughout history at the Rite of
Manifestation, and verified by the Orb of Arin. Every time Arin speaks
during the Rite, the scroll expands. When the Orb is present, the words
change from black to gold."

Mujahid smirked. "You're telling me that with a quill and some ink I
could take control of your order?"

"The scroll is immutable. You could place it in fire and it wouldn't burn."

"And these," Mujahid asked, indicating the loose parchments.

"It's impractical to carry the scroll everywhere, so scribes have copied the unverified words of Arin into these documents for further study. They contain every communication that has taken place since the theft of the Orb forty years ago."

Something wasn't right. If the number of parchments were any indication, there were more proclamations during the last forty years than in all of recorded history prior to the creation of the Great Barrier. Either Arin had a lot more to say lately, or someone other than Arin was doing the talking.

"Arin speaks only during the Rite of Manifestation—"

"Once per year," Jonathan said, finishing Mujahid's sentence. "Yet these parchments suggest Arin has begun appearing to the archmage dozens of times per year."

"Forgive me, Archbishop. It's been many years since I last gazed on the Book of Life. May I examine these?"

Jonathan nodded.

Mujahid read for more than an hour, comparing proclamations from decades ago with the most recent ones, trying to find some change in the pattern.

He searched for common themes, but the recent proclamations covered every minutia of life. Perhaps the lack of a common theme might be the evidence he needed? Evidence of what, however, he didn't know. He turned to the last sheet of loose parchment.

His heart raced when he read a declaration that mentioned his ancestral home. When he comprehended what he was reading, he allowed himself a small laugh. The proof he had sought for forty years was right in front of him. He offered a silent prayer of thanks that he hadn't marched on the Pinnacle.

Jonathan's eyebrows lifted when Mujahid laughed.

"Nuuan would love this," Mujahid said.

"I'm sorry?" Jonathan said.

"Do you believe in the truth of divine proclamations, Archbishop?" The question was rhetorical. Mujahid was well aware of the Order's beliefs.

"When a proclamation is verified by the Great Orb, it is beyond question."

"Have you ever known two or more proclamations to contradict one another?"

"Of course not. One of them would be false."

"What if a proclamation made a statement that, by definition, could not be true?"

"The same question phrased differently, is it not? I assume this discussion is academic, Lord Mukhtaar. So allow me to clarify and say that what you are asking is impossible if a proclamation has been verified."

"Humor me."

"I would question the source, and instruct my priests to do the same. Demonic influence in world events isn't unheard of—you of all people are aware of this, *Lord* Mukhtaar."

Mujahid ignored the remark. There was a legend the Mukhtaar Lords allied with demons. Another claimed they were demons themselves in league with Hasat'Tan. Neither was precisely true, but the poor man would never sleep again if he knew the whole truth.

"But the end result is you would not attribute the words to Arin, correct?" Mujahid asked.

"I believe that is what I said."

"Read this out loud for me." Mujahid handed Jonathan the parchment.

Jonathan cleared his throat and started reading. "People of Erindor, mark this day. The city of Paradise has been destroyed. Its orb of power lies in ruin, and the magic of death scatters." Jonathan lowered the parchment. "Forgive me, Lord Mukhtaar, but I fail to see the humor here."

"What would you say if I told you this proclamation contains a statement that is absolutely false?"

Jonathan inched closer. "I'm listening."

"The city of Paradise never had an orb of power in its possession, Archbishop. But the settlement of Paradise *Minor* did."

"What? Let me see that." Jonathan leaned in close and examined the document.

"The city of Paradise is the ancestral home of my clan, and only a Mukhtaar Lord, and those to be tested, know its location. I can tell you with certainty that Paradise stands, and its orb of power is not destroyed...because it never contained an orb of power. The Mukhtaar orb was housed in a different location, a small permanent settlement on the outskirts of Paradise."

Jonathan's expression changed and Mujahid could see the man starting to comprehend.

"It...no," Jonathan held the parchment closer to his eyes. "They destroyed the wrong city."

"They destroyed the wrong city," Mujahid repeated and smiled. "When the Great Purge began, we brought our clan members close to our ancestral home, to provide them with as much protection as we could. But Nuuan, in a moment of brilliance...or deviousness, thought it would be best to ignore custom. He spread the word that this small settlement was, in fact, our ancestral home of Paradise. Not Paradise Minor. Until this moment, he and I were the only two people in Erindor who knew otherwise. Now tell me, Archbishop, do you believe the gods would know the true location of Paradise?"

"Archmage Kagan believed the lie," Jonathan said. "It was right in front of us."

"Don't be too hard on yourself. You had no way of knowing. My brother's deception uncovered something sinister beyond imagining. I'm afraid your initial suspicions are confirmed. These so-called divine proclamations are forgeries. And that can mean only one thing."

Jonathan's face drained of color. "By Arin, I was right. The archmage has found a way to counterfeit the Book of Life."

And that meant Kagan was far more powerful than Mujahid had given him credit for. Kagan was a tyrant, but a false prophet too? To forge a page in the Book of Life required a power beyond imagining. Kagan would have had to find a way to defeat mystical safeguards devised by Arin himself. If Mujahid had followed his instinct and marched on the Pinnacle alone, Kagan would have destroyed him.

But now Mujahid knew what he was up against. He couldn't guarantee the outcome, but at least he could prepare.

"I am at a complete loss, Lord Mukhtaar. For the first time in my ministry I have no idea how to shepherd my flock."

"I can't offer you counsel on that subject, Archbishop," Mujahid said. "But I will tell you what I must do. I will seek the king's assistance in accomplishing what I failed to do forty years ago. A tyrant and false prophet sits on the Obsidian Throne. And I cannot allow this to stand."

CHAPTER TWENTY FIVE

Y ou learned a valuable lesson today," Lamil said.
Nicolas didn't want to hear it. He was numb, as if he were
observing someone else from a distance. Detached. Empty.
He walked closer to the Orb of Zubuxo.

"You are a necromancer," Lamil said. "When life finally leaves your
body, you will make the journey to the Plane of Death with the blood of
many men on your hands. It is the horrible certainty of our vocation."

Vocation. Nicolas heard that word many times growing up Catholic,
used by well-intended priests seeking new recruits. Vocation meant
many things to him, but being a killer wasn't one of them.

"Let's just agree to disagree."

Lamil looked Nicolas up and down in a gesture that was familiar to
Nicolas now. A gesture of thoughtful consideration, as if the speaker
were choosing his next words with care.

"Our vocation is to take on the sins of our penitent," Lamil said. "You
know the namocea. You do not merely witness the evil that person
commits...you *desire* it as much as they do, because for a brief moment in
time you *are* the person you summon. You never feel clean again, do
you?"

Nicolas stared straight ahead.

"Yet with each summoning," Lamil said, "you must strive to make it part of yourself in a way that pushes you closer to perfection, not farther away. The great challenge of our office is to take on the sins of the universe without becoming evil ourselves. Some fail. There are evil necromancers out there whose souls are as dark as the robes they wear. Never forget it. The midnight blue reminds us that we, too, are capable of much evil on the path to perfection."

Nicolas tried to calm himself by retreating into his cet. How could the siek, of all people, believe that killing was the right thing to do?

His calm exterior crumbled and his cet slipped away. He tried to force his mind into submission—the wrong thing to do, but he didn't care. He wanted to beat on something, even if only himself.

"There's something else I've learned from all those lifetimes," Nicolas said. "No one's beyond redemption, no matter how bad they were. Why did I have to be the instrument of Jurn's death? Was there no other way to learn the lesson?"

"Too much too soon," Lamil said.

"No!" Nicolas punched the Orb of Zubuxo, and his energy well drained like a water tower whose bottom fell out. The orb had pulled all the necropotency out of him. The deafening shriek of ripping metal exploded through the temple.

The sound faded and the world folded in on itself.

A bright light at the center of an abyss became a vortex of alternating black and grey cloud that pulled Nicolas deeper. He felt at peace within the swirling violence. He belonged there.

The mouth of the vortex swallowed him and a pinpoint of light grew larger in front of him. The pinpoint became a star burst too bright to look at, so he covered his eyes.

He felt ground underneath him and air circulating against his face. When he opened his eyes he was looking up.

The sky was black and starless, like the sky over the room of many doors in his hall of power. A small, red sphere appeared in the starless void and grew larger as it rushed toward him until it covered most of the visible sky. It was a desert planet, covered in red and orange terrain—

and not a drop of water that he could see. It came to a stop and rotated, casting light downward in rays like sunbeams through a cloud.

He stood on a high cliff of lifeless charcoal-grey ground that extended for miles to his sides and behind. In front lay a vast plain, tens of thousands of feet below, stretching into the distance ahead. The plain writhed like a snake, but as he stared he saw it wasn't the plain that was moving. An ocean of people stood on the plain, each facing away from him.

Most of them weren't human. He felt small, insignificant. His problems seemed childish now, as if the universe itself would laugh if he mentioned them.

Every time the desert planet in the sky rotated the beams of light would strike the rear of the plain, below the cliff he stood on, and countless souls would materialize, causing the plain to fill. When it reached its capacity it would shift and stretch to accommodate the millions who were coalescing from the rays of light.

He traced the sloping plain downward to a titanic black throne, taller than any mountain in his memory. Was the throne's height measured in feet or miles? He couldn't tell, but the answer soon became moot. The plain expanded once more and the empty throne grew along with it.

To the left of the throne was a mammoth black gate that grew at the same rate as the throne.

He knew where he was. Siek Lamil had spoken of it many times; the plain filled with souls, the giant throne, the gate...and the last thing Nicolas remembered touching was the Orb of Zubuxo.

He was standing over the Field of Judgment on the Plane of Death. The souls he saw were the countless multitude of penitents in need of purification. The throne belonged to Zubuxo, the God of Death. And if that was true, then the gate must be the entrance to the Plane of Peace. All the theology Lamil had taught was true...to the letter.

But what did it mean? What of his own religion? He wasn't the best Catholic in the world, he wasn't even sure how much he believed, but he was damned if he'd ever stop thinking of himself as Christian.

The field darkened. He looked back to the planet, which had been the source of much of the light in this place, and saw it retreating. It vanished, leaving the starless sky empty, but another took its place and rushed toward him. This one had vast oceans, and thick polar caps. It came to a stop and rotated, shining bright beams of light that struck the field before him, manifesting countless souls on the ever-expanding plain.

If he kept watching, would the Earth fill the sky and deposit its dead on the plain below as well?

Movement caught his attention. Something had noticed him. A ghost-like humanoid figure floated toward him on the cliff, its body more cloud than solid.

And he knew the person.

It was the skeletal warrior that killed the crag spider the day he met Mujahid...his first day in Erindor. He sensed a connection to the warrior, similar to the necromantic link, but subtle and delicate.

Fear bubbled to the surface. The connection he sensed was the feeling of the necromantic link during the namocea. He had never taken control of the warrior! Had the skeleton come back to kill him?

Power surged through his mind and filled his well. He unleashed the energy on the skull symbol and it rushed forward like a bull springing from a pen. That bag of bones was in for one hell of a surprise this time.

Nothing happened.

It was as if the necropotency had taken on a mind of its own and refused to leave him. He was doing everything right, but nothing worked.

The warrior drew closer, but his image shifted and blurred. It grew sharper, like a picture coming into focus, as flesh appeared on its bones from the inside out, beginning with internal organs and ending with fascia and skin.

Nicolas's fear grew, but something told him there was nothing to fear.

The old warrior stopped a few feet from Nicolas and smiled. A jagged scar ran down his forehead, through one of his eyes, and onto his cheek. White hair cascaded onto broad shoulders that partially concealed a two-handed sword extending up from his back. Armor of darkest black formed around him, as if coalescing from dust in the air, and settled onto his body.

"I've waited for you, priest," the warrior said. "My name is Kynthelig. We once met as master and servant, but today we meet as brothers. Through your summoning I have paid the last of my debt to the God of Death, and I await passage through the gate, as do many down below. But the Plane of Death fills with souls faster than they can be purified."

Nicolas was dumbfounded. The man wanted to thank him, not kill him. He looked at the vast ocean of souls and felt a permeating hopelessness. All of these people were stranded here, unable to return to their lives, and unable to move forward. How could all of the necromancers combined ever hope to purify them?

"The God of Death hides his face from us," Kynthelig said. "Many here feel he has abandoned us, and fear the Plane of Peace is forever closed."

"How long has it been?" Nicolas asked.

Kynthelig gave him a questioning look.

"When did you last see Zubuxo?"

"Time has no meaning here. But I have never seen Zubuxo."

Nicolas realized he had no idea how long he'd been standing here. Had it been minutes? Days? Years? No matter how hard he tried, he couldn't pinpoint how much time had passed. It felt as if everything was happening *now*. Past and future combined into an eternal present.

Kynthelig turned to the multitude. "There are tainted ones among us now." He pointed to the ever-expanding plain below. "Look there. Watch the purest ones."

Nicolas looked where Kynthelig was pointing. A new throng of souls appeared on the plane. Differentiations existed among them that he hadn't seen before. Some wore garments of jet black, like Kynthelig, while others wore white and every shade in between. The imagery wasn't what he expected, given his Catholic upbringing. Kynthelig was pure, yet his armor was black.

"I don't understand what I'm seeing," Nicolas said. "Aren't the ones wearing white the purest?"

"The question of a child, not a priest."

Something about the word *child* caused a shift in Nicolas's perception. When he looked back at the plain below, he noticed that one section stood out from the rest, and within it the garments were the blackest of all. But he sickened when he looked closer.

They were infants floating above the ground in black swaddling clothes.

A bright flash of light reflected off one of the children, as if lightning had struck nearby. When the light faded the child writhed and cried as if in pain.

When the second flash struck, the infant's black garment turned grey. It was almost unnoticeable, except that it was no longer the darkest in the group.

A third flash struck the child, and Nicolas saw the source. A white door had opened on the planet above, and a brilliant beam of light shot out, striking the child in the chest. The child's garment grew lighter with each strike. But the garment wasn't the only thing changing. The child's demeanor was changing as well.

The strikes began to provoke a violent reaction, and the infant lashed out like a feral animal. The infant stood—something that should have been impossible—and swung its arms at the other children, but it never made contact. Its hands passed right through anything they touched.

"What's happening to that baby?"

"She is tainted now, priest," Kynthelig said. "The hellwraiths will come for her soon. This place is no longer appropriate for her."

Two shrouded beings approached the child from opposite directions of the plain. They had no discernible lower bodies, and the only feature Nicolas could see were two pinpoints of brilliant light where eyes should be.

"They come now," Kynthelig said.

The hellwraiths flew above the multitude of souls. When they were next to the child they shrank to twice the height of a full grown man and hovered beside her. The souls standing near scurried away and formed a circle, leaving the hellwraiths and the girl at its center.

One of the wraiths produced a great whip that looked like a rope of shadow, absorbing the light around it. The other wraith approached the girl, reaching out with ephemeral hands to grab her.

The child flailed, screaming, and Nicolas expected her arms to pass right through the wraiths as they had with the other spirits. This time, however, her arms made contact. As she touched the hellwraith she threw her head back and cried. The hellwraith lifted her up and flew into the air, leaving a trail of shadow behind him. When his arms enveloped the girl, her clothes became darker and her body shuddered. It carried her toward the throne, to a door that had opened on the side opposite the gate. The remaining wraith followed, stowing its shadowy whip in its cloak that flowed down around legs that didn't exist.

"A spirit I once knew, know, and shall know again called this *the great evil*," Kynthelig said. "He said it was an abomination of magic, a perversion of necropotency. He blamed himself for abandoning the priesthood for what he called life magic."

A cold chill passed through Nicolas as Kynthelig spoke those words. Mujahid told him that life magic was a perversion, taking life rather than granting it. Was he seeing, first hand, its consequences?

"What can you tell me about life magic?"

"Only what you witness here," Kynthelig said. "It takes life, purity, innocence. The result is what you see. The spirits taken by the hellwraiths are never seen again. Sometimes they vanish before the hellwraiths can take them. Whether they are the luckiest or the most unfortunate I do not know."

"This can't be allowed to continue."

"But it does, priest, and I fear for my own soul," Kynthelig said. "Please. I beg of you. Say the words before it is too late for me."

Nicolas knew what Kynthelig was talking about. He had spoken *the words* many times over the last few months, but Kynthelig wasn't under his control.

"I don't think what you're asking for is possible."

"Then I, too, will be tainted by the great evil, and the hellwraiths will drag me away."

"There's no link," Nicolas said. "There's no way for me to know the state of...."

He stopped. What he was about to say wasn't true. The state of Kynthelig's soul was written all over the old warrior in perfect black. If Nicolas were truly a priest, then shouldn't he be able to minister to this man? Shouldn't he have the power to set things right? And what was the strange connection he felt? It must mean something. Besides, what could it hurt?

He decided to try the unimaginable. No magic. No necromantic link. Just the words of a priest with good intentions.

He placed his hand on Kynthelig's shoulder and said "Spirit, I release you from your penance."

The world around him changed and he felt himself moving through space at a rapid rate. The sensation lasted only a moment, if moment held any meaning here.

Voices rose up around him, saying, "priest, priest", and Nicolas was no longer standing on the impossibly-high cliff. The mammoth gate rose above him like a mountain with a sheer face. The spirits nearby pressed forward as one, but some unseen force kept them from advancing any farther. He recognized many as human, some as cichlos, but there were too many different species to count. There were some that didn't resemble life forms at all; animated rocks, sentient whirlwinds, and puddles of liquid metal that periodically solidified and walked. The feeling that he was a tiny part of an infinite universe overwhelmed him.

Multiverse, he corrected himself. *Whatever the hell that means.*

An ear-splitting, metallic sound rang through the air causing Nicolas to jump. The giant gate creaked open.

"You have saved me," Kynthelig said. "But there are countless others. The great evil comes for them."

"I won't allow that to happen."

"Zubuxo must be found. Only he can control the hellwraiths and open the gate for all."

"You better go," Nicolas said. "I have no idea how long that thing stays open."

Kynthelig laughed.

Nicolas realized his mistake. It was difficult to wrap his head around a place where time had no meaning.

The warrior bowed and walked toward the open gate. Nicolas looked past him, through the gate beyond, but he couldn't see anything past the threshold. Nothing existed beyond that point, like the strange archway leading to Mujahid's estate.

A colossal angelic figure appeared at the gate. The being stood half the height of the gate itself, towering above the plain. Nicolas couldn't make out any features on its face, but he couldn't have missed the two body-length black wings.

As the warrior approached the gate, the angel shrank to Nicolas's height. A surge of power passed through him and the angel's face became visible. Her skin was alabaster. Her face wasn't long, and it wasn't gaunt, but in perfect symmetry with her wide blue eyes and slender, upturned nose. Long, curly red hair stood in sharp contrast to the pitch-black gown she wore, spilling down over bare shoulders, down over arms covered in colorful symbols that spiraled to the tops of her hands. She was almost as pretty as Kaitlyn.

Almost.

She gestured toward the inside of the gate, and the warrior passed over the threshold and disappeared.

"Zubuxo is lost, Nicolas," she said. Her voice was lilting, like a pleasant melody. "He waits for you. We try, but there is only so much my kind can do."

She swept her gaze across the multitude of souls. Her wings spread as if to embrace the plane in perfect night. The symbols on her arms and across her upper chest began to glow lavender from within. A single black tear fell from her eye and splashed on the ground below. The obsidian splash became a wave, and a fountain of clear water appeared in its place. Spirits gathered around and bathed in the fountain, and their clothing turned from grey to darkest black.

Nicolas heard his name from behind and turned. Dr. Murray stood in the crowd that was pressing toward the gate, his clothes not quite as black as the others.

Nicolas had to do something. He couldn't leave Dr. Murray here knowing those hellwraiths could come back.

"Dad, wait!"

He turned to the angel, hoping the creature could help him, but she was gone and the gate had closed without a sound. When he turned back to the crowd, his father was gone.

The words of the angel rang in his mind. "Zubuxo is lost."

He heard a great tearing sound and the world retreated. Darkness closed around him and he drifted into unconsciousness.

Nicolas sat up. He half-expected to see the hellwraiths flying above him, but all he saw was Siek Lamil helping him up next to the Orb of Zubuxo.

"How long was I gone?" Nicolas asked.

"If you mean unconscious, only a moment," Lamil said. "When you struck the orb, you created a small loop of energy. You broke away and fell unconscious for a moment. Your head hit the floor and you started muttering something about Zubuxo being lost."

"No. That's not what happened."

"My eyes never turned from you. Neither of them."

"I stood on the Field of Judgment. It was exactly the way you described it. I saw the throne of Zubuxo. I saw the gate to the Plane of Peace. I opened the gate, Siek. The angel told me Zubuxo is lost. I was there for...for..." He tried, but he couldn't find a frame of reference to indicate how long he'd been gone.

Lamil extended his hand toward the Orb of Zubuxo, stopping short of touching its surface. He looked back at Nicolas and pulled his hand away.

"I must inform the elders."

"You believe me?"

"You are many things, Nicolas, but a liar is not one of them. It has long been known that the Orb can transport a person to the Plane of Death. No one who has used it to take the journey remains alive to speak of it. Except for one."

"This has happened before?"

"Walk with me."

Lamil walked toward the arch leading to the high priest's chambers and Nicolas followed.

"Tell me what you saw," Lamil said. "In detail. Leave nothing out, no matter how insignificant."

He recounted the entire journey as they walked. The siek grew anxious when he mentioned the hellwraiths.

"You were wise to merely observe. How the Gates of Abaddon have opened, I cannot say. Only a Lord of Hell can command them."

"Gates of—"

"You once asked me about the Third Law of Necromancy, and I told you it was not the proper time."

"Too much too soon...again."

"What is the First Law of Necromancy?"

"You're really going to do this now?"

"What is the First Law of Necromancy?"

They spent the next few minutes covering the details of the first two laws as they walked. Nicolas could recite them backwards if the siek asked him to.

"The Third Law of Necromancy states *there is no death*," Lamil said. "Repeat it."

There was no denying the truth of that statement now. Nicolas had seen too much to think otherwise.

Lamil looked Nicolas up and down. "Repeat it, student."

"There is no death."

"Correct. Given your recent experience, do you feel as if you understand?"

"It makes sense in a way I can't explain."

"When you walked the Plane of Death, did you feel as if you were surrounded by death?"

"I felt death energy everywhere."

"That is not what I asked, and you should know better."

The Plane of Death had a dreamlike quality about it. Every time he reached for a feeling or an image, it would slip through his fingers like water.

"It was a strange place," Nicolas said. "I saw things I can't describe. But those people were alive. That angel was both beautiful and terrifying as hell."

Like Kynthelig, the warrior he sent through the gate, the angel wanted him to find the missing god. He looked back at the Orb of Zubuxo, and a strange thought occurred to him. The siek wouldn't go for it without some convincing, though. He needed to make him see it was the only logical choice.

"Mujahid once told me that no one but a god could create an orb of power. Do you agree with him, Siek?"

"I have no knowledge of any species creating an orb of power, yet orbs exist. To agree or disagree would require a leap of logic, for it would require me to have knowledge of every species in the multiverse. I make no such claim. Nevertheless...I feel as if the answer is yes."

"Do you think it's safe to assume the gods create their own orbs? I mean, if that really is the Orb of Zubuxo, then Zubuxo would be its creator and not some other god, right?"

Lamil looked Nicolas up and down, and then faced the orb.

"No assumption is safe when it comes to the gods, Nicolas. Your dialectic, while commendable, is unnecessary. Say what you wish to say."

It was worth a try. He'd have to be more direct.

"Siek, has any priest, in your knowledge, ever thought to cast the arrow on the Orb of Zubuxo?"

Lamil looked from side to side in a gesture Nicolas hadn't seen before. Perhaps the siek had never considered this possibility.

"What you are suggesting is not a valid use of the *guide* symbol," Lamil said.

"With much respect, Siek, I didn't ask if you thought it was valid. I asked if it had ever been done."

Lamil smiled. "A fair objection. The answer is no. No necromancer, to my knowledge, has ever cast the guide symbol on the Orb of Zubuxo. But consider what you ask. There would be no reason to do so. There are only two known uses for the guide, and you are aware of them both."

"But the gods are different." He wasn't sure where he was going with this, but thinking out loud was helping.

"I would agree with that statement," Lamil said.

"I think we just need to change our understanding of them. The gods can't ever die...not the way we can. I'm suggesting they live along a continuum of life and death. The more I think about my experience in the Plane of Death, the more I feel right about this, Siek. What can it hurt?"

"It is never good to channel energy into an orb of power. This has been understood from the dawn of understanding."

"I'll release the power at the first sign of trouble."

Lamil looked Nicolas up and down. He seemed to be struggling against some inner conflict. But he pointed toward the orb. "You may try it, but I will restrict your flow of power with a shield."

Nicolas started walking back toward the orb. "Fine. I just have to try."

When they reached the orb, Nicolas took a deep breath and cleared his mind. Something was squeezing his well of power—probably Lamil's shield. He created a pathway to the arrow—*guide*, he corrected himself—and allowed the smallest amount of power to trickle along the surface of the orb.

Nothing happened. He repeated the process for good measure, but again nothing happened.

"It's going to take more power, that's all," he said.

"Nicolas...."

"Please. Trust me. I didn't used to think it was possible to walk from one world to another. Maybe there are some things you think are impossible that are actually possible?"

Lamil drew his shoulders up.

"I can feel it," Nicolas said. "Just let me use more power."

Lamil looked down and the squeezing sensation stopped. Power flowed into the guide and out onto the surface of the orb. When it encircled the orb, a vicious wave of nausea passed over Nicolas. He gritted his teeth, attempting to ride the wave, but it grew stronger. He was about to release the power, thinking Lamil may be right, when the spinning came to an abrupt stop.

He knelt and started feeling the floor with both hands.

"What is it?" Lamil said. "What did the arrow tell you?"

"*Guide*," Nicolas said and smiled. "When I arrived here on that first day, I was led by an undead cichlos. He made it so I could breathe under water. Can you do that for me?"

"I can."

"Then get ready to take a swim, Siek. The guide is leading me straight down through the floor of Aquonome."

Nicolas and the siek descended for nearly an hour. The bone-crushing pressure of the lake would have killed him without the magic of the undead cichlos, and the water was frigid and pitch black. Necropotency allowed him to see, and the temperature was bearable as long as he held power, but the power made him feel every individual drop of water against his body, like tiny beads.

Through the murk, a great yellow wall, pulsating with inner light, rose from below and to the west, turning inward on itself in a gentle curve. It disappeared beneath them, creating a straight line where yellow met nothing, leaving the wall on one side and a void on the other.

The great barrier, Nicolas projected to Lamil. *It isn't a dome at all. It's a sphere.*

It would appear so.

The Cichlos didn't know?

There is no reason for us to travel this deep. There is no food for us here.

The closer they approached, the more power flowed into Nicolas's well. The source of necropotency was so massive, it was as if every living thing on the planet had died in one place. But it wasn't just necropotency. There was another power. A power he'd never felt before. The hum of energy was deafening, even through the water.

A cacophony of voices entered his mind and he lifted his hands to the side of his head, trying to block them out.

He who walks between worlds, said a female voice.

Who are you? Nicolas said.

We cannot leave here until you bring down the sky, the female said. *Our sacrifice protects the children. I...must go.*

The guide in his mind's eye winked out of existence. He had come within feet of the lake floor and could see the barrier plunging into the ground next to him. The ground where the barrier penetrated shook, and the lake bed vibrated like rocks on an archaeologist's sifter. He was close enough to touch the barrier if he chose, but he was sure it would kill him if he did.

One thought haunted him—if the guide led him here, it could mean only one thing; Zubuxo was on the other side of the barrier...or perhaps *inside of it*. But there had been more than one voice talking to him, and one of them was a woman.

He drew power from the barrier and his thoughts came into sharp focus.

It was obvious to him why the archmage took the Orb of Arin. It contained Arin's power, just like Zubuxo's orb contained Zubuxo's power. The archmage would need its power, the power of the god of life, to construct a barrier of this magnitude from *life magic*.

Even the earthquakes made sense. The barrier was moving and vibrating continent-sized chunks of land beneath the surface of the planet.

The cause of the diminishing power of the gods as well as their absence was clear to see. The truth was the gods were *never* gone. They were here all along, *inside* the barrier. And as far as he could tell, they sacrificed themselves for the sake of children.

The unborn, he corrected himself. *But what does that mean?*

He didn't know. But as they began the ascent to Aquonome, he understood something else.

He understood how to get back home.

Nicolas didn't care if the high priest liked it. He just needed the man to do it.

The high priest had been reluctant to call the elders together, but Lamil asked Nicolas to stay behind while he persuaded the high priest to relent. After more than an hour of waiting, they emerged from the high priest's quarters.

"I concur that what you discovered is disturbing," the high priest said. "But what you ask is not easy to grant. You ask me to grant aid to the people who stranded us here. The people who hunt us like animals."

"Sabba," Nicolas said, "I can only imagine how you feel. I know the atrocities they committed against you and I respect your judgment. But I can't do this alone. And if I don't succeed, you'll never see Terilya again. The fate of everyone in Aquonome hinges on the success or failure of my mission."

"Tell him the rest, Nicolas," Lamil said.

Nicolas looked back at Lamil with uncertainty. This was going to get someone's attention.

"The throne of Zubuxo is empty, Sabba," Nicolas said.

The priests surrounding the high priest gasped and argued among themselves.

"This is blasphemous," one of the priests said.

The high priest waved his hand at the angry cichlos and faced Lamil. "Is this true?"

"Nicolas has never given me reason to doubt his integrity, Sabba," Lamil said.

"How do you know this, my son?" the high priest asked Nicolas.

Nicolas was taken aback for a moment. This was the first time the high priest had ever addressed him in such a familiar fashion. He looked at Siek Lamil for approval.

"Go on," Lamil said.

Nicolas recounted his journey to the Plane of Death, and subsequent trip to the bottom of the lake. By the time he was finished, everyone in the room was speechless.

"This is not possible," one of the priests said. "He was hallucinating, nothing more."

"It is not merely possible," the high priest said. "It is understandable. It explains much of what none of us could comprehend. Nicolas merely gives voice to the fear buried within our hearts. He has grasped what every master necromancer in Aquonome failed to see."

The high priest stood next to Nicolas and faced the other priests. Lamil appeared surprised by the gesture.

"If what Nicolas says is correct," the high priest said, "then the fates of Erindor and Terilya are merely the beginning of a much larger problem. If Zubuxo is not restored to his throne, all living beings will be condemned to undeath, unable to pass into the Plane of Peace."

"I have to put an end to this," Nicolas said. "The Orb of Arin is the source of that barrier. And if the orb is at the Pinnacle...." He let the sentence go unfinished.

"We will do whatever we can to assist you," the high priest said. "There is the issue of your training we must address."

"Sabba, no," one of the priests said. "The last time—"

"Is he ready?" The high priest turned to Lamil, ignoring the priest's comments.

Lamil nodded. "There is nothing else I can teach him."

"Then it is decided. Nicolas, you are to be elevated to the midnight blue. You will take your rightful place among the master necromancers of Aquonome."

Had he heard that right? How could he be a master necromancer?

"Your ordination will take place tomorrow. Tonight you will spend in meditation. Siek Lamil, see that he is ready at the appointed time."

"Of course, Sabba."

The priests withdrew, leaving Nicolas and Lamil behind.

"That was...most unexpected," Lamil said. "Though it doesn't surprise me. There is little more I can teach you. The rest you must learn by experience."

Nicolas didn't know what to say.

"Don't look so surprised. I doubt anyone here is. Come, let's discuss your preparations."

Nicolas followed Lamil into the training dome.

I knew you'd get there before me," Toridyn said. "No one's ever mastered two symbols in less than a year. Crazy. What's your secret?"

"Ignorance and immaturity didn't hurt," Nicolas said.

"Funny," Toridyn said. "Fine. Keep all the glory for yourself."

Nicolas tried his best to smile, but it was difficult.

"So...you're really leaving?"

Nicolas nodded. "I don't have a choice, Tor. I don't know what's more important, getting back home or bringing that damned barrier down. But I can't do either here."

Toridyn was about to say something, but was interrupted when Siek Lamil entered the room.

Lamil was carrying something under his arm, but Nicolas couldn't tell what it was.

"Do you remember the responses I taught you?" Lamil asked.

"I'd be lucky to remember my name right now."

"Wear this. Then follow me. Both of you."

He handed Nicolas a white garment, like an alb that priests and altar boys wore. Nicolas changed and they marched out of the dorm.

When they entered the temple dome, a large crowd had gathered. Three student formations spread out in front of the Orb of Zubuxo in silence. Lamil led him to a point between the orb and the formations, and then faced the high priest.

A priest stepped forward and handed Lamil a large square of dark material. Lamil took and unfolded it into a large, midnight blue robe. He held it open, behind Nicolas, and Nicolas slipped his arms into it. It buttoned in front, from top to bottom like a priest's cassock, but there was something else. It was identical to the robe in the mosaic at Mujahid's estate.

The ordination ritual began and the high priest intoned the words Lamil told Nicolas to expect.

"Nicolas Ardirian," the high priest said when Nicolas was dressed. "You hold the powers of the priestly caste, but you have not been elevated to the priesthood. Do you seek elevation?"

"Sabba," Nicolas said, hoping to get all the words right. "I seek to be counted among the priesthood. I seek elevation."

"Siek Lamil Jiskossa," the high priest said. "Is Nicolas Ardirian, your student, worthy of elevation?"

"Sabba, all cichlos—" He stopped as if uncertain of how to proceed. "All *people* are weak and unworthy of elevation. We elevate for the sake of others, not for the sake of the priest."

Nicolas kneeled and the high priest and his assistants chanted the names of the gods, invoking their blessing on him. Each time they named a god, Nicolas felt something strange near his well of power, as if the boundary of the well was being pulled or pushed against.

When the invocation was over, the high priest stepped forward and held a hand above Nicolas's forehead.

A subtle hum reached Nicolas's ears, and a black aura formed around each of the webbed fingers of the high priest's hand. The aura grew larger and enveloped Nicolas in shadow, making it impossible for him to see. The boundaries of his well of power grew outward like a balloon being inflated, and something burned at its core. When the expansion was complete, the aura vanished and he could see the high priest once more.

The high priest handed Lamil a midnight blue cowl. Lamil placed the cowl around Nicolas's shoulders and fastened it in front.

"Nicolas Ardirian," the high priest said. "Rise as priest, *sab*, master necromancer."

Nicolas stood up on legs that were shaky at first. His well of power was full when he entered the temple, but now that the ritual had expanded it, he felt as if it were empty.

"Priests of Zubuxo," the high priest said, no longer chanting. "I present to you Sab Nicolas Ardirian."

Applause filled the temple changing the atmosphere from solemn to joyous. Nicolas wasn't sure how to react to the applause. He had never been good at receiving praise from people. When the applause died down, he smiled and shrugged awkwardly.

Toridyn was smiling so broadly Nicolas thought he was in danger of unhinging his jaw. In a burst of excitement, Toridyn rushed forward and engulfed Nicolas in a bear hug.

Nicolas laughed. "Ok, happy fish. I think that's probably too much for the occasion."

Lamil gave Toridyn a disapproving look as he released Nicolas, but Toridyn kept smiling.

"Sab Nicolas," the high priest said. "May the robe and cowl you wear be an ever-present reminder of the dangers and challenges you will face in the execution of your priesthood."

The high priest extended his hand, and Nicolas realized he was trying to shake hands according to the human custom. Nicolas reached out, surprised by the gesture, and gave the high priest's hand a firm shake.

"I'll fix this, Sabba," Nicolas said. "I'll confront my father, and I'll bring down that barrier."

Nicolas had never been so sure about something in his life.

CHAPTER TWENTY SIX

Mujahid had filled Donal in on the details of what he discovered at the Temple. As much as Donal sympathized and agreed action was necessary, he didn't have the resources to sustain a war.

"Perhaps the best action is to ask for terms from the archmage," Donal said.

Mujahid shook his head. "We cannot allow him—"

"If I oppose the Pinnacle it is the people who will suffer. Those people you see walking the streets, afraid of their own shadows...those people are my only vassals."

"You have more vassals than you know, and their weapons are far more effective than steel. At least hear me out before you decide."

The king leaned back in his chair and looked away.

"For forty years, necromancy has been driven underground," Mujahid said. "My people, once the pillars of our society, live in caves and travel under cities for fear of being tortured and executed. But your kingdom is different, Majesty. That is why I asked my brother to come here."

Donal stared at Mujahid, saying nothing.

"Where do you think most of the necromancers wound up after the Purge? The other two nations would arrest them with few questions asked. But in Tildem...."

"They'd live in peace," Donal said. He looked up at the ceiling as if considering something.

"Your kingdom has been a thorn in Kagan's side since before you were born," Mujahid said. "One way or another he will remove you from power. An army gathers as we speak. It flies the Red Dragon of Religar, but you can rest assured Kagan holds the reigns."

Donal shook his head. "I cannot afford this war, Lord Mukhtaar. The cost in lives alone would be too great. And even if I could muster the force we need, with what would I pay them? Maintaining a single city has stripped my resources bare. I cannot afford to oppose Kagan directly."

"You already oppose him. You look the other way at necromancy. You ban his Pinnacle guard from your borders. You harbor a banished archbishop in the most influential temple in Erindor. Like it or not, Majesty, you are already at war with Kagan, regardless of the lack of formal declaration."

The king remained silent for a moment, and placed his hand on the back of his head. "If the necromancers went to ground here when the Union and Empire hunted them down...."

This was Mujahid's chance. He had to strike now. "Act boldly. Release a proclamation legalizing necromancy within your borders. Escalate the conflict between yourself and the archmage and you will raise an army the likes of which the world hasn't seen since the Necromancer Wars."

Donal sat deep in thought for several minutes. "Will they follow you?"

"They are bound by sacred oath," Mujahid said. "But these men and women practice the old religion. They need no oath to know what is right."

"If this fails, Lord Mukhtaar, it will mean the end of my kingdom."

"If you fail to act, then the end of your kingdom is already at hand."

Donal exhaled. "It was always going to come down to this, wasn't it?"

"Your Majesty, I know—"

"You'll have your proclamation. Let's hope I have my army."

Mujahid prayed Nuuan had found more priests.

Gods, where is my festering brother?

Ｔhe royal proclamation sent shock waves through Tildem society. The atmosphere of fear began to lift as news spread of the return of the old religion, and Mujahid began the task of removing the death piles. He instructed an army of volunteers in the method of interring corpses in makeshift mausoleums along the city's walls, built from pieces of collapsed building and debris from destroyed walkways. If Rotham on Orm was to be defended by an army of necromancers, those crypts would be more valuable than arrows and boiling oil. The local Arinian priesthood joined in the effort, lending whatever assistance Mujahid required, but there were too many dead to purify for a single necromancer.

He had the royal tailor make him a midnight-blue robe. It would be good for other priests, still uncertain about revealing themselves, to see a Mukhtaar Lord had no fear of identifying himself as a necromancer.

The librarian Saul was never found, and this disturbed him. He had seen some strange things in his days, but ghosts were the creation of fanciful imaginations. The dead didn't return to life under their *own* power.

Two weeks after the proclamation Mujahid remained the only known necromancer in Rotham. The people may be relieved that necromancy was legal again, but it didn't take a military strategist to know what would happen if the Religarian army arrived before he could muster a force of necromancers.

He swore as he approached a death pile. If the priests in hiding didn't trust Donal's offer of amnesty, this would be a short-lived resistance. He vowed it wouldn't be as short as their worthless lives if he ever found them. Tildem deserved better than this. Donal's kingdom was the last great hope for the survival of the old religion. Mujahid couldn't do it alone. He needed a powerful ally. A king. And this was how the clan repaid his efforts, by ignoring that king's amnesty and hiding themselves away.

He scowled at one of the volunteers before catching himself. He was in a foul mood, but he couldn't allow himself to take it out on them.

Someone cleared his throat behind Mujahid. "Ahem."

A diminutive man, standing barely four feet tall and wearing brightly colored floor-length patchwork robes, approached Mujahid from the street.

"Good day, good sir," the man said. "I presume I am addressing none other than the infamous Mujahid Lord Mukhtaar."

Mujahid raised an eyebrow.

"Ahh yes. The infamous eyebrow of the infamous Lord Mukhtaar...practitioner of the darkest arts. Bane of Shandaria. Demon of Religar. Rapist of...innocents or livestock or something in Caspardis, however the story goes. But my presumption was correct. You are, in fact, *the* Lord Mujahid Mukhtaar."

"And what makes you think I'm a necromancer, much less a Mukhtaar Lord?"

"If the eyebrow wasn't enough, I dare say the midnight blue is a dead giveaway, man." The man laughed and acted surprised at himself. "*Dead* giveaway. Amusing."

Mujahid smiled and chuckled...not because he was amused, but because the gods had a cruel sense of humor, and today they were in rare form.

"I don't know you, sir," Mujahid said. "So I'm going to extend the courtesy of a warning. If you choose to continue speaking, and the next words out of your mouth do not sufficiently impress me, I'm going to bugger you with your own head."

The man smiled a toothy grin. "Then allow me to introduce myself, *buggerer* of little people." The man bowed as if he were on stage. "I am Digby, *master* necromancer, drinker of wine, dread pirate of...no, that's someone else...ravager of women—yes, that's me—and, I jest not, bosom friend of your brother, Nuuan Lord Mukhtaar."

Mujahid raised his other eyebrow. "That was...sufficiently impressive."

"Superlative. Now that both my head and my arse are safe, we can get on with more serious matters. And know, good sir, there are few things I take more seriously than the drinking of women and ravaging of wine. I've raised it to an art form, you see. Why the whores of Arin's Watch actually call me—"

"More serious matters, Magus Digby?"

Digby deflated. "Yes. Well. Stories for later, I suppose." His expression grew serious. "There are problems up north. Big problems. Your lord brother sent me ahead to warn you. He's dealing with the situation as best as he can, but you need to be aware."

"North. Three Banks?"

"Religarian forces captured Three Banks and blockaded the river a week ago. And they weren't alone, my Lord. The Pinnacle has joined them."

"Tell me they stopped there."

"They stopped there." Digby smiled, making an exaggerated show of touching his teeth together.

"You're lying."

"Of course I'm lying, man, you think Kagan's daft? His force separated in twain. One half marches west, and the other marches here with Religarian soldiers in tow as we speak. This is total conquest."

"And what of the others? There must be other priests who have heard about the proclamation."

Digby shrugged.

Mujahid swore. After a moment, he placed a hand on Digby's shoulder. "You make a strange first impression, Magus Digby...*master necromancer*. But you're a sight for sore eyes. Come. There's work to be done."

Six weeks after the proclamation, not a single priest had come forward except Digby.

Mujahid had found a friend in Digby. The flamboyant man was a hard worker and a highly-skilled necromancer. He placed Digby in charge of the backlog of funerals, and the man worked without rest to perform the rites. Whenever he questioned Digby about Nuuan, however, Digby would smile lasciviously and say, "You know Lord Nuuan."

Mujahid hoped to be in command of a dozen or more necromancers by now. He swore as he and Digby climbed up the ladder to the top of the north wall. He swore again when he saw the Religarian army spread out on the dusty plain beyond the wall.

Tildem was outnumbered four to one.

He wielded considerable power, and Digby was a force to be reckoned with as well, but two necromancers wouldn't decide the outcome of this battle.

Where were the siege engines? The army Tithian showed him had dozens of catapults and ballistae, if not more. He supposed it didn't matter. All the empire had to do was blockade the city and wait.

The wall might be able to withstand one or two waves of attack, once the siege weakened them, but no more. Where was Nuuan? If he couldn't find twelve necromancers in Tildem, then an ascended one would be their equal. But where was he?

There was no longer any denying it. Mujahid had failed. He had failed the king, and he had failed the soldiers. Worse, he had failed the people of Rotham, who never asked him to bring war to their doorstep. It was time to deliver the news to Donal. The man's kingdom was coming to an end, and he had a right to know.

"You," he said to a nearby soldier. "Find your commander and ask her to join me below as soon as possible."

"Yes, m'lord."

"Fear not, my Lord," Digby said. "These are my kind of odds. Besides...they haven't seen my secret weapon yet."

"I am afraid to ask."

"It wouldn't be secret if I told you, now would it?"

"Join me in a few minutes down below. You may find the tactic I intend to employ here...distasteful."

"I have often been called distasteful myself. Now that I think on it, so has my secret weapon. Perhaps you know too much already."

Mujahid climbed down from the wall. Digby's humor had a way of making him feel better.

The command center was nothing more than a circle of tents along the main thoroughfare that led to the north gate, but it provided the king and his advisors a place to meet close to the wall.

Mujahid passed the outer guard and entered the king's tent.

"Does it begin?" the king asked.

"Sieges are nasty things, often lasting months," Mujahid said. "If they attack now it's because they know something we don't, or their commander is a complete idiot. They outnumber us, but not enough to throw bodies at the wall as if they have an endless supply. No...they'll starve us out."

An explosion of foul language outside the tent made both men look up at the entrance. Mujahid filled his power well and ran toward the noise. Several guards were lying on the ground, and five robed people stood over them, their heads hidden by large black hoods. Mujahid was preparing to expel a wall of force as the person in the center looked up and revealed his face.

"Brother," Nuuan said. "Your face looks like a slapped arse. I thought you were expecting me?"

"What in Arin's name did you do?" Mujahid asked, checking for signs of life on the guards.

"They acted like I needed permission to see you."

"Arin's festering—a little less heavy-handed next time?"

"Ahh, give us a hug now," Nuuan said, moving forward with open arms.

Mujahid embraced Nuuan. "Your timing is impeccable, as always. Where have you been?"

Nuuan gestured toward the robed figures standing behind him. "Raising an army." He made a show of looking over Mujahid's shoulder and around the command tents. "Where's that cross-dressing postulant I left you with?"

Mujahid showed Nuuan the talisman.

"Arin humping an orb," Nuuan said. "I read the proclamation. Has the boy king lost his senses?"

"Sometimes I wonder how crazy this boy king is," Donal said. He must have followed Mujahid.

"Your Majesty," Nuuan said and bowed. "Forgive me."

Donal waved the comment aside. "My ego remains intact, Lord Nuuan."

"Are they versed in battle tactics?" Mujahid nodded toward the necromancers.

"They'll do."

"I've learned much in your absence, brother," Mujahid said. "Things you won't believe."

"As much as I appreciate the help, Lord Nuuan, five extra people hardly tips the scales." Donal said.

"You've never seen necromancers conduct a coordinated attack," Mujahid said. "The last Necromancer War took place decades before your birth."

"My brother's trying to say the odds have evened up a bit, Majesty," Nuuan said. "May I have a private word with my brother?"

"Please," Donal said, and gestured toward his command tent.

They stepped into the command tent, and when the flap closed behind them, Nuuan grabbed Mujahid by the shoulders and spun him around.

"Have you lost your mind?" he said in a hoarse whisper. "You want to risk what few priests remain to save this man's kingdom?"

"And just what would you have me do?"

"We throw up a ring of bones, march straight out of here, and dig a festering hole, like we always do."

"Like we always do."

"Don't give me that look. I'm not some new recruit ready to cower at the feet of the great and terrible Mukhtaar Lord. And I know you too well to be convinced of your angelic innocence."

Mujahid knocked Nuuan's arms aside and turned away.

"It's how we survive," Nuuan said. "We dig a hole and live where others fear to tread."

"It has to stop. The hiding. The destruction. It has to stop sometime, brother."

"And you think you're the one to stop it? Did you ascend a little higher than I did that day?"

Mujahid turned on Nuuan.

"These people are facing overwhelming odds. I don't know if we can save them, but how can you ask me not to try?"

"Alright already," Nuuan said. "I was convinced at *overwhelming odds.*"

Mujahid exhaled. Nuuan could be as quick to calm as he was to anger.

"I know you too well to think you don't have a plan," Nuuan said.

"Death's Vise."

"Death's—" Nuuan stopped himself and put a fist up to his mouth. "You haven't told Digby yet, have you?"

Mujahid shook his head.

"Well, gird your loins. There's history there. And trust me, he's the last person you want to see in a homicidal rage."

"I knew there was more to him than he was letting on."

"Brother, you don't know the half of it." Nuuan turned and left the tent.

The atmosphere hadn't changed much during their short conversation. The tension was palpable.

"By your leave, Majesty, I would like to address these men," Mujahid said.

Donal nodded.

Digby approached with Commander Yuli, Guard Captain of the Rotham Militia. She was dressed in fitted leather armor and carried a long bow. Her blond hair was pulled back into a long braid that ran down just beyond her shoulders.

"Do you mind, brother?" Mujahid asked.

Nuuan shook his head.

"Priests, Commander," Mujahid said. "Gather around, all of you. As you do, I want you to take a look at this place. Get a look at the streets...the buildings."

The small crowd looked around. Some kept looking over their shoulders nervously towards the wall.

"Most of you are too young to remember what Rotham was like before the barrier went up," Mujahid said. "This city was once the gem of Erindor, and so were its citizens. If a traveler was found wandering, he'd find himself surrounded by an escort of people, all debating which route would find his destination the quickest."

There were a few nods, but most stood expressionless.

"But not anymore. People looked at me with fear in their eyes the day I rode into this city weeks ago. Fear! Why should any man, woman, or child fear a priest?" Mujahid pointed east, toward the far off Pinnacle and Obsidian Throne. "They fear us not because of who we are, but because of who the false prophet says we are. The people believed they heard Arin's holy words, when it was Kagan's words instead."

Nuuan's eyes grew wide. "What? You didn't—"

Mujahid held up his hand. Now was not the time for explanation. "'The archmage usurps the voices of the gods. What will happen when the last necromancer draws his last breath? What will become of humankind then, or the countless other forms of life we have purified in the exercise of our office?"

The priests had begun nodding with each point he made.

"Brethren," Mujahid said. "It has fallen to me to ask you to do something that may run counter to your training. And there is a strong likelihood you will lose your mind in the process."

"That affects me little, Lord Mujahid," Digby said. "I lost my mind many years ago." He looked up at Commander Yuli and smiled. "But fear not, sister. The gods replaced it with extraordinary sexual prowess."

"Call me sister one more time and I'll cut your *prowess* off and wear it as an earring."

Digby swallowed and the other priests erupted in a round of laughter.

When the laughter died, Mujahid spoke. "If battle comes, you will each live hundreds of lifetimes within a span of hours...minutes, if the gods favor us. Your teachers instructed that it is not possible to summon more than one penitent at a time. That teaching...is a lie."

Most of the necromancers reacted as if they couldn't believe what they were hearing, but Digby didn't seem surprised by the revelation. His smile faded and his face became expressionless. His eyes looked as dead as any corpse Mujahid had ever seen.

"Each time death's journey takes you, your mind will splinter," Mujahid said. "Until all that remains is the evil you witness. You will no longer recognize the difference between reality and the summoning. You will become that which you hate the most."

Stillness descended on the small group. Digby's face remained expressionless.

"When these walls are challenged," Mujahid said, "and we run out of corpses to raise, you'll have to perform *pure* summonings—without a corpse—and death's price will be all the greater because of it."

Murmurs arose from a few of the necromancers but Nuuan gave them a stern look.

"Hold fast to this reality," Mujahid said. "If the madness takes you, it will be too late."

Mujahid never thought he would find himself ordering Death's Vise. It ran counter to everything a necromancer stood for. But it was Rotham's best chance for survival.

Nuuan faced the other necromancers. "Some of you don't have two halves of a mind to rub together as it is, and I should know."

Digby chuckled.

"So if you forget who you are, come ask me," Nuuan said. "I'll write your name in the dirt with your own entrails. Maybe that will jog your memory."

"What in Arin's name is Death's Vise, Lords Mukhtaar?" Donal asked.

Given the looks on their faces, the other necromancers had the same question.

"A festering meat grinder, Majesty," Nuuan said. "And they'll never expect it because it puts us on the offensive. You mind?" Nuuan asked Mujahid.

"Please," Mujahid said. "I have no stomach for it."

"It's why Lord Mujahid requested two *centuries* of archers, Majesty," Nuuan said.

Mujahid inhaled sharply.

"What, you thought I wouldn't notice?" Nuuan said. "The archers concentrate fire on both the rear and the van at the same time, dropping as many as they can. We raise the bastards up as fast as they drop and leave them wild...we don't control them. We let nature take its course."

Donal's jaw dropped. "Feral beasts," he said.

"Precisely, Majesty," Mujahid said. "The penitents in the vanguard can't mount the wall, and they're filled with a blood lust for mindless slaughter. So they turn to the rear and begin killing anyone and anything they can get their hands on."

"Meanwhile," Nuuan said, "the evil bastards at the rear are doing the same, only they're coming forward toward the van. They meet in the middle—"

"And slaughter one another," Donal said. "Brilliant."

Nuuan snorted. "Hundreds of uncontrolled penitents. If you ever wanted to see pure chaos, that's as close as it gets."

"And they're the least of our concerns," Mujahid said. "The toll taken on the priests is beyond imagination. Some will go mad and become homicidal." He glanced at Digby when he said that. He didn't intend to, but he couldn't help it. "Nuuan and I have seen it happen...during the Necromancer Wars. What my brother said earlier was no idle threat. If we see anyone acting strangely, we'll put them down like a maimed horse and consider it a mercy."

A debate ensued amongst the other necromancers, but Digby remained silent. His eyes never left the ground in front of him.

"Silence doesn't suit you, Magus Digby," Mujahid said. "You've been a friend these past weeks. I would know your thoughts."

Digby never raised his head, but he lifted his eyes toward Mujahid.

For a brief moment, Mujahid saw madness behind those eyes.

"The Necromancer Wars," Digby said. "Horrific. Mindless slaughter lasting for days with no respite. The dead need no rest. Priests falling in battle, only to be raised and turned into mindless killing machines. Battle after battle, wading through body parts and excrement as deep as my knees. Corpses of our allies rotting and unburied to be used as ammunition. Your own family members...normal one moment, insane the next. Watching as your leader feasts on the fetid corpse of a fallen priest as if it were roast adda...and knowing he doesn't realize what he's doing. These are my thoughts, Lord Mujahid. They haunt my every waking moment, and I will carry them with me for the rest of my days. And now you know them."

Digby smiled and blinked. The look of madness was gone, replaced by his usual jocular grin.

"But like I said earlier," Digby said. "I misplaced my better senses long ago. What do I know? If Death's Vise is what you command, then Death's Vise is what I shall give you. If there ever were a mind worth losing, it is mine."

"How are you old enough to have seen the Necromancer Wars, Magus Digby?" one of the necromancers asked.

Digby looked away, but Mujahid wondered the same thing. Only a Mukhtaar Lord could transfer life, and Digby was no Mukhtaar Lord.

"We'll need to plan this carefully," Nuuan said. "I'll command the—"

Loud shouts from the wall warned of attack. Archers took positions behind the merlons in the crenelated wall above.

"To the wall," Mujahid said. "Now!"

He didn't know why the empire had chosen to attack, but he'd save those questions for later. Right now, he had to get to the wall. He had a few hundred lifetimes to live before this battle would be decided.

CHAPTER TWENTYSEVEN

They ran between the command tents as arrows rained down from the amber sky, a task made more difficult by debris from shattered buildings littering the streets. Mujahid hoped the Religarian commander was as dumb as his strategy was.

"Digby," Mujahid said. "Concentrate your efforts on the vanguard. Take these two with you." He nodded toward two other necromancers.

Digby and the two priests climbed up the wall and out of sight.

When they reached the wall, Mujahid's well of power filled faster than it should have.

A battlement crumbled next to him.

A ground assault on the wall wouldn't destroy the structure. Something was wrong. It wasn't the Religarian soldiers who were dying. It was the Tildemen on the wall.

Mujahid cursed. He'd failed again.

The empire's catapults hurled boulders toward the city, destroying more battlements. He should have known the empire wouldn't charge the wall en masse. Only an idiot would order such a move. But where in the six hells did those siege engines come from?

As Mujahid crested the wall, it was obvious the enemy commander was no idiot. The bulk of the empire force had moved beyond the range of the Tildemen archers, making their bows useless.

The battle for Rotham on Orm had begun, and *Death's Vise* was no longer an option.

So much for plans.

A boulder struck a battlement next to Mujahid, and he had to leap out of the way to avoid the resulting shrapnel. The wall couldn't take much more.

The necromancers raised the dead Tildemen soldiers, and Mujahid signaled for them to take control. If Death's Vise wouldn't work, then they had to use the undead to their best advantage.

Another powerful blast shook the wall. Mujahid had to do something, or this would be a short siege indeed.

"They have us by the balls like this, you know," Nuuan said. He crouched behind the battlement with Mujahid and Yuli.

"The wall is already weak from the quakes," Yuli said.

"They didn't bring those catapults with them," Mujahid said. "They teleported them here. That can mean only one thing."

Nuuan cursed. "Festering life magi."

"But this could work in our favor. If they were expecting a quick breach...." Mujahid spread his hands.

"They wouldn't have time to flank us," Nuuan said. "Yuli, meet me with a century of archers at the western gate. And run like your arse is on fire. Digby, you're with my brother."

Nuuan rose to leave, but Yuli stopped him.

"If you're going to flank them, Lord Mukhtaar, we should set a diversion," Yuli said.

"Make that *two* centuries," Nuuan turned and ran along the wall to the left.

"Death's Vise may work yet," Mujahid said. "Nuuan will be heading to their rear. I'll take a century with me to the east, below the wall, and start attacking their vanguard."

"You can't sneak two hundred archers over a barren plain," Yuli said.

"Open the gate," Digby said.

"What?" Yuli said.

"A diversion only works if your enemy doesn't expect it," Digby said. "Do you think they expect us to open the gate and welcome them with open arms?"

A boulder struck a nearby battlement with massive force, and it crumbled into dust as if it had been pulverized.

"We're betting with the city here," Yuli said. "Rotham will fall if the Mukhtaars don't succeed."

"I'm sorry if I have misunderstood our present situation," Digby said. "But I was under the assumption defeat is a foregone conclusion and Death's Vise is a last ditch effort to save our collective arses. Was I wrong?"

Yuli looked away.

"When the two centuries reach the northern wall, order the gate opened and the men to lay down their arms," Digby said. "I might be able to use my secret weapon after all."

"Do as he says, Commander," Mujahid said.

"I don't like this, but I'll see to the archers," Yuli said. "One century to the west gate and one to the east. If this fails, Lord Mujahid—"

"Then nothing changes but the timing of our defeat."

Mujahid set off toward the east gate, taking two other necromancers with him. The streets were deserted, and it didn't take long for them to find their destination.

The sound of boots striking the dirt grew louder and soon a full century of archers stood before Mujahid in the small plaza.

"Lord Mujahid," one of the archers said as he stepped forward. "I'm Centenaur Eric, leader of this lot."

Mujahid had seen better soldiers in his day, but these men were far from green.

"Did Commander Yuri inform you of our strategy?"

"Yes, m'lord."

"Follow my lead and be prepared to fire the moment I give the command. And then I want you to do something that just might save your life."

"My Lord?"

"Kill me."

"What?"

"If for even a moment I behave in a fashion that seems threatening to you or your men...that will be the only moment you get before your life is forfeit."

The Centenaur swallowed and nodded.

The sound of battle grew muffled outside the eastern gate. The dull crack of boulders striking a distant wall echoed on the stone streets.

They jogged north under the deserted eastern wall, and the sound of destruction grew louder. Mujahid signaled for everyone to stop when he reached the northeast tower.

The enemy's siege engines were too far away to be hit and too far away to hit the wall. They had to be magically enhanced.

A commotion rose among the enemy forces, and he could see the vanguard marching toward the wall. Many of the soldiers had looks of disbelief on their faces. The northern gate must be open now. The soldiers within would be making a show of surrender. The diversion was working.

Mujahid gestured for everyone to follow him as he headed farther east, down the embankment that kept the city elevated above the plain. He just needed to give the archers a clear view.

Laughter erupted in the enemy vanguard.

Digby was running back and forth, naked from head to toe, his bowed legs moving faster than Mujahid thought possible. After performing several cartwheels, and pantomiming being ravaged by the northern gate, Digby ran back into the city. Some of the soldiers in the van doubled over with laughter, but most looked at each other with confused expressions.

This was the moment Mujahid needed. Digby's *secret weapon* had worked.

Mujahid looked over his shoulder at Centenaur Eric. "Now."

One hundred arrows launched toward the vanguard. Mujahid signaled and the other two necromancers entered the battle.

When the first of the undead rose, the imperial soldiers didn't realize what was happening. One moment their fellow soldiers were laughing next to them. The next moment they would rise, striking at anyone within arm's reach.

A surge of death energy emanated in waves from farther out to the north. Mujahid watched the other two necromancers with a discerning eye as they raised penitents in quick succession. But it was early in the battle. The effects of madness would be difficult to detect. He summoned his own penitents into the mix.

The number of undead on the field grew at an alarming rate. The Religarian forces remained confused after the first three volleys of arrows. They had no idea where the attack was coming from.

 The undead slaughtered everything in reach with a sadistic fury, ripping their opponents apart by hand as often as using a weapon. Some were killed by empire soldiers, only to be raised and thrust back into the fray. Soldiers fled as they realized what was happening around them.

As necessary as this was, Mujahid's stomach sickened. Each of those reanimated corpses was a person who was suffering and confused. He had to fight his natural instinct to help them. He had a job to do, and thousands of lives depended on him. The dead would take care of the dead. He had to take care of the living now.

He focused his concentration and looked back toward the battlefield. Many of the fleeing soldiers were cut down by a surging swarm of death. The thirsty, barren field turned crimson beneath their feet, and a hideous mud formed and clung to boots and armor.

An empire soldier...an officer by the look of it...had ridden into the van and was shouting orders. Soldiers turned this way and that, but found themselves under attack by dead allies they thought were still alive. The only way to know for certain who was dead and who was alive was by the degree of injury sustained.

An arrow took the officer straight through his right eye, and he slumped off his mount. Mujahid channeled power into the corpse and summoned the officer back from the dead. When the namocea was over, Mujahid took control. He commanded the man to remove the arrow from the gaping wound and toss it aside. Without thinking, he attempted to get the officer to remount, but the horse would have no part of it.

He cursed himself for his ignorance.

Animals could always tell the difference between the dead and the living. The giant warhorse reared up on its hind legs and tried to trample the undead officer.

Mujahid called the soldier off, and the horse bolted backwards, crushing several men in the process. Mujahid cast power forward and the men rose, one by one, no longer fettered by the moral constraints of life, and no longer in possession of anything resembling sanity.

A sharp, stabbing pain took Mujahid in the thigh, and he looked down to find an arrow protruding from the muscle. He looked up to the wall to find the source of the attack and cursed. A Tildem archer was fighting a losing battle with one of the necromancers and had misfired.

So it begins, Mujahid thought as he looked at the now-insane priest.

His newly-raised penitent sensed his distress and began running toward him.

Mujahid had to do something. If the Religarians saw the commander running this way, they would follow.

He ordered the penitent to return to battle, and filled his energy well.

He sent a wall of force in the direction of the archer and the necromancer. The blast caught both of them, tossing them backward down the embankment. The fallen necromancer rose and lunged toward the archer.

Mujahid recoiled as wisps of power moved past him from the tower above. The insane necromancer was lifted off the ground as if bound by mystical ropes.

Mujahid looked for the source of the power.

Digby stared back at him from the tower. The expression on his face was deadly, but something was holding him back. He must be looking for permission to kill the other priest.

Mujahid nodded.

Digby made a sweeping gesture toward the killing field below the wall, and the necromancer flew into the midst of the carnage. A nearby penitent reared back and threw himself at the fallen priest, ripping the necromancer's throat out.

Mujahid had never witnessed such an adept display of telekinesis in all his years of necromancy. There was more to Digby than the man let on.

Mujahid channeled power into the dead necromancer and ordered him into battle. He told himself that he needed to control these penitents, but he knew it was a lie. The insane necromancer had affected him, and he wasn't expecting it.

A stabbing sensation brought him back to the present. If he didn't do something about his leg soon, the injury would be permanent. He was going to have to remove the arrow himself.

Motion caught his eye and he looked up to see Digby leap from the crenelated tower.

Mujahid screamed at him to stop, but it was too late. The man had gone insane. He must have thrown himself off the tower in a moment of clarity. Mujahid wanted to turn away but something stopped him.

Digby wasn't falling.

The diminutive priest slowed his fall with another masterful display of telekinesis. When he reached the ground, he ran to Mujahid's side.

"Are you aware there's something pointy sticking out of your leg?" Digby said.

"I thought you mad."

"I just threw myself off a wall, man. Of course I'm mad."

Mujahid gripped the arrow by the shaft. "Are you ready?"

"The question, my Lord, is are *you* ready?"

Mujahid ripped the arrow from his thigh. His flesh tore as the barbed point ripped through his leg. His vision swam, but the unmistakable vibration of power entered his leg.

Digby was healing him. He shouldn't know how to do that.

Mujahid's energy returned and the wound started closing.

"I'll be ok from here," Mujahid said. "Thank you."

"You're a mighty necromancer, Lord Mujahid, but not even that thick skull of yours is hard enough to stop arrows. You're too important. Don't die."

With a single push of his legs, Digby leapt into the air and ascended back to the tower.

Mujahid was speechless.

Shouts of "to the King" went up near the northern gate.

King Donal charged into the midst of a group of Religarian soldiers, who had made it past the line of undead and were threatening the gate. His swordplay was masterful, but his sword wasn't the weapon Mujahid was interested in. A penitent fought at Donal's side.

The king was not only personally leading his men into battle. He was leading as a necromancer.

Smoke had begun to blot out the amber sky, and as it began to cloud Mujahid's vision, three Religarians charged King Donal. A crushing blow from a war hammer the length of a man broke Donal's sword in half as the smoke grew too thick to see through.

There was no way to get to the king now. Mujahid hoped Donal's guard was up to the challenge.

The acrid odor from the smoke burned Mujahid's nostrils, and he turned to find the source.

Fires had been set at the vanguard and the rear in an attempt to separate the living from the undead. If he didn't stop underestimating this Religarian commander, they would all pay the price for it.

The blaze had engulfed many of the living along with the undead, but the undead penitents were taking the most damage. There was a clearly-defined corridor of living soldiers, caught between the wall of fire at the van and the wall of fire at the rear. Fire had destroyed the siege engines at both ends, but the ones in the central corridor were standing. The empire had been shaken by Death's Vise, but they were regrouping, and if Mujahid didn't change his tactics the temporary gains would mean nothing.

The Religarian commander had ordered his archers forward, and they were targeting Tildem archers at the rear and eastern flank. It would only be a matter of time before the Religarian forces overwhelmed the wall. Tildem would fall.

Nuuan came running along the rear of the enemy force. He cast as he ran in an apparent attempt to raise the archers as they fell. But in order for it to work, he would have to control every one he raised, and there was no telling how many he had already summoned during the battle.

Mujahid was weak, but he was running out of options. He commanded his penitent necromancer to begin casting toward the enemy force. An undead priest may not be able to summon a penitent of his own, but he could wield a healthy amount of necropotency.

The necromantic link evaporated, leaving Mujahid disoriented. He looked out onto the smoke-covered battlefield through columns of fire. A group of life magi were killing the undead soldiers with bursts of fire that vaporized anything in their path. The tide of battle was turning, and not for the better.

Archers and infantry fell by the dozen as flames enveloped a large section of the wall. The remaining catapults hurled burning payloads that burst on impact, spreading liquid fire with an accelerant that Mujahid couldn't identify. Tildem infantry gathered in preparation for the inevitable breach.

Mujahid had to shake this fear that had risen inside him. Risk of insanity or no, he couldn't stand here and do nothing as Rotham fell.

He took a deep breath and cast necropotency out into the field, summoning as many undead as he could in rapid succession, living one lifetime after another. If he failed here, all of Erindor would be doomed to an uncertain fate. The darkness closed in around him, as his mind grew closer and closer to the point of fracture.

Lifetime after lifetime, atrocity after atrocity, he stood on the embankment once more. How much time had passed? Four thousand years? Five thousand years? He raged with evil absorbed over the course of untold millennia. Every rape, every murder, every genocide twisted and deformed his soul until he no longer knew anything of Mujahid or Mukhtaar Lords, Pinnacles or Archmages. He wanted to kill the little flying man. He wanted to rip him apart with his bare hands. Maybe he would tear his heart out and eat it. He had done that many times in the last thousand years. He had grown to like the taste of human flesh, succulent and warm. He would start by setting Digby on fire. That would be fun. Digby would burn and dance, and this time he wouldn't escape.

Mujahid filled his power well and prepared to cast.

Something rose up from deep within his being. The boundless rage had broken free of its shackles and rushed to the surface, a malevolent force that fought to take control of him. He saw no flames, but it was as if he were on fire. It felt as if his bones wanted to break free from his body.

Pain exploded in his face, and brilliant lights danced before his eyes. He landed on his back and his head hit the ground with a solid thud. The evil that had threatened to consume him slipped away.

"You try that again and I'll kill you myself," Nuuan said. "You won't have to go crazy first, you idiot! By the fetid sweat on Zubuxo's—what the hells were you thinking?"

Who was this vulgar man screaming at him?

Nuuan. His brother.

Tildem.

The Pinnacle.

The tyrant.

Memories rushed back in a torrent of images.

"Nuuan?" Mujahid said, groggy from the punch to the face. "What in Arin's name are you doing here? The rear?"

"Never mind that now. It's too late."

"How?"

"Look," Nuuan said, pointing toward the battle.

Mujahid turned toward the battlefield and his eyes widened in horror. The absence of any necromantic links confirmed what his eyes beheld. Not a single undead warrior remained standing on the field. They weren't fallen...they were gone, destroyed by the fires that ravaged the field. Several thousand Religarian soldiers remained, and they were advancing.

Rotham would fall. There was nothing Mujahid could do about it anymore.

"You need to go, brother," Nuuan said. "Get your arse out of here and back into the city."

"We'll go together."

"I'll be staying."

Motion caught Mujahid's attention and he turned to see Digby walking toward them with the two necromancers that had been helping Nuuan at the rear. They each had the same deadpan expression on their face.

"What are you going to do?" Mujahid said to no one in particular.

"I'll see you again, brother," Nuuan said. "May be a while, though."

Mujahid panicked. He wasn't accustomed to panic.

"Now go," Nuuan said. "Quickly, before it's too late. Get back into the city and wait."

"Nuuan."

"Trust me, brother. Stay in the city until the fog disappears. You hear me? Wait for the fog to pass."

"What fog? What in Arin's—"

"Go!"

Mujahid nodded and turned back to the wall. For reasons he couldn't explain or understand, he started running.

He didn't want to leave Nuuan there. His brother was stubborn. He'd never talk the man out of whatever plan he had concocted. But he trusted Nuuan. Even if he didn't know or like what he was planning.

A burning sensation in his chest distracted him for a moment. Was it a remnant of nearly going insane? He ignored it and kept running.

The wall was peppered with large holes. Mujahid entered through one of the demolished sections and ran toward the command center at the northern gate.

A half a block from the command center, soldiers were staring out at the battlefield with looks of disbelief.

The Religarian army had turned around, as if some unseen threat approached them from the rear. A semi-transparent dome rose from the center of the field, growing to cover a group of people beneath it.

Mujahid ran into the eastern tower, which was still standing, and climbed up for a better look.

What he saw defied explanation. Nuuan and his three companions had fought their way to the center of the battlefield, and one of them...Digby, from the look of things...was releasing energy from his hands that splayed out and formed the dome. Volleys of arrows bounced off the structure as if striking stone.

At the center of the dome was Nuuan. He was sitting on the ground, ignoring what was going on around him. The dirt on the battlefield churned, as if dozens of miniature vortexes were rotating just beneath the surface.

Nuuan collapsed. The necromancers under the dome ran to his side. Digby ran toward him as well, and the transparent dome vanished with a thunderous explosion that filled the battlefield with a thick, red fog.

Mujahid's chest grew warmer, and again he ignored it. Was this the fog Nuuan had warned him about?

A nightmarish sound rose from the battlefield. It was impossible to see what was happening through the fog, but from what Mujahid heard, he was glad he couldn't see. The sound of a thousand blades filled the air, intermingled with the screams of men watching their doom approach. A sickening, slicing noise rose up from the field and rain poured down on the fog-shrouded areas, swirling the fog into a series of damp red vortexes.

An errant drop struck the side of Mujahid's face and he wiped it off. When he pulled his hand away, he realized something about the texture of the rain wasn't right. He held his hand up and stared as blood dripped down his finger.

The individual swirls of red fog, which had been scattered among the Empire soldiers, coalesced into a bloodthirsty vortex in the center of the killing field, drawing the horrific cloud into a tornado of blood and human remains. When the howling wind reached an ear-shattering volume, the vortex stopped spinning and began to collapse in on itself, layer by layer, until all of the blood and gore existed as a single point in space.

The point vanished, and stillness settled on the field. Not a single Religarian remained. What the vortex left behind of the Religarians wasn't recognizable as human. It was a mixture of flesh, liquid and mud oozing together to create a macabre lake of death.

The warmth in Mujahid's chest threatened to distract him from his horror, and he shook it off.

Where was Nuuan? Panic rose as Mujahid considered the possibility that his brother was a part of that grizzly lake. He took a moment to get control of himself, going over the last things Nuuan had said. Nuuan never made a promise he couldn't keep.

A cheer rose up from the Tildem army, but Mujahid couldn't take his eyes away from the battlefield. In all his years of necromancy, he had seen more strange things on this day than in all previous days combined.

The heat in the center of his chest had grown unbearable, and he couldn't take it anymore. He pulled his robe outward and looked down the neck to see what was causing it.

The Talisman of Archmages was active. Nicolas was alive.

Oh how the gods mock me.

He hoisted the talisman out of his robes and studied it. Nicolas was traveling toward Arin's Watch.

The boy remembered.

Mujahid looked down from the tower and saw the king standing in front of the gate, disheveled and staggering. A wounded soldier stood on one side, and a penitent stood on the other. Mujahid climbed down the stairs and joined him.

"Majesty," Mujahid said.

Donal swayed and nearly fell. He held up the hilt of his shattered sword.

"Somebody broke my sword," Donal said. "Dirty *bastard* broke my sword."

Mujahid made his way down from the tower and held the talisman up for Donal to see.

Donal leaned against the wall for support.

"I must leave for Arin's Watch," Mujahid said.

"You'll not travel alone," Donal said. "Commander Yuli will accompany you with a small force."

He hadn't realized the bruised and bleeding person standing next to the king was Yuli. She had a cut over her left eye and was struggling to see.

"Aye, Majesty," she said. "I'll go."

"Rally the necromancers of Tildem, King Donal," Mujahid said. "The future of Erindor depends on it."

"I intend to," Donal said.

"If my brother should return...." Mujahid had to choke back a lump in his throat.

"I will tell him where you are, and what we saw here," Donal said.

Mujahid nodded and joined Yuri.

They gathered what supplies they could, and within an hour they had left Rotham behind through the eastern gate.

CHAPTER TWENTY EIGHT

Nicolas had emerged from the turbulent Sea of Arin through an underground waterway known only to the cichlos. They'd told him where to find the switchbacks leading to the top of the sheer cliff face near Arin's Watch, where'd he see a monolithic statue in the distance across the sea. He was told it was a statue of Arin, but it was too far away to tell.

He surprised a starving crag spider while climbing up the switchbacks and had to deal with it, but the cichlos had warned him about those as well.

What he wasn't expecting were the Religarians. They were patrolling the cliffs several miles from Arin's Watch, away from any roads or ports. Some mounted, some on foot. They must be aware of the switchbacks as well. He saw them too late to avoid them.

They were young. Too young to recognize the significance of the robe he wore. He should have worn something less noticeable, but it was a part of him now. He was a necromancer. And he had no intention of hiding that fact.

There were close to twenty of them. His stomach churned, which surprised him. He expected fear to be gone along with his innocence. He should know better.

"Identify yourself," a mounted soldier said. His mount wasn't as long as an adda-ki, but the creature's six legs were more muscular.

Nicolas called to mind Kaitlyn's picture, and his rolling stomach began to settle.

The world outside fled along with the fear and anxiety, and he dwelled within his cet. There was nothing but peace there. Peace and power, intermingling as if one could not exist without the other, two forces in perfect balance. They intertwined around the image of Kaitlyn and embraced her.

"I'm under the authority of the Emperor of Religar and the archmage," the soldier said. "Maybe a jail cell will loosen your lips?"

Not gonna happen, asshole.

Nicolas had seen the inside of too many jail cells in Erindor. He didn't know which would scandalize the nuns at the orphanage most—his ability to raise the dead, or his two stints in jail since leaving them. He chuckled when he realized it would probably be the latter.

"You find us amusing?" the soldier said.

Nicolas stopped chuckling. "You're marching an army through somebody else's country like you own the place. Yeah, that tickles me a little."

Another mounted soldier came forward and drew a sword. "We don't have time for this."

"Suit yourself," Nicolas said. He embraced his power, preparing to attack, but hesitated for a moment, looking for any possible route of escape. When he found none, he swore.

I don't want to do this again!

The mounted soldier raised his sword and swung.

Nicolas expelled two narrow, sharpened cylinders of necropotency at the mounted men.

His attacker fell to the ground clutching his throat, blood flowing in rivulets between his fingers. The other mounted soldier slid off his mount soon after, and his compatriots backed away. They turned in confusion, as if looking for an ambush.

The telekinesis weakened Nicolas. Manipulating necropotency like that was draining. He was taking his newfound power for granted, and power was no substitute for brains. If he didn't perform a summoning now, he wouldn't have any energy left to survive the fight.

He raised the dead Religarians, his mind aging a half century in a moment. Through their memories he understood what was happening and why they were here. Arin's Watch was in the hands of Religar now, and a bloody field paved the way through its western gate. That explained the presence of a crag spider so close to a city. But the soldiers had seen two conflicting versions of the events that took place.

His penitents attacked and two more Religarians died before the others realized what was happening. The necropotency from their corpses flowed into Nicolas in a steady stream.

"Six hells! He's necromancer," a soldier said.

Cries went up at the word *necromancer* and the group erupted in chaos. Several soldiers raced toward him with swords drawn, but the rest fled to the rear.

The sound of shouting and hooves grew louder as a larger group of Religarians approached from behind the first. The first patrol must have been nothing more than a scouting party.

Nicolas raised another penitent.

When the namocea passed there was a surge of necropotency. Something had changed. There was more ambient power than there should have been. People were dying nearby and he couldn't see how or why.

Several Religarians fell from their mounts, unseated by arrows that punctured their light armor. Within moments the edge of the cliff was swarming with Tildem soldiers and undead.

I'm not the only necromancer here.

Nicolas didn't see where the help had come from, but if they were attacking the Religarians, then they were his allies. He combined his attack with theirs and went after the larger force, pulling men from their saddles with ropes of necropotency.

He wielded necropotency instinctively, willing it into shapes and patterns governed by the ebb and flow of battle.

He looked around for the other necromancers that must be there. There had to be a small army of them, based on the number of undead. He picked out the translucent necromantic links, using the trick he learned in Aquonome, and saw several blue lines extending to some point behind him.

The last Religarian fell, and Nicolas exhaled.

A man cleared his throat. "What is the Prime Duty of a necromancer?" the familiar-sounding voice asked. *Mujahid!*

Nicolas smiled. "The Prime Duty of a necromancer is to raise the dead and help them achieve purification."

Nicolas turned and saw Mujahid smiling back at him in front of a dozen or more archers. He wore a brown robe, unlike any he had seen before. It had a hood that looked big enough to cover four heads, and it hung half way down his back.

"And how is the old siek these days?"

Nicolas embraced Mujahid.

"You should have told me about the cichlos," Nicolas said. "I thought you were dead, by the way."

"No," Mujahid said. He stepped back and placed both hands on Nicolas's shoulders. "It was I who thought *you* were dead. And I had far better cause to believe it. When the talisman went dark...." He shook his head. "I didn't know until a few days ago that you were alive. I'd love to hear how you managed that little trick of concealment."

Mujahid didn't know? But he'd been to Aquonome too. Was there anything else Mujahid didn't know about the cichlos?

It was strange seeing his old teacher. It felt as if several lifetimes had passed since he last saw the man, and in a way that was true. He had learned his place in the universe since then, and discovered what his purpose was.

"How'd you get out of Caspardis?"

Mujahid's face became serious. "With help from a guard."

Nicolas understood. He didn't need the details. "I learned a lot from the cichlos."

"Obviously," Mujahid said. He narrowed his eyes as he stared at Nicolas's robe. "Does the siek know you have that or did you abscond with it when you left Aquonome?"

Nicolas turned his gaze toward the yellow sky. "I have to bring that thing down. One way or another."

"We are of one mind. I'd like you to meet someone. Commander Yuli, Guard Captain of the Rotham Militia."

The woman named Yuli approached and nodded. This woman was no stranger to battle. He could see it in her walk. Confidant strides. Every step had a purpose. Just like the countless warriors he'd raised from the dead.

"Nicolas Ardirian," Nicolas said, extending his hand for Yuli to shake. "Necromancer...and Heir to the Obsidian Throne."

Mujahid looked at him with surprise on his face.

Yuli took Nicolas's hand and gave it a firm shake. "Well met, Magus Nicolas. Do you have news of the siege at Arin's Watch?"

"There is no siege," Nicolas said. "My penitents saw a cloud of demons that came out of nowhere and destroyed everything in sight. Well, one saw demons, the other saw blades. I saw it through their eyes, and I still don't know which one is right. It was the fog from hell, though, I'll tell ya that much."

Mujahid and Yuli exchanged an odd look.

"We saw the very same cloud," Mujahid said. "It lifted the siege of Rotham as well."

"Siek Lamil told me about a smaller barrier that protects the Pinnacle," Nicolas said. "Can we get through it?"

"If we have the key, yes."

"Say what?" Nicolas asked.

"Remember the *tithe* I said you'd need?"

Nicolas thought back. Mujahid *had* spoken about a "tithe from Pilgrim's Landing" back in Caspardis.

"You have to present the priests at Pilgrim's Landing with a gift in order to get into the Pinnacle," Mujahid said. "A tithe. The priests at the Great Temple take the tithe and *bless* it...or so Erindor believes."

Yuli's posture stiffened.

"They place the tithe and a small orb, no larger than my fist, into a locked container and give it back to the pilgrim to take to the Pinnacle. The orb is the key."

"Looks like we need one of those orbs," Nicolas said.

"I'll handle the tithe," Mujahid said.

"We can find a ship in Arin's Watch, now that the siege is lifted," Yuli said.

Mujahid tugged at his brown robe. "I brought some extras along. They'll help us blend in."

Nicolas looked at the dead Religarians and the Prime Duty echoed in his mind. The next few hours would last several hundred years. "Let's clean this mess up and be off to Pilgrim's Landing."

CHAPTER TWENTY NINE

Nicolas watched as Pilgrim's Landing, and the statue of Arin, grew larger in the distance.

The island was an enormous rock, jutting up from the sea all spiked and jagged, like a bunch of skyscrapers packed too close together. There was no way to avoid it if they wanted to. The Sea of Arin funneled all ships to the southern dock, forcing them between crags sharp enough to tear a hole in the hull of the ship. The only way around the island was through it or over it.

Pilgrim's Landing grew out of the face of the island itself. Several stone-carved piers along the southern dock formed platforms where ships could tie their mooring lines. A large ship anchored along the northern dock, which was visible less than a mile north of the southern dock, rocking back and forth with the swell of the sea. The face of the rocky island was peppered with arched passageways and ornately-barricaded landings that protruded from tunnels entering the mountainside. At the top of the mountain the gargantuan statue of Arin, wearing his great winged helm, was carved out of the rock face, and the largest landing of all jutted out from the mountainside next to its right. The helm was a translucent stone that reminded Nicolas of quartz.

"The Temple of Arin," Mujahid said as he gazed toward the giant statue. "The Great Orb once illuminated the helm from within, like a beacon. Now...." Mujahid stopped and sighed. "We'll be docking soon. Change into the extra priest's robes."

Nicolas thought back to the voices under Aquonome and wondered if one of those voices was Arin. Mujahid had to be told, just in case, and now was as good a time as any.

"I've been to the Plane of Death, Mujahid."

Mujahid's eyes narrowed. "I missed our banter, boy, but we have precious little time—"

"Zubuxo is missing. I think he and the other gods are *inside* the barrier. And it has something to do with the unborn kids I saw in the Plane of Death."

"And I thought you were crazy before—"

"The hellwraiths take them. The life magic takes—"

"Hellwraiths?" Mujahid snorted. "Can't be hellwraiths."

"Listen. It takes everything we do as priests and...*undoes* it."

"The Abaddonian Gates are sealed. Whatever you saw, they weren't hellwraiths."

"I don't know about any Abaddonian gates, but do white-eyed evil bastards with black whips and no legs who come and drag your ass off ring a bell?"

Mujahid scratched his chin. "Those are hellwraiths." He swore. "This changes everything."

"Oh no it don't. I'm still taking that barrier out."

"The hellwraiths are *my* business to deal with. I just didn't think it would be so soon."

"What would be so soon?"

"Just find the Great Orb. You'll know what to do. You saw what happened in Paradise."

"That's what worries me. That orb is my only way home."

Mujahid spent the next few minutes giving Nicolas details of the Pinnacle's layout, including a description of the hallway leading to the sanctuary; polished stone and portraits of old archmages. As large as Mujahid claimed the place was, the Great Orb's sanctuary wasn't going to be difficult to find. It was a straight path, if he took the right entrance.

As they drew closer to the dock, Nicolas slipped a large brown robe over his own, and Mujahid inspected him.

"Good," Mujahid said. "Some Arinian priests take a vow of silence. You're one of them. So shut up for a change and let me do the talking."

"Nice."

"They won't trouble us. I'll give them some gold, they'll give us a tithing box. But, take this dagger just in case. Hide it like this for now." Mujahid showed him how to use the sleeve for concealment.

It wasn't getting to the Pinnacle that worried Nicolas anymore. It was whether he'd have the strength to do what needed doing once he got there.

N icolas stared out over the ship's bow toward a yellow dome that stretched across the horizon and several hundred feet into the air.

The Pinnacle barrier.

Somewhere under that dome was Archmage Kagan. His father.

But not my dad.

His dad would never be capable of bringing a world to ruin to suit his ego. Dr. Murray; the man who dished out food at a soup kitchen when he wasn't excavating archaeological sites. His dad; the man who adopted him as a teenager when everyone else just waited for him to turn eighteen and leave St. John's children's home for good. No, his dad could never sit on a throne and exalt himself while the rest of the world decayed around him. Even Siek Lamil was more of a father figure to him than Kagan could ever be.

I wonder what Kagan looks like.

It was a stray thought, but one he couldn't help. The man was, after all, his father. Were they the same height? Did they have the same wavy hair that grew wavier with length? Maybe the same nose, narrow with a slightly pronounced bridge?

He squeezed his eyes shut and turned away from the barrier. Any thought of similarity between him and the tyrant disgusted him. The feeling of wanting to be anywhere but here overwhelmed him, but that just made him angry with himself for even considering it. He opened his eyes and let the light from the Pinnacle barrier flow into him.

I ain't going anywhere until this is done.

He took a deep breath and studied the barrier once more.

Choppy waves disappeared into its base without as much as a splash. He hoped the ship would pass through without it killing them, but the more he thought about it the more he realized *not passing through* wasn't the thing to fear. The siek never said the cichlos couldn't enter the barrier...he said they vanished when they tried.

Three buoys rose out of the sea as black shadows against the yellow dome. That must be how they regulate traffic through the barrier. The buoys marked two channels for ships, one for entering the Pinnacle and one for leaving.

Nicolas stood closer to Mujahid as the ship approached the barrier. He didn't know the range on that tithe box, and he didn't want to learn the hard way.

The ship's bow entered the yellow wall and the barrier crept toward him. Everything became simple. All he had to do was wait.

He closed his eyes as the barrier surrounded them. Necropotency surged around him like a whirlpool, and he opened his eyes, afraid he'd see the entire crew dead on the deck, but no one had died. He saw the ship and the crew, as well as Mujahid standing next to him. But everything else was the same shade of bright yellow. The uniformity was such that there was no way to tell how far it extended, or if it extended at all. The only evidence of distance was the space between him and the bow and the crew members.

A male voice boomed in his mind.

He who walks between worlds.

It was a voice he heard under Aquonome the day the siek took him to the Great Barrier.

Bring down the sky. Save the children.

Nicolas reached up and grabbed his head. The voice was powerful...and sad.

"What is it?" Mujahid said.

"I hear voices. *Loud* voices."

Mujahid frowned, as if someone had just told him that hot was cold.

A crackling sensation rippled across Nicolas's skin. The yellow vanished and he looked out over the bow. His chest tightened as he caught his first glimpse of the Pinnacle.

Resting atop a foundation of solid stone, the Pinnacle complex was the most prominent feature of the island. A massive city upon a mesa, it stretched more than a mile across the mountaintop and dwarfed everything around it. The complex was as much a temple as it was a fortress, with tall minarets rising up beyond its fortified wall. A lofty helical tower, with arched windows, spiraled up from the center and tapered toward the top. It reminded Nicolas of the minaret at the Great Mosque of Samarra, though this was at least twice the size in every direction. It reflected the yellow light from the barrier sky like a golden beacon. Its spirals alternated in shade and created a barber pole effect that reached toward a soaring beam of amber shooting into the sky. Crackles of multicolored energy soared upwards along the beam toward the pale yellow barrier and disappeared into it.

The Great Orb was up there. Nicolas couldn't see it, but he knew it. He knew it was the source of that amber beam. It was the source of the barrier. It was the source of all the trouble in this world.

But the Great Orb wasn't the only thing that waited for him beyond that fortified wall. Kagan waited among the minarets, among the council magi and pilgrims.

He wouldn't have long to wait.

I'm home, father.

CHAPTER THIRTY

When the ship docked, Nicolas noticed something odd. Pinnacle guardsmen patrolled the area in much smaller numbers than he had expected.

"Shouldn't there be more guards?" Nicolas asked.

Mujahid shook his head. "This is an island of magi, Nicolas, surrounded by waters that are virtually impassable. When the Barathosian Empire sent their armada, even they were smart enough to avoid a direct confrontation with the Pinnacle. If an attack is going to come for the Pinnacle, it won't come by sea or sword."

"That's something else I'm afraid of," Nicolas said.

"Let Commander Yuli and I worry about the Pinnacle guard. Your goal is the sanctuary at the top of the central tower. You're dressed like a priest of Arin, so use that to your advantage."

Nicolas nodded, uncomfortable in the bulky brown robe with over-sized hood, and walked down the gangplank with Mujahid.

"Remember," Mujahid said. "Enter with the pilgrims through Bishop's Gate on the west side of the fortress. It's reserved for the religious orders. They'll lead you to a large room at the bottom of the tower...cavernous, by most standards, and you'll see a great spiraling staircase leading up. Take it. And be careful. There are men and women in that fortress who have forgotten more about magic than you will ever learn. Oh, and you'll need this." He handed the tithe box to Nicolas

"What about the patrols? Isn't someone gonna stop me?"

"I'll keep them busy. No one here knows what you look like...not even your father. People will look at you and see a priest of Arin. You still have the dagger?"

Nicolas nodded.

"Well don't be afraid to use it."

Nicolas headed toward the west end of the dock, but stopped when Mujahid called out to him.

"Good luck, Nicolas," Mujahid said. "Remember Lamil's teachings. Cling to the things that give your life meaning. They define you and make you powerful. And remember this...you're still my postulant, regardless of that festering robe they gave you. Get yourself killed and I'll make sure you live to regret it."

Nicolas smiled and headed toward the staircase.

Do you think he can do it?" Yuli asked.

Mujahid pulled power into his well. On most occasions it was something he did without thought, but this time it brought him comfort to direct the flow of the energy with purpose.

"We'll give him as good a chance as we can, Commander, even if it means we die trying."

"Looks like we're going to have that chance sooner rather than later," Yuli said. She nodded toward an approaching Pinnacle guard patrol.

Mujahid pulled off his Arinian robes and exposed the midnight blue necromancer's Robe of Mastery. The symbol of ascension ignited in his mind.

"Now it begins," he said.

He cast the power forward and hoped it would buy Nicolas the time he needed.

An enormous torrent of energy flowed past Nicolas. Mujahid must be drawing the guards to the dock to keep them away from the sanctuary.

Nicolas pulled his hood up as he climbed the grand stairway that was carved into the stony foundation of the Pinnacle. The stairway switched back on itself several times as it made the hundred-foot climb above the dock. Mist from the sea no longer reached him here, but the smell and taste of salt in the air remained. He slipped on the shiny stairs and chided himself for not being more careful. It would be pretty sad if he came all this way only to slip on some stairs and break his neck.

The steps looked as if someone had carved them with a machine, so perfect were the edges, and the stone banisters were engraved with ornate scroll work. A glint of light caught his eye from one of the steps and he looked down.

The light emanated from within the stone, as if the rock were lit by some internal energy source. Back in Austin this wouldn't have struck him as odd at all. But in Erindor? There was magic involved here.

Several guards passed him, saying "Father."

Mujahid was right. They only see a priest of Arin.

Nicolas kept his hands folded in front of him and nodded back.

The top of the staircase emerged onto a rectangular plaza dominated by the Pinnacle fortress that surrounded it on three sides. Everything was a rich, dark-brown color. Highlights and bas-reliefs were layered in gold, in stark contrast to their darker surroundings.

A stone stairway, spanning the width of the plaza, rose up to a marble colonnade on the far end, where four monolithic doors hung open. That must be the primary entrance to the Pinnacle, and it was an entrance Mujahid told him to avoid. The twisting passages within would lead him away from the main tower, rather than toward it.

Two grand arches bordered the east and west sides of the plaza. Bishop's Gate, the gate for pilgrims, was somewhere beyond the western arch, so he headed in that direction.

An enormous surge of power raised the hair on his arms, and shouts went up throughout the plaza.

"Necromancers at the dock!"

Nicolas looked over the edge of the plaza and glanced down toward the dock more than a hundred feet below. Mujahid had raised a penitent, and it was slicing through Pinnacle guard two at a time. A green cloud descended on several of the guardsmen and they dropped to the ground, clutching their throats. Another cloud descended on the stone staircase leading down to the dock.

He picked up his pace and walked through the arch, but he had to resist the urge to run when he turned the corner.

More than a hundred guards were running toward him, making their way into the plaza. He glanced over his shoulder and saw the same thing happening at the eastern arch.

He lowered his head and kept walking, but he couldn't shake the certainty of what was about to happen.

There's no way Mujahid and Yuli will survive this.

Pinnacle guardsmen poured down the stairway as Mujahid offered a silent prayer to Shealynd. The symbol of ascension burned with fury as he channeled a continuous flow of power into the disease trap he laid over the staircase. The trap pulled power from him at an extraordinary rate when the first wave of guardsmen entered and collapsed to the ground. He broke the link to the trap and allowed it to consume whatever energy it had left. Corpses lined the pristine marble staircase and the number grew as guards fell by the dozen.

Mujahid turned inward and started raising the dead. Two corpses rose on the staircase. He sent the attack command and both corpses bounded up the stairs toward oncoming guards.

"Now," he yelled to Yuli.

The commander shouted orders and several of her men launched volleys of arrows up over the staircase.

"Is this wise?" Yuli asked. "We're shooting blind. We could hit anything up there."

"If it's up there, we *want* to hit it."

His penitents were moving through guardsmen like skilled warriors battling new recruits. It had been decades since the Pinnacle Guard had done battle with a master necromancer, and their lack of training was showing.

It wasn't the Guard that Nicolas needed to worry about, however. It was the Council. The older Council magi were once powerful necromancers themselves, before the Great Purge, which forced them to forsake their vows or be banished. They would know what to expect from an inexperienced priest. And no matter how far the boy had come in his training, he was inexperienced.

But not Mujahid.

Mujahid was a Mukhtaar Lord, forged in the undying fires of Paradise, and raised by Rite of Testing to a state of ascendancy. He had paid a dear price for his ascension, in ways no man living save one could comprehend.

Mujahid was no inexperienced priest. Today the Council would pay a debt to society for their crimes against humankind. Today they would know the wrath of a Mukhtaar Lord.

He filled his well and advanced up the marble stairs to the plaza.

Nicolas slipped into a group of pilgrims as they entered the Great Hall.

The palatial hall was separated into two halves, one comprised of several large, sunk-in sitting areas, ringed with polished travertine stone banisters, and the other a banquet area with rows of glazed-granite tables and benches. The walls, ceiling, and floor all looked as if they were carved from a single piece of polished rust-brown marble.

A group of women gathered in the closest sitting area. They were speaking with animated gestures.

"I'm well past my time now," a woman said. "I think I'm pregnant."

Most of them smiled when they heard the news, but an older woman didn't share their excitement.

"Don't set your hopes as high as last time," the older woman said.

They passed the group before he could hear the rest of the conversation. Why would they tell a pregnant woman to not be happy?

The base of the helical tower was on the far end of the room...right where Mujahid said it would be. Arched openings running up the outside wall allowed natural light to illuminate the spiraling stairs inside.

His group would pass the base of the stairs on their way to another shrine, so he slowed in an effort to fall back to the rear. He had to do something about the guard that followed them, though.

He dove into the stairwell, releasing two ropes of necropotency behind him. With a strong mental tug, he pulled the guard into the stairwell behind him with one rope while using the other to gag him.

Nicolas dragged the guard behind a half wall, then pulled the dagger from his robe.

The guard's eyes bulged, but the mystical gag kept his screams from being heard.

"I'm so sorry," Nicolas said.

Nicolas thrust the dagger into the guard's throat. He backed away as the life drained from the innocent man.

What have I become?

When the last shred of life left the guard, Nicolas raised him and bounded up the spiral staircase toward the sanctuary, losing count of the number of turns it made.

A cloaked man in leather boots, wearing a talisman like Mujahid's, ran down the stairs toward him.

There has to be a way through this without killing everybody I run into!

The words of Siek Lamil echoed in his mind. "You will make the journey to the Plane of Death with the blood of many men on your hands."

He shot a cylinder of necropotency toward the man's throat.

The man vanished, and a wave of power passed through Nicolas's chest from front to back.

It happened so fast that Nicolas had to look twice. He cursed under his breath and continued up the stairs. There was no going back now.

A great shudder forced him to the ground as another barrier quake started, but the quake fueled his determination. He would put an end to these quakes and to Kagan as well.

Mujahid looked at the Pinnacle guardsmen gathering in the plaza and knew, in his heart, that he was defeated.

"Get us out of this alive and I promise I won't make jokes about you playing with dead things," Yuli said.

"Let's just hope we bought him enough time," Mujahid said.

Shouts arose from the guardsmen.

Mujahid watched with a mixture of surprise and anger as three undead emerged from the eastern arch and sliced through the guards like master swordsmen.

"That damned boy," he said. "I told him to go straight for the central tower and forget about us."

"Fear not, Lord Mujahid," a voice said from behind.

Tithian.

"The *damned boy* is right where you sent him," Tithian said. "I left him on the central stairs a moment ago. I think I scared the both of us. In fact, I think he tried to kill me."

"Three penitents," Mujahid said. "Not bad for a rusty life magus."

"My people are cleaning up the guard on the east end, but they can't do it all. They're spies and assassins, not soldiers, and certainly not magi."

"You were right. I...you should know, that's all."

"In your own words, old friend, let's survive this war first, then we'll tend to forgiveness."

Mujahid nodded. "Where do you need us the most?"

"Make your way through the eastern arch to the tunnels. We can draw the council out from a position of strength and cover. You have the proper sigil?"

"I taught *you* of sigils, if I recall."

Tithian smiled and vanished.

The ground rumbled as the quake continued, and the stairwell filled with dust.

The way the tower was tapering, he should be getting close to the sanctuary. He made one more turn around the spiral staircase, clinging to the central wall, and a travertine-lined corridor came into view as he rounded the curve.

This was the place Mujahid told him about.

Portraits of magi set in bas-relief lined the corridor on each side. The passage ended in a large arch with two massive stone doors. They hung open to reveal a multi-hued orb of cascading light in the room beyond. As the liquid light flowed over the orb's surface it broke around swirls of energy that radiated every color of the rainbow. A beam of golden yellow as wide as the orb rose straight up from the top. The amount of energy it radiated was incalculable. He'd experienced this much power only one other time—near the barrier wall under the city of Aquonome.

This had to be the Great Orb of Arin.

So why were the doors open? Kagan must have heard that rumpus going on out there.

The ground around him shook, but the Orb of Arin seemed to be permanently fixed in the air, unmovable by any natural force.

He approached the orb, expecting to be attacked at any moment. Mujahid warned him that Kagan would be close to the orb, especially if there was a disturbance on the island. But Nicolas was alone. He filled his well with power to enhance his senses.

As he walked closer to the orb, a war of emotion erupted inside him. He could leave. If this orb was anything like the Orb of Zubuxo, then all he had to do was reach out and touch it. It took the Cichlos back home. It would take him home too. Back to Kaitlyn. He could put all of this behind him and hold her in his arms once more. It had been almost a year since he last saw her. Was she waiting for him? Did she think he was dead?

The heir. He who walks between worlds...Nicolas.

The voice resounded through his being as if it possessed him. It was different this time than under Aquonome. In the sea, a cacophony of voices had bombarded him, but this time a single, majestic voice entered his mind.

You have come. And now you must bring down the sky.

"But I don't know how."

You are not alone.

A blanket of energy hit his back and wrapped around him. The power drained away from him, emptying his well until the last drop of necropotency vanished. It was a shield of some sort.

He spun and saw a tall, slender man standing in the doorway.

The man wore a plain black head cover that laid flat against the top of his head. It was shaped like a zucchetto worn by a Catholic bishop, except broader, covering more of the head, and without the stem on top. Tufts of silvery hair poked out from beneath the cover. A red scapular trimmed with black wrapped around his shoulders and hung down to the center of his chest, where he clasped his slender fingers together. His black, floor-length cassock hid his shoes, but they clacked against the stone floor when he stepped.

"I believe you are my son," the man said.

Kagan. He set a trap for me and I walked right into it.

"That makes you the son of a god, you know," Kagan said. "It also makes you the sole heir to my throne. It would be wise for us to get to know one another, wouldn't you agree?"

Nicolas seethed. Kagan was the reason he was here, the reason this world had destroyed itself, and he was the cause of all the pain Nicolas saw on the Field of Judgment.

One of them would die today. And Nicolas would make damned sure it was Kagan.

Mujahid led Yuli and the remaining men through the eastern arch to a small plaza, bordered on each side by Pinnacle buildings. The hidden entrance he had shown Tithian decades earlier was just ahead.

A guard across the plaza shouted.

So much for stealth.

Dozens of Pinnacle guardsmen rushed from the barracks on the far side of the plaza, drawing swords and shouting battle cries.

When Mujahid looked at the barracks, for the first time in decades, it was as if everything he hated about this place, every bad memory he had, came flooding back.

He thought about the day they banished him and stripped him of an office he never asked for. He thought about Kagan's tyranny, and how the archmage usurped the voice of the gods themselves. He thought of all the dead, trapped in a hellish existence, waiting to be judged by a god who could no longer help them. And he thought of his brethren—men and women of Clan Mukhtaar, who suffered agonizing deaths at the hands of Kagan's agents for no other reason than their faith.

He thought of Nicolas, too...the infant, ripped from his world and birthright...the young man, torn away from his true love and the only home he had ever known, thrust into a conflict he didn't ask for or cause.

He thought of all these things, and something snapped. The carefully-crafted prison that kept his rage in check came crashing down, and he made no move to stop it this time. He welcomed it. He encouraged it.

Now. Now is the time for you to be free.

The hatred flowed through him, and he smiled. They would all suffer. These guardsmen defended Kagan, and that would cost them their lives.

The symbol of ascension ignited in his mind and he raised his hands over the plaza. He heard the guardsmen shout as one before they charged.

He wove threads of energy through symbols of power, forming patterns he had never attempted before. The hatred was leading him to hidden recesses in his consciousness that, until now, were undiscovered...and his smile grew broader.

Symbol after symbol ignited and pulsed with power as he imbued them with necromantic energy. He flooded the dancing symbols in a crackling bath of arcane force, channeling more power than he thought possible, until the pain in his head grew unbearable.

And still he smiled.

He heard Yuli's battle cry, as if from far away, and archers releasing arrows into the charging patrol. He listened as soldiers on both sides fell. It no longer mattered if they were friend or foe...they added to his power. Power was all that mattered. No one would live. A Mukhtaar Lord decreed it so.

No...the being he was becoming decreed it so.

And still he smiled.

He cast the power forward, summoning the entity that demanded to be summoned.

Time slowed its eternal march until it stopped. He turned to his right and saw men with mouths wide open, their arrows hanging in the air as if frozen in a wall of translucent ice. He turned to the oncoming charge of Pinnacle guard, and watched as some of them hovered over the ground, caught in mid step.

It didn't matter. None of it mattered. Only power mattered. Only hatred mattered. Only the being he was becoming mattered.

And still he smiled.

The entity was inside him, allowing him to operate outside the confines of time, and growing stronger at an alarming rate. The absence of the namocea disoriented him, but clarity soon followed.

He knew what this was. The ancient Mukhtaar Chronicles spoke of it as myth. Transfiguration. The Legendary power of a Mukhtaar Lord.

When the entity's rage grew to the point of consuming him, the part of his mind he controlled fought back, and he imagined himself casting the entity's essence forward, using the symbols of power like a sieve, until the being was both captured and empowered by them.

Violent, wracking pains tore through Mujahid's limbs as every bone in his body broke and shifted, shortened and elongated into shapes that defied human form. He grew taller and wider as his own bones ripped through the skin on his back and began to stretch and fold inward, forming skeletal wings devoid of flesh. He screamed in agony as his blood rushed from the exposed wounds in his back and streamed down the length of his legs.

And still he smiled.

Flesh tore from his body and disintegrated before it could touch the ground, and his internal organs liquefied and evaporated. He could taste his own flesh as it melted away from his jawbone and ran down what was left of his throat into the sacred fire that burned at the center of his body. His lower body fell away, leaving the tail of his spine exposed, and he floated in midair as the liquefied flesh dripped to the ground below. The pain was exquisite.

Light altered around him. The shadowy areas of the small plaza rose up and sped toward him, and soon he was shrouded in darkness—a darkness that burned with the heat of a thousand suns. The shadows merged and formed a cloak around his now-skeletal body. He gazed out over the crowd, standing three times his normal height, and the pain grew stronger still.

And still he smiled.

From deep within, a voice...whether it was his own or something alien, he didn't know...told him that he must survive the transformation, or he would die like a novice failing in the halls of power. This was his new hall of power. This was the destiny of a Mukhtaar Lord.

Time resumed and the oncoming patrol slowed their charge, staring upward at him with looks of abject terror. Yuli backed away, mouth agape. The part of him that refused to believe what was happening wanted to turn and see what Yuli was looking at, but he knew the truth. He had transformed into something terrible. There was little of Mujahid left. He was a Lord of Hell now, transfigured by the sacred fire within.

A power came over him that was both alien and familiar. It pulsed through his skeletal arms and guided his spectral hands through a series of complex gestures over the crowd of Pinnacle guardsmen. The sweet scent of freshly-cut roses overloaded his olfactory senses until he could smell nothing else. It was such a welcome smell after the pungent scent of his burning flesh. He must surrender himself, become one with his cet, and allow the gods themselves to guide his mind.

Many of the guards turned to flee.

He cast power forward, and the marble ground erupted into shards that transformed into skeletal hands large enough to encompass a man's thigh. The deathly hands grasped the guards in vise-like grips that would not be broken. The guards swatted, screaming in fear, but the gripping hands grew tighter.

The hatred that dwelled inside helped him see the possibilities, and the possibilities were limitless. He was a god.

Something was wrong. He remembered this. It was a memory long dormant, now returned to the forefront of his mind. The Rite of Testing had transformed him and manifested those changes in unexpected ways.

His field of vision changed, and he found himself looking out over a sea of fire that was not of this world. It felt real to him, but he knew it was a vision. The sea was contained within an earthen dome that rose miles above the tallest flames. He remembered this place—the sacred fires of Paradise. The Rite of Testing always ended here...at the sea of fire. A voice declared that Mujahid would soon become one with the sacred fire. The Rite was coming to an end. The memory hidden in his mind since that day came roaring to the surface. He remembered the Rite...and how it ended...all too well now.

The vision left him, and he opened his mouth in wonder as the fires of Paradise grew within him, warming him with a mystical heat that fused the cloak of shadow to his spectral body.

He exhaled a cone of fire into the patrol of guardsmen, lighting them like kindling. Nothing burned hotter than the fires of Paradise, not the combined fires of the six hells, nor those of the seventh hell that few knew existed. The fire would consume everything...he would see to it.

The screams were terrible as the guardsmen stood there, burning alive and unable to do anything about it. Their pain was brief, however, as the sacred flame consumed and liquefied their bodies, before transforming them into a macabre vapor.

He had become death incarnate, and the power within kept growing, seducing him, teasing him with thoughts of domination, as if all he had to do was reach out and take it.

Something inside was trying to be heard. The entity was telling him not to listen, but for the first time he questioned the entity...for no other reason than he hadn't questioned it before. And that was unlike him. A realization came to him like a bolt from a crossbow.

This is wrong.

A shock rippled up his spine and he became more aware. The entity was a hellwraith, and he had dealt with their kind before. The wraith had almost won, but it hadn't counted on Mujahid's nature. Mujahid was the lord, not the wraith. The wraith was his to command, not the other way around.

If he didn't do something soon he'd be lost. The wraith would consume him, shredding his soul, as it had several Mukhtaar Lords before him.

He thought back to the Rite of Testing. So much of his memory of it had been taken from him when he ascended, yet some remained. To be one with the fires of Paradise required...self-knowledge and control—perfect balance between self and lack of self. Yes, that was it.

He stopped smiling.

He knew who he was. He knew what he was. He focused his mind and spoke the sacred words taught by Zubuxo.

"I am Mujahid Lord Mukhtaar, priest, Lord by Rite of Testing, cast into the sacred lake of fire by the hand of Zubuxo. I am one with the sacred lake, one with the fires of Paradise, a necromancer ascendant. I call upon my dominion over the seventh hell and command you to relinquish your control. We are as one...but you are no more."

The sacred fire consumed him and all he could see was pure light. It flowed around him and through him. It warmed him and made him feel whole.

His flesh returned as if it had never left, and he collapsed onto the ground when the final word left his mouth. The smell of roses faded and the acrid smoke of burning flesh returned. He was confused for a moment because he wasn't burning.

A new construct formed in his mind, starting at his well of power, and radiating outward through the sphere of power symbols. A ring, or rather a thin sphere was beginning to take shape around all of the symbols of power, containing them and binding them together. He probed the sphere and recoiled when he sensed the presence of the hellwraith. The presence was mindless, however, and the sphere would allow him to transform at will, but with complete control. He touched the stone surface of the plaza. Yuli knelt over him.

"He lives," Yuli said to the others. She moved her head closer to Mujahid and spoke in a whisper. "Whatever you were saying was gibberish to me, but two guardsmen survived the fire only to drop dead at the sound of your voice."

Mujahid wanted to speak, but his voice wouldn't obey.

"Who was the woman behind you?"

Woman? There was a woman? He remembered smelling roses, but he didn't recall a woman.

"She was doing something with your hands...moving them around. The whole place smelled like a rose bush."

Something must have caught Yuli's eye, because she stood, barking commands at her men.

Five council magi had stepped out of the barracks.

A volley of arcane power struck Yuli, throwing her back through the eastern arch into the plaza beyond.

The magi advanced, shouting as they tossed volleys of explosive energy.

Mujahid lay on the ground of the plaza, too drained of power to make the transformation again.

He would have to do this the hard way.

CHAPTER THIRTY ONE

Everything I need to know about you I learned out there," Nicolas said. "In the world you almost destroyed."

"Did that traitor tell you about the Barathosians?" Kagan said. "You can't possibly know what we were up against. The armada would have destroyed us. And they're still out there, on the other side of my barrier, waiting to decimate everything in Erindor."

The floor rumbled, sending particles of dust through the beam that reached up from the Orb of Arin.

"Looks like you beat them to it," Nicolas said.

Nicolas had wondered if their hair or nose would be similar, but Mujahid had been right all those months ago. It was the eyes. Looking at Kagan's eyes was like looking at his own. But it didn't matter. He could never think of this person as his father.

"You betrayed your own gods," Nicolas said.

"You think gods are worthy of undying loyalty? They were no longer worthy of mine, I can tell you that. They would have allowed our complete destruction. They would have nullified my office...your birthright, Nicolas. That name...*Nicolas*...how did you come by it?"

Nicolas wouldn't answer him. He didn't want to give him the satisfaction. He tried to draw power into his well, but the shield was blocking him. He could feel necropotency. But he couldn't touch it.

"I'm not interested in your office, and neither are those people suffering on the Field of Judgment."

"I was hoping you would be spared the superstitions of this world, but—"

"Life magic hurts them, and you know it. It robs them of their purification."

"Mukhtaar lies, designed to hold on to an ancient religion that no longer has any place in this world."

"I've seen it with my own eyes. I've stood on the Plane of Death, and I've seen the Field of Judgment. I watched as the hellwraiths came and took people. Took children."

"This is worse than I thought. Not only do you believe his lies, but you are delusional as well." Kagan smiled and it made Nicolas feel dirty. "Think about this logically. Traveling to the Plane of Death is a one-way trip. And it requires the use of an object that no longer—"

"The Orb of Zubuxo did the trick."

Kagan's smile disappeared.

Tendrils of energy entered Nicolas's mind.

See anything you like, Kagan? Perhaps you'd like to see what I saw beneath Zubuxo's throne? Nicolas concentrated and sent every image he could recall through the telepathic link into Kagan's mind.

The tendrils withdrew and Kagan staggered.

"The traitor managed to train you. Was he hiding the orb?"

"The gods are more powerful than you give them credit for."

Kagan stared through unblinking eyes. "They raised *our* bloodline to this sacred office centuries ago. They made a covenant with our family. Did the Mukhtaar Lord tell you that? Listen to me. Justifying myself to a boy. And how is that possible? You should be a man of forty years, yet I'm looking at a person half that age."

Nicolas couldn't have answered Kagan's question if he wanted to.

Kagan continued speaking but Nicolas was no longer listening. There had to be a way through the shield Kagan had placed around him. There had to be a reason why he could feel the power, even if he couldn't channel it.

He thought about his lessons under Siek Lamil, trying to remember anything that might help.

Knowing the siek, he'd probably start by quizzing me on the laws.

The laws. The Third Law of Necromancy said there was no distinction between life and death, and he had learned that lesson better than anyone. But something didn't add up. There may be no distinction, but everything died just the same. Animals. People. Vegetation. They all wound up dead.

He embraced his cet, waiting for the clarity that would follow. He thought of all the strange things he'd seen these past months. Bizarre four-legged turkeys at Mujahid's estate. People with eyes like cats. The tiniest trees, too tiny to be useful.

Animals. People. Vegetation.

Four-legged turkey. Vegetables tastier than anything —

How did I miss that?

The cycle of life and death existed inside him. His digestive tract contained death because he consumed life for nourishment. Even his cells were in a continuous state of death and rebirth. The undead cichlos, Cisic, had told him a priest could never be separated from his power, and now he understood. His own body had been the source of that ever-present energy following him wherever he went, but existed just beyond his reach.

He turned his mind inward on his own body, combing through dead cells and partially digested food, and gathered every drop of necropotency he could find. It wasn't much...but it was enough to help.

He summoned a penitent.

A fraction of a second later a six-foot tall skeletal warrior materialized, unarmed and unarmored.

Kagan took a step backwards, and the newly-summoned penitent dove for him.

Kagan was more adroit than Nicolas imagined he would be. The older man side-stepped many attacks and countered with his own. Nicolas concentrated on the shield, probing the mystical fibers that wove together into an unbreakable bond. His penitent wouldn't last long against Kagan. If he planned on accomplishing more than a diversion, he had to bring the shield down.

No. He needed to *untie* it.

He sent tendrils of energy around the shield's interior, examining its properties and looking for weaknesses. The shield surrounded him, but there was something different about the portion that covered his chest, as if it weren't as solid as the rest.

It made sense. When the shield first went up, it hit him from the back and wrapped around to the front. He concentrated his efforts directly in front of his heart.

The necromantic link vanished, and his penitent along with it. His time was growing short now. He had attacked Kagan, who was climbing to his feet. There was no going back.

He started manipulating the fibers of energy in front of his chest, freeing threads of vitapotency from what felt like tangles.

Touching the vitapotency was odd. Unsettling.

Necropotency felt like a footprint, much the way Lamil and Mujahid described it. But vitapotency felt like the foot. And there was something else...something disturbing. The power seemed *aware* of him.

Foot and footprint. Can't be a coincidence.

A cloud of smoke appeared in front of him. It transformed into an enormous ghost-like hand that inched its way toward him.

"I had hoped you would be happy here," Kagan said. "You defied the odds and somehow managed to find your way back after so many years. And the first thing you do is attack me? Unprovoked?"

Foot and footprint. This has to mean something.

"It was in this room, forty years ago, that I learned of your kidnapping," Kagan said. "It seems fitting that future generations will know this place as the room where I found you dead."

The ghostly hand inched closer to him.

He remembered back to his time in the Plane of Death, back to his first experience of vitapotency. Why had it targeted children?

Foot and footprint. No. It can't be.

The energies were two sides of the same coin. Both channeled life. Necropotency channeled life after it had passed away from this world. So vitapotency must channel life *before* it enters the world.

He understood. And it was so simple. If a necromancer channeled necropotency into death...then maybe a life magus should channel vitapotency into life.

My god. Is that why there are so few children and so many stillborn?

With great effort he concentrated on the pregnant woman he saw in the Grand Hall. He formed an image of a spark igniting a blaze and willed the vitapotency toward the woman's unborn child.

A sense of giddiness emanated from the threads of vitapotency, and for a moment he thought he heard a child's laughter.

The vitapotency rushed away and the shield evaporated. Kagan backed away with a dazed look.

The ghostly hand was less than an inch from his chest.

Something caught Kagan's attention at the entrance of the room.

"You're no god." The voice came from behind him, and it was a voice Nicolas had never heard before.

Whoever this guy was, Kagan looked as if the man was the last person he expected to see.

"You'd do well to watch your words, Tithian. I'll forgive the—"

"If you're a god, then this paltry display of the arcane should pose no challenge to you," Tithian said.

The ghostly hand struck an invisible barrier in front of Nicolas. It struggled to penetrate but couldn't.

Power flooded back into Nicolas's well, and he expelled a wall of force that struck Kagan, lifting him off his feet and tossing him back against the far wall.

He turned his mind inward once more and fashioned a blanket of necropotency identical to the shield Kagan had created. Except this one was compressed into a ball no larger than the head of a pin. He hurled it at Kagan and the compressed energy struck the archmage in the chest, connected to Nicolas by a small tendril of energy. Nicolas willed the ball to expand, and as it grew inside Kagan it spawned smaller, microscopic versions of itself that shielded every cell in Kagan's body.

Kagan was powerless. There would be no way out of this shield.

Nicolas faced the Orb of Arin. The swirls of light danced across its surface in every color imaginable. He'd experienced what it was like to use the Orb of Zubuxo. All he had to do was release a small amount of power and touch it. His greatest desire would come true. He would hold Kaitlyn in his arms again and never think about this place. They'd get married and be happy together for the rest of their lives. He would finish his degree and become an archaeologist, as he always wanted, and honor the memory of Dr. Murray.

The dead Dr. Murray.

The dead.

Countless dead stood upon the Field of Judgment, waiting for purification from necromancers who were being hunted like animals. Nicolas had seen them. He'd stood with the dead and spoken with them. He'd watched as they were defiled by life magic, made dirty even after they were purified. He remembered the cries of the children as the hellwraiths carried one away. Was Dr. Murray standing somewhere on that Field of Judgment destined to face the hellwraiths as well?

The ground lurched as the quake raged on.

He thought of all the villages he passed through, lying in ruin. Everywhere he went it was as if people were refugees in their own cities. He thought of the death piles that Mujahid had told him about, and wondered how many other cities had become victims of Kagan's quest for power.

Tears rolled down his face and he thought of Kaitlyn. He reached into his robe and pulled out the picture she had given him. All of his hopes and dreams were in that face. He looked into her eyes and saw his own future.

But it was just another future that would never be, because of the sin of a single man.

This wasn't his fight. He could walk away. He could go home. He never asked for this.

But if he let this world destroy itself for his own benefit, then he would be guilty of the same sin. How many futures would *he* destroy if he gave in to his desires? How many lives would never be lived? How many children would never be born?

He would never be able to live with himself. And if he became that person—the kind of person that *could* be happy with that decision—then he didn't deserve Kaitlyn.

The tears flowed freely. Mujahid was right. He knew what had to be done.

Tithian stepped forward, and Nicolas thought he was about to kill Kagan.

"No, Tithian," Nicolas said. "Please. This is something I have to do."

Tithian hesitated, and for a moment Nicolas thought he'd misjudged the man. Maybe Tithian wasn't a friend at all.

Tithian's eyes moving from Nicolas back to Kagan. He nodded and stepped back.

"What have you done to me?" Kagan asked.

Disgust welled up in Nicolas's throat like a lump. He wanted nothing more than to summon a penitent who would rip Kagan apart in a shower of blood.

"Do you have any idea what I have to do?" Nicolas said. "What I have to sacrifice to atone for your sins?"

"If you're going to kill me boy, then kill me."

Nicolas faced the Orb of Arin once more. He basked in the energy it gave off. It was calming. But peace was no longer possible for Nicolas. His life would never know peace again.

He closed his eyes and opened himself to the power of the orb. Where once his well of power was like a bucket, now it was like the bed of an ocean. He reached out and drew more and more power until that ocean was full to overflowing.

"Gods have mercy, the power," Tithian said. His hair whipped around his head by a mystical wind.

Necropotency coursed through Nicolas, and his body trembled as he tried to consume even more, but no more would come. He had reached the limit of his abilities, and he would use all of his power to see this to fruition. If he died in the process, then so be it. He was dead already.

He opened his eyes and watched Kagan scoot back along the floor. The archmage's face had turned ashen.

Nicolas had been right about the gods. The gods couldn't die. The gods simply *were*. They existed. And he would raise them the same way he had raised so many others.

Blasts of vitapotency exploded all around.

The Tildemen archers dropped two of the five magi, but the arcane volleys increased in frequency, forcing Mujahid and the Tildemen back into the main plaza.

More archers dropped as they retreated. They didn't have enough people to take out the remaining three magi, and Mujahid would add little value. The transfiguration had left him exhausted, and it seemed as if he couldn't draw necropotency into his well.

When they reached the main plaza, the four monolithic doors leading into the Pinnacle stood open.

More than one hundred Council magi had spread out on the steps leading up to the doors. The entire Council had shown up for the fight.

Mujahid offered a silent prayer that Zubuxo would show him mercy when he arrived on the Field of Judgment.

Nicolas opened his well and emptied it into the symbol of the skull. When it would absorb no more power, he cast it forward, stretching it over the surface of the Orb of Arin. A great beam of necropotency radiated from his outstretched hands.

"No!" Kagan screamed.

A loud hum filled the room as the beam fed into the orb. When the hum reached a volume that threatened to burst his eardrums, silence descended.

He had heard that mystical silence in Paradise, right before—

The orb exploded into billions of tiny fragments, and the shock wave threw Kagan backward into the stone wall. It sounded as if the entire building would crumble down on top of them. The wave parted around Nicolas and Tithian, however, and a feeling of peace entered his mind.

When the explosion ended, Nicolas looked to where the orb had been hovering in the air. It had been obliterated, except for one small section that now lay in ruin on the floor.

A beam of sunlight penetrated the room through a gaping hole in the ceiling. The ubiquitous yellow glow was gone. The sky was as turquoise as the stones the Native Americans sold at the trading posts near the Grand Canyon, and it was the same shade as the hide of a shriller.

He had destroyed the barrier.

A strange sensation tickled the back of his neck. It was the feeling he'd get when someone was watching him.

The smell of fresh roses filled the air.

A cataclysmic explosion rocked the plaza, and Mujahid had to dive behind the battlements on the staircase to avoid the debris that was raining down. A gaping hole had been torn in the side of the central tower, and several portions of the roof had collapsed. The council magi were a mass of confusion, some running farther out into the plaza, and others back into the Pinnacle.

The island grew brighter all around him, and he had to shield his eyes.

"Gods in paradise," Yuli said. She was staring up into the sky.

He followed her gaze, and when he saw what she was looking at, he lowered his head and offered a prayer of thanksgiving.

The barrier was gone.

But something else was happening—something so unexpected, so beautiful, that Mujahid could only stare and laugh.

Hundreds of people appeared on the shores of the Pinnacle, cichlos and human alike. They seemed disoriented, glancing around and staring at their bodies, as if they were getting used to their own limbs. Many had begun to laugh and cry. Others embraced one another as if reuniting with long lost friends.

It all made sense now. The barrier never killed anyone. It *took* them. And now it had brought them back...everyone it had ever taken.

For the first time since coming to terms with Mordryn's disappearance, Mujahid wept.

"Commander," one of the Tildemen shouted. "The Council is boiling the sea."

Mujahid knew that wasn't right. As soon as the barrier collapsed he sensed the magi stop casting. He faced the dock.

Waves crashed against the shore where no waves had existed earlier. Something was disturbing the sea from underneath.

A wall of water rose up from the sea and struck Mujahid and the Tildemen.

Man-sized objects shot out from the sea as if giant crossbows were fired from just below the surface. Water rained down, obscuring Mujahid's vision as the objects kept coming.

He wiped the water from his eyes.

Dozens of undead cichlos were shooting out of the water, landing on the docks, and charging the staircase.

In the midst of the churning water, blue-cowled cichlos were emerging and walking up onto the shore, directing their penitents.

The necromancers emerged from the water, and it wasn't long before they were battling the Council magi in a direct confrontation. The Council was in full retreat, fleeing back up the steps and into the Pinnacle, but that didn't stop the cichlos from chasing them.

An old cichlos necromancer climbed out of the water next to Mujahid. It had been years, but Mujahid would know this cichlos anywhere.

"Siek Lamil," Mujahid said.

Four undead cichlos materialized next to Lamil and charged into the battle, followed by four more, then four again.

Mujahid examined the siek for signs of insanity. No man could withstand twelve summonings in the span of seconds.

Lamil harrumphed. "Were you planning to assist or stare at me for the remainder of the battle?"

"How did you do that?"

"What is the Prime Duty of a Necromancer?"

Mujahid smiled.

CHAPTER THIRTY TWO

The god Arin stood resplendent in his golden winged helm. His brilliant, white armor reflected the Erindorian sun, and he radiated an aura of peace.

Tithian dropped to one knee.

Nicolas was uncertain of what to do, so he dropped to one knee as well.

Two other beings materialized. The first was a woman who radiated a scent of fresh cut roses. Brown hair cascaded down to her shoulders in tight curls. Her eyes were a piercing blue that glowed with an inner light. The second was shrouded in darkness and wore a cloak made of shadow. He couldn't see the being's face, but he had no doubt it was Zubuxo, the God of Death.

Arin squatted next to the orb fragment and picked it up. An expression of pure fury passed across his face, but the aura of peace returned.

Arin stood. His eyes, rust colored a moment ago, flashed a brilliant yellow. They cycled through every color of the rainbow before returning to rust.

Every hair on Nicolas's body stood on end, but nothing happened from what he could see.

Arin spoke, and his voice was soothing, as if all the cichlos of Aquonome were singing in unison.

"Why are you unable to channel, Archmage?" Arin said.

"Arin," the woman said. "Now is the time for mercy."

Nicolas had no frame of reference for what he was witnessing. Were the gods of Erindor, Terilya—and who knew how many other places— really standing before him? And what did this imply about his own beliefs?

"You cannot channel, Archmage, because your son is a greater magus than you are," Arin said. "We did well to choose you, Nicolas."

Arin's eyes were kind, but they were sunken as if weary from witnessing millennia of joy and horror.

"I sent the Barathosians to teach you the true nature of vitapotency," Arin said. "You paid them back with murder."

"Arin," the woman said.

"You didn't capture us, you vain man," Arin said. "We went willingly into the barrier so that it would feed on us instead of the countless unborn."

"Arin," the woman said.

"You traded my words for your own twisted version, all while invoking my name with mock piety."

"Arin, please," the woman said.

Arin turned and his countenance changed. The aura of peace radiated from him again.

"There were others on your path, Nicolas," Arin said. He extended his arms and the scent of saltwater filled the room. A cool sea breeze danced across Nicolas's face.

Mujahid, Yuli, and Siek Lamil materialized in the room.

"Siek?" Nicolas said. He couldn't believe it.

Mujahid and Yuli fell to one knee when they saw the gods. Lamil bowed his head but did not kneel.

Nicolas's heart sank. He'd promised the cichlos he'd help them, but the orb was destroyed.

"You amaze us," Arin said to Nicolas. "Even in your moment of greatest loss, your heart turns to the plight of others."

The woman reached out to touch Arin. Tears pooled in her eyes.

Arin faced her. "Have you ever witnessed anything like this in Erindor before, Shealynd?"

So that's who she is. Shealynd, the Goddess of Love.

Arin closed the distance between them and gently grasped Nicolas's upper arm.

Flesh and blood. He feels like any other man.

Tithian and the others bowed their heads lower.

"Do you see this man, Zubuxo," Arin said.

Zubuxo removed the shadowy hood covering his face. The god had the appearance of an old man, with a long white beard that ran down to the center of his chest, but his eyes were two black orbs.

"You know my mind," Zubuxo said.

The archmage floated off the floor, pulled toward Arin by some divine force.

"So many cry out in anger, victimized by your atrocities," Arin said. "So many are doomed to live out their penance in the six hells because of the damage you did."

"Please," Kagan said.

"You owe a price too great to count," Arin said. "You will be cast into the hells for eternity, and you will serve in whatever manner the Mukhtaar Lord deems worthy of your wretched nature."

Nicolas shouldn't be bothered by Arin's judgment, but he was. Kagan had caused a lot of evil. He should be happy to see Kagan get what he deserved. But eternity was a long time.

Kagan's mouth was open as if trying to scream, but no sound escaped it.

"Take him," Arin said.

Nicolas remembered the argram, the first creature he'd ever successfully summoned. As evil as the creature's acts were, acts which resulted in the downfall of a civilization, he had made some small progress during his time with Nicolas.

"Wait," Nicolas yelled.

Kagan hung in midair, a look of horror on his face.

"I've seen more than enough evil, Arin," Nicolas said. "And if there's anything I've learned, it's that no one is beyond redemption. Tossing him into hell is just revenge, as far as I can tell. It doesn't help him, and it sure as hell ain't gonna help the countless people he's hurt."

Shealynd smiled.

"What are you asking of me?" Arin said.

Nicolas took a deep breath. "If the Prime Duty of a necromancer is to raise the dead and help them achieve purification, then how can I sit back and watch someone be thrown away because of the evil they've committed?"

Lamil placed a hand on Mujahid's shoulder and smiled.

"Yes," Kagan said. "That's mercy. Don't throw me away, my Lord. You're a good son, Nicolas."

Nicolas gave Kagan an icy stare. "You'll pray for hell after you hear what I've got in mind."

"I'm listening," Arin said.

"Make him my penitent," Nicolas said.

It was Zubuxo that smiled this time.

Kagan's eyes widened. "No. Not that. Don't make me live like that."

Arin lowered his hand. "So be it."

"No!" Kagan yelled and became silent as if someone had cut off his breath. His eyes rolled back and he collapsed onto the floor of the sanctuary, dead.

"Rise," Arin said.

Nicolas felt a rush of power sweep past him toward Kagan's body, and a faint blue necromantic link appeared.

Kagan's corpse stirred, awkwardly at first, like a newborn horse trying to stand for the first time.

"I believe this is yours," Arin said.

The necromantic link detached itself from Arin and rushed toward Nicolas. When it struck him, it formed a bond in his mind. Kagan was there, at the opposite end of that link, powerless to act against Nicolas's will.

"And now you must decide, Nicolas Ardirian," Arin said. "I would have you inherit your birthright. Serve us as Archmage. Help us restore this broken world."

Mujahid turned to Nicolas and smiled.

"But know this," Arin said. "The worst is yet to come. The Barathosians will return, and their intentions will not be to teach and guide this time. They will come to kill and conquer because of Kagan's sin, and I will not take away their free will."

"But...can't you convince them to stop at least?" Nicolas said.

Arin smiled and glanced toward Kagan and back again.

Nicolas understood. Even the word of a god wasn't enough to stop human pride from doing its worst.

He could turn down the offer and let someone else worry about the future. He could try his best to move on and forge some semblance of a life in this alien world. But *Kaitlyn* was his entire world, and that world was gone forever. If he was going to pay the price of that future, then he would take nothing less than the salvation of a world in return.

Shealynd looked down, as if deeply troubled.

"I'll do it," Nicolas said. "But there is one thing I would like to change, if I may?"

"Give it voice, and we will see if it lends itself to change."

"My name," Nicolas said. "I don't want to be associated with Kagan or his dynasty. I have no interest in perpetuating that name, and I don't want to think about him every time someone says it."

"And what would you be called?"

"My name is Nicolas Murray. *Murray* is the name of a good man. A decent man who didn't have Kagan's sort of evil in him."

He thought of Dr. Murray and smiled. He bet the old man had no idea he'd be the start of some dynasty on an alien planet somewhere.

"So be it," Arin said. "You will be the patriarch of a new dynasty—the Murray dynasty."

"Arin," Shealynd said. Some form of voiceless communication passed between them.

"I will not," Arin said. "What you wish is not wise."

"Zubuxo," Shealynd said. "You above all know the intimate secrets of humankind. What is the one thing that keeps the greatest of evil at bay?"

"Love, Goddess," Zubuxo said, without hesitation. "Those who require the least purification possess it in great quantities."

"Nicolas loved Kaitlyn so perfectly, that he let her go when Love of others demanded it," Shealynd said.

"Arin," Zubuxo said. "You object."

"The children were taken for a reason," Arin said. "But this is your gift to give or take. Not mine."

Children? What children?

Shealynd smiled.

"Nicolas Murray," Zubuxo said.

When the God of Death spoke, a fire rose from the center of Nicolas's being, and it was as if a red hot brand touched his mind, burning something indelible into the recesses of his consciousness.

A new symbol of power took shape in his mind in the form of a door. But it was different from the other symbols in more than appearance. It had a power source of its own, like a built-in energy well.

The fire vanished, and the pain along with it, but the door glowed in his mind's eye.

You are a good and faithful priest, and you will rise to heights you have not fathomed, the voice in his mind said. *Trust in the Mukhtaar Lord, for your life will depend on it someday. I have granted you a gift given to no other human. Use this gift wisely.*

"I will," Nicolas said.

Mujahid looked at him and raised an eyebrow.

Arin tossed the last remaining piece of the great orb to the floor, and it broke into dozens of smaller pieces with a loud shatter.

"I will recreate the orb," Arin said. "Once more will it light the way across a treacherous sea. But it will not be alone."

Lamil looked up.

"Its twin will reside in Aquonome," Arin said. He looked at Lamil. "Your chimeramancers will not have to make the great sacrifice after all, Lamil Jiskossa."

Lamil had never mentioned chimeramancers, although he *had* implied the orb wasn't the only way back to Terilya.

Arin stepped back between Shealynd and Zubuxo.

"Serve him well, Mukhtaar Lord," Arin said. "His need of you will be great in the days ahead."

There was no sound or movement, or any other indication that they were leaving. They simply vanished.

"I must return to Aquonome," Lamil said. His eyes beamed. "The elders must begin work on a new temple."

Nicolas glanced up and stared in wonder at the turquoise sky above. The symbol of the door burned in his mind, and he knew it was time to use it.

"Mujahid," he said.

"Yes, Archmage," Mujahid said, smiling.

"Oh please. You practically changed my diapers. What's with the *Archmage* stuff?"

Mujahid smirked. "If a diaper is what I think it is, then you exaggerate. That is work best performed by a penitent." He nodded toward Kagan, who remained expressionless.

Nicolas sent a series of commands through the necromantic link and Kagan left the room.

"Where's he off to, then?" Mujahid asked.

"I told him to find a broom."

Mujahid raised an eyebrow.

"Someone has to clean this mess up."

Mujahid and Tithian chuckled.

Nicolas smiled. "I need to ask a favor, Mujahid. Will you be my Prime Warlock and govern while I'm away? I may have a lot to learn about politics, but I know this place needs a strong hand on the wheel."

"I'm honored by your request. But I would serve you poorly by accepting. Especially when there's a much better candidate right here in this room."

Mujahid reached out and placed a hand on Tithian's shoulder.

Tithian gave Mujahid an incredulous stare.

"I was wrong to doubt you," Mujahid said. "And I've been away from the Pinnacle for forty years. There is no one better suited for the job."

"If you will accept, Holy One, I would serve you in all humility," Tithian said.

"Whoa," Nicolas said. "Slow your roll on the *Holy One* stuff. Talk like that is what started this mess to begin with. If Mujahid says you're the man for the job, then yes, I accept."

Tithian bowed his head. "I only hope you will hold me in the same esteem someday, Holy—Archmage."

"About this *Mujahid* business," Mujahid said. "I don't care who you think you are...you're still my postulant, for Arin's sake. I'm *Lord* Mujahid. And that goes for you too, Tithian."

Nicolas smiled.

The orb's explosion had torn a hole through the wall of the sanctuary more than fifteen feet in diameter. Mujahid turned and looked through it, out toward the Sea of Arin.

"I can help Tithian hold the Council at bay for a time," Mujahid said. "But eventually they're going to want to see their new archmage. There's a coronation and installation to consider. Where are you going?"

"I think I'm going home. But I'll be back as soon as I can."

"You make it sound as if you'll be gone a long time."

"I'm only twenty-one years old, Lord Mujahid. Maybe twenty-two—I don't know what month it is anymore. But to you I'm forty. For all I know I'll get back home and...I'd rather not think about it."

"Be well, Nicolas...*Archmage*," Mujahid said.

Nicolas nodded. He was about to extend his hand, but he was overcome by the urge to give Mujahid a hug. He stepped forward and embraced the startled Mukhtaar Lord.

"Thank you, Mujahid," Nicolas whispered. "I owe you my life."

Mujahid smiled and stepped back, leaving his hands resting on Nicolas's shoulders.

Nicolas gazed once more at the turquoise sky, marveling at its rich color. Light reflected off his robes and he remembered he was wearing the robes of a priest of Arin. He had experienced so much in these last few months that he never stopped to consider how his appearance must have changed. He was leaner, with more muscle tone, and his hair and beard had grown out. He doubted Kaitlyn would recognize him...if he managed to find her again.

His thoughts turned inward to the door in his mind. He took one last look around the sanctuary and his eyes came to rest on Mujahid. He smiled and imagined the door opening.

The Pinnacle vanished as he fell into blackness.

CHAPTER THIRTY THREE

The darkness exploded in a cascade of light and sound.
Nicolas squinted in pain and blinked to clear the blurriness from
his eyes. There was something soft underneath him. A cushion of
some sort.

He shifted his weight and heard a squeak.

I know that squeak.

It was his bed in Austin.

As his vision cleared, he could make out the figure of someone facing
away from him.

*Why would someone be inside my apartment? Wait...is this even my
apartment anymore? Oh, damn, when's the last time I paid rent?*

The blurry image resolved into a girl in a black dress. The feelings
came flooding back in a rush as if he'd never left.

"Kait," he whispered.

"Nick?" she said as she turned around. Her eyes were bloodshot and
her makeup was running.

She drew back and covered her mouth when she saw him.

An intense wave of hunger hit him and he doubled over.

"Food," he said.

Kaitlyn reached around the corner into the kitchen and grabbed a banana from the fruit bowl.

He almost forgot to peel it.

"Nick? Oh my god!"

Time rushed back in a torrent. His internal clock told him he'd been gone no more than a moment, yet every experience he had in Erindor remained.

"I'm so sorry," he said.

"What just happened? God, your hair. That's it. You're going to the hospital."

He'd been gone a year and she was worried about his hair? It took a moment for him to realize she was wearing the same black dress as the last time he saw her, all those months ago.

No...just a moment ago. Damn, this is confusing.

He stood and drew her into his arms. "I thought about you every day."

She pulled back and stared at him through narrowed eyes, placing a hand on his cheek as she felt his beard.

"What are you talking about?" She said. "You get pulled through that thing over there, wind up behind me, and now you look like Jesus! What's going on?"

Paws against his hip announced Toby's presence.

Energy filled his well of power from the direction of the window that looked out over the street.

The accident. Mr. Landing.

He approached the window and drew the curtain aside to get a better look. The paramedics were covering Mr. Landing's corpse and shooing bystanders away.

The visions he experienced when Landing died, before he had awakened to his necromantic power, were as vivid in his memory as if they had just occurred. He remembered the goodness of the old man, and the love he had for his grandchildren.

Then he recalled the horror in the jungle, the decades of guilt and self-loathing. Landing never forgave himself for shooting that child. He spent most of his life keeping people away, because he believed he was unlovable, unworthy of forgiveness.

The Prime Duty of a necromancer is to raise the dead and help them achieve purification.

Nicolas invoked the skull symbol and channeled power into the lifeless corpse.

The namocea released him, and Nicolas commanded the corpse to rise. The sheet stirred as if by a breeze and the corpse stretched its legs.

No one noticed at first.

But they noticed when the dead man stood up.

Several onlookers screamed as the once-lifeless corpse stood staring at Nicolas's window. The paramedics hesitated at first, seeming confused, then rushed to Mr. Landing's side. One of them shouted for a stretcher.

Nicolas commanded Landing to be still and allow the paramedics to do as they would. It wouldn't matter in a few minutes anyway.

Toby growled a low growl.

"It's ok, boy," Nicolas said.

He opened the window and leaned out into the fresh air.

"What's happening?" Kaitlyn asked.

He smiled at her and held up his hand. "I'll explain everything, babe. I promise. I just need some fresh air."

Two necromantic links existed in his mind now. He still had a connection to Kagan, but communication was impossible. He focused on the second link instead, and probed it for the penitent's first name. It was always there, in the dark corners of their consciousness, even if they had forgotten. Landing wasn't dead long enough to have forgotten, though: Paul.

Paul, Nicolas said. *The child wasn't your fault.*

What are you, said Paul through the necromantic link. *How is this possible? Am I dead?*

I'm your guide, nothing more. The child wasn't your fault. You need to forgive yourself, or you'll never have peace.

Nicolas sensed great loss and sorrow returning from the link.

It was evil, what I did. Pure evil! I don't deserve peace. I'm the worst sort of evil. The child killin' sort.

You don't know pure evil. I do. I've seen it. Let me show it to you. Forgive me, but it's the only way I know.

Nicolas called to mind images of violence and evil that he had witnessed first-hand through the namocea. Some were of the greatest evil Nicolas had ever experienced. He cast those aside. They would be too much for Paul, and the man would have no context in which to understand what he was seeing. He gathered all of the images together—

images of genocide, rape, murder, torture, betrayal—and sent them, as one, through the necromantic link.

Fear and horror returned from the link.

Dear god. Make it stop, Paul said.

Nicolas withdrew the images.

I'm sorry, Paul. But you needed to see true evil to understand that you're not even close. What you did was an accident. The child wasn't your fault.

It wasn't my fault?

No.

A flood of relief passed down the necromantic link into Nicolas, and he knew Paul's time was drawing close. He'd succeeded.

The child wasn't my fault. I wasn't much more than a boy myself. I tried to make up for it. I tried to give my kids, and their kids all the love that precious child never had the chance to receive. Something's changing.

Nicolas smiled. *For you, everything is changing.*

"I want you to see this," Nicolas said to Kait.

She seemed hesitant.

"Please, trust me."

She glanced out the window and covered her mouth with her hand.

"He's alive?" she said. Her hand muffled her voice.

"Of course he is," Nicolas said and smiled. "There is no death, Kait."

She looked at him as if he wasn't speaking English.

"I release you from your penance, my friend," Nicolas said. "Go on to your reward."

Paul's body transformed into pure spirit, radiating a heatless, painless white light.

"Are you seeing this?" He asked.

At first Kait didn't answer, but the truth was apparent as soon as he saw her face.

"He was a good man. He understands that now. I helped him to understand. That's what I do. That's what this was about."

"Help *me* understand," she said in a whisper.

Paul's spirit smiled. "Thank you."

Toby stood on his hind legs and placed his front paws on the window sill. He bayed in Paul's direction.

"For what it's worth," Paul said, "Toby's a great dog."

And with that the spirit of Paul Landing vanished, leaving no corpse behind. The crowd was silent, and many stared at the place Paul had been standing.

Kaitlyn looked at Nicolas with wide eyes, her mouth hanging open.

Nicolas took Kaitlyn by the arm, led her back to the center of the room, and held her close. She melted into his arms. All he wanted to do was stand there forever, but that wasn't possible. He had a lot to say, and it would be a long story.

There was no way to explain it all without sounding like a crazy person.

But there was *another* way.

"I have something amazing to show you."

She looked up at him with those wide, almond eyes, but her body stiffened.

"Do you trust me, babe?"

She relaxed and nodded.

He stepped back and took both of her hands in his. "Get ready for a wild ride."

Toby barked.

"You too, boy," Nicolas said. "Come here."

Toby grabbed his *gatorpickle* toy and jumped up on Nicolas's leg.

Nicolas put one hand on Toby's head and willed the door in his mind to open.

Once again, Nicolas tumbled into blackness. But this time, the blackness seemed just a little brighter.

EPILOGUE

Admiral Unega stood upon the foc'sle of the Barathosian man-of-war *Vengeance*, surveying the horizon.

The Land of Cowards, as his people knew the Three Kingdoms, was no longer protected by its shield. And now the false archmage would pay for his crimes against the empire. He would answer for the death of Yotto, the Glorious One's son, with his own life. The Barathosian navy would descend upon the Three Kingdoms with the fury of a thousand red dragons, laying waste to everything in its path. No building would remain standing. No person would remain alive. Not even their livestock would survive. Such would be the Glorious One's orders.

"Inform the chimeramancers," Unega said in his barrel-chested voice. "It's time."

The first officer clicked his heels and went belowdecks.

The Diamond Throne would have its vengeance, and Admiral Unega would be the instrument of its delivery.

THE ROAD TO
Dar Rodon
A TALES OF THE MUKHTAAR LORDS STORY

NAT RUSSO

AMAZON #1 BESTSELLING AUTHOR OF NECROMANCER AWAKENING

The Road To Dar Rodon

Mujahid Lord Mukhtaar didn't mind the dust of the desert road he traveled. Of all the cities in the Religarian Empire, Dar Saricon was one of the few he enjoyed visiting. He shook the dust off his hide boots as the road emerged from the desert onto a plain east of the city.

Many once called Dar Saricon the *Gem of the Desert*. Its sandstone city walls and buildings had glistened in the desert sun. Now the wall appeared as if the city had been under siege, ragged and partially rebuilt after several quakes had shaken buildings to their foundations. Most of the houses and inns beyond the wall remained intact, but the ones closest to the shore, precariously perched on the cliffs overlooking the Sea of Arin, had collapsed into the cold, salty water.

The gusting wind kicked up dirt and dust behind Mujahid and scattered it into the nearby sagebrush, pressing his black hood against his head. At least the wind had been at his back for this journey.

Maybe the gods heard the prayers of the Priests of Arin after all. They'd prayed over him before he'd left Dyr Agul. "May the winds be always at your back," they'd chanted. He'd have to thank their counterparts in Dar Saricon for seeing to the needs of the coven in his absence. Peaceful monks, those priests. Mujahid wondered what he'd do without them.

A sand funnel formed nearby and danced away from him, gliding across the desert floor and spiraling up into the magical yellow barrier that covered the sky of Erindor.

No, Mujahid didn't mind the dust, or the wind, or the heat of the Religarian desert. Not if that was all he had to endure to take care of his people. The Archmage may have forced necromancers into hiding a year ago, but Mujahid had a responsibility to the necromantic covens that had been scattered around the countryside. They needed his leadership now more than ever. Besides, the Dar Saricon coven was special.

The children at Dar Saricon had taken to calling him "Uncle Muj," much to the dismay of their elders. While it was inappropriate to address a Mukhtaar Lord casually, Mujahid loved those kids, and he wouldn't dream of making them fear him over something as trivial as a title. Their duty, as far as he was concerned, was to be kids. They had plenty of time to learn their place in the hierarchy.

The hierarchy. He hoped there'd be a hierarchy left by the time the children were old enough to take their place within it, and hope was in short supply these days. Those children were among the last remaining remnants of his faith in the world. He couldn't understand why the gods had abandoned him and the necromantic priesthood they'd created.

No, that was going too far. The gods wouldn't abandon him.

But they *had* allowed a tyrant to declare the holy necromantic priesthood illegal. They had some explaining to do, and someday he'd hold them accountable.

He stumbled as the road leveled out and turned toward the eastern entrance of Dar Saricon.

The uneven city wall spanned hundreds of yards, north and south, and was a patchwork of sandstone bricks, mud, and mortar. The sunlight, though scattered by the yellow barrier, was bright, and Mujahid had to squint to see any detail.

Two guards manned the main gate in the distance, and a solitary woman approached on the road ahead.

Whoever she was, she was having a hard time walking, and Mujahid doubted it had anything to do with the wind. She had gathered her tan robes above her ankles and was staggering toward him.

He calmed his mind and gathered ambient *necropotency* into the empty well of power in his mind. If this woman recognized him, she may call for the city guard. He'd have to be prepared to defend himself or escape with haste. There wasn't much power out here, though. He'd need to get closer to the city for that. The city held far more dead than this empty road, and wherever the dead rested, there was *necropotency*.

He lowered his head to conceal his face within the hood of his black robes. If he had to channel the power, the sacred light of ascendancy would shine forth from his eyes and give his identity away. Another necromancer could channel without anyone being wiser. Not so for a Mukhtaar Lord. Ascendancy came at a price.

As the woman drew closer, a gust of wind pressed hard against Mujahid's back and lifted the woman's hood away from her face.

Gods! It was Yasmine Bazzi. Her husband was a good man and talented necromancer. Mujahid had read bedtime stories to her children, which was one of the reasons he was happy to be on this trip in the first place. But what was wrong with her? Why was she struggling to walk?

When she was no more than two paces from him, she stopped and swayed, and Mujahid caught her in his arms as she fell over.

"What happened to you, child?" Mujahid asked.

Her eyes rolled back and Mujahid shook her gently.

"Yasmine," he said. "What happened?"

Mujahid sent small tendrils of *necropotency* into her body and cringed when the power found the source of her injuries. She was bleeding inside her skull. If he didn't heal her soon, she would die. But to heal her, he would need to take life from something else. Something sentient.

He laid her down on the road, one hand covering her forehead, and glanced around. A bird or snake would suffice, but there was nothing except dirt and sagebrush.

He shook his head. There was no other way. *He* would have to be the sacrifice.

He looked toward the city guards, who were leaning against the wall and talking. Typical. They were probably too young to have ever seen battle. The merits of staying alert were only a theory to them.

Alert or no, it didn't matter. He had to take the chance. He couldn't let this poor woman die on a dusty road away from her family.

He turned his mind inward to the symbols of power that floated above his well of *necropotency*, and opened a channel from the well to the symbol of the vortex. When the power embraced the symbol, he cast it into Yasmine, who absorbed the power with a shudder. The energy drained from his body. But it was more than energy. It was his life force.

His muscles grew weaker and wrinkles formed on the back of his hand. If he didn't cut the flow of *necropotency* off soon, he'd be too weak to recover.

Yasmine opened her eyes, and when she saw Mujahid she tried to sit up.

Mujahid would have none of it. He forced her to lie flat on her back.

"Rest, child," he said.

"My lord," she said in a raspy voice. She covered her eyes with the back of her hand, following the ritual of Clan Mukhtaar.

Mujahid released the power and sniffed. The woman held to the ritual, regardless of her injuries. He didn't care for it, being treated like a saint. Not one bit. But he knew it brought comfort to his people, so he tolerated it.

"The light has passed," Mujahid said.

"May it bless us in its passing," Yasmine said.

Mujahid took a water skin from inside the sleeve of his capacious black robes and made Yasmine drink.

"Tell me what happened, child," Mujahid said. His muscles ached. He must have aged five years during that healing.

"Lord Mukhtaar," Yasmine said. "I knew one of you would come. But it's too late. They're dead."

"What's too late? Who's dead?"

Yasmine's lips trembled.

"My babies," she said. "They're gone!"

Mujahid held her as she wept. What could she possibly be talking about? What had happened to her children?

When her weeping subsided, she spoke. "My lord! The Priests of Arin betrayed us!"

Her words turned Mujahid cold, and not even the desert heat warmed him. Betrayal could mean only one thing. But the Arinian Priests were friends. What could have happened to make her think these kindly clerics would cause the deaths of her children?

"I don't understand, child," Mujahid said. "Please. Try to explain."

Her sobbing came in waves, but eventually slowed enough for her to speak.

"In the early hours of the morning they came," she said. "While the coven slept. I was out buying food from the farmers, but I saw! The farmer's boy didn't get there in time, by the six hells he didn't...but why? Why would they do such a thing?"

"Slow down," Mujahid said. "What happened while the coven slept?"

"The Pinnacle Guard burned the safe house down! No one lived. And it was the festering Priests of Arin that brought them there. I saw them! There was nothing I could do. Nothing I could—"

"You saw them? What did you see? I need to know precisely."

"They came with the guards, my lord. I swear it! They led them straight to the safe house. I watched them!"

Mujahid handed her his water skin. "Take this and listen carefully. This will be difficult, but I need you to do something.

"Anything, my lord."

Mujahid untied his coin purse from his cincture and handed it to her.

"Go back into the city," Mujahid said. "You need—"

"No, Lord Mukhtaar! Anything but—"

"Listen child! You must make your way to the docks and buy passage to James's Landing. Find the coven there and warn them."

"No, my lord—"

"You must! It will be difficult, but I know you don't want the same thing to happen to the children of James's Landing. Collect yourself here awhile. Drink that water. Every drop!"

"What will you do?"

"I…can't believe it."

Yasmine looked at Mujahid with a pleading expression as her sobs came anew.

"Take heart, child," Mujahid said. "I know you'd never lie about such as this. But I have to see it with my own eyes. They're our friends, the priests of Arin. They're…our *friends*."

Mujahid covered his face and headed toward the city.

He lowered his head as he neared the guards, but they didn't act interested in anything except holding the wall up with their backs.

The city was busy at this time of day, as vendors sold food and other wares from their fabric-covered vending stalls on both sides of the *Sharea Ar-Ra'isi*, the central avenue leading from the gate to the docks. A fragrance vendor called out to him, approaching with a tray of vials, but Mujahid kept his head down and ignored the man. The safe house was his only concern right now.

He prayed to Zubuxo, the god of Death, that the coven was alive and well. Yasmine had to have misunderstood what she saw. It didn't make any sense.

The closer he got to the safe house, the *less* he believed her. The Arinian priests weren't capable of turning over innocents to be slaughtered. It violated everything they believed in. Everything they professed.

As he turned into the narrow alley leading to the safe house, his pulse quickened. Something was wrong. There was too much concentrated *necropotency* for this part of the city. His sweat turned cold. The only place that would hold this much ambient power was the city crypt, and that was blocks from here—much too far to fill his well of power.

He lifted his head and had to suppress a wave of nausea.

The safe house lay in smoldering ruin, and the Pinnacle Guard wasn't very careful where they spread the flames, from the look of the neighboring buildings.

His thoughts raced as he tried to understand what he was seeing. This wasn't possible. The priests couldn't have caused this!

The pulsing of his heart blocked out the sounds of the city. If the Arinian priests did this, he'd find out. One way or another. His palms stung from digging his fingernails into them.

Mujahid's legs shook and grew weak, and he landed on his knees in the middle of the alley. Pain radiated through his jaw from teeth clenched shut, and when the pain reached its zenith, his balled fists trembled until the only way he could release the tension was to punch the ground in front of him and cry out.

"Why?"

He collapsed into the dirt.

It was less than a year ago that he'd played with Yasmine's children in this very alley. They were no more than eight or nine years old. And now they were nothing more than piles of ash under a collapsed, burned out building. A building that was supposed to keep them safe. A building that Mujahid himself had *assured* them would be safe.

Yasmine was right. The Arinian priesthood's betrayal had cost the lives of dozens of necromancers and their families.

A breeze swept through the alley, blowing dirt and ash into Mujahid's face. As he blinked the dust from his eyes, something landed on his arm.

It was the brown stole of a priest of Arin.

As his racing thoughts slowed and his mind grew numb, he came to a realization. He would have to do something he thought only his brother capable of doing.

Mujahid stood, shook the dust off his robe, tossed the stole onto the dirt, and stepped out onto the *Sharea Ar-Ra'isi.*

Those festering priests had taken people dear to him, and now he'd make them answer for their betrayal.

It was time to pay a visit to Dar Rodon. It was time the Arinian mother house faced the wrath of a Mukhtaar Lord.

The wagon came to a stop at a small intersection on the desert road to Dar Rodon. Mujahid had ridden for more than a week with a miner headed towards the northern peaks, where the Mines of Abder Razi and its precious gems tempted the adventurous and foolhardy. But this is where they'd part ways. Mujahid wanted a payoff of a different variety.

Those slithering priests may not have used magic and force in their betrayal, but the blood of Mujahid's friends was on their hands nevertheless, and he would make them pay that debt of blood when he got to Dar Rodon.

As he stepped off the wagon onto the stone-paved road, he couldn't get the image of the ruined building out of his mind. Had the children suffered, or had their murderers shown them the mercy of quick deaths?

His mood soured by the minute.

Dar Rodon was days away to the north and east, and he had no idea where or when he'd be able to find another wagon or obtain a mount.

Just when he thought things couldn't get any worse, he saw a priest of Arin sitting on the side of the road up ahead, pulling long brown robes around his corpulent body.

Mujahid quieted the growing rage. This wasn't like him. He wasn't the sort of man to wish for someone's death.

But now one of those festering priests was within reach on the side of the road.

He hadn't expected to see one so soon, but he should have. This road would be bustling with pilgrims from now until after the solstice, all headed toward the Shrine of Arin and all its rituals. They'd wind their way through the red clay mountains and stop at shrines along the way, eventually emerging from the vast Religarian desert at the capital city of Dar Rodon.

Part of him wondered if any of these pilgrims knew what had happened. Did they know the evil their priests were capable of committing?

Arinian priests didn't carry weapons forged from steel or woven from magic. Their weapons were their tongues. By their tongues they seduced the world and murdered innocents. Mujahid would see an end to that, one way or another.

The priest of Arin had soured Mujahid's already lousy mood, and the self-loathing guilt Mujahid had carefully tucked away bubbled to the surface. If only he'd been there. If only he'd seen the betrayal coming. Those families had been counting on him. He was their Lord, and he'd failed them. The Arinian priests were supposed to be friends of Clan Mukhtaar, but instead they'd chosen to turn the coven over to the Empire for execution.

He'd love nothing more than to get his hands on this fat priest on the side of the road—no doubt plump from the food bought with the last pennies of some poor, faithful family.

But the priest would have to wait. Mujahid needed to get to Dar Rodon before anyone discovered who he was. If this priest realized Mujahid was a banished Mukhtaar Lord, head of the twelve necromantic clans, then he would alert an Imperial guard patrol, who would, no doubt, be along shortly. The Empire knew how important these pilgrims were to its coffers. This road would be heavily patrolled.

The priest was chatting with a diminutive man in patchwork robes, sitting atop a tan *adda*—a six-legged, lumbering beast of a mount that looked like a giant, muscular cat. The man couldn't be much taller than four feet.

If Mujahid was quick about it, he could avoid them altogether.

He walked faster, but as he passed the two men, the tiny rider spurred the *adda* southward toward Dar Saricon, removing any chance of escaping the priest's notice.

"You there, good fellow," the priest said. His old voice grated on Mujahid, but it held the confidence that whomever he was addressing would respond.

Typical, Mujahid thought. He ignored the old man, hoping he'd take a hint.

"I say *you there*, good sir," the priest repeated.

The thrumming of *adda* hooves drew Mujahid's attention to an approaching guard patrol.

He stopped. Ignoring the priest now would draw more attention to himself. He did his best to hide his contempt and faced the priest, who had climbed to his feet.

The old priest was shorter than Mujahid, rounder, and he stood with a slight stoop, made pronounced by the long walking staff bearing much of his weight. His brown Arinian robes, pulled tight by his copious belly, would split if he tried to bend over. The narrow brown scapular stretching from his waist to his neck was partially concealed by a flowing grey beard and a bushy mustache that hid his mouth.

But it was the priest's eyes that Mujahid found disturbing. They contained far more joy than they deserved.

"Can I help you?" Mujahid said.

"It's a long way to Dar Rodon. I'm sure we'll help each other before this journey is through."

"I doubt that, sir."

"Why the hurry? You walk as if there were a fire behind you."

"I hurry because there's a fire before me."

The priest wrinkled his mouth, as if in consideration. "Father Dominic. And you are?"

"Samael," Mujahid said, offering the alias he had created when his real name had become too dangerous to use.

"Well met, Samael. Tell me of this *fire*."

"It's a long story."

"It's a long journey."

Mujahid was going to hate this walk. He was tempted to cast a rope of *necropotency* around the man and bind him to the ground, but he couldn't use magic here. There was latent power all around him in pools and pockets of death. But the sacred light of Ascension would give his identity away. And that was the least of his worries with the approaching guard patrol.

"I prefer to travel alone," Mujahid said.

"You wouldn't strand an old man on the side of the road, would you?"

"Guilt is a weapon I'm immune to, Father."

"Guilt isn't a weapon, my son. It's a compass."

"Pretty sure I could kill a man with a well-placed compass."

"As I am sure I could guide one with a well-placed weapon."

Damned priests and their festering tongues, Mujahid thought. *Better to have the viper next to me where I can see him.* "Can you keep up with me?"

Father Dominic smiled. "With Arin's strength, I'll manage."

"You'd better. I'm not serving as your walking staff when the weight of *Arin's strength* causes that one to splinter out from under you." Mujahid started walking, hoping the corpulent priest would decide not to follow.

Father Dominic chuckled and caught up to Mujahid. "I do say, I apologize if I've done something to cause offense, good sir, though I can't imagine what that might be."

Mujahid stopped and pointed at the priest's chest. "Your *kind* causes me offense. The whole lot of you should be rounded up."

"There's too much of that going on these days for my liking."

"Too much offense?"

"Too much rounding up, if I'm not mistaken."

"And what would you know of it?" Mujahid asked.

"More than you'd believe. And what of you? You certainly seem to know something of it."

Mujahid cursed himself. Another slip like that could give up the lie. It was time to change the subject.

"Let's get something straight," Mujahid said. "If you're going to join me on this walk, there'll be no talk of Religion."

"Wouldn't dream of it."

"Good."

"Are you making the pilgrimage? The Shrine of Arin is magnificent, as befits his eternal holiness. The Grand Blessing is said to elevate a person's mind so they can perceive the true nature of the gods."

"Why do I feel like we've been walking for days already?" Mujahid said.

"I'm sure you have been. It would have taken you days to get here from Dar Saricon."

Father Dominic's words were like a dagger to Mujahid's heart. Did this priest have something to do with the destruction of the coven?

Mujahid rounded on Father Dominic. "What do you know of Dar Saricon?"

Father Dominic smiled and nodded toward the south. "I know it lies at the other end of this road."

"Don't lie to me."

"That's how roads work," Father Dominic said.

"What?"

"You begin in one place and wind up somewhere completely different."

"I said *no Religion*, priest. Now what of Dar Saricon?"

"Religion? I was speaking of civic infrastructure. What Religion do you know of that worries itself over roads?"

"I don't have the time or the inclination—"

"I've heard things." Father Dominic started walking.

Mujahid grabbed Father Dominic's arm. "And just what have you heard?"

Father Dominic faced him, no trace of his former smile left.

"Travel with me," Father Dominic said, "and I'll tell you. But not until we reach the wadi up ahead."

"Now listen—"

"The wadi, Samael."

Mujahid didn't want to be attached to this festering priest any longer than necessary, but he needed answers as much as he needed justice for those families.

"Fine," Mujahid said, letting go of Father Dominic's arm. "At the wadi. But no farther."

Dominic thumped his walking staff on the ground and continued walking.

"Bah!" Dominic said. "Roads as a religious reference. If I *had* been speaking in metaphor, I'd say it was a touch more philosophical than religious, wouldn't you? A road is *clearly* a process by which—"

"Blessings of Arin upon you, Father," a mounted Imperial guard said in a shrill voice. "The road ahead is crowded."

Mujahid cursed. This priest had him so tied in knots that he was losing sight of what he was doing. Even if he didn't see the guard coming, which he should have, the musty smell of the guard's *adda* should have been plenty of warning.

As if in response, the *adda* opened its toothy maw and bellowed, receiving a pat on the head from the guard in return.

Mujahid stepped away. Those festering animals had a tendency to spit when you least wanted them to.

The guard, as well as his six companions, was dressed in traditional desert robes, which consisted of long, billowing white fabric that ended with a tail flowing up and over the guard's left shoulder. A portion of the fabric wrapped up from the back and formed a spacious turban that provided ample shade for the guard's head and face. Two sheathed scimitars hung from a belt around the guard's waist, reaching down to his knees. There were few things more effective than a show of steel to make casual criminals think twice about taking advantage of unwary pilgrims.

"Many thanks," Father Dominic said. "How far to Dar Rodon?"

One of the guards, whose turban was hanging behind his head, looked away from Mujahid, but he turned back quickly.

This wasn't good. That guard was getting suspicious, and Mujahid thought the man might recognize him.

"Three days on foot," the first guard said. "But the Oasis of Zarush is only an hour away, beyond the sacred wadi where we camp. You should see about obtaining mounts there. Always mounts to be had."

"Trouble ahead?" Mujahid asked.

"The usual," the guard said. "But don't worry. There's enough of us to handle any trouble between now and the solstice. You'll make it safely to Dar Rodon, as long as you refill your drinking skins at Zarush. We can protect you from the cutpurses. The heat is your own concern."

The guard with the hanging turban circled them on his mount, examining Mujahid up and down.

Mujahid tucked his chin in an attempt to shield his face. He didn't want to kill a guard for doing his job, but there were greater issues at stake. Far greater.

"Come, my friend," Father Dominic said. He put his arm around the back of Mujahid's head and nudged it down as he led him away. "We don't want to keep the guards from their duty."

If Mujahid didn't know better, he'd say Father Dominic was trying to hide him.

The turbanless guard hesitated. "Father, would you give us your blessing before we leave?"

"Blessings, my child," Father Dominic said without turning around.

"Come now, Father," the guard said. "What sort of blessing is that?"

Father Dominic gave Mujahid a pat on the back and faced the guard.

"May the holy light of Arin's helm illuminate your path," Father Dominic said, "and may his strength be your strength."

"What of the winds?" the guard asked. "It would be nice to have them at our backs. I do not hear the rest of the blessing."

"Arin bestows hearing on the deaf."

"As his power should—"

"And he takes sight from those who see," Father Dominic said, his voice tinged with something like *anger*.

The guard whimpered and Mujahid turned around.

"What did you do to me?" The guard asked, frantically rubbing his eyes. "I can't see! My eyes!"

The other guards looked concerned by their compatriot's cries, but seemed confused by what had happened.

"The desert is such a dangerous place when the wind blows," Father Dominic said. "I'm sure it will pass."

The blinded guard rubbed and blinked his eyes. "I…what did you do to me? I can see again!" He seemed scared, but he wouldn't take his eyes off Mujahid.

Father Dominic put his hand around Mujahid's neck and turned him around.

"Come on, you fool," a guard said. "The priest was nowhere near you."

"He cursed me! You saw it!"

"He's an Arinian. I saw a superstitious idiot rubbing sand out of his eyes. Enough of this."

The patrol leader spurred his *adda* away, and the rest of the guards followed, judging by the receding sound of hooves on the dry dirt.

"I'm telling you I've seen him before!" The suspicious guard yelled loud enough to be heard as they left.

Mujahid hoped the guard was talking about Father Dominic, but hope was something he didn't put much faith in these days. Nevertheless, he hoped it would be the last he saw of those guards.

When they were safely out of earshot, Mujahid shrugged the priest's arm away.

"How did you do that?" Mujahid asked.

"Please," Father Dominic said. "Not you too? I didn't take you for the superstitious kind."

"Don't give me that. I know enough of the arcane to know magic when I see it."

"You heard the guard. I'm an Arinian priest. If you know as much of the arcane as you claim, then you should know I don't have magic."

Mujahid couldn't deny that. Priests of Arin had no mystical power whatsoever. Unlike necromancers, who passed the art of necromancy from parent to child through ancient bloodlines, any man who was willing to dedicate himself to Arin and live a celibate life could become an Arinian priest.

Perhaps Mujahid was mistaken. After all, he hadn't sensed a surge of *necropotency*, which would have been the tell-tale sign of magic use. Still, he'd have to watch this priest. He'd made the mistake of trusting them in Dar Saricon, and innocent families had paid for it with their lives.

"Magic isn't the only mystical force in the universe, Samael," Father Dominic said. "You ignore this at your own peril."

"Pick up your pace," Mujahid said. "I'd like to see the Oasis of Zarush before my dotage."

"Why the rush? It's a lovely day."

"We'll be feeling the effects of the sun soon enough."

Mujahid glanced up. The true sky of Erindor had been turquoise no more than a year ago, but no longer. Now it was a uniform yellow. The priest didn't need to remind him of mystical forces. Mujahid didn't question the gods' existence. He questioned their relevance.

How could the gods allow such a tragedy to happen? How could they sit idly by and watch the death of their ancient priesthood, the *necromantic* priesthood, and do nothing to stop it? Who would purify the dead now? Who would console the grieving families? Certainly not these Arinian fools!

Mujahid shook his head and looked down at the road. Staring at the yellow sky always ended the same way; with Mujahid devoid of hope.

"We'd better heed their advice and refill our skins at Zarush," Mujahid said.

"Do you know the story of Zarush?" Father Dominic asked.

"I said no Religion, old man."

"It's just a story."

"A story about a saint. I'm not daft."

Father Dominic *harrumphed*. "Zarush was no saint, let me tell you."

"Zarush died a thousand years ago. What do you know of his sanctity?"

Father Dominic smiled. "Time is a funny thing. It doesn't always behave."

Mujahid smirked.

"I like that," Mujahid said. "I'll have to remember it."

Father Dominic didn't know how close to the truth he was. The process of raising a dead *penitent* caused the necromancer to relive the entire life of the person raised within the span of a moment. It was disorienting at best.

"It's true the popular histories paint a saintly picture of Zarush," Father Dominic said. "But the secret histories of my order are another matter."

Mujahid spun toward the priest, stumbling when he took his eyes off the sandy road. It was unusual for a Priest of Arin to admit the existence of such histories, much less be willing to recount a story from one of them.

Father Dominic's smile was wide enough to swallow a dinner plate. "Zarush nearly died in this desert…on this very road! The goddess Shealynd appeared before him in the sacred wadi, as he breathed his last, and she told him to take heart. 'Fear not,' she said. 'Go east to a crossroads, and pray to the triune gods; Arin, Shealynd, and Zubuxo,' she told him. 'The desert will be marked,' she said.

"Zarush questioned his own senses! More, he questioned the goddess! 'How can I know this is real?' he asked her. 'I will leave you my sign, and all will know the truth,' she said. When she vanished, a beautiful rose bush appeared where she had been standing, where nothing had ever grown before. And so Zarush took heart. The strength he took from Shealynd carried him out of the dry wadi, over the dunes to the east, until he came upon the crossroads."

"You have your books confused, old man," Mujahid said. "Everyone knows that story."

"It wasn't just an oasis of three pools that appeared in this desert that day," Father Dominic said. "It was love."

Mujahid chuckled. "Love. I'll tell you something my brother once told me. 'Love is like a Shandarian pepper. Feels great filling your belly, but painful in the end.'"

Father Dominic laughed. "Your brother sounds like a wise man. That or he eats too many peppers."

"I don't know about wise, but he has a lot of sayings involving his arse."

"It was love that stopped Zarush from living his life like an arse."

"Calling your saint an arse now?"

"I told you before. Zarush was no saint. He was an assassin. And one of the greatest wielders of staves the world has known."

Mujahid widened his eyes. "Well *that's* not in the popular histories."

"He was on the way to Dyr Rahal—"

"Never heard of it."

"Small fishing village on the coast, south of Dar Rodon. Don't interrupt me. As I was saying, he was on his way to Dyr Rahal to kill a man."

Though Mujahid was hot and dehydrated, a chill passed through him. It wasn't every day he learned a well-known saint was a killer. "I thought he was on his way to Dar Rodon to distribute his wealth among the poor."

"Would you like to finish the fake story, or shall I tell you the real one?"

"And who was this man he was going to kill?"

"What's more interesting is *why* he was going to kill the man."

"Do tell."

"Years before his encounter at the wadi, he had made enemies of a powerful warlord."

"How?"

"Stole some gold. Stop interrupting. It's rude."

"Excuse me." Mujahid drew his shoulders back as they walked. "So, *Saint* Zarush was a thief and assassin. Lovely bunch of —"

"*He stole a warlord's* gold. Fearing for his life and the lives of his wife and children, he fled to the desert, where he found a cave in which to hide. Only he and his closest friend, Mostafa, knew of this cave. One day—"

"Wait," Mujahid said. "*Saint* Mostafa The Fisherman?"

"I said stop interrupting, Samael."

"Has anyone ever told you you're a horrible story teller?"

"My story telling skills are exemplary, young man! It's your listening skills that need—"

"You were telling me about Zarush and Mostafa."

Father Dominic blushed. "Yes. So I was. Wait, where was I?"

"Zubuxo save me from the addled," Mujahid said, massaging his temples and wishing his empty water skin was filled with ale. "The *warlord.*"

"Yes. That's right. One day, the warlord took his band of thugs and found the cave Zarush was hiding in. Zarush knew it was over. With much wailing, he prostrated himself before the warlord and begged for the lives of his wife and children. He told the warlord he had spent the gold, but would offer his life in return."

"Well he ended up in a wadi talking to a goddess, so I doubt the warlord took him up on the offer," Mujahid said.

"The warlord told him that Mostafa—who was a poor man with little to spare—had already paid his debt in full. When Zarush asked with what coin Mostafa had paid the debt, the warlord told him Mostafa had paid with the lives of Zarush's family."

"So, Saint Mostafa sold them out."

"The story isn't over," Father Dominic said. His voice changed to a barely audible whisper. "Saint Mostafa sold them out."

"That's what I just said!"

"*I'm* telling the story. Anyway, the warlord wasn't quite finished with Zarush, oh no he wasn't! He climbed down from his *adda*, and in three giant strides of his great legs, closed the distance between them and slashed Zarush across the face with his scimitar."

"That explains some of the drawings of Zarush. Wasn't exactly a handsome man."

"Oh yes. He was badly scarred. And when he recovered, Zarush swore an unholy oath to make Mostafa pay for the lives of his family. He set off across the desert—"

"And ended up in a wadi talking to Shealynd. Tell me *that* part is true."

"That part is true." Father Dominic grinned. "But it's what he discovered at the oasis that warms my heart to no end."

"A bound and gagged Mostafa?"

Father Dominic chuckled. "Love."

Mujahid narrowed his eyes at Father Dominic.

"You think I jest," Father Dominic said. "But I assure you, I'm very serious. What happened to him at the oasis changed the course of his life, and this country, irrevocably."

"You mistake my impatience for disbelief. Get to the point."

"Zarush made his way toward the crossroads, as Shealynd commanded. But before he reached them, he was overcome by a desire to lie down on the ground, as if the divine hand of Shealynd herself had forced him down. For the second time in his life he lay prostrate, but this time he prayed. A globe of light surrounded Zarush, and a thunderous boom filled the air to the east as a great ball of fire fell from the sky. When it struck the desert floor, the sand removed itself from the crossroads, creating a bowl in the desert, with four roads leading into it. When the sand had finished scattering itself to the corners of the world,

Zarush remained unharmed within the globe of light. The globe vanished from sight, and Zarush heard a monstrous rush of water. Three sacred pools formed, where they remain to this day."

"And this changed his life, how? His family was still dead, Mostafa was still free, and all he had to show for it was a nasty scar on his face."

"Unfortunately, no one knows."

"What? Now listen here, old man, you started this tale. I expect you to finish it."

"What do you want me to say? Zarush never told a soul what happened when he reached the oasis that day, but we do know something important."

"And what is that?"

"He searched the world for Mostafa, and eventually found him."

"Finally. A happy ending."

"Indeed. They rekindled their friendship, and you know the rest of the story."

"Rekindled their—Mostafa sacrificed Zarush's family!"

"It certainly—oh, here we are."

As they crested a hill, the paved road came to a plateau. The surrounding desert extended for miles in every direction. In front of Mujahid was the sacred wadi; a large ravine spanning several hundred yards that gouged a crooked path north and south through the central desert of Religar. It was dry at this time of year, but in a few short weeks it would flood with fast-moving waters from the northern rains, bringing an end to the pilgrimage season.

Mujahid's gaze traced the road to Dar Rodon into the ravine, across the sacred wadi, and up a system of switchbacks on the opposite side, where an imperial guard patrol was making its way down into the wadi. Beyond the patrol, the road twisted for several miles across a desert plain, until it reached a small pucker in the ground, where the sand turned ever so slightly upward on the horizon—the Oasis of Zarush.

Voices carried up from the wadi and Mujahid's eyes were drawn to the bottom of the ravine. One group of pilgrims had stopped and prostrated themselves in front of a large, oblong hedge, which curved around and off the road leading through the wadi. Another group rocked back and forth in ritual prayer in front of the hedge,

"Come," said Father Dominic. "You must see the sacred rose bush."

Mujahid was impatient to get to Dar Rodon, but he couldn't abandon Father Dominic if the priest knew something about what had happened in Dar Saricon.

Resigned to staying with Father Dominic regardless of the delay, Mujahid followed the priest toward the edge of the plateau, where the paving stones ended and a dirt trail began.

They started down the narrow switchbacks, hugging the side of the cliff away from the wooden posts and makeshift rope railing. They had to press flat against the cliff as returning pilgrims made their way up the trail on *adda* that were nearly as wide as the trail itself. Several times, pilgrims stopped and asked Father Dominic for a blessing, which he offered with an enthusiastic smile and dramatic wave of his hands. He had a tendency to get embroiled in lengthy conversations, though, which Mujahid had to interrupt.

"We have a destination to reach, Father," Mujahid said, as a pilgrim began to tell Father Dominic her life story.

The woman offered a bow and continued up the trail.

"No need to be rude," Father Dominic said. "She was just saying —"

"I'd rather not be on these switchbacks if that guard patrol returns. And I certainly don't want to be here when they meet up with their friends on the other side. Besides, how in Arin's name could you hear what she was saying with all the talking you were doing?"

"Why the concern?"

"Because if you intend to stop and talk the ears off every —"

"I was talking about the guards."

There was an awkward pause as Mujahid considered his words.

"I've seen enough miraculous blindings for one day," Mujahid said. He gestured along the road, wanting to hurry the priest along.

Father Dominic smiled and hobbled down the path.

After several turns, and several hundred feet of descent, the trail flattened, and they walked out into the wadi, which had been pounded into a hard, flat surface by millennia of pilgrimages. Red cliffs towered over the ravine, their smooth walls swept by countless years of winds. The cliffs would have kept much of the wadi in shadow were it not for the ubiquitous yellow glow from the magical barrier that covered the sky and dispersed the sunlight.

That barrier may have covered the world in yellow, but it covered Mujahid's life in a black cloud of despair. He knew the world was ending, and there wasn't a festering thing he could do about it. And it wasn't only Mujahid who lacked hope. He could see the despair settling over the very land of Erindor, in the trees that were dying in the highlands and the flowers that didn't bloom this year. He could see it in the quake that had leveled the city of Agera, and the dilapidation of Dar Saricon, no longer the *Gem* it once was.

The rage was bubbling, threatening to boil over. True, the Arinian priests had betrayed the priests of Zubuxo…the necromancers, but the Archmage had betrayed the entire world by creating that monstrosity in the sky.

His brother Nuuan had been right. All that was left was vengeance. Vengeance for the destruction of the necromantic coven in Dar Saricon. Vengeance for what was being called the *Great Purge*—the systematic hunting of necromancers and putting them to death on the orders of the Archmage. And who best to take vengeance than a Mukhtaar Lord?

"Perhaps you shouldn't look *up* anymore, Samael," Father Dominic said.

Mujahid shook the dark thoughts out of his mind. "What?"

"Every time you stare at the sky you look like a person marching to his death."

"We all march toward death."

"Not as quickly as you, it seems."

"Don't get me started on your beloved Arinian priesthood, *Father*. They're a part of this mess."

Father Dominic stopped and turned so suddenly Mujahid bumped into him.

Mujahid saw impatience on the priest's face for the first time. But he saw something else too. Something powerful.

The impatient scowl on Father Dominic's face gave way to a serene smile, and whatever Mujahid had seen in the old priest's eyes was gone.

"Come now, Samael," Father Dominic said. "We're here."

Father Dominic led him through the crowd toward where the pilgrims were praying. When they reached the front of the crowd, Mujahid got his first good look at what everyone was staring at.

An emerald green hedge grew up out of the dry, cracked desert ground, spanning more than twenty feet across and ten feet high. It curved around on itself on both sides and stretched another forty feet into the wadi. People had formed a line that disappeared around the other side of the hedge.

A row of guards in voluminous white desert garb stood along the hedge, keeping pilgrims from approaching it too closely.

"Why all the steel?" Mujahid asked. "I thought this was a holy place."

"It's said a Rose of Shealynd never dies," Father Dominic said. "And when one is picked from the hedge, another takes its place within moments. But only a priest of Shealynd is allowed to touch the hedge. The guards are here to make sure of it."

"Am I the only one here who doesn't see any roses."

Father Dominic smirked. "Legend holds the roses only appear when the goddess is present."

"Convenient logic," Mujahid said. "I'll give you that."

One by one the pilgrims in line moved around the hedge as if in a queue.

"Is walking around the hedge some ritual I'm unaware of?" Mujahid asked.

"The sacred hedge encloses a small shrine of Shealynd. Pilgrims may enter one at a time and pray to the goddess."

"Well *Shealynd be praised* and all that. Let's leave them to it and make our way out of the wadi."

"Arin forbid," Father Dominic said. "I intend to spend a few minutes inside that shrine. And so should you."

"You're more addled than I thought. It will take an hour or more with that line."

Mujahid's stomach did a somersault, and he grabbed the skin of water tied to the inside of his sleeve. He must be getting dehydrated, but the festering skin was empty.

"What line?" Father Dominic asked.

Mujahid looked toward the hedge and saw the queue was gone.

"See?" Father Dominic said. "Just a few minutes of your time."

Mujahid nodded grudgingly. "Make it quick."

"I'm not sure I can walk there by myself, my son." Father Dominic's voice grew shaky. "Come with me in case I grow weak."

Mujahid sighed and nodded toward the hedge. "Let's go, then."

Damn these priests and their manipulations.

They followed the curving hedge deeper into the wadi until they came to a five-feet-wide opening, flanked by two guards and covered by a red curtain.

Father Dominic looked up and down at the hedge.

"It's been a long time," Father Dominic said. "A long time indeed."

A priest of Shealynd, a man in his middle years, stepped out through the opening and placed his hand on Father Dominic's shoulder. Mujahid had seen these priests at the Pinnacle, prior to being banished. The priest wore the traditional red robe, gathered at the waist with a green cincture. A red scapular, trimmed in green, hung down to the center of the man's chest and wrapped around his back.

With any luck, Mujahid would go unrecognized.

"The love of Shealynd be with you," the priest said.

"And with you," Father Dominic said in reply.

"Speak the truth of your heart to the goddess, for no sound will travel past the curtain," the priest said. He stepped aside and Father Dominic ambled past the curtain and into the shrine.

"You look familiar," the priest said. "Have you been to the shrine before?"

It took a moment for Mujahid to realize the priest was speaking to him.

"First time," Mujahid said.

The priest looked down with a confused expression on his face. A moment later he smiled and looked up. "You've been to the mother house in Dar Rodon."

Mujahid shook his head and looked away. This was getting uncomfortable. And *dangerous*.

"No," Mujahid said.

The priest hummed and tapped his foot. After several moments of silence, he snapped his fingers. "The Pinnacle! I must have run into you at the Pinnacle."

Mujahid would have few choices if the priest recognized him. He had to stop this now.

"Now that you mention it," Mujahid said, "you seem familiar to me too." Mujahid smiled and nodded dramatically. "I remember now. It was the brothel in Agera. I *knew* you looked familiar! You had a thing for redheads, am I right?"

The priest's eyes widened.

Mujahid lowered his voice to a whisper. "Between you and I, friend, if you took a tumble with Alona, you'd...do well to see a physician."

"Vile creature!" The priest said as he stepped away from Mujahid. "Sounds like some of us need this pilgrimage more than others!"

Mujahid shrugged.

The curtain flapped open and Father Dominic stepped out.

"You're next, Samael," Father Dominic said.

Mujahid waved his hand. "No, that's quite all right. We need to be on our way."

"I won't hear of it," the priest of Shealynd said. "Duty is duty! You won't complete the ritual if you skip the shrine, and it's my duty to see you complete it."

"I don't think that's—"

"If you don't complete the ritual, you'll be ineligible for the Grand Blessing," the priest of Shealynd said. "Now get inside. End of discussion! The love of Shealynd be with you, for the love of...Shealynd."

"You too," Mujahid said.

Father Dominic cleared his throat.

"*And with you*," Mujahid said.

The priest of Shealynd smiled and stepped aside. "Speak the truth of your heart to the goddess, for no sound will travel past the curtain."

Mujahid stepped into the shrine and pulled the curtain shut behind him.

The inside wall of the shrine was no different from the outside, and it completely surrounded him. Though there was no ceiling, and the pilgrims praying outside had been loud enough for their voices to carry up out of the wadi, it was eerily silent inside the shrine.

Mujahid's gaze turned toward the yellow sky.

He remembered how Clan Mukhtaar was once the crowning gem of the necromantic priesthood, raising and purifying the dead as was their duty. Necromancers had been a vital part of society, and now...

Now they were hunted, tortured, and executed.

Those families in Dar Saricon thought they were safe. Mujahid had trusted the Arinian priests, and they'd repaid that trust with betrayal and murder.

The rage roared back to life, and his heartbeat thrummed in his ears. He'd follow that fat priest to Dar Rodon, enter the Arinian mother house and burn it to the ground. He'd raise the dead, all right. He'd raise enough *penitents* to tear the Great Temple down. Then he'd travel to the Pinnacle itself and take care of the tyrant at the center of it all. The Archmage.

Mujahid's heart was racing and his arms trembled as he balled his fists.

The truth of his heart? He'd give Shealynd a *divine earful* of the truth of his heart!

"Why?" Mujahid shouted. "Why did you let this happen? We served you! Each of you! We did everything you asked! How could you abandon us to a madman? Do you watch from on high as the world spirals into decay? Is the sound of our weeping pleasing to your infernal ears? Do you feast in the heavens while we—"

His vision swam and the hedge in front of him transformed into a wall of vapor. He rubbed his eyes thinking the dehydration was playing tricks with his mind, but as he drew his hands away, images began to play across the vapor in wisps, coalescing into a picture of Dar Saricon. This was where the Arinian priesthood had discovered the necromantic coven and informed the local authorities.

The vapor twisted into the shape of a Pinnacle Guard patrol approaching the coven's safe house.

Why was he seeing this? Why were the gods torturing him so? Wasn't it bad enough he couldn't be there to do anything about it? Now he had to watch it play out too?

The guards came with their torches and swords, followed by those pompous, self-righteous Arinian priests. It was precisely as Yasmine described. He seethed as the priests huddled together away from the guards, no doubt deciding how best to stay out of the fray and let the guards take the brunt of what was to come. *Cowards!* They didn't have the courage to participate in the destruction they had caused. He watched as—

What was this? Two priests broke away from the others and entered the safe house through a hidden passage. It was an entrance they shouldn't have known about. An entrance known only to the coven's leadership and their close friends. The priests who stayed outside called the guards away from the safe house, and they were yelling and waving their hands in grand gestures.

As Mujahid looked at the house, the roof in the image became transparent, and it was as if he saw inside the building from the perspective of a god. The two priests were conferring with three others who had gotten there first. And those three had been placing corpses on the floor. Corpses from the city crypt!

One of the priests spoke solemnly with a group of four necromancers. The necromancers, weeping, said their goodbyes to their families and friends, and then walked out of the house toward the guards. The other

Arinian priest — *could this be?* — led the remaining coven members out through the secret passage, out into the street behind the safe house, and down toward the docks, where a Shandarian ship marked with the Arinian symbol of the Helm of Arin waited to sail them safely away.

The image faded and Mujahid wiped moisture from his eye.

The Arinian priests saved the coven. The coven's leadership sacrificed themselves so the rest could get away. They placed corpses in the building to fool the Pinnacle Guard into thinking they had slaughtered everyone.

For the first time in decades, Mujahid felt shame.

How could he be so ignorant? He'd seen it countless times during the *namocea* — the process by which he'd lived the lives of the dead he'd raised. He'd experienced, time and time again, how people were rarely what they appeared to be. And yet he'd judged these Arinian priests to the point of wanting to commit murder on a massive scale.

He closed his eyes and a breeze played across his face, carrying with it the aromatic scent of fresh roses. Strange, as he had seen no roses earlier.

When he opened his eyes he staggered away from the hedge toward the center of the shrine.

Thousands of thornless roses, each the size of a man's head, had bloomed and nestled within the emerald green leaves of the hedge.

He wasn't alone. He couldn't see anyone, but his survival instinct was sure of it. Someone else was in the shrine with him.

A woman!

He couldn't see her, but he knew. A sense of peace filled him, calming his racing heart and frayed nerves. And when he thought he'd imagined it all, that none of this could be happening, a voice filled his mind.

You are beloved amongst your brethren, Mujahid, the woman said. *Be at peace.*

Mujahid looked around the shrine, but the voice came from all directions. "Peace? How can you ask me to be at peace when the world I love is being destroyed?"

Listen and remember, the woman said. *In Erindor's time of greatest need, He Who Walks Between Worlds will come to bring down the sky. The banished lord from Paradise will cradle him like a babe until the water takes him. And when the living sea consumes the Temple of Lies, the lost will find their way home.*

"I—"

Go, the woman said. *He who was blinded now sees.*

The presence left, and all Mujahid heard was the racing of his heart.

Had he received a prophecy from Shealynd herself? But what could it mean? Surely *this* was Erindor's time of greatest need, but who was "He Who Walks Between Worlds?" Paradise was the ancestral home of the Mukhtaar Lords, and Mujahid *had* been banished from the Pinnacle. But *Temple of Lies*? What was the goddess talking about?

He had to get control of himself. This was too much to absorb all at once. He repeated the words, but he knew he'd never forget them. They were indelibly etched into his consciousness.

The goddess had given him something else as well. Was it *cautious optimism*? He dared not call it *hope* yet, but…but maybe it *was* hope.

Shealynd had been right. Mujahid was seeing more perfectly than ever before.

He pulled the curtain aside and stepped out of the shrine.

The priest of Shealynd was lying prostrate on the ground, along with the guards and all of the pilgrims. The only person who remained standing was Father Dominic, who was displaying his customary huge smile.

"You *do* see the roses *now*, do you not, Samael?" Father Dominic asked.

Mujahid smiled.

Cries went up through the crowd of pilgrims beyond the hedge, and the sound of hooves trampling the dry ground echoed off the red clay canyon walls.

"Where are they?" A man yelled.

Mujahid knew that voice. It was the guard from earlier. The guard whom Father Dominic mysteriously blinded.

Seven hells! She said blinded, *not blind!* He knew that guard would end up causing trouble.

Mujahid touched Father Dominic's shoulder. "Can you move quickly?"

"What in Arin's name for?"

"Priest, if you don't follow me out of this wadi, those guards are going to give you a scar much worse than the one on Zarush's face."

"But why? Even if—"

"They...look, there's no time. The guard you blinded recognized me, and that doesn't bode well for either of us. Let's head farther into the wadi. They'll be expecting us to use the switchbacks instead."

"Recognized you?" Father Dominic hesitated for a moment, and his expression was indecipherable. But he nodded and started walking.

Mujahid had been afraid this would happen. That nosy guard must have finally realized who Mujahid was and told the others. They'd missed an opportunity to take down a banished Mukhtaar Lord, and they wouldn't make that mistake again. And with the other guard patrol making its way into the wadi from the eastern side, their numbers would be bolstered.

As they walked farther into the wadi, Mujahid reached out with his mind, searching for every drop of *necropotency* he could find. He allowed the power to flow into the well that rested at the center of his consciousness—that place surrounded by arcane symbols he could weave together to create necromantic spells—in preparation for the battle to come. There was no way he'd make it out of the wadi in time.

A bend in the wadi up ahead might offer them some concealment, but it was only a matter of time before the guards caught up.

As if punctuating his thought, the two groups of imperial guards converged at the hedge and turned into the wadi. It wasn't difficult to find two people walking *along* a dry river bed when everyone else was *crossing* it.

"Faster," Mujahid said.

"This walking stick isn't made for racing, Samael."

Mujahid cursed and stopped. If he kept moving, he might walk out of range of whatever source was feeding him *necropotency*, and then he'd be powerless. No, whatever he was going to do, he had to do it now.

"What are you doing?" Father Dominic asked.

"It's no use. All running will do is make us die *over there* instead of over here."

Mujahid reached inside, past the dozens of arcane symbols he had mastered through the years, until at last he touched the *symbol of ascension*, etched by sacred fire into the heart of his well of power. He ignited it, careful to turn his face away from Father Dominic. The sacred light of ascension would shine from his eyes now, and he was damned if he'd give up his identity after working so hard to conceal it.

Mujahid cleared his mind of everything except the approaching guards and the wadi. He needed something big.

"Keep walking," Mujahid said.

"I thought you said—"

"Just keep walking."

Mujahid considered his options. He could summon a *penitent*, but that would remove all doubt that he was a necromancer. And a single *penitent* against all those riders would be near useless. He could pull a rider or two from their mounts with strands of energy, but the problem remained…there were too many of them.

He turned inside and examined the symbols of power for inspiration.

Two symbols caught his attention. The symbol of the Shield, and the symbol of Disease. He had never tried this combination before, and something about the idea seemed…*dirty* to him. Small, controlled disease spells made people healthier and stronger by rendering them resilient to the greater sicknesses—a helpful trait when a person worked around the dead. The disease symbol was never intended as a weapon. But if he combined it with the shield…

He set aside thoughts of what was *right* and *proper*. Right and proper had their place, but now it was time to survive.

He wove a thread of *necropotency* through the shield and disease symbols and cast the combined magical fields forward toward the oncoming riders.

A sickly yellow-green wall of mist spread out from the center of the wadi, stretching toward each side of the ravine.

The riders in front couldn't have suspected how deadly the mist was. As the first of them struck the mist wall, rider and *adda* alike fell to the ground, choking and erupting in boils and puss.

A small amount of power drained from Mujahid.

So that's *how it works.* He should be able to gauge how much power remained in the disease shield.

The wall grew wider, and another wave of riders struck it and fell before anyone realized what was happening.

Mujahid's face went cold as the wind shifted direction and blew a portion of the disease cloud back toward him and Father Dominic.

Uh oh. I didn't think about that.

"You'd best move faster, Father!" Mujahid shouted.

As the disease cloud spread across the wadi—and crept toward Mujahid and Father Dominic—it lengthened back toward the riders, engulfing more in sickness and disease.

A small group of guards had noticed what was happening and turned their *adda* toward the canyon wall, racing to outflank the disease cloud.

"They're coming!" Mujahid shouted.

Five of the riders made it through the gap between the disease cloud and the canyon wall before it closed on the remaining Imperial guardsmen and dropped them from their mounts, clutching their throats as their eyes swelled.

This wasn't right. Mujahid couldn't shake the strange sense of peace and hope he'd carried from the shrine of Shealynd. Something…divine…had reassured him and given him something to believe in. As far as he could tell, it was Shealynd herself who had done the reassuring! Though a part of him wanted to doubt, he knew what he experienced was real and certain. The prophecy would be fulfilled, and that meant these guards would not prevail.

He withdrew the *necropotency* and dispersed the cloud of disease, hoping he'd never be put in a position to use that combination of symbols again. The guards on the ground were hurt, but they'd recover in time. For now they were out of the battle, and that was good enough.

"Father," Mujahid said. "You'd better—"

Father Dominic had begun running toward the Imperial guardsmen with the agility of a much younger man, dodging large rocks and trenches in the wadi floor.

Mujahid raised his eyebrows.

"These are far better odds, *Samael*!" Father Dominic yelled as he ran past with a grin.

Father Dominic raised his staff above his head and twirled it as he ran. He stopped several yards in front of the approaching guards, and when the staff had completed several spins above his head, he took it in one hand, spun it rapidly, and planted it firmly under his right arm. His left hand extended in front of him in a defensive posture.

This is no priest of Arin, Mujahid thought.

"Stand aside, Father," a guard said as he trotted his *adda* forward. "It's your friend we're interested in."

"No one brings harm to *my* friends," Father Dominic said. His voice had changed. It was deeper. Younger.

Father Dominic raised the staff above his head and the sky darkened.

"You would do well to leave us in peace," Father Dominic said. "I wish you no harm, but I will not allow you to take my friend. He is too important."

A couple of the guards laughed.

"Oh, I know of his importance, Father," the guard's leader said. "And the Archmage would have him executed. Step aside, or there'll be two executions this day." He spurred his *adda* forward and the other guards followed.

Father Dominic twirled his staff, and a dark cloud swept into the wadi from the south. A globe of light formed around him and Mujahid.

As the cloud drew closer, Mujahid could see the darkness wasn't a cloud at all. It was boulder-sized chunks of dirt and rock. They passed harmlessly around Mujahid and Father Dominic and slammed into the remaining guards, pulverizing them into the wadi floor.

When the last of the rocks disintegrated, the globe of light faded.

Mujahid approached Father Dominic, who had remained motionless throughout the maelstrom of dirt.

"Would have been nice to know you could do that sooner," Mujahid said.

Mujahid couldn't see Father Dominic's face from behind, but he knew the priest was chuckling from the way his head bobbed and his shoulder's shrugged.

"I'm sure," Father Dominic said. "But then how would you have learned the lessons you needed to learn...*Lord Mukhtaar?*"

Mujahid reached for *necropotency*, preparing to fight if necessary. He was beginning to like the priest, but it never came to a good end when people knew his identity.

"Fear not," Father Dominic said. "You won't need to use your considerable skills against me. You'd find they'd do you no good anyway."

Father Dominic turned, but the face Mujahid saw wasn't the face of the old priest. It was a much younger version, and this version had a long scar that ran from one side of his face to the other.

"Zarush," Mujahid said.

Father Dominic...*Zarush* smiled.

"The world grows more dangerous with every passing day," Zarush said. "You must grow in wisdom, Lord Mukhtaar. You *must* learn there is a time and place for aggression as well as pacifism. Each is a weapon you must learn to wield. I suspect everything depends on it. I don't know what the goddess told you. Such matters aren't for me to know. But I know that whatever she said is best heeded."

"It was a prophecy—"

"No," Zarush said. "As I said. Such matters aren't for me or anyone else to know. But perhaps whatever it is will guide you when you reach Dar Rodon."

Mujahid looked up at the switchbacks leading out of the wadi and out toward Dar Rodon. The rage was gone. He knew the truth now. The Arinian priesthood wasn't his enemy.

The shame of what he had once intended to do in Dar Rodon made him lower his head.

"This road leads not to Dar Rodon," Mujahid said. "Not for me. Not anymore."

"Mostafa didn't sacrifice my family, my friend," Zarush said. "He saved them. While I was in hiding, he used powerful magic to make the warlord believe he was seeing my dead family. A magic known as *enchanting*. And you're the only soul I've ever told. Let's keep it between us for now. I'll see you again."

"Enchanting?" Mujahid asked. When he turned toward Zarush, Zarush had vanished, leaving nothing behind except his walking staff.

Mujahid picked the staff up and examined it. It bore the symbol of the Shandarian Union. A cat's eye on a red field.

"The Union," Mujahid said. "Perhaps it's time to put down some roots."

Mujahid started walking. It was a long way to the Shandarian Union.

As he climbed up out of the wadi, he hoped he'd come across another Arinian priest along the way. Perhaps…just *perhaps*…they could have a long talk about Religion to pass the time.

ABOUT THE AUTHOR

Nat Russo was born in New York, raised in Arizona, and has lived just about everywhere in-between. He's gone from pizza maker, to radio DJ, to Catholic seminarian (in a Benedictine monastery, of all places), to police officer, to software engineer. His career has taken him from central Texas to central Germany, where he worked as a defense contractor for Northrop Grumman. He's spent most of his adult life developing software, playing video games, running a Cub Scout den, gaining/losing/gaining/losing weight, and listening to every kind of music under the sun.

Along the way he managed to earn a degree in Philosophy and a black belt in Tang Soo Do.

He currently makes his home in central Texas with his wife, teenage son, mischievous beagle, and newly rescued Shepherd mix.

Official Website: http://www.erindorpress.com
Wikipedia: https://en.wikipedia.org/wiki/Nat_Russo
Facebook: http://www.facebook.com/NatRussoAuthor
Twitter: @NatRusso
Newsletter: http://madmimi.com/signups/95405/join

A HUMBLE REQUEST

Life seems to get busier every year, and the thought that you've invested some time in my scribblings is a humbling one. Thank you, sincerely, for spending your invaluable time in the world of Erindor.

If you enjoyed your journey with the Mukhtaar Lords, the cichlos, even the Barathosians...I'd like to ask you to take one more moment to leave a review on Amazon, or any other venue of your choice. And please tell your friends! I will owe you a most sincere debt of gratitude.

Many thanks,
Nat
Pflugerville, Texas
May 2016..

ALSO BY NAT RUSSO

Necromancer Falling: Book Two of The Mukhtaar Chronicles

The Road To Dar Rodon

www.ingramcontent.com/pod-product-compliance
Lightning Source LLC
Chambersburg PA
CBHW050906250626
47155CB00001B/127